BLOOD OF LIONS

Knights Templar Thrillers
Book Three

Daniel Colter

SAPERE
BOOKS

BLOOD OF
LIONS

Published by Sapere Books.

24 Trafalgar Road, Ilkley, LS29 8HH

saperebooks.com

ISBN: 978-0-85495-143-7

To Jill Moore, for the many years of support, and for never doubting.

ACKNOWLEDGEMENTS

To my beautiful wife Melissa, for the praise, criticism, and unfailing humour. To the team at Sapere Books — thank you, and top-notch work as always. And to a growing list of fans; I hope this one is as enjoyable as the others.

CHAPTER 1

Acre, August, the year of our Lord 1186

The king is dead.

Templar knights stood solemn guard over the king's dark cherrywood coffin. Bright silk brocades spilled over the sides. On the silks lay a jewel-encrusted sword and a triangular shield bearing the insignia of the Kingdom of Jerusalem — a yellow cross on a white field with four smaller crosses nestled into the cross's corners. Sword and shield were pristine, shiny as the day they were made, for the slumbering boy had never hefted them.

One of the Templars stared at the shield, too small for his own arm, and ignored the lords and counts and princes who had come to pay their respects.

Laggards never respected the lad when he lived.

The knight held a scabbarded sword, chape propped on the ground, and leaned on the blade like an old man leans on a cane, though he was no feeble old man. He was broad-shouldered and long-armed. His hair was black as jet, short and ragged, his beard long and tapered. Marble-like knuckles bore the lumps and scabs of a swordsman. Scars crisscrossed his face in straight furrows of varying length and gave him a menacing air. His French, when he spoke, lilted with a Gaelic accent.

"Three days of waiting."

"Three days of dying," a second Templar amended. He was taller and thicker than the first man, like a bear is to a tiger, his hands and face likewise marred by their shared vocation. "Fought to the end — tough lad, I'll give him that."

The first knight, Finnláech of Struan, or Finn, kept his gaze nailed on the shiny little shield. He had been there when they raised the boy king. Templars guarded him on the journey from Nablus to the Church of the Holy Sepulchre, then stood by as the boy took the throne meant for a man. He sat on the gilded chair, stick-legs straight out, while the Patriarch told him what to say and he repeated the words in a shrill but grave voice. Young Baldwin was keen, and given time, and with counsel, might have ruled in love and wisdom all his days.

But the boy king, like the leper king afore him, proved sickly and frail. Physics of all sorts came. Saracens. Jews. Greeks. He was bled. Stuffed with concoctions of herbs. Kept in shaded places to save him from the heat, and when that failed, hauled into the sunlight so it might fortify his constitution. Priests prayed unceasingly. All to no avail. God must have been harried by more pressing matters than preserving the life of a king. The illness worsened abruptly and forced Young Baldwin to bed, where he wandered between this world and the next for three days.

Candles made a column of light around the coffin. The rest of the cathedral lay in shadow. Shapes stood in the darkness, and therein shifted and schemed with one another in the flickering candlelight.

"Look lively," the second Templar whispered. The whisperer was Rollo of Caen, Finn's brother-in-arms, and he nodded toward a lean figure moving toward them.

Joscelin, Count of Edessa, Seneschal of the Kingdom of Jerusalem wraithed from the dark.

The count had been the boy king's guardian. He nodded at the Templars, respectfully enough, though his gaze went through them. A hand slid over the cherrywood in passing, as if the lingering touch confirmed what lay inside, then carried on to Princess Sibylla, the dead king's mother. They shuffled aside to converse in whispers and nods.

Altar boys came and lit fresh tapers. Light bloomed and a hint of honey, earthy and sweet, bettered the air. Finn leaned on his sword. Time passed. The tapers wilted to half their former selves. A cord of skull-shaped prayer beads dangled from his wide, battered leather belt. He was contemplating taking up the beads when Sibylla eased into the candlelight.

She gazed at Finn over the coffin. Black robes swathed her slender body. Full lips stood out below hollow cheeks. Kohl lined her eye sockets. Flowers and vines adorned her skin, painted in red henna, and with the black eye sockets gave her the air of a painted skeleton. He returned her gaze, neither arrogant nor submissive, and she arched a brow at a Templar who would not avert his eyes from a princess. She favoured Rollo with her gaze, then came back to Finn, as if assessing them for some task known only to her.

And what does she see? Unkempt beards. Sun-browned faces. Rigid postures. Dark mail. Men of war — dull of mind, easily twisted to the whims of well-bred folk.

Sibylla slid her palms together and bowed her head in prayer. She was still and quiet, and only God knew her entreaties. She made the sign of the cross and graced Finn with a crisp smile before sauntering into the darkness.

Murmuring voices drew Finn's ear.

Joscelin moved to the foot of the coffin. There he conversed with Raymond, Count of Tripoli, Prince of Galilee, and the king's regent.

Raymond employed local people in his household. Ate local food. Spoke Arabic like a Saracen. Carried a *saif* of watered steel, made in Damascus — which rumour said was a gift from the Sultan. Tonight, he wore a brimless cap, baggy cotton trousers, a silk shirt, and over it a flowing *jubbeh* made of red damask. Hand-tooled boots, slightly curled at the toes, adorned his feet. At Young Baldwin's coronation he had looked vigorous, as a man in his early forties should. Now, a year later, he looked tired, his previously thick brown hair thinning.

"By the terms of the leper's will, I am to remain regent until the new king is chosen," Raymond said. "Do you agree?"

Joscelin dipped his chin.

"And do I have your support for the kingship, if I vie for it?"

"Of course." Joscelin paused a beat. "Though I am not the Holy Father, nor the emperor, nor the sovereigns of France or England." King Baldwin's will specified that, if Young Baldwin passed without an heir, the next king would be selected through arbitration of the Holy Father, the Holy Emperor, and the kings of France and England. The count gave a soft smile. "You are the best candidate, certes, but not the only candidate."

"Sad but true. Gerard will prop up his fool."

Gerard de Ridefort was the Templar Grand Master. His fool was Guy of Lusignan, Sibylla's husband, who had been fated to rule until Baldwin the Leper denied his succession. Now Gerard schemed to place a dupe on the throne so, with a blameless face, he could control the kingdom. Everyone but the dupe knew it.

"One must gain the Wolf's favour," Joscelin added, and Raymond nodded.

The Red Wolf of Kerak, Raynald of Châtillon, was Lord of Oultrejordain — and a madman, folk said, filled with hate for the Sultan and any other who prayed toward Mecca.

Two knights from Finn's banner, Hector de la Roca and Serlo of Bellême, came from the nave to stand with him. The four Templars were silent as ghosts, still as statues. Joscelin and Raymond carried on with their muttered scheming. Finn eyed the shield and longed to be anywhere else; the words of these men tormented his ears like a song from the devil himself. *The constant squabbling and tugging on strings … will it never end?*

"I can help you in this, kinsman." Joscelin nodded sharp, as if just coming to a fateful decision, then grasped Raymond's elbow. "Go to Tiberias and call a council of the nobles. Argue your right, remind them of Guy's many faults, and they will see the truth in it." He laid a hand on the coffin. "The Templars will carry this to Jerusalem and see to Baldwin's burial. During the funeral, I will parlay with the Wolf and gain his favour. The old families will abide, follow the drift of things, for few fancy Guy as their king. After they have accepted you as legitimate, come to the city and receive your crown."

Raymond chewed his lip. "Without the Holy Father's blessing?"

"Hard times call for hard deeds. Besides, the Pope, the emperor, the kings — who are they to meddle in our affairs? Outsiders. Foreigners." Joscelin rested a ringed finger on his lip, , as if to acknowledge talking of a coup was no small thing. "The nobles of Outremer know what is best for Outremer — or most do, I should say. Doubters will find their way, sooner or later, or be forced to it. Either method works. And once you are seated on the throne, the Holy Father will bless your reign. He has no other choice."

Raymond stroked his grey-streaked beard. Joscelin, with no beard to stroke, assumed a confident bearing.

"Your loyalty is welcome — most welcome. What would I owe?"

"I am certain, as king, you will provide a fitting reward for your loyal subject." Joscelin gave an oily smile. "For now, let us right this tipping ship, afore it founders."

The two men nodded, clasped hands, then strolled away. The air in the chapel eddied and swirled, in the dark places especially, as if the death of the boy-king opened a gaping hole men rushed to fill.

Hector and Serlo came close. Rollo gave Finn a sideways stare.

"You gawk like a simpleton," Finn said.

"What is Joscelin about?" Rollo whispered. "Loyal subject? The Joscelin I know wouldn't piss on Raymond if he burst into flames."

No-one answered. No-one knew.

"Sibylla looked like the cat that just ate the bird," Rollo muttered.

Finn said nothing. He eyed the small, triangular shield and pondered how Young Baldwin would have used it. *Not well, I wager. Too gentle for this world of war.*

What of the others? Guy would hurt himself with it. Raymond … now he knew when and how to use a shield. It was a versatile tool and could hard-block an enemy's blows, deflect weak hits, or smash a nose, jaw, or arm with the rim or bottom point.

Blessed are we, then, that Raymond fights for the crown.

"Something smells bad," Rollo said. "And for once it's not me."

Finn smiled at the lame jest, though it died quickly.

"Master Gerard. His stink is all over this." The Templar Master was striking, bright-eyed, as if carved by the hand of an angel. Memories of his gaze — arrogant, vulturine, conniving

— soured Finn's thoughts. "I wager his schemes will, once again, drag us into a cesspool."

At first light the Templars rode from the Templar Castle, at the harbour, and turned north. Acre was awash with sights and smells. Wide cobble streets were lined with vendors and churches and tradesmen, and thronged with folk from sundry nations and tribes, hawking, arguing, cajoling. They gave sombre nods to newly sunburned pilgrims. The souq was a beehive with many species of bees — baggy-trousered Persians, Pisans in doublets and pointy shoes, fat-turbaned silk traders from Tamilakam, even glowering Afghans hawking lumps of turquoise.

Young Baldwin had lived past the souq, at the north end of Acre, in Palace Beauregard. Another person whom Finn was fond of lived nearby — Emma of Cherbourg.

He had met her not long past, when Master Gerard charged him with finding treasures described in the Copper Scroll. Emma and her husband, Adrien, were relic hunters and led the attempt. It ended poorly. Adrien turned on the Templars and died for it. Emma was shot by an errant Templar bolt in the mayhem. The wound to her body healed, though the wound of her husband's betrayal festered.

Finn did not find gold but, mayhap, discovered the hiding place of the Ark of the Covenant. Instinct told him to leave it untouched, which he did. Neither did he report it to the Order. Still they trudged out of the Judean Desert with a treasure — Sam, a bright-minded foundling with dark hair. The lad was not meant for the life of a Templar, so they placed him in the Temple in Jerusalem, where his wit could be honed to a razor edge.

The Copper Scroll quest did not go to plan, through no fault of Finn's, yet the Master remained sour and refused his blessing. Rumour claimed brother knights hunted relics in ruins near the Dead Sea, in the wastelands of the Judean Desert, and in the catacombs under Jerusalem. He wanted no part of it. Relic-hunting led to nothing good. *Let the dupes search.*

Now Finn guarded Outremer, patrolled an endless network of roads, and escorted wealthy Christians from Acre to Jerusalem. Pilgrims were his flock, their safety his vocation. He knew every stretch of road, every blind corner haunted by bandits, every climb where raiders lurked.

Sometimes his labours put him with Emma, like today.

Finn lived by a vow of chastity. What he and Emma shared was not of the body — it was a soul bond, forged by shared miseries and triumphs. She had saved his life, twice, and he would walk through fire for her. He came to her when he could, though not as often as he liked. He enquired after her health or asked for details of the ongoing translation of the Copper Scroll. At least those were the reasons he gave for visiting. The truth was that being with her lent a spark to otherwise drab days.

This morning Emma told him the scroll was proving a hard nut to crack. Timothy of Yorkshire, a man with a mind keen as a whip, led the translation. A Jewish scholar of renown helped with the more difficult parts.

"Can you fathom that?" Emma shook her head. "A Jew. Not welcome in Jerusalem, the city of his birth, yet the Order values his knowledge enough to *allow* him access to an artefact made by his people."

Finn gawked at her sky-blue eyes and half-heard her say she was moving from Acre to Tiberias for the spring and summer. She owned a villa at the lake, and from there managed her relic trade with wealthy nobles and the Order. Their thirst for holy artefacts was endless. Greasy napkins venerated as mandylions. This or that saint's bones. The sole from Mary's sandal. Finn, unlike most Templars, found the practice absurd, even tasteless. Emma did not, and claimed research sifted the real from the fake. They agreed to disagree.

She asked if he would visit her. He said he would.

A Templar comporting with a woman bent a Templar's vow of chastity, though many did more than bend their vows. Finn and Emma, in a futile attempt to quash rumours, took breakfast on the porch of her villa, where folk could see nothing untoward was happening. Rollo and their sergeants, Lugh and Jerol, sat nearby, eating bread, cheese, and olives.

Owen, a newly arrived sergeant, tended their horses. He was young and lean, fair of hair and dark of mood, and born in Strathpeffer, not far from Finn's home in Alba. He had spent years as a wanderer and served no lord — a polite way of saying he was a wolf's head. Owen, to no one's surprise, was tight-lipped about what winds blew him to Outremer.

Neither had Finn doled out much of his past life. Of his youth he spoke little. Alba was a misty, poorly known land to those of Christendom. Rumour abounded. Myth swirled. To his comrades, Finn seemed a scarred, ink-marked ruffian from some distant, outlandish demesne. This notion he did little to remedy. Let them gossip. Keep them wondering. Partly it was an attempt to be humble. But by his way of thinking, in a world where folk are oversold and overblown, it was also advantageous to maintain a degree of mystery. Owen's presence threatened some of that, as though another Scot might somehow expose him, and Finn found this vaguely troubling.

The rising sun peeked over the rooftops. Rays of light chased shadows from the roadway. Finn raised a face to the warmth and felt the first caress of the sea breeze from the harbour. The scent of lavender, myrrh, and almond oil wafted from Emma. He breathed in, eyes closed — tranquil moments were rare and never lasted long.

Finn breathed out slowly. "We must get to the road."

Emma, as was her wont when pondering, rubbed at her ear — large for such a petite woman. "You are to guard Young Baldwin on his final journey?"

"All the way to his tomb."

"And after?"

"Back to patrols and escorts."

"So few to protect so much. Your Order receives fewer brothers lately, it seems."

"Aye." Finn had lost half of his banner during the Copper Scroll debacle and, except for Owen, was yet to be assigned replacements. "Christendom forgets the cause, I fear, and we make do with less and less."

Emma opened her mouth to speak, decided better of it and smiled instead.

"Speak freely," Finn said.

"I am not one to tell you your business, but —"

Finn laughed at that, and Emma narrowed her eyes before carrying on.

"Arlo returned from abroad. He saw hoofprints on the road outside Tiberias."

"How many?"

"Two thousand, or thereabouts."

Finn glanced to Arlo, Emma's guard and agent in the relic trade. He was a Poulain, a local-born Frank, and salted by years as an oathman to Raymond of Tripoli. Arlo could count hoofprints and was savvy enough to fret over their number.

"No Christian armies are moving there. We are under a truce with Saladin, so…" Finn shrugged. "Perhaps Raymond is shifting troops to the frontier?"

"Talk of war is like mud in my ears. I only know we have peace. And thank God for it."

Finn wanted to say a truce is just a lull in which men prepare for the next war but did not. "I'll pass Arlo's news to the Master, though certes he is already aware."

"Certes." Emma's flat tone said she had little confidence in Gerard. "Rumour says the Sultan is fond of Raymond. That Raymond is a secret Mohammedan and prays toward Mecca. That he has special … agreements, with Saladin."

Finn snorted. "He is no Mohammedan. He schemes. Buys time. A skilled warrior subdues his enemy without fighting."

"You admire Raymond." It was not a question.

"I do. He is the kingdom's best chance at staying a kingdom. A man who knows when to fight — and when not to."

Emma stared a moment. "The north-east road is in Raymond's domain."

Finn stayed silent.

"The tracks headed south-west, Finn. From Damascus. Not toward her."

"We'd know if it were Saracens — they fart, we smell it."

Emma rolled her eyes at the coarseness.

"Unless a delegation, with a large force, was invited in secret," Finn said slowly. "Which could happen when there is no king to bless or curse the endeavour … or when a man already thinks himself the new king."

Raymond is treating with Saladin. Without the blessing of a sovereign or the favour of other nobles. Finn recoiled from the thoughts. *Is that good or bad?*

He dusted breadcrumbs from his palms and stood. "I thought you said you knew nothing of war?"

"I said it was like mud in my ears — messy and unwanted, but not unknowable."

He quirked a brow in appreciation of the riposte and put three fingers to his brow in a farewell salute.

"Try not to shoot any innocent Christians," Emma said with a teasing smile.

The road from Acre ran through fields of swaying wheat. Trees of several species lined it. A black mulberry, old enough to be from the time of Jesus, threw a generous circle of shade. Templars loitered within. Rollo curled at the trunk, sleeping like an overgrown puppy, strands of his long chestnut-coloured hair lying on his cheek.

Finn and Rollo had set aside their Templar mantles, worn for Young Baldwin's viewing, and now wore cappas, loose robes that hung to their shins. The robes were belted and slit front and back below the waist. Its sleeves reached their wrists. The near-white robes, with red cross pattées, marked them as Templar knights and covered their mail, which kept the sun from heating it and baking them like bread in an oven.

Three Turcopoles, native-born Christians, rode in from scouting the route. Elias led. He was a not a comely man. His body lacked any measure of softness, as if his skin had been peeled away to leave only brown muscle and sinew. Protruding brows covered beady eyes and a bulbous nose. A black, pointed beard made his long chin curve up like a scythe.

Finn told Elias of the hoofprints on the Road to Damascus.

"No Christians should be moving east in number. Sandpigs?" Elias's voice was as rough as his face. He hitched a shoulder to say it was nothing for him to fret on. "How's Emma?"

"She heals well," Finn said.

"Emma." Owen waggled his brows. "Why don't you just take her inside and give her a proper healing? None of us will tattle."

Finn spun on his heel and struck with his fist.

Owen's head snapped back. Then he was on his back and blinking at the tree branches above. Finn dropped to a knee, grabbed a fistful of tunic and heaved him upright.

"Disrespect her again," Finn growled, "and I'll break every bone in your body and toss you in a cesspit."

Rollo, woken by the ruckus, opened an eye, then closed it again with a sleepy smile.

Owen glared, and Finn gave him a hard shake. "Hear me?"

"Aye."

"Aye what?"

"Never disrespect Emma."

"Never disrespect any woman, you arse. Emma especially."

Owen showed his palms, a token of surrender and apology, and Finn shoved him down.

Owen flapped a hand for Lugh to haul him up, but the Irishman shook his head and grinned meanly. "She's one of us, ya eejit. We've been through some shite together. Mock her again and I'll be first in line to stomp on your bones."

Finn propped an arm on the trunk of the black mulberry and breathed, slow and deep. He wanted to shake Owen until his head snapped off and clattered away. *God's wounds, can't a man visit a woman without everyone assuming they're dallying? Jesus befriended Mary Magdalene. Certes they never dallied.*

Rollo snored as Finn watched the road. A pillar of dust showed there. The dust would be from Hector and Serlo, and Denis of Lusignan, the new Under Marshal. He had slumberous, heavy-lidded eyes, round shoulders, and pear-shaped hips. He never ceased grinning and had one for every occasion — a happy grin, a confused grin, a surprised grin. Even an angry grin, strangely, though it only made him look like a simpleton.

Young Baldwin came with them, certes, carted along in as fancy a cart as could be found on short notice. Priests would trail. Finn thought he could hear the flock of crows even now — singing psalms, signing the cross every twelfth step.

Rollo stopped snoring. "They coming?"

"Aye."

"That arse Denis with them?"

"Aye."

"Do you think it's true — he's Gerard's cousin?"

"Aye. How else does a fat cockscomb, fresh from his vows, climb so quickly to a position sought by others more qualified?" Finn stepped to Fagan, his destrier, and slipped a boot in the stirrup. "And who better to spy on underlings than one's kin?"

"Spy on us for what?"

"Anything. Everything."

CHAPTER 2

Horses ignored Baldwin. Men did not. No odour came forth, even in the hot sun, for the coffin was well-made. But one could forget the earthly husk decaying in that box. The boy king's shade lingered. At night he bothered Finn's sleep. Baldwin was not wrathful, nor content, though he would not depart until his body lay at rest.

Other Templars joined them on the Road to Jerusalem. Jean of Provence and Mael of Aleth, old comrades, came from La Fève, a Templar castle in the Jezreel Valley. Jean was Castellan there, and in years past had been Finn's battle companion and second-in-command. They embraced. Jean and Rollo did not; over the years their relationship had swung between loathing and acceptance. They exchanged their usual greetings.

"Brother Rollo."

"Brother Cackhand."

Mael smirked at Rollo's solemn mockery of Jean's left-handedness, and the Breton's mutilated chin quivered as he struggled to hold in his mirth.

Joscelin did not show — despite his promise to escort the boy king to Jerusalem with the Templars. Finn wagered Raymond would be more than a little fretful, if he knew. On the second day, Denis, bored with escorting a coffin, rode for the city with his attending knight and sergeant. No one missed him.

Finn twisted in the saddle to take in his banner of men.

There were two knights besides himself and Rollo. Hector was Finn's second. He was also the second son of a noble Catalan family. Learned, quick of mind and body, dark and rangy as a wolf. Too often Finn thought Hector would make a better leader than himself — and likely he would. Serlo, a Norman, was sculpted muscle with a shaved head and long beard. Stern. Obedient. Fearless. He rationed words like a miser rations gold. The four suffered much, their martial bonds forged in fire, hard as steel. They savvied each other's strengths and weaknesses like husband and wife. A half score of sergeants and Turcs rounded out Finn's band.

At the end of the third day, the Marshal, Jakelin de Mailly, rode from the city and met them before Saint Stephen's Gate. The dying sun painted the sky with streaks of oranges and reds. The hues made Jerusalem's walls glow.

"God be praised," Jakelin said, and embraced Finn.

"Forever and ever," echoed the rote reply from a dozen lips.

Brothers came from the Temple and took Young Baldwin. Finn watched the cart roll away, pulled by a lone sway-backed mule, and felt a tremor of sadness and unease. The lad's spirit went along, Finn felt, for the mood lightened. Priests walked behind and their psalmody filled the streets. Finn spoke no more than a few words of Latin, and his ignorance made the dead tongue hypnotic and lulling. Today the psalmody sounded cold and ominous.

Jakelin spoke Latin, though, and his lips moved in silent time with the song. He was a master of war. A swordsman of renown. A devout and humble man. And a man Finn aspired to be. A shock of silvery hair topped his head and gave him a severe mien, made more severe by eyes the colour of a winter sky. His wintry gaze fixed on Finn.

"You are commanded to stay at Saint Stephen's Gate." He shifted to Jean. "You are ordered to David's Gate. Guard them through the night. Brothers Geoffroy and Beranger will watch Mount Zion and Jehoshaphat."

"Guard them from Saracens?" Jean asked.

"Not Saracens." Jakelin took a breath, eased let it out. "Balian of Ibelin. And Raymond. Maybe Reginald of Sidon. None are to be allowed in by order of Master Gerard."

"Raymond. Balian. Reginald." Jean lived studiously by the Rule, which forbade Christians to fight Christians. He rubbed a palm over the back of his neck. "We fight Christians?"

"Not unless we have to." Jakelin spat, a coarse act from a man so mannered. "Use lethal force only to defend yourself. Pray our presence is deterrent enough."

"Why not city guards to guard city gates?" Finn asked.

"They are not trustworthy."

"Marshal, what is afoot?"

"Many things, Brother." Jakelin placed a palm on his chest and patted, perhaps sympathizing with field brothers ever left in the dark. He edged close. "Count Joscelin is in Acre. He never left. His men occupy Tyre. This morning, he and others declared Sibylla as Queen of Jerusalem. Civil war threatens, certes, so to delay it Raymond and his allies must be kept outside the walls. For now."

Finn fixed Jean with a look and shook his head, as if to ask, *Civil war... won't that be fun?*. Jean replied by hitching up a shoulder.

The Marshal stared into the darkness beyond Saint Stephen's Gate. "The Lord shows me my death, in my dreams," he said unexpectedly, voice cold and distant. "I stand alone in a field of stubble. Mamluks ride at me in waves. I sing a psalm while reaping them. The dead pile at my feet. Blood runs in the furrows."

A shiver chased up Finn's spine. "How does your dream end?"

"A warm embrace, strangely. Then arrows — the dogs fill me with arrows."

"I prefer a happier ending," Jean said. "The knight slays the beast and rides away on a white charger? A banner rescues their brother, perhaps?"

"Dreams are nonsense, I say." Rollo wandered up, tugging his chest-length beard through a hand. "Last night I dreamt the Holy Father was a monkey, wearing the gold cross and a silk zucchetto. All the churchmen were monkeys, too. Thousands of them. Getting into everything."

Jakelin ignored that and carried on in the hollow voice. "Every man dies, though a man is not judged by the way he died, only by the way he lived."

Warriors foreseeing their death, with clarity and to the day, made eerie tales told around many a Templar campfire. A brother Finn once knew had predicted his demise down to the weapon that claimed him and where it struck. Neither ridicule nor reason could loosen this morbid conviction. Three days after the dream, he rode to his doom. Finn suffered another shiver. But the salted knight takes dread's cold hand, holds it close, converses with it until an accord is reached. And so he did.

Jean made a scoffing sound, surrendered to lunacy beyond his ken, and corrected course. "We will guard the gates, Marshal."

Jakelin nodded and came back to the present. "Do the Master's bidding, Brothers, and we will see what the morrow brings."

Finn stood at Saint Stephen's Gate. The Syrian Quarter sprawled behind him. Jews had been driven from it in 1099 to make room for Syrian Christians. Few folk lived there now —

at least few honest folk. Hucksters, whores, and thieves held their revelries unchecked by God or by man. Watchmen, bribed with debased coins, found better-lit places to watch. A venture there would find dark alleys no wider than a man's wingspan, pillared houses half in ruin, all of it echoing with song and laughter, curses and shouts.

Saint Stephen's Gate was a stout wooden door set in a keeled stone archway. A portcullis could be dropped to shield the door. The door was oak, by the grain, bleached on one side by the western sun and darkened on the other by smoke from sentries' fires. They were to leave the gate-door open, to avoid raising the bile of common folk, yet somehow gently dissuade Raymond or Balian's men from entering. At Terce they could bar the doors, a routine practice, and keep them barred until Lauds.

Denis ambled toward them, grinning, knight and sergeant trailing like hounds.

The Under Marshal had arrived in Outremer not long past. His cappa was eye-blindingly white, its hem crisp, and he lacked the vaunted Templar beard. Porcine bristles spiked his jaw. A florid face boasted what was likely the first of several jowls.

"Folk back home call him Denis the Stout," Finn said.

Rollo snorted. "Wouldn't Denis the Fat be more fitting?"

"Too true. Do you remember him in the training yard? Sweating. Blowing like a carp. Swings a blade like a butcher."

Denis heeled in before Finn. "All is well, Brother?"

"Aye, Under Marshal."

Denis planted his hands on his hips and regarded the men. Finn sensed something idiotic was about to be said; he was not wrong.

"Makes me proud to lead men such as yourselves," Denis said. "Brothers from across Christendom, united in a common cause. Normans and French mostly, as you know, but others flavour the stew. Bretons. Catalonians. English. Ruddy-faced Danes and Norwegians. My favourite spice is you Scots and Irish. Doughty fighters. Fine figures. And your language! So melodic." He turned to Lugh. "Say something for me, Brother."

Lugh looked up, as if gathering his thoughts, then prattled something in Irish Gaelic.

"Honey in my ears. What did you say, pray tell?"

"Aye, do tell," Finn prompted, knowing very well what Lugh had said.

"You are the epitome of a French knight, Under Marshal." Lugh offered a short bow. "Skilled with sword and lance, as well as verse and song."

"Ah, how kind — and how mannered!" Denis bowed in return.

Finn glanced away to hide his grin, for what Lugh had actually said was, 'You are a fat French fop, likely to cut yourself with your sword, or fall on your lance and stick it up your arse.'

"Rooster, is it not?" Denis asked Lugh. "How did you earn such a byname?"

Lugh was his birth name and Rooster his byname, earned from his habit of shaving the sides of his head and leaving the top in a crest — like a giant cockscomb.

Lugh ran a palm over his straw-coloured hair before answering in a flat voice. "No idea, Under Marshal. Folk always just called me that."

Denis beamed and clapped Lugh on a shoulder. "I like you, Rooster. I do." He shifted to Finn, still wearing the smile. "*Avoir la pêche*, Brother. *Avoir la pêche*."

Finn shook his head as Denis strolled away, no doubt heading to David's Gate to ensure Jean was as skilled as Finn at guarding a portcullis backed by two double doors. Rollo explained *avoir la pêche* literally meant to 'have the peach,' but figuratively meant to be in top form. To have good morale. Such a daft phrase, with either meaning, should never have been uttered by a Templar, that was for certain.

Finn's mentor, Robert, had preached that leaders were one of four types. Keen. Dumb. Lazy. Diligent. Two could be melded. Most men were dumb and lazy. Some were keen and diligent. These were best used in low- or mid-level leadership. Brothers with a keen mind and laziness got the highest roles, for such men had the intellect and calm needed to make hard choices but live with the consequences. One had to beware of brothers who were dumb and diligent, though, for they would only cause mischief.

Denis showed sizable doses of both.

Time passed as Finn pondered the finer workings of leaders and followers.

"Look alive," Elias said from his perch above the gate. "Riders coming."

The clatter of bridles and the thump of hooves grew louder until horsemen emerged from the darkness and reined in. Their surcoats bore a red cross on a cream-yellow background — the livery of Balian of Ibelin.

Finn, Rollo, and Lugh moved into the archway. Finn glanced at Hector. "Form behind. Stay put unless things get messy."

Hector said something about just shutting the door, but Finn ignored it. His senses hummed with the prospect of violence.

"The city is barred," Finn shouted. "Come back tomorrow. Or next week. Or never."

The lead rider dismounted and tossed his reins to another. He strolled into the light, smirking. His voice, when he spoke, was as ugly as his smirk. "Barred? By whose order?"

"The Templar Master."

"Templars run the city, eh? Since when?"

"Since now."

"I'm Padrig, first-sword to Balian, Lord of Ibelin." Padrig had stringy dark hair and small, pale eyes. He was a Poulain — Breton and Saracen, probably, but all devil. "This ain't your city. And we ain't leaving."

Finn gave a short nod, as if he had expected as much. "You the new king?"

"You know I'm not."

"Then beat feet."

"Beat what?"

"Feet." Finn raised a hand and with his fingers mimed a man walking away.

"Ah," Padrig said. "Now you're being rude."

"Not all knights have manners."

Padrig jigged a thumb over a shoulder, at the men behind him. "We could toss you aside and push through."

"Unlikely." Finn made a show of glancing over his shoulder at Hector and Serlo. "You see, I have friends too."

Padrig squared his shoulders and stomped close — too close. "Move. Now."

Finn glared at Padrig but spoke to Lugh. "Remove this rakefire from my face."

Lugh placed his left hand on the rakefire's shoulder.

"Remove your hand, dog, or —"

Lugh punched with his right fist, at an angle, andit ploughed across Padrig's nose. Padrig staggered and dropped to his arse as two men leapt past.

One of Padrig's men came at Finn.

He was tall, thin as a reed, and the ugliest man Finn had ever seen — uglier than Elias. Forehead was slanting and bulbous. Nose flat and lumpy. One eye glared at Finn while the other glared at Rollo. He led with his right foot and right hand.

Left-handed, ugly, and walleyed. What did his mother do to anger God?

Finn was pondering that when a left fist clipped his chin and a right thumped his cheek. He bobbed and shuffled and threw a punch that fell short of Walleye's nose. Finn glanced at the man's eyes, and while trying to decide which eye to watch, took a hard strike to his forehead and another on his chin.

A cack-hander fights all wrong — leads with his right, counters with a left cross, steps left instead of right. His front foot is on the outside and he can strike with both hands. Finn slid back while his wolf mind, the one in charge of fighting, shifted and hunted for an opening. *You are taller than this man and longer armed*, thought the wolf.

Walleye jabbed with his right, probing, and when his left tensed Finn punched with his long right. It beat Walleye's left, barely, and landed with a satisfying thump. A glancing left caught his ear as he stepped to the outside, then Finn ploughed in with a crushing right to the nose, a left hook to the ribs, and a hard right to the chin. Something cracked together — front teeth — and Walleye went over in a stiff fall.

Bells were ringing, sharp and buzzy. *City alarm bells?* Finn shook his head — which only made the ringing worse. *No, you muttonhead. Walleye rang your bell.*

The second man was all over Rollo.

He was as tall as the Norman but heavier. They met in a flurry of slaps and shoves, like two rutting bulls. Rollo landed a fist on Bull-man's eye. He grunted, not hurt much, though surprised. And mad. He landed a hard left on Rollo's forehead. Rollo planted a left uppercut, took a glancing right on his shoulder, missed with a right. The larger man crowded and worked his arms — left, right, left, right, uppercut.

Rollo took it and came away with a savage grin. Blood smeared his teeth. When Bull-man glanced up, Rollo struck straight between his eyes, pivoted and slammed a right elbow into the side of his head.

Rollo held, expecting Bull-man to stagger off all loose and raggedy, ready to be finished with another flurry of blows. But he glided sideways, agile as a cat, and landed a hard shot to the ribs. Air whoofed from Rollo.

Serlo, no small man himself, blurred past Rollo and shoulder-checked Bull-man, knocked him back. Hector caught Finn and Rollo by the collars of their hauberks, and like an angry mother dragged them inside the arch. Finn spared a glance. Serlo shuffled backwards, right arm cocked, left arm out. Bull-man came on with long strides. Padrig's nose looked like a badly made pancake, flat and lumpy, though at least he was on his feet. Not Walleye. He lay flat on his back, one hand resting on his chest and the other thrown to the side. The oak door slammed shut and the stout locking bar clanged loud as a smith's anvil.

Rollo wheeled on Serlo. "You arse, I had him!"

Serlo, notoriously spare with words, shrugged, then mimed wiping his brow to say Rollo should see to the blood streaming from the cut over his eye.

Finn slumped against the wall while Lugh poured a bucket of water over his head. He blew spray from his moustaches, resisted the urge to shake his throbbing head, instead dragged fingers through his wet and spiky hair.

"Couldn't stand idle as you took another thumping," Hector said. "Besides, it's past Terce, and you could have just shut the door instead of brawling."

"Rollo needed the exercise."

"Didn't think of it, did you? Or were you just spoiling for a fight?"

Finn smiled sheepishly.

"No fun in a closed door." Lugh tossed aside the bucket. "Certes it'll be a long, boring night from here on."

Gerard de Ridefort reclined on the wall inside the king's citadel. He had arrived in the late afternoon; now darkness fell around him. Waiting was no hardship — he was skilled at it. *This night is years in the making.* A tremor of anticipation made his chest tingle. Raymond. Cécile Dorel. Many years past she had inherited her father's fief of Botrun, in the County of Tripoli. Raymond, Count of Tripoli, promised Gerard Cécile's hand in marriage, and with her would have come Botrun. *Bastard broke his word, though, and married her to some hedge-born Pisan merchant.* A bride price of ten-thousand bezants was enough to tip the scales. It was more — much more — than Gerard could muster. Even now his ears reddened at the shame.

A key rode on a cord around his neck; he stroked it through his Templar mantle.

Patience. Revenge. They are weapons, sharp as any sword, and lethal when wielded by one with the skill to use them properly. And there is Outremer itself to consider...

Kings render swords unneeded, or this is how it would be, in a perfect world. Outremer was not perfect. Far from it. The land was ancient but the folk young — at least the newcomers were, and still battling for their place in it. Saladin lurked beyond the frontier. This meant swords and might ruled here, not wisdom and love, and few men would obey a woman, especially in war. To preserve the kingdom, the nobles, ever fickle, had to rally behind a king.

That is the way of it. Always has been. Always will be.

Guy ambled into the torchlit courtyard.

Gerard came off the wall to meet him. "God's blessings, Lord Guy."

Guy's soft brown hair curled around a diamond-shaped face and eyes like jade beads. He nodded curtly. "I have been summoned — by my wife, if you can believe it."

"I can." Gerard veered into shadow. Guy followed like a puppy. "Sibylla has done well," the Master said. "For herself. And for you. She and Joscelin handled Raymond with aplomb. He is in Tiberias, scratching his beard and wondering when the other nobles will arrive. She wooed the Patriarch. Even now Heraclius warms the sacred anointing oil and dusts off the crown and cape. All goes to plan."

"To plan?"

"Aye. Our plan. Remember?"

"Of course," Guy said, a little too quickly.

"Then certes you remember I vowed, not long past, you would be King of Jerusalem. The Order is your ally in this and did all it could to aid you — even finding the coin to fund your kingship. Brothers guard the gates, and the walls, and the streets." Gerard smiled. His teeth were shiny, pointy, and white. "The hour is nigh when I fulfil my vow."

When you become my king.

"Aye. You said those things. But men promise many things." Guy bit his lip and swallowed. "What do you see in me?"

A fop. A laggard. A dupe.

"A king," Gerard said, and raised a majestic hand for emphasis.

Guy drummed his fingers on his chin, then glanced away.

Do not lose your spine now. Not now.

Guilt and pride made strong motivators. Gerard played to them now. Guy, like many, had come to Outremer to make amends with God and to build a name.

The Lusignans had been, many years past, dispossessed by Eleanor, Duchess of Aquitaine, once Queen of France, and presently Queen of England. Treason was the cause for dispossession. One fine day, the Earl of Salisbury was escorting her to Poitiers when the vengeful Lusignan brothers, Guy and Geoffrey, attacked her entourage. They hoped to capture her and hold her ransom. The ill-advised plan went bad. The Earl gave Eleanor his charger, which was faster, and for his gallantry was lanced in the back as she escaped. Guy de Lusignan, rumour said, was the cowardly murderer. William Marshal, perhaps the finest knight to wield a sword, was there and swore Guy led the sordid affair. Lusignan became *persona non grata* in Christendom. Now he stood at the cusp of becoming King of Jerusalem.

"God gives you the means to make amends." Gerard made a theatrical flourish to the east. "Saladin lurks there, in the darkness." He swept a hand over an imaginary throng in the courtyard. "Thus gentle folk need a strong ruler, now more than ever, to bring them light." He raised a hand to the heavens, eyes closed in rapture, and whispered, "God forgives those who are worthy. And He has chosen you to be the bringer of light, to be the protector of Jerusalem — you, Lord Guy."

Guy's gaze meandered up the stone tower, rising high into the dark sky. He spoke in a soft and shaky voice. "God chose me. I dare not refuse."

Gerard dipped his head in something near a bow, held it a beat, then looked up with a sombre expression on his face.

Guy gaped at the citadel. "I must see her."

They climbed the stairs. Two guards bowed their heads as Guy swept past, Gerard at his heels. The landing was empty, but the great hall was thronged with men — and Sibylla. She stood in the centre of the room, head bare, green eyes shining in the lamplight.

Beyond her sat a vacant throne. Baldwin had ruled there — rotted there.

The leper's stench taints this place, thought Gerard. *I shall have servants cleanse it.*

Guy strode into the room, then slowed, as if intruding on something not intended for him. Sibylla scowled and was about to reply to some query just spoken. Muttering voices faded and Sibylla, seeing Guy, gave a wide smile.

"Ah, Lambkin, you have arrived."

An avenue opened through the nobles, and she sauntered through it to embrace her husband.

"Lambkin." Guy held onto Sibylla like a child to his mother. His gaze swept the nobles, now on bended knee, heads bowed. "They bow to their queen," he said.

"No. They bow to their queen and *king*," Sibylla whispered in Guy's ear.

Gerard could not hear her words, but he knew them all the same. *Tomorrow the Patriarch will make me queen, and place a second crown at my side, and bid me choose whichever man I think worthy to govern the realm. Nobles oppose you. To appease them, I vowed to set you aside and choose another. Though I will not. I will select you, Lambkin.*

36

Gerard finger stroked the key riding on his chest as he strolled from the room. Outside, he stared up at a blanket of stars, crisp and silver and blinking in the heavens. His retinue, two knights and a sergeant, loitered by the wall and they came to him now.

"All ended well, Master?" a knight asked.

"Aye." Gerard made the sign of the cross and kissed an imaginary crucifix. "Very well."

Now. One more task afore this night is done.

CHAPTER 3

Finn stood at Saint Stephen's Gate. Revelries echoed from the Syrian Quarter, distant, sporadic. Walleye's thumping had made his head throb, and tired of its ache he meandered away from the ruckus, to the first intersection. The inner city was quiet as a tomb. Bats flew looping courses through the streets. Beggars and curs slept in ragged piles in the dark alleys. A watchman's brazier glowed like a nest of rats' eyes, but of the guardsman there was no sign.

Finn was about to turn back when Denis's knight and sergeant hustled past, heading toward the Temple. Sometime later they came back with Denis. Neither took note of a lone Templar in shadow. Other brothers came. Jakelin de Mailly too. Finn stepped from the darkness and the Marshal saw him, held a hand flat and patted the air, like one would tell a dog, *Sit, stay.*

Rollo walked to Finn's side. "What's afoot?"

"Don't know."

They waited, for what they could not say, then shouting drifted to their ears. Someone yelled. Loud banging. More yelling.

"The Hospital is not far," Rollo said. "Could it be under attack?"

Finn tilted a head in vague reply. They began walking. The ruckus grew louder. They found themselves behind a throng of Templars, filling the street before the Hospital. Finn was taller than most, Rollo taller than Finn, but both had to stand on their tiptoes to see over the crowd. A score of Hospitallers dressed in braes and tunics arrayed in front of the barred door. Axe handles filled their hands, or mallets, or rocks.

"Give me your key, de Moulins!" someone yelled. It was Master Gerard. "I will not ask again, you dim-witted churl, and I will not leave until I have it."

The insult to the Hospitaller Master, Roger de Moulins, did not fall on deaf ears. Hospitallers surged; Templars replied in kind.

"No!" Jakelin shoved into the space between. "Hold! God withholds his blessing from quarrelling brothers."

"Will he bless your treachery?" a Hospitaller shouted.

A rock hit Jakelin in the chest, and he grunted and staggered. A knight batted aside a rock aimed for Denis's head. The clatter of rocks on shields sounded like a brief summer rain.

"Hospital lads are a bit tetchy," Rollo said drily, and stepped left to avoid a stone bouncing over the ground toward him.

"Last chance, de Moulins!" Gerard bellowed at the window. "Give it freely or I will take it. I will break down your door and climb your stairs and pry it from your fingers, if I must."

Silence.

Gerard flailed a hand in a gesture that was part anger, part resignation, and Denis barked, "Shieldwall! Shove them aside; chop out the door!"

Templars formed. Shields clattered together woodenly. Hospitallers called them to the dance with taunts and jibes.

Templars and Hospitallers scrapping over ... what?

"This is madness," Finn said.

Something arced out the window and landed between the Templars and Hospitallers. The tromp of boots stilled. Gerard trod into the silence and bent and picked up the thing. He hefted it to the torchlight — a bronze key.

Rollo scowled. "Lads were going to break heads over a key?"

"Not just a key," Finn said, comprehension coming in a rush. "The royal insignia are stored in a coffer. Three keys are needed to open it. The Patriarch of Jerusalem holds one. The Templar Master holds the second. The Hospitaller Master holds — or held, I should say — the third. And now Gerard holds all the keys needed to crown a king."

The coronation proved a drab affair. No hymns. No incense. The Holy Sepulchre, ever a sacred place, was sullied by the crowd of devious men. Templars arrayed in a neat row, stiff and staring as ivory pieces on a board game. No Hospitallers came in silent protest of the illegitimate affair.

Sibylla sat in the middle of it all on the gilded chair; her crimson robe lay at her feet like a pool of blood. An empty chair sat to her right. Heraclius, the Patriarch, approached and placed the crown on her head. He was a bloated, wrinkled old bag, and his hands trembled with the effort. She flinched as it settled, as if it weighed more than expected. Latin words were recited. Sacred oil anointed her forehead.

The Patriarch gestured at a priest, and he came bearing a second crown on a silken pillow. This Heraclius took and set on the empty chair.

Finn glanced at Master Gerard, standing at the head of the row of white knights. His blue eyes gleamed with a strange light; his body strained beneath his cappa, as if he were about to shove the Patriarch aside to place the crown himself.

"Queen Sibylla, with this crown," Heraclius said, and paused to wheeze, "nominate the man who, in your wisdom, will best lead the kingdom with judgment, prudence, and bravery."

Sibylla surveyed the room with a dramatic, sweeping gaze, until it settled on Guy. She beckoned him forward and he knelt before her. She placed the crown on his head.

"I, Queen Sibylla, choose as king Guy of Lusignan, the man who is my husband. For I know he is a worthy man and of upright character. He will rule his people well. While he lives I cannot, before God, have anyone else, for as the scripture says, 'Whom God has joined, let not man put asunder.'"

Some of the nobles erupted in cheers and shouts of hosannah, as though they had seen something noble and good. Many gawked, aghast, or gabbled in outrage.

Guy eased into his gilded chair, next to his queen, stiff and straight-backed in a pose of magnanimity and grandeur. He beamed like the idiot he was and gave a king's wave — arm bent, wrist turning back and forth, exposing the front and back of his hand. The gesture was too stiff and likely much-practised in a mirror.

Images of Young Baldwin needled Finn's memory — pale-faced, reciting in a sombre and piping voice, making kingly gestures of which he did not understand the import. *At least the lad sensed he was underwater, looking up.*

Joscelin scurried to Guy's knee, no doubt already calling in favours due. Raynald, the Red Wolf of Kerak, stood with his arms crossed over a surcoat of yellow, red and blue. Finn had seen him at Montgisard, where he led the king's army, and he was little changed. Long-haired. Thick-chested. Ruddy-faced.

Seeing the man launched a parade of memories. In 1182 Raynald had connived to sack Islam's holiest places, Medina and Mecca, and drag Muhammad's body from his tomb. He failed, though the attempt made him a Devil to Mohammedans — and to some Christians. Saladin vowed to kill the madman, too.

Allah preaches mercy and vengeance. His followers take both to heart and vengeance, especially, is never forgotten. *Don't I know it.* Finn had killed one of Saladin's kin, who vowed to take his head, and years later the vow yet haunted him.

Rollo, Hector and Serlo gathered round Finn, sharing dull glances but saying nothing. The coup was done. A king was made, and every day the fraud remained king, the more entrenched he would become. Seeing Guy propped on his throne set loose a writhing worm of worry in Finn's chest.

"Guy cuts a fine figure; do you not agree?" Gerard strolled into their midst; Denis hovered a step behind. No one replied, so Guy answered himself. "He is majestic."

Majestic? Pitiful!

Gerard gave a thin smile. The smile conveyed much. Arrogance. Contentment. Want. But not humour. It made the worm in Finn's chest burrow deeper.

"Do you assume Raymond will abide this charade?" The query escaped from Finn unbidden. Gerard nailed Finn with a warning stare, and Finn held it for a moment before adding, "Master."

"What Raymond thinks is of no importance to me, Brother. Though perhaps you would favour me with your opinion — will he attack us?"

"He has cause. But he is too wary. Too sensible." Anger had replaced worry in Finn's chest. "Sibylla holds the ports, which is no small advantage. But half of Outremer sides with Raymond. The Balians. Reginald of Sidon. Humphrey of Toron. Others." He paused. "Real fighting men. Salts. Not the buffoon you imposed on the kingdom. Your meddling pits Christian against Christian, at a time when unity is needed most." Another pause. "Master."

Gerard's smile withered. "You overstep, Brother Finn. I am God's humble servant and do not meddle in worldly affairs."

Liar.

Gerard stepped close. Wine and wax and sweat wafted with him. "You would do well to remember Raymond, in his arrogance, made a truce with Saladin — a truce for Tripoli but not for the kingdom. He is a secret Mohammedan, too, and prays toward Mecca. Our agents report it."

Finn shook his head at the oft-flung aspersion.

Gerard eased back, glanced at Raymond. "I should order an attack on the fool."

"Don't you mean King Guy should order an attack?"

Gerard was caught flat-footed and could speak only the expected.

"I advise the king. As Templar Masters have always done." Nobles streamed by. Gerard glowered at Finn as they passed, then spoke low and sharp. "You took a vow of obedience — remember? Thus my orders are your tasks. An opinion, should you form one, is a treasure best kept to yourself. Fail and I will have you removed."

Finn had been banished once, by Master Odo, and bullying was a strategy favoured by Masters. Banishment and threats were nothing new. None of it worried him; he would never climb to a higher station, nor did he seek to. But all the blustering taught him a hard truth — the Order needed him more than he needed the Order.

"I remember my vows, Master," Finn said, "and why I took them. We all have cause for what we vow and what we do. Sometimes these causes are even noble."

The Master's eyes narrowed to slits. "Men will not follow a woman to war, nor follow a secret Mohammedan. I grasped that, others did too, and we acted in the interest of the kingdom. Guy is the only viable king."

The only king you could control, you mean. Finn stayed silent and smirked, knowing silence and arrogance got under a superior's skin.

"You defiant arse. I should —" Gerard balled a fist, then turned it into a jabbing finger. "This repays Raymond for Botrun! For Cécile!" His voice had risen to a shout, and nobles shuffling by pasted on flat smiles. He offered them a dip of the head, then came back to Finn with a glare. "Certes you, among all brothers, understand revenge?"

"I do. And I learned much while taking it." Finn paused to sift his memory. "Brother Marcus, the Godliest man I've known, once said to me, 'Torment your enemy with forgiveness, the thing he wants least, and leave the wrath to God.' I struggle to live his advice, as you know, which only makes it a harder truth."

Gerard, rebuked by an inferior, could only sputter. He snarled, readying to bite, but instead turned on his heel and stalked away. Denis trailed and cast Finn a baleful glance over his shoulder.

"The Master loves us," Rollo said, and chuckled. "Certes he will soon promote us."

"Promote us to a farm to pull weeds, or maybe the docks to unload ships." Hector pursed his lips and nodded to himself. "Docks. It will be the docks."

"I don't think so." Finn idly twisted the tip of his beard in thought. "More likely he will snatch labourers from the docks and press spears into their hands. The Master lacks muscle. He can't afford to send fighting men anywhere but to a fight — and there will be plenty of those."

"I am King of Jerusalem. Kings do not control the weather."
Guy fluttered a hand to pronounce the petition decided.

"I beg your pardon, Sire," the olive grower said. He was a
flaxen-haired Poulain with skin charred copper by the sun. "I
am not asking you to control the weather. I am asking for my
water. My neighbour steals it, from my canal, which rights are
guaranteed here —" he paused to heft a wrinkled parchment
— "and have existed for sixty-three years. They were granted
by King Amalric, and —"

"Enough." Guy gave the man a withering stare. "My lands
are tortured by endless drought. All of them. This you know.
So. The water will be communal until conditions improve." He
flicked his fingers. "You may go."

The olive grower stomped out, huffed at Finn in passing as if
his woes were Finn's fault.

King Guy lacked a king's guard; men were being trained for
the honour. In the meantime, Templars served as guards, and
today Finn had drawn the short straw. The kingship remained
tenuous, despite the coronation, and Master Gerard fretted his
new puppet would have its strings cut before he could put it to
use. Finn, Rollo, Hector, and Serlo stood in the shadows
around the throne.

The trick for playing guard, Finn learned, was being invisible.
Keeping still but using your eyes to seek the man staring too
intently, too long, or the man with, a hand tucked within the
sleeves of his robe. The day was spent watching an endless
parade of petitioners. He prayed for an assassin, just to break
the tedium, but only poor folk came to plead on deaf ears.

"King Guy," the chamberlain said. "Brothers Bellicus and
Loy, of the Cistercian Order, petition your attention as envoys
of Raymond, Count of Tripoli, Prince of Galilee."

Guy and Sibylla shared a look, stared, nodded, all in the silent language of married folk. The king twitched up a finger. "Admit them to our presence."

Two Cistercian monks filed in. Three men-at-arms held at the door.

The Cistercians were referred to as the White Monks because their habits of undyed wool appeared white or grey. The Cistercians, like the Templars, lived by the Rule of Saint Benedict and of Saint Bernard. Poverty. Severity. Humility. The first monk, forgetting humility, strode toward the throne and offered a terse twitch of the head. He was lean as a skeleton, as were most Cistercians, with ever-moving eyes.

"Lord Guy." The monk lingered on the word 'Lord,' and paused while the murmur of threats and warnings coursed around the room. "I am sent by Raymond, Count of Tripoli, Prince of Galilee, to remind you of King Baldwin's will. Recall the new king is to be selected by the Holy Father, the kings of France and England, and the Holy Emperor. He bids you adhere to King Baldwin's final wishes."

"Too late for all that." Guy sat forward and tapped the crown on his head. "I am king, as you see. Selected by the Patriarch of Jerusalem and the Holy Orders. Thus I am selected by God himself."

Finn thought it a weak case. As did the Cistercian.

"You trample Baldwin's will. This is an outrage. A betrayal of…"

Finn stopped listening. His skin tingled — someone was staring. He scanned the room. His gaze landed on one of the monks' guards, staring back at Finn from the doorway. Abram. The man gave a grin and a nod.

Abram was little changed. Neither tall nor short, hair black as jet, eyes grey as stone. Ink marks beautified his hands and arms and chest. He wore a *jazerant*, a mail shirt sewn between layers of cloth, the inner layer padded and the outer layer black linen decorated with swirls of silver thread.

Abram had been a Mamluk — a child-slave, humbled and broken, remade as a warrior-slave. He purchased his freedom, then as an agent of the Order guided Finn on the hunt for the traitor, Robert of Saint Albans. Templars and Mamluks were bitter enemies. Some said it was because they were too alike; others said it was because every knight needs an enemy of equal skill. Finn had hated Abram, at first, but over time they formed a grudging respect, then friendship. Now he considered Abram a brother, though he had not seen, nor heard, from his brother since their hunt for Robert ended.

The White Monk was still scolding, louder now. Finn caught Rollo's eye and held up a fist to say, *Hold here.* Finn and Abram shuffled outside, where there was much embracing and slapping of backs.

"Playing lap dog to kings now, aye?"

"Better than playing lap dog to White Monks," Finn countered, and Abram nodded to concede the point. "Thought you'd headed home," Finn added.

"Nothing for me there. Besides, I was nine or thereabouts when last home, and I'm not certain I could find my way back." Abram was born a Svan, a mountain tribe in the distant, wild Caucasus Mountains, until snatched away by slavers. "I've hired myself out. Fought here and there. Ended up with Raymond. He is friendly to my kind and, more importantly, pays well for men who know their way around sharp steel."

Abram was skilled with the blade — impeccably so, in Finn's estimation.

Voices echoed in the chamber. The White Monk was humbly shouting.

"What's next?" Finn waved toward the citadel. "After this, I mean."

"Tiberias. Raymond wishes to visit his wife. She has a lady in Sibylla's entourage."

Abram meant a spy. Everyone used them. Christian. Saracen. Men. Women. Sometimes agents doubled their fee and worked both sides against the other. Finn had recent experience dealing with agents.

"Saladin had an agent in Tiberias," he said, the words slipping out unbidden.

"Had?"

"Rumour says a Christian crept into his villa and chibbed him," Finn said.

"Where?"

"Two in the kidneys, one behind the ear. Lights out. Never fails."

"No, I meant where was the villa?"

"Edge of town. Another agent in Jaffa three nights later. Nablus after that."

Abram bunched up his brows. "You are well informed."

"Rumour. As I said."

"Templars had nothing to do with knifing agents?"

Finn flashed a grin and changed course. "Does Raymond treat with Saladin, as men say?"

"Certes. He'd be stupid not too. Why fight what you can befriend?"

"Prudence in that. Risk too."

"Guy is a loggerhead." Abram flicked an errant lock of hair out of his eye. An inked crescent moon and three stars shone on the back of his hand. "He will doom this kingdom. Only Raymond is strong enough to make war or peace."

"Aye," Finn whispered. "But what does he plan?"

It was Abram's turn to say nothing and grin. But Finn could guess. *Certes something stews in Raymond's pot...*

The ruckus inside surged. Shouts. Curses.

"Something tells me you'll be leaving soon," Finn said.

He waved over the sergeant holding Abram's weapons. The man handed over a straight-bladed *saif*, plain but well-made, and a *qama*, the horn-handled short sword carried by men from the Caucasus. Abram nodded his thanks and tucked them into the red sash he wore as a belt.

The monks' other guards came out. The first was a tall, dark-skinned Moor. The second was black-haired with pale eyes — Armenian, by his look. Both showed ink-marks, like Abram, which marked them as retired or disgraced Mamluks. Abram introduced them as his brothers, and both offered dips of the chin, which Finn returned.

"God keep you, brothers," Finn said.

Abram did not believe in God — any God — but touched two fingers to his forehead and smiled politely. "Take care of yourself. And give Rollo a slap in the face for me." He leaned toward Finn's ear. "I still owe you my life. Do not think I have forgotten."

Abram, like Finn, had sought vengeance. He killed a Mamluk traitor and suffered wounds doing it. Finn fought to reach him, dragged him to safety, and coaxed him back to life.

Finn waved a dismissive hand. "When will you have the chance to repay the debt, eh?"

"One never knows," Abram said. "Expect the unexpected and you will never be surprised."

Finn was filled with an icy dread. Was a dream the cause? His mind grasped at swirling wisps and fleeting notions he could sense but not seize.

Then he smelled it. Rot.

He forced open his eyes and there was Robert — a darker smear in a dark corner of the room. The apostate came often in the days after Finn killed him, to taunt or mock. His hauntings were rare now. Finn's mind told him he was dreaming. Alone except for Rollo. And what used to be Robert. First a mentor, later a murderer and a traitor. At the end, he was prey Finn hunted and killed.

"Are you awake?" came the gravelly rasp.

"I am now," Finn said.

In life, the Englishman had been well-groomed. Not so in death. A Templar cappa — worn in mockery, Finn suspected — hung from him in brown-stained rags. Ribs and other bones shone white under the rents. His face was skeletal, though bits of flesh and sinew clung to his cheekbones and jaw. Oddly, his luxurious hair remained, combed neatly to one side, which only made the skeletal face more grotesque.

"My lord comes for you," Robert said, and clacked his teeth for emphasis.

"Leave." Finn had long since grown weary of Robert's riddles.

"My lord comes for you," the spectre repeated.

Finn sighed. "Saladin?"

"He is a lord, aye."

"He was your lord."

"In life. Now I am dead."

"Which lord do you mean? Certes not the Lord, for no heretic would be in His presence."

"The Lord is master of all, but there be many lords in the afterlife, just as in life. Some are not kind. Mine is one of them."

"The Devil? He comes for me, you say?" Finn laughed, though it came out brittle.

"He does. Remember Tomas? His MacDougall kin? They remember you."

In the darkness hovered the familiar faces of four men — eyeless, earless, tongueless. Finn's handiwork. They moaned and flailed their mutilated heads.

"May you forever wander deaf and dumb and blind," Finn growled, as he had that ugly night, and as he did every time the spectres visited him.

Robert made a dry wheezing sound intended as laughter. "Poor Tomas," he said. "You are stubborn and never forgive. I wonder if you will be forgiven?"

Silence. Finn prayed Robert had left. He had not.

"My lord comes. He brings pestilence, and famine, and death. War too. It builds, like liquid fire, soon to flow forth and scorch the earth." Robert ran his finger bones though his thick hair, a habit in life, though a grotesque tic in death. "I tell you this, Finn, from the love we once had, so you may see to your soul and reset your course afore it is too late."

"How kind of you."

Finn waited for more, but the spectre was gone, back whence it came. He lay a long time in his bedroll, awaiting the light.

CHAPTER 4

Autumn turned to winter. Folk celebrated its passing. Cool nights were welcome, certes, though days remained warm and dry as a bread-maker's oven. Drought tormented Outremer — as it had for years. Crops failed. Animals suffered. Dust blew. Rain was an eerie tale spoken around campfires to awe children.

Through it all, Raymond schemed, and Guy schemed, and agents passed to and fro.

Raymond proposed Humphrey of Toron, husband to Sibylla's half-sister, Isabella, as king. The Council of Nobles agreed. Humphrey did not. He wanted the crown like he wanted a nail in the head and in secret went to Guy and swore fealty. The king, in a rare moment of wisdom, forgave and forgot. The whole affair yanked the spine out of the rebellion, though, and in a slow stream nobles came to King Guy on bended knee.

Raymond did not. His allies did not.

"The elder Ibelin brother won't serve a half-wit." Rollo said. "Heard he went to Antioch."

"Aye?" Hector shook his head. "Shame. He was Outremer's best knight."

"I'm Outremer's best knight," Rollo said, and Hector arched a brow at that.

They were on the Road to Jericho, escorting Father Henric to Castle Kerak, and debating a crumbling kingdom as they travelled. Gerard said the chore was suited to Finn because, 'you are arrogant, as are the folk in Kerak, and you shall get along nicely.' The jest fell back on Gerard, for the road meant freedom — from Guy's puffery, from Gerard's venom, from the city's cloying walls.

Father Henric had recently been sent to Outremer by the Holy Father, Urban, as an advisor to the king — and as a spy. Guy promptly named him king's envoy and ordered him to the road, mostly to keep his nose out of the king's business. Henric was a small man with lively eyes, and was fitted for the occasion with a freshly plucked tonsure, a crisp brown habit, and freshly made turn shoes. He rode a palfrey stiff as a board, bounced and battered his arse, and like a child rattled off endless questions about this or that. At night he sermonized, or recited the Holy Book, which helped everyone get to their bedrolls early and sleep soundly.

Henric grew skittish with each passing hour, for he hunted a wolf — Raynald, the Red Wolf of Kerak.

He ruled Oultrejordain, a broad, ill-defined desert to the east of the Salt Sea. Kerak was his lair. From there he preyed on caravans travelling from Cairo to Damascus. The Red Wolf had done what wolves do — hunted and sacked a large *Hajj* caravan. Guards were massacred, *hajji* enslaved, booty hauled off. Some folk claimed he ravaged Saladin's sister, though Finn smelled the lie in it, for they would be at war if such a foul deed had been done to the Sultan's kin.

"How old are you, Brother Finn?"

Henric's question brought Finn's wandering mind to roost. He tugged up the hood of his cappa to shade his face from the sun. "Thirty-one, I think."

"And how do you find your life? As a Templar, I mean."

"I live humbly. Want for nothing. Serve others."

"This pleases you?"

"It does."

"Where do you sleep?"

"Wherever I am."

"You own nothing?"

"Not the mail on my back, nor the roof over my head."

"Is Jerusalem not your home?"

Finn shrugged. "Sometimes it is. Our temple is there."

"We brought nothing into this world and take nothing from it," Henric said. "But if a man has food, and clothing, and friends, he can be content. Timothy wrote this."

"A wise man," Finn said, suggesting he had read Timothy, which he had not.

"Indeed." Henric gave a thin smile. "You live much like our saviour did — except for the sword and the bloodshed and the killing."

"Aye. Except for those."

"I wonder what our saviour would say of that?"

"He might say, 'Well done, my son.' For you see —" Finn sifted his memory, then recited one of the few scriptures branded there — "God is a god of war."

"Exodus, chapter fifteen." Henric arched a brow to indicate he was impressed. "Saracens innumerable. Skulking along the frontier, the Devil lurking just beyond. I find it all dreadfully frightful. Though I suppose it does not frighten you?"

"Couldn't practise my trade if it did."

Finn did not fret over his trade — war. Instead, he craved it like a drunkard craves wine. He often wondered why that was. Madness? He was not mad — or at least he did not think so. Belief? Aye. Training? Certes. But most of all, he had long since accepted he would die here, in Outremer, and acceptance made mortality comforting. He did not seek death. Neither did he fear it. Every warrior needed to accept it as a probable outcome, morbid though it may be, for otherwise he could not fight.

"Trade. What an amusing term for war." Henric smiled to soften his words. "So many places to practise your trade, I imagine. Why here? Atonement for a grievous sin committed in a corner of the world?"

"Grievous *sins*," Finn corrected, "and it was a far-flung corner of the world."

He gazed sideways at Henric's knowing, sunburned face.

Ah, youthful iniquities, the good Father must be thinking, Finn thought. *Same story for many a Templar. Wrath. Murder. Greed. Or was it evils of the flesh? A dash of each, perhaps? Certes defending God's kingdom will remit them all.*

Yet God's kingdom was infested by greedy, scheming nobles, the Order led by an arrogant, vengeful man. Finn had served three Masters. They all carried defects. No man is perfect. But Gerard's flaws were sundry. Obeying him tried Finn's vow of obedience and, with every devious act, splattered him with complicity and guilt.

Bitter experience remade the naïve knight, and through wiser eyes, Finn savvied the true Gerard. Now Finn fought for his brothers, whom he loved, and for the people who could not fight for themselves. He would fight, for it was what he did best, though he questioned his reward.

"What reward do I seek for my labours?" Finn gave the expected reply. "Paradise."

Henric bowed his head. "'To the one who is victorious, I will give the right to eat from the tree of life, which is in the paradise of God. He who...'"

Finn's mind drifted from the sermon — as it often did these days.

Does the holy word wear thin in my ears? Or am I just worn thin?

Oultrejordain, known in ancient times as Edom and Moab, stretched through the Negev Desert from the tip of the Gulf of Aqaba to the Dead Sea. It was a hard land, like the people in it, the landscape barren and marked by endless expanses of bare earth, mountains worn to nubs by eons of desert winds. Deluges, when they came, carved ravines off the spiny ridges and slopes. Deep wadis intermingled on the low ground in sundry coils.

Rollo spoke the inevitable. "What a hellhole."

Henric took the bait. "You are sadly mistaken, good sir. This is holy ground."

"Been here many a time and am yet to see anything holy. No water. Serpents the length of your leg. The only satisfaction I find here is in the work."

"Which is?"

"Killing Saracens."

It was a tired quip. Rollo grinned to himself, though no one else joined in.

The Templars entered the town of Kerak at the end of the fourth day. They wound their way along narrow cobbled streets set between low stone houses, then neared a staggered two-storey inn, old as the apostles. A dark-eyed man in blue robes stood in the doorway. Finn dipped his chin in greeting; the man replied in kind, fingers touched to his forehead in a greeting common among Mahounds.

Castle Kerak loomed over the town. It sat on a plateau surrounded on three sides by near-vertical hills — like a galley cresting a wave of rock. Finn and Father Henric crossed a wood bridge to the postern gate, set in the wall between two towers. Finn banged on the door and waited. He raised a fist to bang again when the peephole creaked open. A filmy eye gazed out.

"Aye?"

"Brother Finnláech. With the king's envoy, Father Henric, to see Lord Raynald."

"Who?"

"Brother Finn. A Templar."

"Finn? Never heard of her."

"No. *Brother* Finn. Is Lord Raynald here?"

"One should hope so. It's his castle. But he's not seeing anyone. Go away."

"He must receive the king's envoy." Finn tipped his head toward Henric.

"Envoy?"

"Aye. With Templars."

The watery eye blinked.

"God's bones," Finn cursed, and swiped a hand through his hair. "Listen. We —"

"Templars? Why didn't you say so?"

Metal thumped and scraped. The door creaked open. The filmy eye belonged to an usher, stooped, scrawny, with wisps of grey topping his head. He led Finn and his band to the upper courtyard, muttering all the while about folk who mutter too much, and with a flail of his hand bade them wait. The usher shuffled away; a while later he shuffled back.

"Lord Raynald is preparing to sup," he said, "and bids you join him." The usher swept a hand to encompass the sergeants and Turcs. "Food will be brought to these."

"Deaf eejit," Lugh grumbled.

"Eh?" said the usher.

"Indeed," said Lugh.

Finn, Father Henric, and the knights tailed the usher through keeled stone archways and vaulted stone hallways. The way was dark. Sputtering lamps set in wall niches made little difference.

A man lay in the shadows, dead drunk, or maybe just dead. A doorway yawned ahead. Muted conversation and soft notes from a lute echoed. The moist, salty aroma of roasted meat drifted, and Finn's stomach rumbled. They stepped into a spacious hall. Faded tapestries draped the walls. A long plank table spread the length of the room.

Raynald lounged at the head of the table in a huge, battered chair. A grey-haired knight sat at his elbow. Two dogs, Canaans, watched, aloof and indifferent. A handful of younger knights arrayed along the table. Jugs of wine and cups abounded.

A knight was passed out, head back in his chair, mouth yawning. Two others across the table balled bits of bread and tried to lob them into the drunkard's mouth. A toss hit his chin, bounced off, and the tosser swore and slapped a coin on the table. The next piece bounced in and the drunk awoke with a snort, glanced about stupidly, then began chewing.

Roaring laughter. Slapping of knees. Someone shouted, '*Dévorer*.'

Finn had given up alcohol years ago, as part of his vows, and in the sober years since he had realized the sport of drunkards was only amusing to other drunkards. He surveyed the room. *No women. Lots of drink, yet a tense air despite it. This is a council of war, not a supper...*

The usher led them to the centre of the room, and in a too-loud voice announced, "Brothers Finnleech and Himlich, of the Church of ... the Temple."

Raynald and his knights chortled at the senile usher. When the ruckus ebbed, Henric bowed and said, "I am Father Henric, King Guy's confessor, and today his envoy." He swept a hand over the Templars. "Brothers Finn of Struan, Rollo of Caen, Hector de la Roca, and Serlo of Bellême."

"Well met, Brothers." Raynald's long red hair twisted over his shoulder and cascaded onto his chest to mingle with the beard resting there. His eyes shone like blue glass, cold and keen, his jaw square and proud. He fanned a hand toward the chairs. "Sit. Sup with me."

Finn and Henric took seats opposite Raynald, and the other Templars settled to Finn's right. A minstrel sat in the corner and began playing the lute. A vielle and lyre rested on a rack near his knee. He plucked an edgy tune and sang about a young maiden wooed by a knight who by night became a wolf. The player was white-haired, aged, and very good. Henric was beaming, tapping a toe to the rhythm until he saw Finn's stare and put on a stern face.

Servants brought heaped trenchers. Pickled walnuts. Honeyed almonds. Salty cheese. Creamed bream and eels spiced with cardamom. Salt-brined roast pig stuffed with nutmeg, saffron, apple, and bread. Some of the spices were local. The food was otherwise defiantly French — Raynald, unlike many from Christendom, resisted going native. Only his dogs were indigenous.

Henric dove into prayer. "Lord, bless our host, and bless this bounty, that it may strengthen and nourish our bodies..." He even blessed the minstrels' performance, and beseeched any travellers may return safely to their homes.

"Amen." Finn made the sign of the cross and looked up to see Raynald, lounging into the arm of his chair, staring back with a tilted head.

"Have we met?"

"Not with polite introductions, Lord Raynald." Finn paused to gesture down the table at Rollo and the others. "We fought at Montgisard. You might have seen us there. And you might have seen us tending Young Baldwin's coffin."

"Montgisard." Raynald gazed up at the vaulted ceiling and ran a tongue over his yellow teeth. "Now that was a brawl to remember. Bloody fun, aye?"

Finn nodded.

Raynald tapped a finger on the table, then pointed it at Finn. "You're the madman that chased after Saladin."

Finn nodded again.

"What would you have done if you'd caught him, I wonder." Raynald tossed a scrap to one of the Canaans, who snatched it from the air. "Like a dog chasing a cart. To his surprise, he catches it, and has no idea what to do. Bite it? Let it go?"

"Kill it, what else?"

"Would that you had. Would've saved us all a hell of a lot of trouble. And Robert of Saint Albans… Tell me, was it difficult, killing one of your own?"

Finn stared off. Dark memories roiled up like smoke.

The ambush in Arish. Brother Petrus, dead. Robert trying to take Jerusalem for Saladin. The battle at the pass. Brother Michael, dead. Hunting Robert through the mountains and over the Jordan. Abram, leading Finn into Robert's camp under the guise of a prisoner. Fighting his men. Knifing the apostate as he sat in a chair. Dying breath in Finn's face, blood on his hands. More dead brothers. Abram, exacting revenge. Battling vengeful Mamluks. Setting fire to the camp and leaving it wreathed in smoke and swirling ash.

Finn shrugged. "Not much to it, really."

Killing former brothers proved much like killing anyone else, in truth, though the aftermath was proving more arduous.

The minstrel altered course to pluck a rising and triumphant tune, and Raynald said, "What you did might be considered murder, if you were not a Templar."

"I'm immune to the laws of man. Comes in handy at times."

"Templars — what brotherhood of criminals has ever been more cleverly concocted." "Such privilege demands sacrifice, though. Chasity foremost among them." Raynald gave Finn a meaningful stare. "I hear some Templars cavort with women. Test their vows."

Finn ignored him, and the minstrel flowed into a doleful song about forbidden love.

Father Henric cleared his throat.

Raynald continued to stare at Finn but spoke to Henric. "Spit it out, priest."

"Lord Raynald. I am sent by King Guy on a most serious matter. You raided a caravan — a *Hajj* caravan, at that." Henric's voice deepened ominously. "You broke the truce. The four-year truce agreed to in 1185."

"Truce?" Raynald glanced to the older knight at his side. "Oy, Alain, you ever heard of such nonsense?" Alain played along, scrunched up his weathered face and shook his head. Raynald gave up the charade and pointed east. "Satan is there, living in filth, like an animal. The breezes carry his reek to us. And one does not make peace with a reeking, filthy animal."

"There is a truce, Lord," Henric insisted.

"I made no such agreement, nor will I, and I am not beholden to agreements made by others."

"Sacking the caravan caused outrage, Lord. There are grave complications, which you must rectify for the benefit of the people, for the well-being of the kingdom. The king insists. The sultan insists."

"I must do nothing, priest. The caravan is spoils. Taken under the law of war."

"The king strenuously objects to you keeping the spoils and selling the prisoners. King Guy insists you make amends. Otherwise, you give the Sultan cause to break the truce and war will be your recompense — nay, war will be *our* recompense."

"Hmm," Raynald said. "War. That would be bad, aye?"

"Very bad. The king will be most displeased."

"Displeased? Why didn't you say so earlier?"

Henric cinched his eyes, just now suspecting he was being mocked.

Raynald took the moment to make himself clearer.

"Many of the old families opposed Guy. I did not. I made him. His wife made him. The Templars made him. We can unmake him, too, if need be." Raynald pointed at Henric with his eating knife. "I am lord of my land, just as Guy is lord of his. I do as I please, when I please, as I please. None shall stop me. Not Guy. Certainly not the Sultan."

Henric said nothing, tapped a finger on his wine glass.

"You hear me, Father?"

"I hear you, Lord Raynald. And I shall give the king your foolish reply."

"Foolish?" Raynald stabbed the eating knife into the table. The torchlight made his red hair glisten like blood. "Tread carefully, little man. I carve any who insults me — even a man of God."

"Carve one man of God and you must carve us all," Finn said, in a voice soft but cold. "And you will find not all men of God are so easily carved."

The music ended on a dissonant chord. The chatter ended with it.

Raynald fixed Finn with his ice-blue glare; Finn returned his own black-eyed glare. Henric shifted in his chair and made a soft pacifying sound in his throat.

Finn and Raynald kept glaring, until Raynald took up the rib in his trencher and took a grinning bite. "A spanking is all I meant." He mimed a slap at Henric, then fanned a hand at the minstrel, who began plucking a festive ditty. Chatter resumed. Through a mouthful, Raynald said, "Eat, eat, we're all friends here."

Finn shared a despairing look with Henric that said, *That didn't go as hoped...*

Finn tried the pork. Salty with a touch of sweet — rich fare for a Templar, and he ate like an ascetic. A dog padded over and nuzzled his hand, and he slipped it bits of meat.

The usher toddled into the room. "Lord Raynald!" he yelled.

Raynald waved a rib to say, *Speak.*

"The Sultan's envoys have returned. They request an audience, Lord."

Raynald stared at the old man, sucked at a piece of meat wedged in between a tooth, then glanced at Finn. "Sent them away thrice afore. But let us have some entertainment." To the usher, he said, "Bring the dogs afore me. Offer no hospitality. And we shall watch them grovel."

A moment later, eight Saracens trooped in; two stepped forward, a fair-haired youth and the blue-robed man from the inn in town. Kohl lined the man's eyes and turned them into dark chasms. Sharp eyes glinted like a gloved falcon. His beard was long and wet with scented oil.

The envoys lingered, ignored and slighted. Raynald let them stew as he made a show of chatting with Rollo about Montgisard, the charge, and all the Saracens slain. In a too-loud voice he asked Finn to recount the killing of Ahmad al-Taqi. He harkened back to the battle, where his lance had spit the man like a bug on a pin, and his death helped shift the tide. The young man's father, Taqi al-Din, one of Saladin's generals, named Finn *al-Safak*, the murderer, and offered a helmet full of gold for his head.

The blue-robed man shifted his hawk-eyed glare at Finn, and thereafter it never strayed far. The fair-haired youth cleared his throat.

Raynald favoured the young man with a glance, then feigned surprise, as if just noticing him. He hefted a rib. "Pig. Would you care for some? Perhaps a cup of wine to chase it down?"

"We thank you for your hospitality, Lord." The young man had blue eyes and spoke good French. "Alas, pig is forbidden to us, as is wine."

"Forbidden? How surprising." Raynald did not sound surprised. "If you did not come to enjoy my food and drink, why are you here?"

The young man inclined a head toward the blue-robed man and opened his mouth to rattle off introductions. Raynald sliced the air with a curt hand to cut him short.

"Musa. I recognize this man. Distant kin of Saladin, if memory serves. Speak, Musa, for I grow sleepy with each passing moment."

Raynald called him by his *ism*, his name, and purposefully ignored his lineage names, his *kunya*, *nasab*, *nispa*, and forwent his many honorifics.

Musa gave a scathing glare, then launched into a lengthy speech in Arabic. Sharp white teeth flashed in a black beard as he spoke. His gestures were as important as his words, as was the way with Saracens. Each gesture was calculated to augment his words. He brought an arm forward, pursed fingers down, and made stabbing gestures of warning as he talked. He finished with a deft flourish of a hand, like an illusionist at a bazaar, then laced his fingers over his chest and raised a chin.

The younger man began translating. "We are envoys sent by Ṣalāḥ al-Dīn An-Nasir Yūsuf ibn Ayyūb, Sultan of Egypt and…"

The young man waned as Alain, the grey-haired knight next to Raynald, tapped the table and held up a hand for silence. He raised an arse cheek, grimaced, and loosed a long, soggy fart. Laughter coursed around the room. Another fart echoed in a gassy challenge. More laughter.

Alain shrugged. "It's natural. Everyone does it."

The envoys swapped looks from the corners of their eyes, their lips flat and pale.

"You were saying?" Raynald prompted the young man.

"Lord." The young man ran a hand down his silk-clad chest and breathed out. "Musa reminds you of the truce between our peoples. Attacking his caravan breaks this truce. *Hajji* were taken, some killed, wares stolen. The Sultan requests you make restitution. Return what was stolen and he, in his magnanimity, will forgive the offences. He also requests that you free his subjects. Believers should not be slaves. Slavery is not —"

"Where were you born, boy?"

"Born, Lord?"

"Aye. Born."

"Nablus."

"And your mother?"

"Nablus."

"Your father?"

"Also Nablus, Lord. His father came from Gascony."

"So, born in Outremer to Christian parents, which makes you a Poulain." Raymond hitched a brow in mock surprise. "Why, I'd wager you were stolen in a Saracen raid, hauled away as spoils, and are now a slave."

"Servant, Lord. I was a slave but was manumitted, by the gracious will of my master."

"Servant. Slave. Is there a difference?"

The young man had no argument to offer.

"There is no difference in what I have done and what Saladin has done. None. By might I took, as has Saladin." Raynald fanned a lazy hand. "Your Sultan's hypocrisy stinks worse than Alain's farts."

Finn kept an eye on Musa — eyes flicking to and fro, lips cinching tighter at each slight. *He speaks more French than he lets on...* He glanced at Henric, who sipped wine and stared at one of the Canaans, as if willing the dog to speak out against the madness. The king's envoy had been ploughed under by Raynald and lacked the spine to dig his way out.

Musa launched into a long, peppery speech of some length. He finished with another theatrical hand flourish, then shot Finn with a glare sharp enough to draw blood. The young man gazed into nothing.

"And what did your master say?" Raynald prompted, then held up a hand. "Wait. By your frightened mien I can guess — something about bloodshed and war and death, no?"

The young man opened his mouth, but his master's hand stilled him.

Musa glared at Raynald with eyes wide and unblinking. He made a show of placing his first finger and thumb together, facing askance, and pointed with his three remaining fingers. It was a gesture to say, *I will break you*, and at the same time, *This discussion is done.* He stabbed the hand with each point made — now made in halting French.

"The Sultan will hammer your king's gold crown, and with it shoe his war steed. Bats will lair in the palaces of the so-called lords of so-called Outremer, and their whimpering children will flow like water through the hands of slavers. Also you die. Madman. Peace-breaker."

Raynald made a show of yawning, rolling his head side to side as he did.

"Would-be defiler of holy places," Musa hissed, and made a final stab with the three fingers. "Your head will roll in the dust of the desert, by the Sultan's own hand, and your corpse will rot in the sun and dirt, unburied and defiled. This he vows."

"This he vows?" Raynald lunged forward and slapped the table. "I am here. Bid him come for me. I vow *he* will die by my hand! Then I will piss in his dead eyes, and in his dead mouth, and feed his bits to my dogs and laugh as they shit him out."

The young man did not need to translate that.

"I could have you skinned alive and thrown out with the rubbish." Raynald eased back and gave a dramatic sigh. "Alas, you are under the sacred protection afforded all envoys. You will keep your skin. You will not be tossed from the walls."

"Pity," Alain muttered. "They make such a satisfying sound when they hit."

"Besides, I've a task for you," Raynald said. "Carry a missive from me to your master."

Musa's chin jutted in defiant anger.

The Lord of Kerak made a show of stroking his beard. "Tell him…" He gave a dramatic pause. "Tell him to bugger himself."

The room erupted into laughter. Alain pounded the table in hysterics.

Musa flushed crimson at this final offence. He spun on his heel, swirled his robes around himself, then swept toward the door. The young man followed in his wake. Someone flung a pig bone, which bounced from Musa's back and left a smear of grease on his crisp blue robes. The minstrel sprang up from his chair and crept along behind the entourage in shuffling, stop-start steps, strumming a dramatic tune on a viol to mock their departure.

Raynald turned to Finn. "And that, Templar, is how you treat a Sandpig."

No, that is how you start a war. Which is what you want. Finn was appalled at the treatment of the envoys but said the expected in a flat voice. "Your discourse was elegant and well-reasoned."

Folk claimed Raynald was a madman. Ill-tempered. Dangerous. He was all of these. But he was also a savvy leader, fearless, endlessly loyal to his friends. A keen, calculating mind lived behind Raynald's sharp blue eyes, and it deserved a healthy measure of respect.

Father Henric thought otherwise.

"Churl," he said, too softly for Raynald's ears. "Seeds sown in the past bear fruit in the future, though the fruits of war are sorrow and taste of ash."

CHAPTER 5

The night was moonless. Stars carpeted the sky, crisp and cold and bright.

Finn huddled by the fire, wrapped in his cloak to ward off the desert chill. Smoky tendrils spiralled into the night sky, trailed by orange sparks that sputtered and died. He imagined those tendrils like scent trails, from him to out there, and at the other end a blue-robed man raised a bearded chin and breathed in the traces of his prey. The wheel pommel of Finn's sword, Oathkeeper, nestled against his shoulder under the cloak. Finn fingered the naked blade, cold steel, slick with a sheen of oil.

Father Henric's teeth chattered, though with cold or fear only he could say. "But Joseph said to them, 'Don't be afraid. Am I in the place of God? You intended to harm me, but God intended it for good...'"

Genesis, maybe? Finn listened but did not hear. Every so often he threw in a grunt or a nod.

Playing bait was cruelty to the nerves.

Rollo lay faux-snoring in his bedroll, staring across the flames at Finn and grinning like a demon. A deep scar ran diagonally from Rollo's cheek, through his lips, and onto his chin, and the flickering light made it writhe. Serlo and Hector huddled by a second fire nearby. Other bedrolls lay in the dark, only they held bits of kit covered by blankets to form the shape of a man. Sergeants and Turcs hid in the darkness, away from the flames, in a ring of flesh and steel. Sitting by the fire made the knights blind to the night, vulnerable, thus dependent on the lively eyes of the sergeants and Turcs.

"'Bandits will raid Gad,'" Henric continued, teeth chattering, "'but Gad will raid them back.'"

Aye, Genesis, I remember that one…

Raid and counter-raid, trap and counter-trap. The eternal dance of fighting men. Tonight's trap was an old cateran trick used by raiders the world over — Finn had first used it in the hills of Alba. Success lay in letting the prey get close, but not too close, then pouncing just as they pulled back on the bow strings. Arrows and bolts would do most of the work. All that remained after was tidying up the mess.

Time passed.

Henric was somewhere near the end of Genesis, Finn guessed, and ploughing toward Exodus. The bark of a jackal echoed in the dark and Finn's head came up. *Jackal? Trite. I'd have gone with the call of an owl.* He gripped Oathkeeper. Rollo grinned wider and Finn returned a toothy grin of his own.

Henric stumbled in his recitation. "'If there is further … further injury … you shall impose a punishment, a penalty … life for life, eye for eye, tooth for tooth…'"

The jackal barked again, surprisingly close, and another answered in kind. Finn was chilled but a bead of sweat rolled down his nose, lingered at the tip, and fell.

A sudden buzz and a thump and a shriek. More snaps and thrums as arrows flew off strings. Yelps and thuds. A tribal trill in Arabic. The scuffle of boots.

A shadow rushed from the darkness, howling like a death-angel, fire-lit silver coming back in a vicious arc. Finn tossed off the cloak as he leapt up and swayed aside. Sharp death hissed past close enough to shave hairs from his head. He caught a glimpse of wild, kohl-dark eyes, the shimmer of an oiled beard, a swirl of blue robes.

Oathkeeper flashed back and cut across — Musa's head tumbled from his shoulders. The headless body, none the wiser, stomped through the flames before falling in a cascade of sparks and smoke and crimson.

The shooting and shrieking passed in a blink. The horses tethered nearby nickered at the scent of fresh blood on the breeze. Rollo stood wide-legged, sword in one fist, dagger in the other, head swivelling to and fro as he sought a foe. He found none.

"Too slow, all gone," Finn said.

Rollo growled in frustration, then sent up a spray of sand with a swipe of his sword.

Jerol strolled into the firelight with a spent crossbow propped on each shoulder. "Seven dead — the fair-haired lad among them. We are thirteen. They had spine, or were mad."

Seven Saracens gone — like chaff winnowed away in a gust of wind.

"Mad with revenge," Rollo said, and dropped by the sputtering fire. His head shot up. "There were eight of them at Kerak."

"Which means one rode to Saladin carrying the Red Wolf's reply," Jerol said, finishing the thought. "The others trailed us — trailed Finn, I mean."

Father Henric had not moved. He sat with his cloak clutched to his chin, shivering, then nodded toward Musa's smouldering robes. "You killed him ... cut his head clean off."

"Aye." Finn glanced at the head, tottering on its crown. "Would seem so."

Sergeants and Turcs were sauntering in, wiping their blades on scraps of blue silk, a last indignity to the envoys, and grinning at the trick they had done. Lugh stabbed each Saracen in the heart, just to be certain, and patted down each corpse for rings or coins while Finn pretended not to see. Elias came in, trailing seven Arab horses and again as many rounceys. Sergeants dragged bodies into a nearby wadi while Turcs saddled horses and stowed gear. No one wanted to spend the night in a place of blood and ghosts.

The knights sat by the fire with Henric. Finn cleaned Oathkeeper with a linen cloth.

"How did ... you know ... they would come?" Henric's chattering showed little sign of easing.

Finn spelled out the obvious — or what was obvious to a man of war.

Musa wore the colours of Taqi al-Din, close kin to Saladin. Lord Raynald, unable to resist, had stuck a knife in the man's pride and twisted it. His bragging about Ahmad al-Taqi's death, about butchered Saracens, and the bounty on Finn's head had made Musa hot enough to start a fire. It did not take a prophet to see what would come next. Elias had lagged behind, watched the road from Kerak, then reported what Finn already sensed — the envoys had sniffed Finn's trail, the tools of diplomacy set aside for the tools of revenge. Honour dictated it. Hatred ensured it.

"They've haunted us for two nights," Rollo said, "waiting for one of us to trundle into the dark for a piss or a shite."

Henric's eyes flared at that.

"Now you've gone and scared Father Henric," Hector said.

They all laughed — except for Henric, who was deciding life in the king's palace was preferable to life on the road as the king's envoy. Owen and Lugh came for the headless Musa, robes still smoking, and grabbed his arms to drag him off.

"Feigning ignorance invites overconfidence," Finn said to Henric. "An old cateran trick from the Highlands. Learned it from the MacDougalls, then turned it back on them."

Owen's head snapped up at the Scottish clan name.

"Old enemies, the MacDougalls." Finn kept an eye on Owen while dabbing at Oathkeeper. "After years of quarrels they wanted peace, they claimed, though it proved a lie. They killed some of ours — by breaking the ancient law of hospitality, mind you. So we snuck into their glen to settle the score. Crept through the pines, quiet as ghosts, until we found them."

"What happened?" Henric's piping voice dropped to a whisper.

"I'm still here. They're not." Finn flailed a hand to say he had bragged too much. He fixed Owen with a squinty stare. "You know any MacDougalls?"

Owen shook his head, and in Gaelic said, "No. I hail from Strathpeffer. Wouldna ken MacDougalls. Nor Donnachaidh. Like I told ye afore."

Finn waved Owen back to his task. "Don't forget the head."

Alba, also called Scotland, birthed sundry folk. Languages were a confounding mélange. Finn was descended from an old Highland family, Gaelic people. Thus he spoke Scots-Gaelic, but also French-Norman, as most noble-born did. He even managed Scots, which some called Inglis, the tongue spoken by a Northumbrian and favoured in the merchant and craftsmen burghs dotting his homeland. Owen, from what Finn could divine, spoke only Scots-Gaelic, which implied a life outside well-heeled circles. This, combined with what little else he knew about the man, hinted at a life in shadowy and forsaken places.

Rollo squinted at Owen and spoke to Finn. "Strange lad, Owen. Always seems busy but doesn't accomplish much. Like he's waiting for more interesting things to happen."

Now the bodies lay in the wadi, not out of kindness but out of necessity, for Finn wanted to be in Jerusalem by the time

Musa's kin found him. They climbed into saddles and rode into the darkness, while somewhere under the vast eastern sky Saladin waited for word from a kinsman that was already dead.

Winter turned to spring. Templars guarded roads busy with pilgrims and watched for Saladin's attack that never came — though all agreed it must come soon. From his lair Raynald the Red Wolf mocked friend and foe alike. Above Outremer, dark storm clouds gathered.

Finn had returned to the Temple in Jerusalem after a patrol.

Squires set the tables in the refectory while others dragged in a steaming pot. Eating bowls were rough, hand-carved affairs, and each pair of Templars shared one. Knights filed in and took their seats as the green-robed chaplain commenced prayer.

"Blessed are you, Lord our God, maker of heaven and earth. Bless this daily bread, and grant that all who eat it may be strengthened and nourished, and grant your faithful servants..."

Finn did not hear the chaplain's words. Worldly thoughts filled his head; Raynald's arrogant mien; Gerard's false smile. The Master was headstrong, often reckless, always mad for the Order. Now he just seemed mad.

"...and Lord, bless the Holy Father, that he may..." The chaplain was in fine fettle and, if past performances were any indication, would plod on for a while longer.

Rollo faked a snore and Finn ignored it. The Master's words from the coronation echoed in his head; "I should order an attack." *Attack a Christian? Are we becoming rabid wolves, feeding on one another instead of sheep?* Laying a hand on another Christian was cause for losing the habit, yet the Master, leader of the Order, proposed just such a sin.

A chorus of "amen" brought Finn's mind back to the present. Squires ladled steaming food into bowls and stacked bread on plates.

"Pottage — what a surprise." Rollo thumped the table with his palm. "God blesses me. He does. Bland. Mushy. And so damned much of it!"

Something grey and wet slopped into Finn and Rollo's bowl. Finn flourished a hand to say, *All yours, Brother.*

Rollo picked up his horn spoon and pointed it at Serlo. "I'm a lover of breakfast. A good start to the day means a good finish to the day, Ma always said. Don't you agree?"

Serlo nodded. Taking to him was like talking to a statue, though with fewer replies.

"Don't overwhelm me with words," Rollo said. "Tough on my ears. Worse on my mind."

The chaplain looked daggers. Silence was expected. Rollo waved a hand in apology, his usual reply to a reprimand, and tucked into the pottage.

The chaplain began reading scripture. "'He reached from on high. He drew me out of deep waters. He delivered me from my enemies and from those who hated me, for they were mightier than I…'"

Jean slid down the bench. The Frenchman steepled his fingers at his lips. It was a mock pose of prayer, used to hide his mouth so he might speak through the fingers — a skill perfected by all Templars sworn to silence.

Jean looked at Finn but tipped his head toward Rollo. "Why must he act the buffoon?"

"It's no act," Finn said through his own prayer fingers.

"Heard that, you arses," Rollo garbled around a mouthful of pottage.

"Buffoon," Jean repeated.

Rollo and Jean abided each other. Neither prized in the other what Finn prized in each.

Jean kept at the mock prayer pose. "Cannot fathom we are going after Raymond."

"What?"

The chaplain was laying into another scripture and Jean stopped to listen.

"'...when evildoers assailed me to eat my flesh, my adversaries and foes, they stumbled and fell. Though an army may encamp against me, my heart shall not fear...'"

"One of my favourite Psalms," Jean said, before turning back to Finn. "You have not heard the news, I see. Master Gerard convinced King Guy to bring Raymond to heel. We ride first thing tomorrow to encircle Tiberias and, if Raymond refuses to take the knee, we will take her."

"Why wasn't I invited?"

"Because you are not the Master's pet at the moment?"

Finn dipped his head to acknowledge the truth there. He stared into nothing, pondering, while Rollo grumbled over his dull meal and the chaplain recited scriptures about gratitude.

Mael, Jean's second, slid onto the bench and assumed the fake prayer pose. "Rider just arrived. From Tiberias. Says Saladin asked permission for Mamluks to cross Raymond's lands."

Jean's fingers dropped. "How many?"

"Seven thousand. Or thereabouts."

"Seven thousand," Jean repeated. "Raymond consented?"

"The truce with Saladin gave him no choice. Raymond said they are to be gone within two days, though, and are to harm neither man nor animal. Saladin agreed."

Finn glanced at Rollo. "The tracks Arlo saw, near the frontier..."

"...envoys, riding to Tiberias, guarded by Mamluks," Rollo finished.

Mamluks were snatched from the cradle, enslaved and trained to arms. They obeyed one master, Saladin, and lived for one pleasure. War. Mamluks and Templars were sore enemies. One of the fiends had carved the deep, long furrow across Finn's face, and he stroked a palm over the ragged scar.

"All that throws a wrinkle into your attack on Tiberias."

Mael dropped the prayer fingers to show a grin. "Odd you should say that, Finn. Master frets we might find trouble and ordered everyone into the saddle — even you."

"Even me. How desperate things must be."

"Here. Here. And here." Gerard leaned over the map and stabbed a finger at the roads leading to Tiberias. "Templars will guard these. Your men," he paused to tap in two places, then made a wide sweep to the east, "will form along these points. Together we will encircle the city, then sweep in unannounced. Raymond will have no choice but to come to you on bended knee, Sire."

Gerard, as a Templar, was not obligated to call a king his sire, for Templars owed allegiance only to God. Yet he did. *Flattery never harms.*

They sat in King Guy's tent on the road not far from Jerusalem. A campaign table stood between them. The table was an artefact of King Baldwin; Guy owned nothing so aged and battered. The map lay over it, held down at the corners by metal discs. Candlelight flickered on three popinjays dressed in bright silks; they wore boots pointed at the toes and carried blades fresh from the smith's fire — the newly formed king's guard. They tried for bravado in their manner but fell so far short even Guy snickered.

77

Gerard realized the king was stroking his chin and staring at the map.

"Raymond will come to you on bended knee," Gerard repeated, "or face consequences for treachery. By hook or crook, you win, Sire."

Guy glanced up. "By hook or crook — I like that. Flemish saying?"

"English."

"Well. I still like it."

The king's gaze flicked back to the map.

Dithering ... again.

"Sire," Gerard said, "the rebel faction, led by Raymond, must be brought into the fold. Your kingdom can afford no doubters, no fissures, no fractures. Unity must —"

Guy held up a hand, then let it wilt until it rested on his knee. "We thank you for your counsel, Master Gerard. Tomorrow we will do as you advise. Close the roads. Encircle the city. Force Raymond to his knees."

Gerard dipped his chin. "There is a saying in Flanders. When faced with a difficult decision, the best thing a king can do is the correct thing; the worst thing he can do is nothing."

The saying was not Flemish; he had made it up. Guy nodded once, and it settled his mind — for now. They sipped wine and mulled over the plan. Gerard, sometime later, stepped into the night full of confidence. *Raymond will be broken and battered ... and I will be there to see it, and he will know it was me.*

His triumphant gaze landed on Balian of Ibelin, standing in the light of a flickering torch. An usher led him toward the king's tent. He heeled in before Gerard.

"Master Gerard. Well met."

The younger Ibelin was lean but ledge-shouldered, like a youth just come into manhood, though he was no boy. Pale crow's feet creased the corners of his eyes and showed the colour his skin before the sun had tanned it. Chestnut-hued hair hung past his ears and he wore a close-cropped beard splashed with grey. Balian's blue eyes were keen yet calm, a little world-weary, perhaps, and the mix gave an air of confidence and competence.

"Lord Balian." Gerard offered a tip of the head. "Come to join the king's sortie?"

"Come to offer counsel — as have you, I see."

"It is the king's will to settle accounts with Raymond — to visit the prodigal son, so to speak. He will not be persuaded from this difficult task."

"Will not be persuaded?" A smile said Balian would wager otherwise. "Well. My king awaits and I must attend him. A good night to you, Master Gerard."

"God's blessing, Lord Balian." Sudden realization swept over Gerard. *Crafty bastard. The king heeds whoever last whispers in his ear, and you arranged to be the last whisperer.*

The tent flap opened and a flood of wan, flickering light shone before it closed. Gerard stood in the dark and thought of Guy, and Balian, and Raymond. He liked none of them, but he especially did not like a king so easily persuaded. *Or at least so easily persuaded by others.*

Gerard began walking toward the rows of Templar tents.

His knight fell in beside him. "We attack on the morrow, Master?"

"Aye. The plan is made." Gerard spoke with a certainty he did not feel. Balian's calm, confident face haunted his thoughts. "It cannot, will not, be unmade now."

Templars formed in the weak light of the morning sun. Golden rays warmed them in hues of orange and red and yellow. White-crowned wheatears flitted through the scrubs in low-flying bands, their calls rising and falling in mirror of their play on the wing. They were piebald birds, with a black body and white crown, thus often called Templar birds by locals.

The morning brought news.

Balian had reasoned and, God be praised, Guy had listened. The king and the Army of Jerusalem were returning home. Balian and Josias, the Archbishop of Tyre, would negotiate peace with Raymond. Templars and Hospitallers, and the masters of both Orders, would be there to lend their weight. A contingent would ride the Northern Road to La Fève, where they would join Balian and Josias, then carry on to Tiberias and Raymond.

"Gerard must be livid," Hector said.

"Aye." Finn grinned. "I pray so."

A settlement was brokered — but now they had to find their way to Tiberias without running afoul of seven thousand Saracens. The Master and other Templars milled up ahead. Jean kneed his mount away, down the line, and Finn stepped out to meet him.

"You are to ride last." Jean gave a mocking grimace. "Gerard said, 'Tell the dirty Scot to guard my dirty arse.'"

"Blessed am I." Finn grasped Jean's elbow. "Guard your own arse today, aye?"

Jean heel-tapped his courser into a walk and spoke over his shoulder. "See you in Tiberias."

"I'll be the one coated in dirt."

Finn's banner waited as the Hospitaller column streamed by. They were a sombre lot, long-bearded, dressed in black robes bearing white crosses. Now came the Templar column. Master

Gerard stared straight ahead, ignoring Finn, though Jakelin reined in on a brilliant white stallion.

The Marshal angled his comely face toward the sun. "A fine day, don't you agree, Brother Finn?"

"None better, Marshal."

Jakelin's face clouded. "Once I offered you counsel, in Jerusalem, afore the battle at the pass with Robert of Saint Albans. Remember? A fight looms, again, and I offer the same words. Think of your men. Pick your spots. Know your time." He nudged his mount away, then steered him back. "Brother Finn, forgive me if I have ever given offence."

The words caught Finn flatfooted, and he managed a lame, "You never have."

Jakelin gave a thin smile as he spurred his mount up the line. His cappa flowed behind him and the sun winked from the pommel of his sword, like an archangel of war. The sight almost brought Finn to tears. Memories of Jakelin recounting his dream filtered through Finn's head. A sudden shiver raked him, despite the sun's warmth, and his mind leapt to his meagre band.

Two sergeants had been assigned to Finn's banner the previous day. Odrich, yet another burly Norman, and Perig, a Breton. Owen was there; taking Finn's fist on his teeth had not caused him to quit the Order. Yet. Finn felt no remorse for striking the malcontent — he had earned it. He was a youth, twenty or so, and Finn figured such lessons were part of becoming a warrior. Owen was no worse for wear, though, and acted like it had never happened. Yet there was a rift between them.

The tail end of the column approached, and Owen stuck a boot in his horse's stirrup.

Lugh placed a hand on Owen's shoulder. "Not yet."

"Obey the Rule," Hector said. "Clauses one hundred and fifty-six to one hundred and sixty, *How the Brothers Form to March*."

Finn held an apple between the palms of both hands, rolled it in opposite directions, and got a crisp snap as it came apart. He handed half to Owen. "Mount when directed by the Marshal. Form by banners, with squires behind carrying weapons, gear, and mounts."

"Ride at a walk to the column," Hector added, "and when a banner takes its spot, squires move to the front and go first."

Owen took a bite of apple. "We eat their dust?"

Rollo tapped the *shemagh* wrapping his nose and mouth. "What do you think these are for?" He took the half-apple from Finn's hand, slipped it under the scarf and took a large bite, then handed the remains back. "Squires carry our kit, so if the column is attacked, weapons are at hand rather than in the baggage."

Owen nodded to acknowledge the practicality.

"Ride in silence. No idle chatter." Hector dipped a head toward Serlo. "Like this one. And if you must come or go, ride downwind."

"Fart downwind too," Rollo said, "so that your gut stench does not stain the noses of the holy brethren. As is detailed in Rule eight hundred eighty-eight, or whatnot."

Finn chuckled at Owen's stern face.

"Lots of rules, eh?"

"So many rules."

Owen stared at Finn, unblinking despite all the dust in the air. "So much retribution for bad behaviour."

"Don't you mean penance?"

Owen grinned. "No. Retribution."

CHAPTER 6

The passage of hundreds of hooves churned the road to powder. The tail end of the column passed through the raised cloud of dirt half-blind. Finn's men tucked in their heads, breathed through their *shemaghs*, spluttered and coughed.

Late morning, they came to Nazareth, where a scout reported the Saracens lingered not far ahead. Christians rode on and passed over the hill behind Nazareth. Not long after, the column lurched to a stop. They waited in the rising heat, sweating and muttering, and in the lull Finn dismounted to re-tie his shield, which had come loose.

The board was piebald, black on the bottom half, white above. The top edge was straight, the side edges straight until roughly halfway down, where they tapered to a point. Tall enough to protect, short enough to be carried mounted. He ran a palm over the curved outer surface, used to deflect strikes rather than take them square and hard. Finn thought of Young Baldwin and his small shield, and wondered if he would have found himself here, riding to confront a Christian, if Baldwin had lived.

"Retying your shield?"

Finn glanced over his shoulder at Denis, who leaned on the pommel of his saddle. "What gave it away, Under Marshal?"

Denis, unsure if it were a jest or a question, settled for fanning a droopy hand. "You are summoned to the front. I would have sent a squire to fetch you, but I wanted a word."

Finn jerked up his chin.

"Master Gerard offers you an olive branch." Denis waited for a response, but ploughed on when all he got was a cold, flat stare. "He gives you the honour of riding beside him. To fight at his left."

Not an honour. He wants a killer to cover his arse, is all.

"Well? What do you say?"

"I'll do as ordered, Under Marshal."

"*Avoir la pêche*, Brother," Denis said, and smiled.

Finn did not trust his mouth, so he kept his lips together.

They rode forward, past more than a hundred knights, past three times that number of sergeants, and past half that number of Turcs. A small rise lay ahead and a score of Templars and Hospitallers clustered there; what lay beyond held their eye.

Finn reined in next to Jean. "What's all this, Brother?"

"Saracens. Camped at Cresson Springs. Al-Afdal leads them."

Al-Afdal ibn Salah ad-Din. One of Saladin's seventeen sons — and a favoured son.

Finn heaved up in the stirrups to see over the sea of heads. The sight was like a horse-kick to the gut. A field of reaped corn spread away. Clods and clarts of dark earth, wreckage from the last ploughing, lined the edges of straight and neat furrows. Stalks lay here and there. At the far end swirled a sea of green and blue. *Kurds, most likely, and mounted Turkish archers.* The left flank teemed yellow — Mamluk yellow.

"We cannot fight a horde," Jean said.

Finn eased back into the saddle. *We can't fight a horde … why not?*

Fighting was his trade. Easy as breathing. It ran in his blood. A knack for sowing chaos was his greatest strength and, at the same time, his greatest weakness. Joining the Order only whetted his appetite for war by adding a veneer of righteousness. A shivery thrill coursed through him.

I'll take a score by myself — Rollo and the others will too.

Success depended on giving a bold charge and dealing the first blow. Front-rankers would die under Christian blades. Hit hard. Hit fast. Rip them open as easily as a rotten sack.

Victory beckoned.

Except it did not.

Five hundred could not fight seven thousand and come out the other side. Not without footmen to guard their back. Not without archers. Finn's head told his heart to sit down. He looked to Jean, who was better at counting things, and the Frenchman held up two fingers to say, *Two thousand,* then jigged the fingers to add, *Give or take.*

So not seven thousand. But still too many.

Finn heel-tapped Fagan into the press, shoving until he could see the masters of both Orders, side-by-side, bracketed by their marshals. Gerard wore his usual gaze — arrogant, vulturine, conniving, though now a glimmer of the deranged danced there too.

Gerard's voice thickened. "We have the high ground. Our charge will hit hard."

"Are you mad?" The Hospitaller Master, Roger de Moulins, leaned forward to fix his counterpart with an incredulous stare. "We are outnumbered. Their middle will bend backward, but their ends will wrap around us." He waved a hand behind him like a tutor lecturing a student. "Do you see archers? Do you see more than three, four hundred footmen? You do not. Which means we have no way to prevent encirclement."

"You were outnumbered at Montgisard yet prevailed."

The Hospitaller shook his head and scowled as if to say, *You were not there; what do you know?*

"I beg your pardon, Master Gerard, but Master de Moulins is right," said Jakelin. "At Montgisard, we pinned their wings in place, or mostly in place, and the —"

"Bah, I have heard the stories, and they do not frighten me." Gerard fixed his Marshal with a sneer. "God loves us. And you love your blond head too much to risk it."

A sudden hush.

Jakelin blinked and gaped. "I shall die in battle a brave man," he said in a voice gone hollow. "You shall flee as a coward."

Gerard opened his mouth but swallowed the words as a faint chant drifted up.

"*Allahu Akbar, Allahu Akbar, Allahu Akbar.*"

The horde had seen them. Initiative, if the Christians ever held it, had flown. Discordant music arose — cymbals, brass drums, trumpets. Faris formed at the right and left. Mamluks settled in the middle. Sunlight shone from their lamellar cuirasses. Finn could not see it from where he sat, but his mind painted a picture of conical helmets, spiralled or fluted to imitate the folds of a turban; mail coifs covering their faces; or metal masks, crafted to resemble a face complete with hand-tooled moustaches and eyebrows.

"The dogs call us to the dance," Gerard said. "Only cowards would refuse."

"Go for the middle." De Moulins scrubbed at his beard in frustration. "Reform. Go again if they are on their heels. Pray God favours us. Rally here, at the high ground, if He does not."

"Footmen come up behind, quick as they can," Gerard added. The Master slapped down his conical helmet, clean and shiny, and nudged his destrier forward. "The rally point is here — though as God loves us, we will not need it."

"Footmen won't make it; we'll be split," Finn muttered to Rollo, and Rollo grunted his reply.

Sergeants began forming behind and Finn twisted in the saddle to take them in. Dusty faces, dirty tunics, yards of beard. But no fear. His heart thumped with pride. Spearmen formed behind the sergeants.

Elias nudged his horse into the press, caught Finn's eye, showed his palms and shrugged as if to ask, *What about us Turcs?*

Finn held up a clenched fist. *Wait here.* He then mimed holding a lance. *Unless you want to pick up a stick and join us?*

Elias laughed his gravel-hoarse laugh.

Finn pushed Fagan into Denis's left, who sat at Gerard's elbow, followed by Rollo, Hector, and Serlo. Jakelin slotted in at the Master's right, with Jean and Mael and the Hospitallers on his other side.

Denis elbowed Finn in the ribs. "Ready?"

Arse… I know where I'm going and what to do when I get there. Do you? "No going back now," Finn said.

Reins served no purpose and were tied off. Knee taps and spurs would guide the destriers. Hands would grasp lance and shield. They formed a *conroi*. Destriers shoved and jostled, leg-yielded to mend the line. Their prey was mounted men, not footmen, so they maintained gaps between each man to allow the passage of horses.

Finn made the sign of the cross, slid Oathkeeper out, kissed the flat of her blade, and sheathed her. *Lord, if you love me, watch over me, I pray.* He glanced at Gerard, who studied him from the corner of his eye. Then the Master gave a savage grin before tying his ventail in place.

Only fools or drunks grin like that, and there is no wine in him.

Quiet settled except for the odd jingle of harness, the stomp of hooves, and the soft murmur of prayer in several tongues. *Not to us, O Lord, not to us, but to your name give the glory...*

Gerard slashed a hand forward and the *Gonfanier* tipped the black-and-white standard. A hundred voices roared the Templar battle cry: "*Beauséant!*"

Destriers plodded out, hastened to a walk, then surged to a trot.

Across the field Mamluks shifted and rippled in time with Templars.

Destriers increased to a three-beat canter.

Arabians replied in kind.

Templars spurred their destriers to a gallop. A hedge of lances dropped in unison.

Mamluks picked up speed, lances clattered down, and the two sides closed fast — flying walls of horse and man and lance.

For a moment Finn was soaring, weightless, the air whistling through his mail coif. Fagan's hooves were a distant thump. He resisted the urge to toss his lance and raise his arms to the heavens. The thump of Finn's heart merged with something feral and primitive, and the marriage of the two made for a fierce and fearless calm. Dirty corn stubble flashed by his feet, dark shafts filled a blue sky.

An arrow tonked off his helmet. Another thumped into his shield. Muted curses.

Templars hurtled through the arrows. The two walls closed the final space and hit with a crash of steel on steel, steel on wood, wood on wood. Fagan's ears flattened to his neck as Finn's lance shattered on a shiny round shield. At the same moment, a lance to Finn's shield rocked him in the saddle. For three heartbeats he reeled and teetered, glimpsed Fagan's hooves blurring over the ground He heaved himself upright just as a spear point grazed his helmet.

The din of the slaughter erupted where once men had grown corn.

Kill, kill, kill, rasped the spectre slumbering in Finn's head that awoke at times of carnage. He slid into *it* — the place where he cut and thrust and parried without thought or remorse.

The great sword came free in time to shove off the swipe of a green-robed faris. Finn knee-tapped Fagan and the destrier turned hard right, wrapped around the arse of the other horse and put Finn at the man's left kidney. He stabbed it, in and out, wheeled Fagan away as the faris folded over.

Steel sheared away a corner of Finn's shield in a spray of white and black splinters. He twisted and swung at a yellow blur and hit a shield. The blow shuddered through the blade and up his arm. Finn's dropping cut to the other side cleaved a hand. A scream pierced his ear. Fagan rumbled on while Finn couched the great sword like a lance and used it to gouge a man from the saddle.

A glimpse of the piebald standard above the press — *Gerard will be there.*

He spurred Fagan toward the standard. Mamluks swirled to his front and Fagan, with no urging from Finn, dropped his head and shoulder-slammed a horse — the smaller Arabian went over in a sprawl of thrashing limbs. A lamellar-covered back shone on the other side. Finn stabbed it, felt scales sunder, snarled as the Mamluk arched up and screamed.

The dust was heinous now, alive, swirling. Shapes moved in it, some friend, most foe. Then it slowed, like they had waded into a field of mud, and the fight became a melee of snarling faces and flashing steel.

The charge is broken. Now the work begins.

Finn jabbed Fagan with both heels, and as he walked back in a straight line, Rollo, Hector, and Serlo fell in at his side. Rollo's mount leg-yielded to tighten the gap. Jerol and Lugh and Amic filtered in behind. They held thus until a pack of Mamluks slipped from the haze, angling left, intent on wrapping around Gerard.

"Ha!" Finn barked, and slapped spurs. Templars pounced in a quick two-beat canter.

The first Mamluk never saw the strike that unmade his shoulder and left his arm swinging. Fagan angled toward another. A bearded face turned, his mouth an O of surprise, as Finn wrist-rolled and cut. He caught a glimpse of a furrowed scar, hairline to chin, as the man fell away trailing drops of crimson.

Rollo — God no! I killed my brother.

But a glance found Rollo at his side, eyes bulging with bloodlust, hacking at a man in lamellar. No Hector. Further on was a white shape in the haze that must be Serlo.

A shout in Arabic and as if by magic Mamluks materialized — hidden in the dust until now.

Something silvery flickered in the corner of Finn's eye and he twitched the shield, shunted off a blow that jarred all the way to his aketon. He reared in the stirrups and thrust over the top of his board. Scales sundered. A shriek of pain. A yellow blur as the man wheeled away. A mail-covered face loomed, too close for the blade, and Finn ducked under the man's cut and smashed him from the saddle with his shield.

"Back! Back!" he yelled, but only Rollo came with him.

And Mamluks — they came too.

Steel rang on Finn's helmet and left his ears buzzing. Another to the side knocked his breath loose with a grunt. He hunched over Fagan's mane in a world gone silent, gasping for air until his lungs shuddered and filled. A sudden din battered his ears. Lugh was screaming, thrusting over Finn, his courser bumping Fagan's rear.

Finn raised himself up just as a whistling edge came for his head. He tucked in his chin and took it on his helmet — screaming, scraping in his ears as it slipped off. The sword's guard tore his cappa and caught in his mail, and he jabbed his great sword low and blind. A hitch as it pierced flesh and cracked bone, then he hauled it back and was rewarded with a moan of pain as the steel came free.

Finn risked a look — no Denis, no Gerard, no Hector. Serlo was afoot. Rollo was mounted, and swirled his blade and cut forward. Blood sprayed. Jerol spurred toward him to close the gap and leaned to slash a faris across the eyes.

Steel gleamed and cut and scraped. Men screamed war cries or shouted gibberish.

Mamluks charged in twos and threes, cut and slashed, wheeled away to do it again. Footmen scuttled in to stab with spears. They were everywhere at once and Finn swung the great sword in glittering, sweeping arcs to drive them back.

Lugh cried a warning and thrust into the neck of a footman about to spear Fagan in the guts.

A horse whinnied and a man bellowed — Rollo, by the timbre. Finn glimpsed a footman, his spear stuck in Rollo's thigh. Rollo twisted back to smash him on top of the head with the point of his shield. He shield-shoved another, knocked him into Jerol, who hacked the man down as easily as chopping wood.

Someone was singing a Psalm with surprising spirit. "I will pursue my enemies, and I will not turn back till they are destroyed. I will crush them, and they will fall…"

Serlo always sings in battle ... but is he in the same fight as me? thought Finn.

Someone else was bawling, "Form! Form! Form!"

Finn looked for the *beauséant*, to reform there, but could not see it.

No ... has it fallen?

"To the right!" Jerol shouted.

The Mamluk charge, unseen until the last moment, hurtled into the Templar flank in a blur of yellow and silver. Bodies of men and horses hit with half-muffled groans and curses. Steel rang and men screamed. Something meaty thumped Rollo's destrier and it went over, crashed into Fagan, sent him stumbling to the side.

A silver mask emerged from the dust cloud. The mouth lifted at the corners, as if amused by some lame jest, though the man behind it was not laughing. His *saif* gouged a furrow in Finn's helmet and almost twisted his head from his shoulders. On instinct Finn countered with a backhanded slash but the silver mask leaned back, then came forward with a thrust Finn managed to bat aside with his board.

Echoey, metallic laughter behind the silver mask fired Finn's ire.

The destrier and the Arabian wheeled and circled like two prize fighters. Then Fagan got his hooves under him and stomped and bit. The Arabian took teeth in its neck and the Mamluk took a sword across the mask. The smirking mask was knocked askew and Finn glimpsed a ruddy face, a blue eye, a pockmarked cheek. Steel came back and blurred forward to punch into the front and out the back — the Mamluk folded over the blade. He groaned and slid away with the great sword still in him.

Finn reached, found the handle of the mace behind his cantle, and pulled it free.

Rollo lay on his chest Jerol rolled him over and hauled him upright. Lugh wedged his courser in front of Jerol, swapping blows with a Mamluk, both screaming high-pitched war chants not understood by the other. A footman came at Jerol's back. Finn spurred Fagan and leaned to cosh the man's neck with the mace.

Mamluks swirled, like surf breaking around a rock, and the surf was filled with men who flailed and screamed and died. The fight flowed away, like the tide retreating, leaving them stranded amidst the dead or dying. A channel opened at his back. The way lay open.

"Go. Ride. Live."

The voice in Finn's ear was clear as a chiming bell. Calm. Kind. A touch weary.

God's voice — must be God.

Lugh had bested the Mamluk, who was rolled into a ball like a woodlouse, the Irishman hacking at his back.

Finn spurred Fagan, grabbed Lugh's elbow and shouted in his ear, "Go!"

The sergeant stared, blinked, and Finn gave his elbow a shake. "Beat feet!"

Lugh flinched, like a man coming out of a dream, and heaved at the Mamluk until he toppled from the saddle. Jerol draped Rollo's arm over his shoulder and pushed him up onto the Arabian while Lugh hauled from the other side. Finn led Jerol's mount over, held it as he climbed aboard, then gave the horse a slap on the rump.

"Meet at the rally point." Finn pointed with the mace. "Up the hill!"

Lugh and Jerol hit spurs in unison, towing a tottering Rollo in their wake.

Hooves thudded. Finn whirled to a bare-headed Mamluk trotting toward him. Sunlight danced on his brilliant lamellar coat. He looked like a giant silver fish.

Finn waved the mace in invitation. The Mamluk whooped and slapped spurs.

Halfway the Mamluk straightened up, his *saif* came back in a glittering arc, and his empty left fist tucked to his body. Finn threw the mace, as practised countless times, and steered Fagan to the side. The mace flew end over end. The Mamluk was a blur and Finn did not see three pounds of flanged steel hit — but he heard the grunt of surprise.

He pulled Oathkeeper and gave a crisp wrist roll that made her flash in the sunlight.

The Mamluk's stallion slowed to a trot. The man stared at his chest, where a fist-sized dent marred his brilliant armour, then his head drooped like a man nodding off to sleep. He melted from the saddle and landed in a sprawl. Finn nudged Fagan over and looked down. The Mamluk rolled onto his back, eyes closed, mouth open and heaving for air.

"How'd that feel?" Finn asked in French.

The Mamluk pried open his eyes, glared his reply, then coughed a spray of blood. Finn kneed Fagan away and spoke a warrior's adage over his shoulder.

"Broken ribs, punctured lung, breathing done."

Fagan plodded toward the rise as Finn twisted in the saddle to eye the dust cloud at the far end of the field. A riot of yellow and blue swirled around a clump of black and white. Clashing steel and screams drifted over the stubble. Closer, in the middle of the field, nine Templars fought afoot against three score mounted Mamluks.

Brothers fight and die on that field.

"Go. Ride. Live."

The voice spoke again, pure and strong, and Finn did as bid.

He murmured a prayer and asked for forgiveness, for his cowardice, for failing his brothers. He spurred Fagan but got only a limping trot.

Fagan lumbered up the hill. Two horses toiled ahead. One towed a sergeant. His boot was wedged in a stirrup, his body dragged through the dirt, helmeted head bouncing and arms splayed behind. Finn glanced down as he came alongside — one of the new sergeants, Perig, the Breton. Dead. The second horse carried the other new sergeant. His hand was tucked under his armpit. His face was pale.

Odrich. "Oy, Brother, you hurt?"

Odrich pulled out the hand — only there was no hand. A stump sprayed blood feebly, in time with the beat of his heart.

"Ain't fair," Odrich said. "God's bones, I just got here."

With that his eyes rolled back and he slid off the horse, and landed with a thud.

Finn wanted to bind his wound, to make the sign of the cross, to do … something. But the sergeants were gone, and in the end he could only nudge Fagan onward.

Bastard Gerard earned us a thumping.

Fagan laboured up the slope and Finn reined him in at the top. Rollo and the others angled toward a wadi at the far side. Big Rollo looked ridiculous on the little Arabian horse. Finn glanced back.

No Hector. No Serlo. No Owen.

But there stood Jakelin, in the middle of the field of reaped corn, his great sword held in a two-handed grip. A dying Hospitaller knelt beside him.

Mailed riders yipped and swirled around them like wolves on a bloodied stag.

God, no... Finn clenched his teeth in dread and impotence.

A mailed wolf broke from the pack and spurred in. Jakelin sprang forward, sword held high, then hunched and sliced on the run. The horse dropped to its knees and launched the rider between his ears. Jakelin pivoted. Cut a man across the middle. Danced back as the horse blew past, the man dropped over its neck. He strolled to the thrown man, just climbed to a knee, and took his head with a quick swipe.

Wolf after wolf made runs at the cornered stag. Each wanted the honour of the kill.

Jakelin held his ground and took his time, lashed out when it was right. A man tottered in the saddle, his horse trotted on a few steps, and the man fell like a sack of rocks. Jakelin shuffled left and cut hard. A Mamluk reeled away grasping an arm twisted the wrong way around.

Finn watched the fight as if in a dream as a Psalm echoed up to him in a baritone voice; *Even though I walk through the darkest valley, I will fear no evil, for you are with me...*

Mamluks rode in, hacked and sliced in glimmers of steel, then pulled back howling and spitting in rage. Jakelin was calm, certain, and glided over the ground like a ghost.

"That," Finn said to Fagan, "is a warrior."

A Mamluk made a run. Jakelin missed and shuffle-stepped in a circle, limping now.

He hobbled behind a dying horse to force his enemy to come over or around it. Three took the challenge — one leapt over, one around either end. The Marshal feinted, swivelled the other way to thrust a Mamluk through the thigh. He took a cut on the shoulder, ducked another, then crab-stepped left. Steel flashed and an arm fell. The blade reversed in a silvery arc to cleave the horse's leg. Jakelin limped to the trapped rider, thrust down, and legs flailed up.

Finn suddenly longed to be with Jakelin, to die with him, to ascend to heaven at his side. He gave a harsh "Ha," and spurred Fagan. The destrier raised a hoof but plopped it back down, turned to fix Finn with an equine stare that asked, *Certes you jest?*

Jakelin's words came to Finn in a whisper: *Think of your men. Pick your spots. Know your time.*

Finn let out a shuddering breath, kneed Fagan away, but spared a last glance. Dead piled around Jakelin like sea wrack wrapped around a boulder. A solitary Mamluk slid from his mount, stuck his sword point-first into the ground, and strolled toward Jakelin with empty hands held wide. The Marshal planted the great sword in a furrow, muddy with blood, and rested an arm on the pommel.

The last thing Finn saw was Templar and Mamluk embracing.

CHAPTER 7

Darkness was complete. Deep. Unbreakable.

The night was cool but sweat made them cold. They dared not light a fire and instead huddled in their cloaks and shivered. Fagan stood next to the Arabian and both, too weary to fight, made a tenuous peace. Horses were left saddled, in case they were needed, though Fagan deserved a rub-down and a bucket of oats. Finn felt guilt at that — as would any horseman worth their salt.

Could use a rub down and bag of oats myself.

The rush of the fight faded, as it always did, and a tired ache settled in his bones. The thrill of the fight mutated into something else — angst, remorse, despair? His hands trembled and he was grateful for the night, which hid his shame, though from experience he knew everyone else's hands shook too. Violent images pounced from the dark. They were too sharp, too raw, and he recoiled from them. Post-battle jitters turned each sigh of the wind into a Mamluk, blade drawn, creeping in to kill.

"So." Rollo coughed, spat. "That went well."

No one replied. They were busy licking their wounds.

Rollo lay on his side, to avoid putting pressure on the spear puncture in his thigh, though his ribs were sliced on the other side, and he could find no way to lie that did not hurt. A clout on the head had dented his helmet and left him dazed.

Finn flinched up a chin at Rollo. "How's your pretty little head?"

"Got hit so hard I lost the hearing in my right eye," Rollo said, and snorted at his own lame jest.

Lugh bore a gash across his leg and another across his arm. Jerol wheezed like a busted bellows. Finn stared into the inky night and remembered times he had seen men wheezing from sundered lungs, with blood in their mouths, and struggled to recall if Jerol had suffered thus. He did not think so — broken ribs, probably?

We ran ... fled. The thought burned like fire.

Finn felt holed and thinned, like old clothes that had been washed, beaten, and wrung over rocks. His mail had held. His helmet had not. The rivets binding the centre ridge were sprung, the nasal bent, the whole thing wrecked. His head throbbed like a drum and a cut on his forehead seeped in time with the beat. Other hits had battered his body. He ached everywhere.

Lugh limped back from the mouth of the wadi, where he had been keeping watch.

"Anyone?" Finn knew the answer but asked anyway.

Lugh shook his head. "We're it." He made a strange sound in his throat. "Dead. So many dead. Reek of it drifts on the breeze."

"How kind of you to lift our spirits," Rollo snapped back.

"That ... arse, Gerard." Jerol sucked in a breath. "Shouldn't ... have attacked."

"Shouldn't have attacked," Lugh repeated in a dull voice.

"Anyone see the arse go down?" .

The question came from Finn with a hopeful tone, and Rollo laughed, then groaned.

"Hector? Serlo? Jean? Elias?"

Silence.

Lugh limped to the mouth of the wadi. Several groups of Saracens had passed late in the day, heading back to the battlefield after chasing Christian spearmen. Templars froze like hares, hearts thumping, holding the muzzles of their horses, and praying the fiends would pass by. They did. The night was quiet — so far, at least.

"No one," Lugh whispered. He hobbled back and forth, back and forth.

Lugh, like most men of war, was supremely skilled at several things. Fighting. Sharpening weapons. Mending kit. Riding horses. At other things, not so much. Waiting patiently, especially, was not a skill he possessed.

"Enough, Rooster," Finn said. "Your lopsided gait is making me sick. Sit."

"Sit? With brothers missing?"

"Sit. Your. Arse." Finn breathed out, angry and hurting.

"Do something useful," Rollo said, "or do nothing."

Rooster has a point. So does Rollo. Do something useful...

Finn scrubbed a hand through his sweat-spiked hair. He heaved himself up, swayed a moment, then began undoing the straps for his leggings and let them fall. He worked the hauberk up with a muffled groan, fought it over his head, then left it in a pile. Mail was a second skin. He wore it always, everywhere, even slept in it when on campaign. His body was accustomed to its weight. It went unnoticed — until it was gone. Now he felt light as goose down and naked as a plucked bird.

Rollo raised his head. "What're you up to?"

"I'm going back."

"Back?"

"Down there. To find the others."

"The hell you are. Sit your arse down, with the rest of us, and wait for daylight."

"Can't abandon the wounded to Saracens."

"You gonna save 'em all? Be the hero?"

Finn ignored Rollo. Loss brought despair; despair brought meanness. The others would try to follow, despite their wounds, despite their grumbling. He hardened his voice. "As banner leader, I order you to stay."

"Bugger your order." Rollo pushed himself up, then fell back, groaning.

"I order you," Finn repeated in a growl. He tried for reason. "Besides, you'll only slow me down, or get yourself caught. One man can go where many will fail."

Darkness was Finn's friend. Had been since his youth. He did not fear it. Back home he was called Black Dog — a twist on *Cù-Sìth*, the devil-dog, bringer of mayhem. Some said the byname was given as a nod to his dark hair and eyes. The truth was far darker.

"You get taken," Jerol said, pausing to cough, "won't no one come to save you."

"Get taken? Dead is what he'll get."

The voice came from the mouth of the wadi.

Owen. His shadow came closer, leading shadow horses — Perig's and Odrich's.

"Where have you been?" Finn asked.

"Laying low. My courser took shafts at the first charge. Went down like someone cut his legs off mid-stride. Pinned me. Elias came, freed me, and sent me up the hill."

"Where's he now?"

"You didn't see his ride?" Owen whistled softly. "Madman, that one. When the Mamluks hit your flank, he and a handful of Turcs stung them in the arse and turned some, or you'd all be dead. Haven't seen him since."

Elias — how many times had that fierce, faithful man pulled Finn's chestnuts from a fire?

Finn sensed the others staring. They warned of horrors real and supposed — from the dead, from errant souls, from the living. He did not need warning of what awaited. His hands had eagerly made some of that mess, but now, for reasons his own, he loathed wading back into it. Yet he knew he must.

He slung Oathkeeper over his neck and adjusted the strap until the handle hung below his left armpit. The biodag was at his hip. Other knives rode in his boots, and on a cord around his neck, and he checked each was snug in its sheath.

"I'll be back afore first light or not at all," Finn said, and made the sign of the cross. "Don't wait for me. Take the horses and go. And give Fagan a rub-down and a bag of oats."

"Do it yourself, lazy arse," Rollo rasped.

Finn was already gone.

Finn sat on a rock halfway down the slope. Sounds drifted up. Chanting. Laughter. Wailing. It was faint, from the far side of the field, where firelight lit shadows that shifted like wraiths. The Mamluks would be worn by the fight and lazing in victory, Finn hoped, though an enemy so close put a sharp edge on his nerves.

Clouds swept the night sky like long, wide cloaks, by turn dressing and undressing the moon. It was waning gibbous.

Stealthy scuffs behind.

"I ordered you to stay," Finn said over his shoulder.

"Didn't hear that part." Owen squatted at Finn's side. "We are the only two that can walk straight. Which means I'm going with you."

Finn said nothing.

"So," Owen said. "What're we waiting for?"

Finn pointed at the moon to say, *For clouds to cover the moon.* Which was half true.

His mind wandered back to dark places, remembered things best left alone.

Finn had been on a field of dead before. His Da was there. Somewhere. Finn would not have a dog gnaw his bones, a raven peck his eyes. He had expected the silence of the graveyard, for there lay dead men, though it was anything but silent. Scavengers, human and beast, robbed the dying and fed on the dead. The wounded begged for water, for their ma, for their God, for the end. A clansman pleaded for the mercy stroke. Finn, then a young man, was too cowardly to give it and slunk off with pained cries torturing his ears.

Finn and his brothers rooted among the dead like pigs after acorns. They saw the terrible things men do to men. They found their old man, after too long searching, and stood there silent and staring. A dreadful way to see him for the last time, for try as Finn might to picture him in life, most often when he remembered his Da it was the Da from that night. Waxy. Mouth slack. Eyes rolled up. Slathered in blood, gone crusty now, and his arm…

Finn shook his head like a dog to clear the images.

The MacDougalls were to blame.

The bastards wanted to parlay, they said, and offered safe passage to a neutral glen. Da had agreed. It proved a trap. The promise of safety during truce, sacred the world over, was stomped into the mud. Clan Donnachaidh carried biodag and sgian dubh, as agreed. Clan MacDougall came armed to the teeth. Da fought hard and died hard. The days after were blurred by drink. Burial. Rain. Grief. Later, barely sober, Finn and his brothers called on their neighbours. More murdered men, cut men, maimed men.

Finn milled thumb and finger into his weary eyes until his vision was a pulsating web of black and orange and red.

"Ever been on a field of dead at night?" Finn asked the sergeant. He gave no time for a reply. "I have. Its hell — bloody, stinking hell. Only the stout walk there. Go only if you're strong of spirit and mind."

"I am." Owen tried for a confident tone, but a quiver in his voice gave him away.

"Strip your mail. We go quiet. Don't get behind me or you'll get chibbed by mistake. Find a spear, a broken lance, whatever." Finn watched the moon and clouds, judging when the latter would cover the former. "Use your stick to roll bodies over. Look just enough but not too much. Recognize someone, give a hoot, soft as a baby owl."

And try not to remember what you see.

Owen began stripping his mail. "What if the man is alive?"

"We'll carry him from the field. Fetch horses. Get gone."

"And if Sandpigs find us?"

"Take a few with you afore you go. Most importantly, don't be captured, for that'll be a long and painful end — very long, very painful."

They started down when clouds cloaked the moon. Finn found hell just as he remembered it.

He used the corners of his eyes, where night vision lived, and avoided the lure of distant fires to preserve his night vision. This he did by keeping his gaze nailed to the ground — which proved no easy thing.

The stench was so thick he could taste it — spilled guts, coppery blood, putrid gases. It would only get worse when baked in the sun. Horrid sounds drifted on the night breeze. Groans. Curses. Cries for water, for the wounded always have an insatiable thirst. A horse nickered in pain, another replied in kind, and the pitiful sounds were enough to make Finn cry.

Spears littered the ground. Finn took one and used it to prod and lift the dead — footman, sergeant, and knight. In whispers Owen explained how footmen tromped after the horsemen, laboured to lend their support, but were hit in the flanks by faris and broken asunder. A few hundred ran to the hills, or for Nazareth, Kurd faris snapping at their heels. Perhaps some made it.

The footmen had tossed their spears aside to run faster.

A pack of shadows scattered. Jackals. They circled, eyes luminescent in the moonlight, and their growls raised the hackles on Finn's neck. He shuffled over to find a headless Templar, sprawled and twisted. Finn saw no one he recognized and moved on. A peek over his shoulder found the glowing eyes gliding back to their meal.

Stealthy scuffing sounds came from behind and Finn whirled. Owen — creeping at his heels.

"Nearly gave you the pointy end of my spear," Finn hissed.

"That'd be bad, at least for me," Owen whispered, and tittered at himself.

"At least there'd be one less idiot in the world." Finn pointed the spear to his left and Owen shifted away from his back.

Lad must be afraid, and who can blame him?

In the lull, someone wittered a looping mantra, in a tongue Finn did not know. *Arabic? Or Aragonese?*

Finn whispered, "*Jésus sauve,*" and got the expected reply; "*Jésus sauve et guérit.*"

They found him further on. A Hospitaller with black eyes and white teeth.

"I can smell me," the man said by way of greeting. He nodded towards his stomach and made a wet, consumptive sound meant as a laugh. "Cannot feel the wound, which is not a portent for my recovery, I suspect."

Gut coils bulged from a gash across his stomach. They shone in the darkness. He could not feel because his legs were twisted halfway round; it was plain his back was broken.

"Doesn't look promising," Finn agreed.

"Give me the blade, Brother. Send me on." The Hospitaller's calm was unnerving.

Those words, once uttered, could not be unheard. Images of the dying clansman pleading for the mercy stroke filled Finn's head. The Hospitaller spoke again.

"Send me. Jesus awaits."

Clouds slid from the moon. Finn took the man's cold hand, and with his other hand pulled the biodag.

"Pray with me first," the Hospitaller said. They held hands as he prayed in Aragonese, which Finn did not understand, though to his ears it sounded elegant and lyrical. The Hospitaller made the sign of the cross and in French said, "The stars are bright. There is Orion. And Taurus. As a lad, I would lie on my back in summer, and hunt stars in the night sky."

"May you pass over Aragon on your way to heaven." Finn pressed the knife point to the hollow at the base of his neck, then rammed it straight down inside his rib basket and into his heart.

Only after he was gone did Finn realize he had not asked the brother his name.

Some things are better left unknown.

Finn and Owen moved on.

They neared the springs. Sounds grew louder — echoey laughter in Arabic, an odd metal clanking every so often, cries or pleas in Hebrew or French. Finn could do nothing for them, whoever they were, so he turned a deaf ear to focus on the grisly task.

A furtive scuffle behind and Finn dropped into a crouch. Owen — creeping at Finn's back, again. "Bastard," Finn hissed in Gaelic. "You almost got chibbed. Walk beside me."

Finn carried on prodding dead men, levering them up and letting them drop. Bodies grew thicker now. Templar and Hospitallers intermingled. He found a knight on his back and missing his head. Another headless brother lay nigh.

Mud sucked at their boots, clogged their soles, pulled at their spear butts. *Hasn't rained in years … that mud wasn't made by water.*

Sibilant whispers filled the dark, like demons, and ahead figures flitted in the dark.

Finn motioned for Owen to hold and dropped into a crouch, spear held low. He stole forward — ghost-walking, he called it. Weight on the back leg. Place the front foot down, outside edge first, roll the foot to the ground. Anything unexpected underfoot and he would shift and try again. When the foot was grounded, he would swing his body, weight over the front foot. Lift the back leg. Move it in front. Repeat.

He crept up on the whisperer — a woman. A surge of primitive dread coursed through him. *Ban-sìth? Or some other she-devil come to torment the dying?*

She squatted in the moonlight, chemise tucked up to show her bare thighs, and patted and slapped at a body. A sliver of steel showed from her mouth — a knife, gripped by the handle, and she hummed as she worked. Other shapes moved in the dark and hummed songs of their own. Together the drone of disparate tunes made a sinister chorus.

Hisses streamed from a second woman, further on, then a gravelly voice. Male. Familiar.

"Now, now," said the woman, soothing, "give us the ring and we won't cut you."

"Try to take it, I dare you."

Elias — only one man owned such a hard, raspy voice. His words came from behind a dead Arabian. Finn reversed the spear in a twirl, cracked the butt end over the first she-demon's head, then hopped over her slumping form towards the second.

She scuttled away with a blurted curse, waving a knife. "Mine! I found 'im — I get 'im!"

"You'll get my spear in your eye, is what you'll get." In a growl, Finn added, "That man is a brother. Leave or die."

She saw wisdom in that, and in the menace of sharp steel, and moved off.

Finn peered over the dead horse at Elias. "Ever get tired of me rescuing your pathetic arse?" he said, and grinned, for once having turned Elias's pet taunt back on him.

Elias laughed, humourless and relieved at the same time. "Took you long enough."

Finn twisted to wave Owen over, but he was already there, spear held in two fists and the gleaming point aimed at Finn's side. A shiver ran through him and on instinct he batted the point away.

"Idiot," he said, and waved his own spear toward Elias, who was trapped beneath his horse. "Help me free him."

They used their spears like picks, stabbed the soil to loosen it, then scooped it out with their hands. The ground had been ploughed for generations and fed shite; thus it was loamy and soft, otherwise Elias's leg would have been crushed to a bony paste. As it was, he could barely stand, and cursed and grumbled until Finn fretted the Mamluks would hear. He said as much.

"Mamluks?" Elias took the spear Finn offered and leaned on it. "They're gone. Rode off after the fight, all full of whoops and song."

Finn nodded toward the fires. "So who's that?"

"Kurds. About three hundred. Stayed behind to chain up the folk from Nazareth."

The metal sounds, the pleading, the wailing — it all clicked together in Finn's head. Elias told how, before the battle, Gerard yelled to the Nazarenes to come, to see the Christian triumph, to collect loot from seven thousand dead Saracens. Many came. Only they became the loot, claimed by Mamluks still very much alive. Now they would be hauled to Damascus and sold as slaves. Finn breathed out a long, shivering breath, and stared into the fires until his night vision was ruined.

Their lives will be brutal and short, and there's nothing I can do to remedy it.

Elias began massaging life back into his dead leg. He raised his prodigious chin and pointed with it. "Jakelin is over there."

The Marshal, when Finn found him, lay on his back, fingers interlaced over his chest in a gesture of prayer. A soft smile rode his lips. Shafts riddled him, snapped off now, which made him look like a giant hedgepig. Jakelin was a brother of legend. A shining star in the Order. Finn dreamt of one day becoming like him. Seeing him thus was soul-rending.

Someone had used a leather thong to tie the handle of his sword into his hands. Finn felt Jakelin's hand, cold and dry, and touched the pommel, also cold and dry. But the steel hummed with a strange aura, like it was alive, and impulse Finn untied the thong and worked the sword free. He hefted it and tilted the pommel to the moonlight. It was tarnished, battered, round and heavy. On it was engraved a prancing stag surrounded by three hammers.

"No one defiled him, nor stole from him," Finn said. His mind must have wandered for a moment, for he did not notice Elias limp up, and he flinched when he spoke.

"Jakelin gave them death and they offered him life."

Elias had played dead, under his horse, and had seen the Marshal's end. He told how the Mamluk came and praised Jakelin's valour and skill, and said he could live — but only if he became a Mahomedan. Jakelin replied, "No, Brother, life at the price of my soul is no life at all." Such a warrior could not be left to fight another day. So, the Mamluk waved archers forward, and they feathered him as he stood with arms cast wide. Out of respect, the Mamluks hauled Jakelin here, arranged him with his sword, and forbade the Kurds from desecrating him.

An image flashed in Finn's head — of Jakelin and the Mamluk embracing. *An enemy who stands, brave, defiant against hopeless odds ... such a man would win my respect too.*

"Jean is over yonder. Mael too."

Elias had whispered, but the words hit Finn like a boulder to the head.

Finn found them near the springs — or at least their heads, stuck on spears to display them as trophies. The row of spears stretched into the distance. Campfires backlit the grisly tableau and the silhouetted heads seemed to float. Their mouths gaped as if screaming at the outrage done them.

Haven't seen a knight with his head. Now I see why.

Three Kurds came and leered and jeered. Finn paid them no heed. He walked the row, took the heads in one at a time, committing their faces to memory.

Many he knew not at all. Some he barely knew. A small number he loved.

There was Master de Moulins, glowering in recrimination, proved right at the cost of his head. And Brother Aldus of Pérouges who, years past, had sailed from Christendom with Finn. Aldus never took a shine to Finn — nor Finn to him. *Can't force brotherhood; certes it'll never grow now.*

Mael, with his scarred chin, gaped down from atop a blood-smeared spear. He had strolled into Robert of Saint Albans' camp with Finn, fought with him, taken wounds with him. Now all he was, or would ever be, rode a stick of wood.

Jean was a few spears further down the line.

Strands of fair hair, what little remained, were plastered to his head. Firelight shone on his bald spot. His mouth yawned grotesquely. Finn almost looked away in tears. But he did not. He stood before his friend, beneath a brother whose soul was kind and pure, and honoured him with his gaze.

Now his soul is flown. Jean is in paradise.

A blood-rimmed hole marked where a shaft had gone into his eye. A hole behind marked where it had come out. The arrow must have been shot close, to do that, and it must have torn through and fallen to the earth somewhere in the rows of freshly cut corn. Most likely it would be tilled under in the spring, buried and lost, where the steel point would rust and merge with the soil. It would feed the crops, as would all the other steel and bones.

Finn wanted to scream, to cry, to take Jean's head and hold it in his lap and whisper loving words in his dead ear. But he was too numb, too was broken, weary, and wretched. His body stayed rooted to the spot like an old, decaying tree, swaying just a little.

"Don't see Hector or Serlo," Elias said. "Nor Gerard."

"Well." Finn turned away from Jean cuffing an eye. "At least we have that small blessing."

CHAPTER 8

The Kurds departed when the morning sky was glowing rosy. Buzzards and kites whirled and squawked overhead. Templars crept down from the hill and shooed the birds away, then collected one hundred and twenty-four heads — Finn knew because he counted each one. They consecrated a place for their slumber at the edge of the field, overlooking the valley.

Footmen had cowered in the hills during the night. Now they filtered down in twos and threes, eyes downcast like fearful dogs. Finn suffered their shame — he had fled too. He set them to work digging a communal grave for the knights.

Finn pondered as he watched the footmen labour. He had thought of Gerard like a squall — nettlesome, blustery, but unlikely to leave any lasting damage. Now, as he stared at rows and rows of brothers, rolled in the cappas, laid out side by side, he was reminded that even a small squall could sink a big ship.

Heads were laid in, then the bodies, facing east because Christ would return thus. Templars and Hospitaller lay together, united in death, if not in life. It occurred to him that someday, probably in the distant future, someone would dig here and find the heads and bodies. Perhaps farmers. Maybe explorers. The grisly find would mystify, be attributed to some arcane ritual, as folk do when the past is unexplainable.

Rollo insisted on clambering into the hole and laying Jean in it. Finn and Lugh handed down Mael, and Rollo and Jerol laid him next to Jean. Finn hoisted Rollo out and they stared into the pit, po-faced, and wiped dirt from their palms. Rollo nudged Finn with an elbow.

Words? You expect words?

Finn's head was full of dark thoughts, resentful thoughts, which could only lead to dark and resentful words. Jean would have known what to say, he always did, but he was not here. After a moment Finn started speaking in a voice as hoarse as gravel.

"Jean of Provence. Poor Fellow-Soldier of Christ and of the Temple of Solomon." He regarded Jean's slack face a moment. "Good man ... no, *great* man. Great Brother. Great friend. Always honest. Always loyal. Never shirked a fight if it beckoned; never sought it either." He breathed out. "I'll miss you. I'll pray for you."

"Aye." Rollo swiped at an eye. Perhaps he had dust there.

Finn sent riders to Jerusalem to give word of the tragedy that had befallen the Orders. It was a bad day for the Templars and Hospitallers, though a good day for feeding the cropland. The reek ripened by the hour, so Finn ordered some of the footmen to dig graves for the commoners, others to collect usable weapons. Townsfolk came to help. Scores of sergeants and footmen and Turcs were laid into scores of pits.

Hard work, digging pits. But better than being laid in one.

Jakelin was buried — Finn set him in a lone grave, rested a crude wooden crucifix on his chest, and heard the priest's Latin prayer. Folk sliced pieces of robe from the Templar Marshal, to keep them and venerate them, in memory of his courageous death. The same folk, in the days after, whispered angels descended and carried Jakelin to heaven in a golden ray of light. Finn said nothing to contradict their tale. Hope was finding a light in the darkness, and who was he to snuff it?

Templars rode out in the afternoon trailing a line of empty horses. Fagan developed a limp for which neither Finn nor Lugh could find a cause, so Finn claimed de Moulins' destrier, Azrael, a black stallion with bright eyes. Fagan stomped a jealous hoof and Finn brushed him down, murmured in his ear, and stroked his nose. A bag of oats was the final remedy. Elias took Rollo's Arabian, Rollo a destrier, and each deemed it a fair trade.

"Cackhand," Rollo said from nowhere. He used his favoured byname for Jean. "You can love someone and hate them a little too."

Finn managed a nod.

"I remember seeing a madman once, naked and sitting in the middle of the street, eating raw hare and green onion." Rollo grimaced at the memory. "He'd chew the hare, swallow, then take a bite of onion. He looked at me with an accusing face, like I was the mad one, like everyone should eat raw hare and green onion in the nude."

Finn rubbed his eyes like a sleep-weary child. He had not slept in forever, it seemed, and would not any time soon. "Your point?"

"We're the mad ones." Rollo jigged a thumb over his shoulder toward Cresson Springs. "And being mad is why we made it through?"

That ... and fleeing. Finn deliberated over what remained of his band.

He had led thirty-three men for what, seven, eight years now? At times he was moved to tears by their discipline, their skill, their sun-darkened faces. Some leaders proved better than Finn at strategy, others in their devotion to the cause. None surpassed him in loyalty to his men, nor in his love for them. There was nothing Finn would not do for them.

War whittled them down, though, despite his efforts to prevent it. Those that were left trudged toward the edge of their endurance. Lugh's leg wound was puffy. Jerol hunched in the saddle and wheezed. Elias scouted ahead, and after every turn in the road Finn expected to find him fallen from his Arabian and lying in a heap. Rollo made a show of riding upright, as a knight should, though each hoof strike must have been agony.

Only Owen was sound of body, though perhaps their stroll through the field of dead had rattled his mind. He rode behind the others. The sergeant looked indifferent to their plight. Finn said as much to Rollo.

"You punched him in the cheese hole for disrespecting Emma. In front of his mates. That can't have settled well."

"Was I supposed to pull him aside, ask him what he did wrong, and how he might do better next time?" Finn made a mock sad face. "Perhaps give him a hug?"

"God's bones, but you can be a hard bastard."

"These are hard times."

"We headed to Tiberias?" Rollo asked the obvious question.

"Aye. To seek Hector and Serlo. And Arse-Master Gerard."

"To get new orders?"

Finn laughed, flat and short. "No. Not that."

"You're going to do something daft, aren't you?"

Finn laughed again.

The Sea of Galilee was a blue gem in a dust-brown desert. Tiberias staggered along its sparkling western shore like a drunken minstrel on stage. Fishing and trade in salted fish brought wealth. It had for centuries. Hot springs, believed to cure maladies, lured diseased pilgrims, and their healthy coin, to wash in the curing waters. Romans built Tiberias on the ancient Israelite village of Rakkath, as named in the Book of Joshua, and here and there bits of the old poked through the new. The city, like most places in Outremer, bore sundry names. Jews call it Teverya. Sometimes Rakkath. Romans named it Tiberias, and this was the name Franks used.

The city, when they reached it, was quiet as a crypt. Folk peeked from shadowed windows, trying to discern if these riders were ghosts or men. A fretted guardsman said inhabitants hid in the city or fled into the hills. Fear of a Mamluk incursion had spread like a pox.

Little life did they find in Tiberias. Neither did they find Gerard. He and Denis were at Cafarsset, a Templar *casale*, outside the city. The *casale* consisted of a scatter of Templar-run farms and a villa with a wall and two towers. A squire led them to the villa's Great Room, where the Master lay, arm wrapped in blood-smeared linen, leg propped on pillows.

Pillows? What Templar owns pillows? Finn glared at the tawdry things. "Master," he said through gritted teeth.

"It warms my heart to see you alive, Brother," Gerard replied, voice cold. "How many brothers are with you?"

"Brother Rollo. Three sergeants. One Turc."

Gerard grimaced and fluttered his fingers as if to say, *Provide your report.*

Finn told how Jakelin died, how Master de Moulins died, how Nazarenes were hauled away in chains. He spared no painful detail. Not the row of heads stuck on spears. Nor the grave filled with headless bodies. Gerard flopped back on a pillow and closed his eyes. Finn fixed his glare on Denis, who returned a dopey grin, oblivious to Finn's ire.

"We misjudged. Our mistake." Gerard opened his eyes, dragged the back of a hand over his brow. "The Sandpigs took us by surprise, is all."

This was your idea — you argued and cajoled and berated for it. Now everyone is dead and its we, and ours, and us? Finn said, "Templars do not ask how *many* enemy but only *where* they are. Mayhap you should've counted this time?" He held a beat, then added, "Master."

Gerard squinted his eyes to warn he was in no mood for criticism. "And you should have stayed by my side, to guard it, as I ordered. Where were you, I wonder?"

Blood surged in Finn's ears like a battle drum. The red mist descended.

"Battles are chaos. Always are. World shrinks to a blade length." Finn hitched a lip to show his pointy teeth. "You would know this, had you ever been in one."

Gerard's mouth worked like a cod dragged to land. Finn hammered away.

"We were at your side. Fought hard to stay there, too. Then Mamluks hit our flank. Broke us asunder. All because you, *Master*, failed to account for them."

Rollo had been leaning against the door jamb; now his limping gait echoed over the flagstones — thump, drag, thump, drag.

"Sundered. Yet somehow you managed to fight free? How valiant." Gerard reared up. "Hear me, you filthy, reeking —"

"No. You hear me." Finn stomped forward and stabbed a finger at Gerard. "Men died. Good men. Better men than you. Because of *your* arrogance! And now, after all is gone to hell, you lack the grit to admit *your* error."

Thump, drag, thump, drag.

"Brother de Moulins agreed," Gerard hissed. "And you did not voice —"

"You lounge on pillows!" Finn's eyes were hot and bright and black. "They support your weak spine, aye? Only a weak leader fixes blame."

Gerard sputtered and blinked.

Rollo grabbed Finn's elbow and hauled him back, just as Denis leapt in front of his Master, hand lifted as if placating a rabid dog.

"Calm," Denis said. His gaze bounced from Finn to Gerard. "Think. For some words, once spoken, cannot be unsaid nor unheard."

The attempt was noble. But too late.

"Get gone!" Spume flew from the corner of Gerard's mouth. His face, already burned by the sun, flushed a dangerous shade of crimson. "Get gone. Now. Or I will have you stripped. Beaten. Thrown from the wall."

"Who will do your bidding, aye?" Finn fanned a hand at Denis and snorted a harsh laugh. "This doughy one? Or the multitude of brothers lingering just outside?"

"Bastard, I'll carve out your heart!" Gerard slapped around himself for a blade but found only pillows.

Denis flailed at Gerard. Rollo yanked at Finn.

The red mist blurred Finn's vision, and his ears thrummed so loud he did not hear Gerard's stream of profanities, threats, and insults. Rollo dragged him into the hallway. Serlo was there, frowning in reproach, and for a moment Finn wondered if it was his ghost come to chastise.

"You can be such an arse," Serlo said, and laughed.

Serlo speaking, let alone laughing, was a rare event. Cursing rarer still.

Finn laughed too — a sound woven with despair, exhaustion, grief.

And perhaps a thread of madness.

CHAPTER 9

The scent of fragrant herbs and flowers wafted through the garden. Rosemary, sugary and resiny, reminiscent of pine, capable of warding off illness and spells. Marjoram, which Franks called Za'atar, was honied and woody with delicate floral tones. And thyme — spicy, aromatic, leathery. An ancient *Ein Shemer* apple tree stood in the middle of it all, with globes of pale-yellow apples, sweet, firm, and ripe for the plucking.

Finn pried open an eye. Small birds flitted through the thyme. One peered at him with a tilted head — red face, black and white head, black and amber wings. *Goldfinch*. Their calls were soft, like slurred musical notes, or liquid tinkling.

Other sounds came to him. Waves lapped nearby. Farther out echoed the faint cry of a gull.

His mind came alive, like a slumbering bear in springtime, and he remembered where he lay. Emma's garden. Gerard had driven him from Cafarsset. So, with nowhere to go, he sought an old friend. She let them in. Fed them. Months past she had sold her old villa, on the bustle of the main road, and bought this villa, nestled against the lake shore. 'Too many memories,' she said. She meant too many memories of her dead husband, Adrien, killed by Lugh after Adrien double-crossed them.

The land neighbouring her villa was bare and level until it reached the lakeshore. Eons of erosion had carved a bay, a dent in the shore, and it served as a small harbour. It boasted an outer breakwater of stone, long and narrow, and a quay for landing boats. A pier jutted from the shore into the lake. Tiberias had three more harbours, each larger, each named, though this baby harbour was ancient. An age-worn trail cut down to it and the whole affair lay hidden from above. Generations of folk maintained the pier. Now sun-browned fishermen loaded boats, sorted nets, rigged sails.

Fishing was timeless. Men had always fished. Always would. The Saviour threw nets for a while, Finn was taught, and also worked wood. *Was He a skilled wood worker? Were his tables and chairs and bowls practical and much-used? Or artistic and stored on a high shelf?*

The three knights sat under the tree and sliced and ate apples. Emma's servant brought fresh-baked pitta, olives, cheese, and salted fish.

"Baked fish. Creamed fish. Stewed fish." Rollo sighed. "Always fish in Tiberias."

"At least it's not pottage," Serlo said. "You could thank God for that."

Rollo made a show of mock contrition, gazed heavenward and made the sign of the cross, while Serlo shook his head at the impiety. Finn waited for Hector to chime in, for the sound of his crisp laugh, then remembered he was not here. Hector was the cool to Finn's fire. As second in the banner, he mothered the men, soothed their wounded pride when Finn took them to task. Finn felt incomplete without Hector.

Serlo told how Hector's destrier was bowled over. He did not see the charge from the flank, thus had no time to slip from the saddle, as knights train to do. He was pinned on rocky ground, leg broken, and took stabs from a spearman trying to finish what the ground had started. Denis saved Hector — and Serlo.

"Denis?" Finn barked a short laugh.

"Saved us," Serlo repeated.

"You jest?"

Serlo gave a sombre shake of the head to say he never jested. "He went battle mad. Frothed. Ranted. One of his blows almost caved my head. He cut a path to me, and together we freed Hector and the Master — and recovered the *beauséant*." He tapped his shaved dome. "Denis might not be the sharpest sword in the armoury, nor the fittest, but he has no fear. None."

Finn harkened back to the Under Marshal's byname, Denis the Stout, and realized it might not refer to his portly body, or *just* to his portly body, but could have something to do with a stout heart. People were often more layered than they seemed.

Serlo had used up a month's supply of words, perhaps two, so Finn gave him time to rest and regain his strength. After a moment, he asked, "What did the barber say?"

"Hector will walk again," Serlo said. "Though how well..."

"Does the barber know healing?"

Serlo shrugged and spoke a Templar adage. "Hands clean, nails trimmed."

Finn knew a brother who passed to the other side because of a broken leg. A bad break turned worse. Rot was the cause. First, they took his leg to the knee, then to the crotch. Next, he got hot and started talking stupid, then stopped breathing and expired. No point visiting Hector, Finn suspected, for he would be under the poppy. Finn had been under it once. It had been an unwonted fog, filled with mad dreams, spirits both moral and wicked.

Finn made the sign of the cross and recited a paternoster. God, the Great Shaper, former of heaven and earth knew all, saw all. Hector's fate resided in His hands — Hector would repair or he would not.

Hector had been carried to Castle Saphet. Saphet sat on a hilltop in the mountains, half a day's ride north of Tiberias. She was a jewel in the Order's crown — one hundred- and forty-foot walls, seven towers, two concentric bulwarks, two moats, water brought by an underground aqueduct. A Templar sought posting in Jerusalem, or Acre, maybe Tyre, but Saphet was next best.

Emma came and sat on a garden bench beside Finn. He glimpsed a flash of pale feet, soles dark with potter's soil. Her head was uncovered, her hair pulled up in a loose pile — scandalous, some would say. She wore a pelisson of light blue cotton, just fitted enough to taunt the eye, and embroidered at the hems with scrolls of flowers and vines. A linen chemise peaked out at her elbows.

Rollo and the others shuffled into the shade at the far side of the garden.

Finn soaked her in, revelled in her calm, in her feminine charm. A sweet air wafted from her, a blend of myrrh, rose, and marjoram infused in almond oil. She was lean and fit, forearms tanned and hands calloused from labouring in the garden. Strength alongside softness never offended Finn's eye. A woman bold enough to own and defend opinions was more appealing still. There was allure in a keen mind, in seeing things from different angles, in being a good listener.

She had all that. Yet she was beautiful in her soul, and this appealed the most.

Emma gave a sympathetic smile and touched the back of his hand. Finn nodded to concede the simple gesture. They sat in companionable silence for a while.

"Your garden is peaceful," Finn said, voice hoarse.

"My mother kept a garden." Emma breathed in. "Herbs remind me of her — and home."

Finn's gaze meandered over her lips. Her sun-kissed cheeks. Her large ears. He realized she was staring at him with a bemused tilt of the head. She had asked a question.

"Sorry, what did you say?"

"I asked, what is your home like?"

Finn glanced away and ran his fingers through his spiky hair, buying time to hone his mind. "My home? Wild. Rocky. Ancient forests cover much of the land. Rains a lot. Sometimes the rain is so fine it doesn't fall, just coats spiderwebs in wet diamonds. And the glens — fields of purple heather go on as far as the eye can see, if the mist is gone."

She smiled. Finn managed a smile, the first in days, and carried on.

"The love a Scot bears for his glen is irrational. Highlanders — mean as a rabid wolf, hardy as iron nails. And proud. So proud. They'll gouge your eyes out when given insult. Grudges last forever. Yet no folk are more caring, honest, or reliable. Cold in winter, though. So cold your..." Finn stopped short of saying, *So cold your cods freeze and fall off.*

"Sounds enchanting," Emma said with a wry grin.

"It is. Possibly one day you'll go there." Finn carried on before she could reply. "Scots defend their glen and raid the neighbouring glen. Yet both glens unite against outsiders." He nodded to the sergeants. "See Owen? And Rooster? Scot and Irish, nigh on kin, yet if they were on home ground, it would be no time afore one chibbed the other and danced in his blood. But here, in Outremer, they are brothers, each reliant on the other."

"Brothers..." Emma's smile faltered. "Brother Owen makes me uneasy. He looks at me like ... like he wants to skin and eat me. You too, when you are not looking."

Finn had seen the same, heard worse, but did not mention knocking Owen to his arse.

Emma took an apple from Finn's bowl, and he brushed her hand in passing. She paused with the apple halfway to her mouth. "Never turn your back to him, Finn."

Gerard stared out the window as gulls wheeled and screeched over freshly ploughed fields. Standing made his leg throb. It was a reminder of his recent failings, so he embraced it and would not surrender to it.

Denis read the lists and gave the bad news — dead Templars, dead Hospitallers, dead destriers. Footmen trudged the road to Tiberias in a steady trickle, Denis added, though they were no consolation. A company of spearmen could be made from any rabble of peasants. Give them a spear. Show them which end is sharp. Point them toward the enemy.

Knights were another matter — losing a hundred was worse than losing a thousand spearmen. Knights took years to train and cost a fortune to equip. And they had to be broken, like a dog, to be loyal and compliant. To obey without thought. Thinking was no good for a knight. Think too much about your place in the Order, ponder the Order's place in the world, and you might become a malcontent. Perhaps a deserter or, God forbid, an apostate.

Such cankers needed to be excised. Burned. The ashes scattered to the four winds.

Denis said Gerard's name, shifted from one foot to the other, but Gerard kept staring out the window. It was a sunny day. Sergeants trained in the courtyard and from somewhere drifted the scent of freshly baked pitta. After a while he asked, "The Scot is gone?"

"Aye. In Tiberias, I hear." Denis gave a tentative grin. "Can you not make amends? Assign penance to humble him?"

"Penance? No. I want him hurt. Badly. Or, better yet, gone forever." Gerard could not say 'dead', but it was what he wanted. "A Templar is obedient. Servile. Meek. Brother Finn is none of these things, alas, and I have not the time nor the energy to mend him. He must be anchored in righteousness or cast aside — God wills it."

"God wills it," Denis repeated.

"Not fit for duty," Gerard added, almost as an afterthought. *Dangerous as a rabid wolf, too.* He would not voice it, but the Scot also made him nervous, hesitant to turn his back.

Finn was noble-born — though you might not know it. Heathen ink marks hid beneath his cappa, literal and figurative stains on a man of God. A cross of Jerusalem was ink-marked on his wrist, and recently, as if to amend for the other sinful marks. *Ink marks!* As if someone so coarse, so deviant, would ever rise in God's Order. For a time, he had thought Finn a useful tool, well suited to the dirty chores not suitable for nobler brothers. He snuffed out the heretic, Robert, and his plan exposed the traitor, Ulmer of Rothenburg. Neither had he made a mess of the copper scroll quest. Yet lately he was defiant. Hot-blooded. *Why did it take me so long to see his true nature?*

Having Finn at his side, at Cresson Springs, had filled Gerard with confidence. The man was a rare killer. The fight had proved glorious — at first. He was going to claim a triumph to rival all others, carve his name into Templar lore, on a par with the first Master himself, Hugues de Payens. Then Gerard was almost cut to shreds by a horde of howling, blood-mad Saracens.

He had not died, though. Which was curious, now he considered it, and further proof that God had chosen him for some grand task. *Only providence can explain why I live when others do not. It is God's will. Yet this arrogant churl, Finn of Struan, dares to challenge me, God's chosen?*

Gerard stood, defiant against the pain in his leg, and stared at the Sea of Galilee. Denis pursed his doughy lips, uncertain what to do or say. After a while, Gerard turned to him and spelled out the plan and Denis nodded to say he understood.

"Do well, cousin," Gerard said, "and God will bless you for your faith and obedience to Him. Have no doubt."

Emma was gone and the darkness returned. Finn's uncle often said, 'God will not give you more than you can bear.' *That might be true in Alba, Uncle, but I'm far from there now.* He lounged in the shaded garden, watched goldfinches play, tried to nap. Recent days had left him hollow.

He burned with shame, too. A vow of obedience required unfailing loyalty; the Rule required humility. Anger drove him to rash words, though, and soiled his vows. Rage came like a wave, irresistible, and could swamp him with its force.

Guilt owned him at times. At other times the unrepentant part of him took savage pride in shouting down the Master. It was plain his arrogance shoved the kingdom close to a steep precipice. *Should have smothered the churl with a pillow and left his battered legs twitching...*

Solace could be found in solitude, so he pulled up the hood of his cappa, putting his face in shade, and walked down the trail to the lakeshore. There he meandered, Oathkeeper cradled in his arms like a drowsy babe, until he came upon a wayside shrine, a small hut made of wave-rounded rock and driftwood. Water sloshed at his heels, and the soft, papery clatter of a dragonfly's wings at his back. A rising breeze cooled his neck, fluttered the tattered hem of his cappa around his shins. He stood there awhile, waiting for what he was not sure, then ducked his head and stepped through the door.

Inside was a child-sized statue carved from basalt. Paint peeled from the stone. Nubs of votive candles, hooks, and weights arrayed before it like pagan offerings. The figure had an X-shaped cross at his back and a fish hanging from his hand — Andrew, Patron Saint of Fishermen, was martyred on an X-shaped cross. He was the Patron Saint of Alba, too, and Finn often sought his favour.

Finn knelt, bowed his head, beard splayed on his chest, and prayed for the Godliest man he knew. *Saint Andrew, first to be called by our Lord, you who died a martyr's death and offered your blood to build His Kingdom, intercede for Brother Jean, that our Lord grant him entry to paradise.* He prayed for himself, even though it was sinful. *Andrew, stir in my heart a desire to save souls, and to do all things for the glory of God. Replace my worldly doubt with heavenly assurance. Amen.*

Finn held his breath and listened, but heard nothing, felt nothing, saw nothing. The hollowness deepened. Thoughts swirled aimlessly — faith, purpose, doubt. He eyed Andrew from under lowered brows, and thought of home and his parents. Pondered what they thought of him, of what he had become, and if they revelled in his deeds or were shamed. Ma would be proud, he decided — she always was.

Her words came to him, soft and distant: *I am your shelter. Come to me in your summer, when your heart is liquid, or come to me in your winter, when your heart is ice. I will share your bliss or mend your ill. And know, child, I will walk through hell to keep you safe.*

Ma led his thoughts to Saint Mary Magdalene. Jean had often told Mary's tale — how she had fled Outremer to escape

127

persecution, landed in the region of Provence, lived in a cave near the town of Marseille. Jean hailed from Provence, as did many Knights of Solomon, thus Lady Wisdom was revered and her teachings were woven into the Order's lore. Some even claimed Templars guarded Mary's offspring to this day.

Finn thought it all a fine story — fine enough for him to venerate Mary, too.

He bowed his head, and a vision of saintly beauty came to him. Calm and warmth suffused him, drove out the darkness, and for a moment his soul tugged at its mortal strings. In the west, the sun fell in a cascade of light. *There is purpose in the setting sun, as there is in the rising sun. I am small in them, yet not small.* Finn fingered his prayer beads, carved like tiny human skulls, and dove into prayer. "Saint Mary, woman of many sins, who became the beloved of Jesus..."

He faltered, the words frozen to his tongue, for the beauty filling his head was not Mary.

It was Emma.

Denis waited at the lakeshore. His attending knight and sergeant lay mouldering at Cresson Springs, and only a pimple-faced squire attended him. Seeing the man was a splash of cold on his calm.

Finn offered a terse nod.

"I have been waiting," Denis said. "Where have you been?"

Finn made a show of scratching his beard in thought. "The Lord said unto Satan, 'Whence comest thou?' And Satan said, 'From going to and fro on the earth, and from walking up and down on it.'"

Denis grinned at that, not certain if it was jest or scripture, then doled out recent news. Balian had carried on to Tiberias without Gerard. He met with Raymond who, horrified by the debacle of Cresson, rode to Jerusalem to reconcile himself with King Guy. Guy, in magnanimity, and for the sake of the kingdom, raised Raymond from bended knee and embraced him. Unity was resurrected — though how long it would live, none could say.

Finn thought it all well and good but wondered what came next, and asked Denis as much.

"Campaign season is upon us," Denis said. "Saladin forms his army."

Finn nodded once to say, *No news there.*

Denis said, "You are to scout for Saladin's army."

"Me?"

"You. Beyond the Black."

To his credit, Finn remained stone-faced, though his gut had dropped to the floor. "Beyond the Black," he repeated, and Denis beamed like a child.

The Black was borderland. Marchland east of the Sea of Galilee. Franks called it *Terre de Suète*, the Black Earth, because of the basalt rocks and rich, dark soils found there. Arabs called it al-Sawad — the Black, and from this came its name. Boundaries between Mohammedan and Christian lands blurred, ever shifted, and over the years the Black had changed hands many times. Borderlands were dangerous, but creeping beyond them, into Saladin's realm, was a task seldom asked and seldom done.

Finn had done it, while hunting Robert of Saint Albans, and almost perished there.

Knights were at their best raging from the back of a destrier or brawling in a shield wall. Other tasks beckoned during times of peace. Patrolling roads, certes, guarding pilgrims, aye. But Templars did not scout — Turcs were the Order's eyes and ears. They owned the skills to creep into the Black and come back.

This goes beyond penance ... this is a death sentence.

Denis, in a rare moment of insight, seemed to read Finn's thoughts.

"Master Gerard remains livid. I argued your cause, of course, for I think you are misguided, not ill-intended. The Master is of a mind to expel you, forever, though I reminded him expulsion would require an inquisition, a ruling, the Council..." Denis fanned a hand to say, *And all the to-do that goes with that.* "Alas, we are at the precipice of war, and the Master grudgingly admits he lacks the time to allot proper punishment. Blessed are you, Brother Finn, for the Master gives you a chance to let the temperature cool and regain his favour."

"Blessed am I." Finn's hard tone said he was anything but blessed. "Am I given additional brothers, Under Marshal?"

"The Order finds itself short-handed." Denis tipped his head toward Serlo. "So much so that Brother Serlo, as of today, is reassigned to the Master's guard. A just reward for his recent valour, do you not agree?"

Finn said nothing.

"Serlo will serve the Master well. He rarely speaks, and never speaks disrespectful words, unlike you." Denis was savouring the moment. "You will conduct a scout with the remainder of your banner and no more. Go beyond the Black. See what you can see. Report to Acre after. Master Gerard and King Guy will be there." He cinched his eyes in warning. "Loss of habit awaits if you refuse. This the Master can arrange with a stroke of his hand. Loss of habit, as you know, requires no inquisition, no ruling from the council."

Loss of habit. It was more than mere penance — it meant being stripped of Templar privileges, and endless humiliations to gain back them back. Eking out an existence on bread and water. Complete silence. Labouring like a slave. Sleeping on the floor with dogs. Dishonour lasted a year and a day. Worse, once the habit was regained, a brother would never again command knights or carry the black-and-white standard. His reputation was stained. His career in the Order forever stalled.

Rollo had lost the habit. Being refused leadership was a long and bitter supper.

Finn realized he was glaring at Denis. "Least you could do is tell me why."

"You know why," Denis said. He tilted his head. "You're not a father, I suppose?"

"Not that I know of. But I've been a man all my life, with a heart, and with pride."

"Well. The Master, like any father dealing with a prodigal son, wishes to remind you that pride has no place in his home. Loyalty and obedience are welcome. Pride and disobedience are not."

Finn kept glaring, and Denis shifted course. "Care for my advice?"

Advice from a muttonhead is the last thing I care for. "Of course."

"Make peace with Gerard. Set aside differences. Start anew."

Finn snorted. He tried to fire his anger. Usually the ember simmered under the surface. Not today. Now he felt indifferent to the Master's pettiness, tired of the Order's endless rules and customs. There was a time he had hungered for reputation, acclaim, respect, but the hunt for them took much from him. And others. Brothers followed while he led them to dangerous places, bloody places. Many had not returned. Finn would lead. It was what he did, and he did it well. But the drive and ambition were gone.

Still, losing the habit, being denied a banner, being lowered to a common brother — no one in their right mind wanted that. Cold settled, a sort of dread, he supposed. Then Emma's smile shone in his mind and he breathed out.

Denis took Finn's calm mien as surrender. "*Avoir la pêche*, Brother."

Anger stirred, just a bit, and Finn made a harsh sound in his throat.

CHAPTER 10

Emma breathed in the bouquet of her garden. She took out her rosary and prayed for things profound and mundane — safety, peace, rain. And for Finn. They had shared much, good and bad, and grown as friends.

Friend. Is that all he is?

Finn was a Scot, a folk of which she knew little, but which hearsay credited with deeds of cleverness and cruelty. He was rife with contradictions. Nigh on illiterate, not tutored in mathematics, philosophy, or poetry. But he owned a keen mind. Capable of treading several paths at once; cunning and calculating, reckless and impulsive. He was endlessly kind and giving to friends, but brutal and ruthless to enemies. Finn could kill or maim men with no remorse. Yet when tortured by Shabh, a woman, his internal code kept his knife from her throat.

Memories of the Wadi of the Dead flared, unwanted, and with an effort she closed her mind to them. To ponder them brought darkness — though always the one shining light was Finn.

"He is a man of God," Emma whispered to herself.

A Templar. Vowed to God. Certes he had given her no promises of love, nor had she asked for such, yet did she not sense in him something more? Soft words. Sly looks. Lingering glances. Or was she deceived? Was loneliness the cause? She had lost two husbands, one to illness of the body, the other to illness of the mind. Fear of loving and losing again filled her, buried but unconsidered, for to study it in depth was too much to bear.

After the death of her first husband, Emma's mother said, 'Loss is forever. You never overcome it. Nor should you. But you learn to live with it, and when you live you can find love, if you seek it.'

Am I seeking it? I think so.

Finn and Rollo and Serlo came up from the lakeshore, then the Under Marshal. Finn wore a dark countenance, Denis his usual dumb grin. Emma tucked away her rosary and went inside to watch from the corner of a window.

Serlo turned to Finn. They talked a moment, then embraced and kissed each other on the cheeks. The shaven-headed Norman tailed the Under Marshal from the garden. Finn and Rollo sat in the garden and conversed as the sun fell. She left them to it.

In the late afternoon, Arlo roasted a lamb, bought in the market. To it he added a dish of finely diced tomatoes, cucumbers, and onions, gathered from the garden, and dressed with parsley, olive oil, and citron. And a warm cake, made with apples plucked from Emma's tree and spiced with a dash or two of sugar and cinnamon. Rollo was mad to sink his teeth into a dish that was not mushy pottage or covered in scales. They ate on a battered plank table lit by sputtering lamps while gnats buzzed and whined in their ears. Arlo was proclaimed a cook of legend — the food proved excellent, the company superb, the wine not bad.

Talk turned to Saladin, and to Guy, and to the Marshal's valiant death. Eyes shone with tears. Voices grew thick. Emma, silent through it all, marvelled at why gallantry fired men's souls, how death could be seen as noble rather than wretched. They planned for war, as men will do, and spoke of brutality and madness as if it were virtuous. Lumps of bread were positioned on the table to mark the various armies. Strategies were put forth, savaged for this flaw or that, then withdrawn for another equally flawed scheme.

Men are children ... but strong, and scarred, and capable of immense damage.

She was quiet, for she held no desire to speak of such things.

Their passion for destruction was infinite, alas, and soon the banter drifted to the tools of their trade. The virtues of the spear for piercing ribs. The mace for breaking bones. The war hammer for sundering helmets. And of swords. Their preferred dimensions for a blade. Whether the blade's cross-section was best as a diamond or with a fuller. And the proper depth of a fuller to make a sword light but not too weak. Over the axe there was much debate. Rollo argued it was a weapon without peer. Finn argued it a yeoman's tool better left at the woodpile. A conversation oft trod, Emma sensed, and one tired though familiar.

"We live in a time of frivolous inventions and false advances," Rollo countered, and tapped Oathkeeper. "Consider this blade. Watered steel, aye, but..."

Emma's mind drifted and her gaze settled on Finn.

He was nodding and idly palming the scar that furrowed his face from temple to jawline. His beard, black as jet, was streaked with a ribbon of white where the weal lay buried, and she realized she had not noticed that before. Black and white — like the Order. He sensed her gaze, glanced over, and a smile transformed his face.

Warmth suffused Emma and a blush crept across her cheeks. She excused herself, bowed her head in reply to the vigorous chorus of blessings and thanks for her hospitality, and strolled from the garden.

"Emma."

She turned. Finn had followed her to the door of the villa.

"Finn."

He shifted his feet. "I... I, uh ... fret for your safety." A grimace, as if his mouth had disobeyed his mind, then he blundered on. "Things are heating up — with Saladin, I mean. You should consider moving back to Acre."

Emma made a show of considering it. "You think Saladin will come for Tiberias? I have heard it said, more than once this very night, that Kerak and Jerusalem are his obsessions."

"They are," Finn said. "But the devil is unpredictable. He lurks out there. Always. He'll swoop in when he sees the kingdom lose her skill in war, when faith becomes charade, when warriors become coin-grabbers. The only question is whence? And when?"

"What a pleasant perspective you have — and all this, just afore my bedtime. I shall sleep peacefully, I expect."

She cocked her head and smiled to soften her words. Finn flapped a hand in mute apology.

"Saladin will not come for Tiberias, I think," he said, softly now, "though it's never a bad thing to prepare. Make plans. Have a man keep an eye on the Black and report movement."

"You are practical, as ever. And do not fret — I will take measures to safeguard myself." She watched Finn, eyes sparking, then bit her lip gently. "Good night, Finn."

He lingered, about to say something, but swallowed whatever it was and said the expected, "Good night, Emma."

Once in her room, she completed her ablutions, then retired to her palliasse. Outside, the war chatter carried on, but soon the garden fell quiet. Someone, probably Rollo, began snoring as loudly as a winter bear — or at least how Emma imagined a bear would snore. She lay comfortably, secure in her room, while Finn lay on the hard ground outside. All that separated them was one wall, an Order, and God.

In the night she dreamt she had misplaced something priceless, though she could not say what, and though she searched far and wide the priceless thing was never found. Emma awoke with a start, filled with an ill-defined dread. Things lost and things unsaid — her mother had once said unresolved things would haunt forever. Finn had prepared a speech, that much was plain, and it was not about Saladin or Tiberias.

Things lost. Things unsaid.

Are they not the same?

The eastern sky was streaked with hues of blue and grey and violet — the first signs of the dawn. Emma arose in a flurry, dressed, and went toward the garden. Her heart thumped in her chest. As she walked, her mind buzzed, mapped out what she needed to say.

The garden was empty. Finn was gone.

They rode from Tiberias in the dark of morning, when the world was most subdued, when the people and the animals and the land lay slumbering. Finn forwent farewells to Emma, anxious to be in the field and to place himself in danger, where improper thoughts would be shoved aside by thoughts of survival. Out there, beyond the Black, things would be simple. There would be no angry, scheming Master, no rules to abide, no paternosters to recite, no need to ponder vows of obedience or chastity.

Emma had stood at the door to her villa, daring him to say something meaningful, daring him to speak his mind. Finn read it on her face, and in her body, plain as gold shining in the sun. He wanted to. But the Templar part of him, the part used to denial and restraint, tied his tongue in knots.

Denis had taken Azrael, Master de Moulin's black stallion, and said he would see the beast returned to the Hospitallers. *Aye ... certes you will.* Finn was on Fagan, no longer limping, and felt restored for it. The familiar was good, a well-known brother even better.

Elias found Yousef, one of Finn's Turcs, on the road outside Tiberias. He had been scattered during the scrum at Cresson Springs, hid in the hills, then spent days walking to Tiberias. Yousef was younger than Elias, more handsome by far, but less skilled at fieldcraft. Both were masters of the recurved Turkish bow. Yousef was met with embraces and slaps on the back. They gave him one of the pack rounceys and redistributed kit to the others. Lugh cinched a strap, then asked the obvious.

"What's the plan?"

Denis had provided no direction. Details were for Finn to sort out or die trying. *The Order expects blind obedience. Independent thought is discouraged — they command, you do.* Yet over time Finn learned success hinged on traits deemed abnormal by the Order. Boldness. Self-reliance. Creativeness. The ability to think on the run. And the sharp mind that went with all that.

"Plan?" Finn shrugged and made a show of pondering it, as if he had given it no previous thought. "Get to the border and cross without being seen. Travel by night, lair up by day. Creep about and see the sights. Avoid a fight. Then meander back to Tiberias." He gave an exaggerated yawn. "Simple."

The men eyed Finn for a long, hard moment before soft laughter coursed through the group.

"Simple." Jerol cuffed an eye. "Thought you were going to say, 'be ghosts in the desert,' or some other stupid shite."

"And end with, '*Avoir la pêche*, Brothers'," Lugh said, and they laughed harder.

It was gallows humour, spitting in death's eye, for nothing about the plan was simple.

They rode south from Tiberias, around the Sea of Galilee, crossed the Jordan River over the bridge of Sannabrah, then turned east toward the Black. It was a day's ride to Cave de Sueth, the last Christian stronghold before going beyond the Black. By turns, they passed groves of olives and fields of grapes and barley, which stretched away as far as the eye could see. The soil was dark and rich — bountiful land, for borderland. A contingent of Templars, stationed at Cave de Sueth, patrolled and protected the folk. *Back home, ground like this would be fought over like gold — and be burned to cinders in the bargain.*

"Idiotic task, this scout," Rollo muttered, while pinching and rolling his reins between grubby finger and thumb. Their punishment gnawed at him. "Shite. Bollocks. Knights sniffing around like a bunch of Turcs, it's yeoman's work — no disrespect to Elias and Yousef."

Injustice had a way of tormenting the long-haired Norman, as it did Finn, though he was in no mood for it today. He hoped the deluge of complaints would sputter and die. They did not.

"Arse-face Gerard sent us here to die. I know it. You know it. Yet here we are, docile as sheep, when we could..."

Rollo let the sentence hang unfinished, but Finn knew what he had in mind.

"Abscond?" There. Finn had spoken it aloud. "Can't say I haven't contemplated it. But fleeing isn't something I can do. Not made that way. Besides, I figure Gerard wants us to run and I will not give him the satisfaction. So. Here we are. Doing yeoman's work." He fixed his gaze on Rollo. "Best if we stick to it, I'm thinking. Eyes open. Mouth shut. When we return, which we will, we'll be like shite in Gerard's pottage. We'll prove ourselves the better men."

Rollo said nothing. Finn prodded. "Or does running feel right to you? If it does," he waved vaguely toward the west, "then you have my leave."

"Bugger yourself," Rollo growled.

"Knew you'd say that." Finn smiled. Rollo would never abandon him, nor would he abandon Rollo. "Ah. The two of us. We used to be legends. Remember? Christian folk spoke our names reverently; Sandpigs whispered them in fear. 'Finn and Rollo, Hector and Serlo, why, they've killed more Mahounds than Noah's flood!' But who cares now, aye? Times have changed. The Order and the kingdom are in decline. Brothers die and no one replaces them. Saladin is strong,Guy is weak. Nobles fight each other when they should fight the devil."

Rollo tipped his head in a gesture that could have meant agreement or denial.

Farmers ploughed a field nearby. Two teams of oxen kicked up a dry, dusty plume that made the sky murky, like a gauzy veil. Finn waved and a man, a stick figure in the distance, hesitated before returning a curt wave.

"This isn't our land," Rollo said. "We don't belong here. Do you ever wonder if we're the bad men?"

"Certes we are," Finn said. "But its fine. The world needs bad men."

"It does?"

"Aye. To take care of the other bad men."

Rollo snorted a laugh at that.

"Cresson opened my eyes, Brother. We can't afford to lose, for we haven't the men. We must win every fight. Saladin can lose and will still have ample forces to come back for more. He need only win once." Finn breathed out. "Even so. I'll not break my vows, for they matter, or nothing matters. I'll find the devil's army, protect the weak, carry on loyal to God's cause. What else is there?"

"Nice speech." Rollo smiled, though there was no humour in it, and it only made his scarred lips and chin gruesome. "But at some point soon, I think, we'll have to fight for ourselves."

And so they rode into the Black, toward Damascus, toward a horde of enemy.

Under a murky sky.

CHAPTER 11

They angled across the Black in one morning and in the early afternoon followed a goatherd's trail into the Yarmuk gorge. There, the Yarmuk River flowed in a narrow, looping ribbon of shimmering green, meandering its way as it had for millennia. The way dropped steadily over rocky slopes until joining a second trail snaking alongside the water. Sentries, perched on a spiny outcrop above, hailed them, and demanded the watchword.

"Glory on high." Finn gave the watchword given him in Tiberias.

"Wrong!" shouted the sentry.

"Glory to God?"

"Wrong again."

"God's high glory?"

"You're getting colder."

Rollo spurred forward, grabbed a fistful of his cappa and yanked it up. "See this? Then you see who we are, and you see we are not Sandpigs. So, we'll pass without more idiocy, or I'll climb up there and kick your arse."

The sentry paused, then waved a hand. "Bit wordy, but it'll do."

"Who needs watchwords when I've got you," Finn said, and grinned at Rollo.

Further on, the trail branched from the river and into a wadi cutting down from the heights above, then out of it and into a series of sharp turns. Each turn took them higher. The track angled, slipped into an S-turn, then turned again. After one last corner, it straightened and climbed along a slope until they gazed up at Cave de Sueth, cut into a cliff face at the top of the ravine. Vertical brown smears on the rock showed the wadi continued beyond the cliff and, when the rains hit, water flowed over it.

Finn reined in and stared from under a hand-shaded brow. Cave de Sueth was not a cave but a series of caves. There were three levels of chambers, each hacked out of the rock and accessed by external timber stairs. Narrow ledges and niches dotted the rock. No doubt internal passages connected it all from inside. It reminded him of the Fortress of Crows, carved into cliffs above Tiberias.

"Around now, Hector would be prattling on about how these caves were enlarged during the reign of King Somebody, in the year Whatever, and how Saint So-and-So later rebuilt them, and how what was once a laura is now a Templar fortification." Finn let his hand drop. "Annoying drivel, certes, yet to my surprise I miss it."

"I don't," Rollo said.

Sergeants met them. Finn slid from Fagan and handed the reins to the first. "Where is Brother Herson?"

Herson de Tuilière, Commander of Cave de Sueth.

The sergeant held Fagan's reins in a fist and the other hand rubbed the destrier's neck, so he jerked his chin to the right. "On the knob. Catching the sun."

"Catching the sun?"

The sergeant nodded and grinned to say, *You'll see.*

The climb to the knob proved short but steep. It was a flat rock overlooking the gorge and the green-blue river. Patches of silvery light shone on the water. A man sat at the edge in the style of an Eastern mystic — legs crossed, upturned palms on his knees. His back was to Finn and he spoke over his shoulder in a measured tone.

"Well met, Brother Finn."

"Well met, Brother Herson."

Finn eased toward the precipice and peered over — his gut flinched at the steep drop, littered with jagged boulders, brown scrub, and the rare, stunted tree. Below him glided a black bird. Its wingspan was longer than Finn was tall. It was the largest bird he had ever seen, and it struck him as odd to be looking down upon the huge, gliding beast. He said as much.

"Griffon vultures," Herson said, without opening his eyes. "Poor flyers, truth be told, but they can glide for days. They nest on the cliffs nearby." He patted the rock by his side. "Sit."

Finn stepped back from the edge and lowered himself to his arse. He studied Herson from the corner of his eye. Lean-bodied. Hollow-cheeked. Weak-chinned. His skin was mottled red, pinked by the sun, his hair so pale and fine that, at first, Finn thought he lacked eyebrows. Herson brought to mind a giant, brow-less lizard lazing in the sun.

He sat still, eyes closed, for an uncomfortably long time.

"You are catching the sun," Finn said, as much a statement as a question.

"I am." Herson's voice was soft and high, like that of a boy. "One must catch it every day. Allow it to merge, through the palms, while breathing it in through the mouth. Little bits of the sun's rays enter the blood, and there they course until they find our inner fire. The sun feeds the fire. Enlivens us. As the sun enlivens the earth."

"I see."

Herson opened his eyes, pale as water, and fixed them on Finn. "Catch the sun."

"Another time."

Herson nodded curtly, to say he expected as much. "Why are you here, Brother?"

"To find Saladin's army."

"Turcs do that. My Turcs are in the field as we speak, and will return any day to report Saladin rallies at Tell Ashtara."

"Tell Ashtara?"

"A mound, to the north-east, said to be the ruins of an ancient city." The vulture drifted higher, level with them, and Herson watched it a moment before speaking. "Saladin used to sally from Cairo. Now he sallies from his new capital, Damascus, and forms his army at Tell Ashtara. From there they march to Amman, then attack Kerak or Montreal, or sometimes Jenin or Nablus. I have been here nine years, three months, and thirty-three days. In those years the Saracens are yet to come this way."

"Just because a man usually does something doesn't mean he always will."

"True." Herson nodded, then said, "You are a man of war."

"As are you."

"I can be. When God bids me, I pick up sword and shield, don the armour of God, and do what I must." Herson's pale eyes rolled reverently to the sky and back. His childlike voice hardened. "Saladin is a man of war. Like you. And like any fighting man, he can see there is no advantage to coming through the Black. Only risk. If this were not so, he would have travelled it already, which means he will not come this way. An old horse does not jump new fences."

"So, you won't be offended if I take a stroll to Tell Ashtara, to see for myself?"

Herson ignored the question. "I wonder, what sins did you commit to anger our Master, that he sends you on a needless and perilous task?"

Finn was about to offer some vague reply about arrogance and unwelcome opinions when it occurred to him — Herson had called him by name before opening his eyes. Which meant he was expecting visitors. Which meant he was communicating with the Master. *Which is as unsettling as Herson's pale, unblinking eyes.*

"What sins did I commit?" Finn gave a tired sigh. "I think you know, Brother."

"Rumour speaks of a hot temper, rash acts, ugly words. There are two sides to every tale, of course, so I am certain a just cause lies behind it all." Herson tilted his face to the sun and closed his eyes. "Yet the Master's tale is always correct, at least in his mind, and must be honoured as the entire truth, even if it is not. Which is why I refuse your request."

"My request?"

"You were about to request some of my men as guides. Local men who know the land. The Master did not tell me your sins, not in detail, but he was clear I am not to aid you. Alas, I cannot spare any men."

"Cannot, or will not?"

Herson shrugged, a gesture that said, *Is there a difference?* He opened his eyes to look out over the gorge and said, "I will not defy the Master."

Unlike me, aye? Finn shook his head at the Master's pettiness, and at his own foolish pride, then pushed himself up.

Herson gazed up from his cross-legged repose. "Would you like to know the secret to long life, Brother?"

"Catch the sun every morning?"

Herson smiled at the gentle mockery. "That helps. But mostly," he said, twitching up a finger, "care for your soul." He raised a second. "Drink wine, though not much." He raised a third. "And never rile the Master."

"Too late for that, Brother." Finn watched the vulture wobble into a turn. He spoke softly. "Brothers watch what

146

their leaders do. It is their example we follow. Gerard sets a bad example."

Finn's band lounged outside Cave de Sueth. Herson, now dubbed the Sun Lizard, gazed down from the uppermost cave. Groups of sergeants took turns marching north-east, laying up a while, then marching back. Always seven, the same number as Finn's band, and always dressed in brown robes and dun-coloured *shemagh*. Saracen spies watched Cave de Sueth from the far side of the gorge. The point of all the coming and going was to sow deception. Sergeants heading out. Coming in. Readying kit. Heading out. Coming in.

Any Saracen watcher must have been muddled after a day of it. Even Finn was confused.

His band began preparing when the sun dropped behind the hill.

Horses became a point of debate. They were surefooted in the dark, if given their head, and would trail the animal in front of them. Men moved quicker with four hooves under them, certes, but quieter without them, and would not have to hide them by day. Rollo argued long and hard for horses. His thigh, speared at Cresson, still pained him and a horse was the remedy. In the end, they left their horses at Cave de Sueth, but only after much debate and a few heated words.

Finn reverently folded his tattered cappa and stuffed it into a saddlebag. White would be easily spotted in the Black. Mail made a soft, slushing sound, so they left it behind and wore brigandines under their robes. They donned brown robes and wrapped their faces with dun-coloured *shemagh* — same garb as the coming-and-going sergeants. Dressed thus, and from a distance, they might pass as Saracens. Swords and daggers, bows and crossbows were their weapons. Each man bore a wool blanket rolled and snugged against their lower backs, a waterskin, and a haversack holding salted fish, dried apple, and horsebread.

Darkness fell and they departed with a curt dip of the head. No words. No prayers. It was twelve or so miles to Tell Ashtara as the raven flies. Finn intended to spend as little time as possible beyond the Black, that was for certain, and aimed to cover eight miles the first night. An easy day's march.

Only they were not on easy ground.

The narrow path out of the gorge was steep and winding. Beyond lay a maze of ridges and slopes interspersed with open, flat fields. They kept to the higher terrain and, when they had to, scurried across the low spots hunched like mice fearing the night owl. Wadis abounded. Enemy patrols too — at least Finn assumed they did. He had not been over this border before. The land here was as strange as the moon. With no local guide they could blunder about, become lost, never find Tell Ashtara. Elias swore he had been there and could find it, but if he could not...

The foreign, dark ground made them tread warily and sniff their way.

They became wolves. Elias was the pack leader and the pack trailed him in a straight line. No one talked. Hand signals spoke for them, mixed with the odd grunt, nod, or shake of the head. Their vision was reduced to the outline of the man in front. Ridge and slope, hill and valley. Rock and scrub, moonlight and shadow.

A Templar's prayer beads, besides counting prayers, could be used to count distance. A furlong was the length of an average ploughed furrow, hence *furrow-long*, which was six hundred and sixty feet. Eight furlongs made a mile. Finn knew, from experiment and experience, how many of his strides it took to cover a furlong. He counted strides, moved a skull-shaped bead down the cord for each furlong walked, and tallied simple arithmetic. God had gifted him a sense of distance and direction and these, with the beads, told him they crept into Saladin's land during the witching hour.

The night passed in a blur of shadows and skull beads.

Dawn showed as an ominous grey smear on the eastern sky. Finn jolted awake — daylight was exposure, and exposure was danger. Elias broke from the track and veered across country, then dropped into a low, meandering wadi overgrown with brush. He found what he wanted in a dense grove of scrub, and pointed at it to say, *We'll lay up there.*

Jerol patted his crossbow and nodded at the lip of the wadi to say, *I'll take first watch.*

The others set to clearing the heart out of the grove but leaving a ring of scrub around it. Branches formed the supports for a shelter, which they covered with armloads of leaves. Elias pointed at where he wanted leaves, scowled, and readjusted the covering to his liking. After more scowling and adjusting, and a bit more foliage, he gave a sweeping gesture to say, *Welcome to my humble abode.* One after the other, they crawled inside. The Turc brushed away their tracks using a branch, and was the last to crawl in.

The night had been long, the march arduous, their senses strung tight. Finn lay on his blanket and let the tension ebb away. Rollo began snoring, then Lugh. Finn was drifting off, nearing peaceful oblivion, but through drowsy lids glimpsed Owen glaring at him. Hard. Finn's eyes snapped open. The sergeant flashed a toothy smile, like a jackal over a fresh meal, then pulled a blanket over his head.

Finn lay awake a while after.

There are many ways to die. Finn pondered them in the shade of their lair; skull-shaped prayer beads slipped through his finger and thumb one at a time.

War took more than its share. A battle did not decide a victor, in truth, but only who survived. Most warriors accepted this. To do otherwise would make the work impossible.

Accidents were more common than one might have thought. Finn knew a brother in Jerusalem, late to Nones and hustling to the chapel, who was killed by a stone falling off a stonemason's scaffold. Wrong place. Wrong time.

Templars were not immune to sickness, either — especially in Outremer, where each illness proved more lethal than any suffered back home. Even popes fell victim to unseen maladies, and in some places a man was more likely to succumb to the coughing disease than a blade.

Boredom could kill. The devil made work for idle hands, folk said, and old Split Hoof was skilled at spreading mischief. Templars were men, after all, thus prone to recklessness. Finn once watched a brother handle a viper on a dare — *God will protect me*, he said. God did not. The serpent bit him on the hand. His arm turned blue, puffed up to twice its size, and he passed after three days of misery. All for a wager.

And then there was murder.

The front of Finn's mind would be focused on the task at hand while the back devised ways to snuff out Gerard. Sometimes Denis was woven into the plot. Then he would realize what he contemplated and remember he was a Templar, and that murder was, as Rollo was fond of saying, 'Useful, but frowned upon.' Finn would make the sign of the cross and recite paternosters. Later, though, he would find his thoughts again meandering into dark territory.

Thinking thus was a sin, worthy of damnation. *I have fallen. Pride is the cause.*

He forced his mind to ponder happier notions. Emma filled his head. Of kindness and softness he knew little, that was certain, but she gave a small measure of both. She had touched his hand, in her garden those many days past, and still he felt the thrill of that lingering touch. His heart was split — one side for God, the other for her. He had made a vow to God, who gave him purpose, put his idle hands to work on a noble endeavour, and awaited Finn in paradise. All good things came from God. Perhaps He nudged Emma and Finn along?

"You're quiet," Rollo said.

Finn held a finger to his lips, then whispered, "We're supposed to be quiet, on account of being beyond the Black. Remember?"

Rollo ignored the mockery. "You've got that look in your eye, the one you get when you're contemplating bad things. Thinking of Gerard, are you?"

"You know me too well," Finn said. "Gerard's pride got Jean killed, and Mael, and others. I can't forgive that. I'm also thinking I've been an arse — more than usual, I mean. My ire put us in a bad place, attempting a task we shouldn't, to make amends with a man I hate."

"Don't waste mental vigour on it — you don't have much to spare."

"Still. I endangered you. And the lads. To no useful end."

"You did," Rollo said, a little too fast. "None of us hold you to blame, though. It's who you are. Time spent in your company is rarely boring. Beats dying in bed. So. Now all that remains is doing our bit, paying our dues, and getting our arses back across the Black."

"Aye. All the same. I'll be less of a contrary man. For you and the lads, at least."

Rollo chortled at that and shook his head.

"No. I will." Finn shifted to better fix Rollo with a hard stare. "I'll leave Gerard be. He is a quick-tongued liar, a backbiter. He plots in the dark. But whatever is done in the dark shall be brought into the light. God will make sure of it."

"Time with the Sun Lizard cooked your mind," Rollo said, and tapped his head. "You're God-mad. Addled. I see that now."

It was Finn's turn to ignore the mockery. "God will cut Gerard down. Not me." He knew that with certainty, but he was uncertain if the cutting would include him.

CHAPTER 12

Darkness was falling.

When the last sunrays of the day kissed the sands, when the oranges and reds melted into black, that was when the lair emptied and the wolves came out to play. Night sent people, worn from the day's labours, scampering to seek shelter and fire, which together warded off fear and induced drowsy contentment. An aged tradition. Old as mankind. But these men, contrary to nature, hid from the day and embraced the night — like the caracal that sleeps away the sun's passage to hunt under the moon.

Night brought urgency. Templars sat in their lair and made plans.

"Me and Adonis," Finn said, and paused to nod at Elias, whose ugly face glared back, "will go to Tell Ashtara. Poke about. See what we see. Yousef too." He fanned his fingers at Rollo and the sergeants. "You'll wait here. All of you. Fewer of us means less chance of being seen."

Rollo bobbed his head side to side in a gesture of tacit agreement. He and Lugh's wounds, taken at Cresson, yet nagged them. Their limping gaits had slowed the night march. Finn would not call them out for it — they had too much pride to suffer that indignity. But Rollo knew it. Besides, Finn had placed them in this mess, and it was on him to bear the brunt of the risk. Leaders should never ask of their men hard tasks they were not willing to do themselves — especially when the leader's impertinence caused the hard task.

Finn gave Rollo a nod. "We'll be gone a day or two, and if we don't come back … well, you know what to do."

"God's bones," Owen said. "We're to lie in this infernal heat, in the dirt, like rats?"

"That's what war is, Owen." A wayward lock of hair dangled in Rollo's eyes, and he paused to tuck it behind his ear. "Lots of loitering in horrid places. Too hot. Too cold. Never enough food, and what you have isn't fit for dogs. Then all the misery is enlivened by sudden, short bursts of intense fighting."

"So at least we have something to look forward to, aye?"

"Aye. Laziness and fighting — what joy they bring."

"Rather not sit here and sweat my bollocks off, all the same," Owen said with a smile, and made to rise. "I'll go with."

Finn's growl stilled him. "You don't have a vote, churl, even if this were a voting banner, which it's not. You'll stay, is what you'll do."

Owen swung from amicable to fuming in a blink, and fixed Finn with a glacial stare.

Jerol turned to Lugh. "Touching. Owen doesn't want to let Finn go. Must be mad with love."

"Finn's the madman." Lugh jerked a head toward Owen. "Leave this eejit. Fine by me. But I'm your sergeant. You left me at Cresson. No way in hell I'm staying —"

Finn held up a palm to quiet the Irishman, tugged at his long black beard, then pointed at Lugh's straw-coloured beard. "I might pass for a Saracen, at least from a distance, and so long as I don't speak. You will not."

Lugh opened his mouth and Finn made a fist to say, *No more, Rooster, it's decided.* He left Lugh grumbling, Owen glaring daggers, and set off with Elias and Yousef.

"That lad, Owen, he doesn't like you much," Elias said as they walked.

"Likes you, though," Finn said. "Hard to fathom. Must be on account of you saving him."

"Eh?" Elias scrunched his thick, hairy brows. "When was this?"

"Cresson. He said he was pinned, and you came and freed him."

"Didn't happen. I remember where I was that night, and it was nowhere near Owen. Maybe another handsome, charming Turc came along and he's confused us?"

"Confused you with another goat-arse-ugly Turc, you mean," Finn said, and Elias spat his reply.

Finn's mind meandered to Cresson, to Owen's insistence on going with him onto the battlefield, the sergeant's twitchy behaviour. Finn assumed him unnerved by the dead, the dark, the reek. Yet, now he thought about it, Owen was ... distracted, more so after finding Elias. *Why would Owen lie about Elias? Was he a coward? Did he hold back, hide from the fight, and concoct the story of Elias as cover?* He shoved the half-formed notions aside and vowed to come back to them later.

They fell into single file and moved toward Tell Ashtara. The moon at Cresson Springs had been waning gibbous and gave off a fair light. Now it was a waning crescent, a weak light, though Finn wished the light gone entirely. Vision took a lesser role in the dark. Hearing and smell became more acute. He peered into the inky night out of habit, but quested with his ears, sniffed the breeze like a dog.

In the darkness we navigate not by sight, but by instinct and faith.

Elias was a wraith, shifting and sliding, and Finn did his best to keep up. Not too close, not too far. They crossed a wadi filled with ankle-deep water. On the other side, the terrain sloped north. Ploughed fields abounded. Green shoots poked through the dark soil and, considerate to the farmer's plight, they tried not to trample them to ruin. Low hills dotted the ground and they flitted from hill to hill. Finn's pacing and prayer beads told him they had travelled a mile. It would be another mile, maybe more, before they reached Tell Ashtara.

Elias dropped into a crouch and his fist shot up — the sign for *hold*.

Finn did the same without a thought, blood surging in his ears, eyes moving but seeing nothing. Elias made a flicking gesture with two fingers, the sign for him to come closer. Finn shuffle-scampered to Elias and was about to whisper, *Aye?* when he smelled it. Death. Drifting on the breeze. Wet copper, the pork-like reek of charred man-flesh, woodsmoke.

They found the source not long after — six lumps smouldering in the ashes of six fires.

Finn had seen dead men. Too many. He had made his share too. War was his trade, death its artefact. This was different. Six men had been broken, their bones smashed, their bodies folded unnaturally and bound in ropes until the size of a large sack, then dangled over a fire and slow-roasted. The ropes, weakened by the flames, eventually snapped and dropped the man-sacks into the coals. A devious torture and a long, agony-filled ending. Cruelty and hatred were needed — and much of each — to do such things to another human.

"Karluks." Yousef spat and wiped a lip. "Maybe Khalajes. Pain feeds them."

Elias shook his head. "Kipchaks. Give enemies no mercy and expect none in return."

Finn scrunched his brow at the back and forth.

"Turkmen," Elias said, the one clipped word an explanation. "Karluks, Khalajes, Kipchaks. All Turkmen. All fight for Saladin."

Turkmen; Turks. A loosely related group of people, with sundry tribes rolled into one name. All fierce warriors, skilled from horseback with a bow or lance, afoot with shield and blade, riding at night — their array of martial talents was endless. Some Turcopoles, like Elias, were the sons of Turkmen.

"My father was Kipchak," Elias said, as if hearing Finn's thoughts.

"Your mother?"

"Arab. Amila tribe."

Finn nodded sombrely to say, *Thought so*, though in truth he had no idea. He crouched to study a smouldering man-sack, and a half-open eye gazed back from the mess, glassy and dry. "Herson's scouts. I don't think the Sun Lizard will get his report after all." He straightened up and made the sign of the cross. "It's on us now. We are the kingdom's eyes. Which means this needless scout just became meaningful."

"Aye, for none of these will be walking anytime soon," Elias said, and snorted at his own dark jest.

They left the dead smouldering where they lay and carried on, more fretted knowing some fiendish breed of Turkmen hunted the night. Finn tried not to ponder that ugly thought, nor remember the pulverized man-sacks. Instead, he focused on counting beads, squinting into the dark, sniffing the air, and questing with his ears.

Time passed thus. How much time, Finn could not say.

"Need to water the flowers," Elias whispered. He veered to the side of the trail, fumbled at his braes, and blew out a lengthy sigh as piss hit the ground.

Finn took the moment to drink from his waterskin. After, the three huddled close, squatting on their haunches.

Elias looked toward the north, the east, the west. "Just a bit further, I wager, and we should tack a bit more east."

"Do you know the way to Tell Ashtara ... truly?"

Finn's query caught Elias by surprise. He sniffled his bulbous nose and scratched his long, bearded chin before replying.

"No."

Finn snorted in amusement and shook his head.

"But," Elias said, holding up a calloused finger, "I know how to angle north and east at the same time. Even you, Frank, could do that. And I know it'd be hard, very hard, to stroll past an encamped army without noticing."

Elias was right in the end, and Finn should not have fretted over finding Tell Ashtara. A bit further and it found them. A lurid glow lit the night sky just over the horizon. Only thousands upon thousands of fires could cause a glow like that; cooking fires, warming fires, fires just because that was what men did when sleeping rough. Light called like a beacon guiding a ship to safe harbour — only no safe harbour awaited.

To the north-east, a thin, rocky ridge clawed out of the ground. Finn tapped Elias on the elbow and pointed at it, and they worked up it in a crouch. Yousef held on the slope to watch their backs, as Finn and Elias crawled the last few feet on their bellies. Finn peeked over, just his eyes and hair showing, and squinted as his vision adjusted to the deluge of light.

"My God," Finn whispered. His eyes were wide and white. "My God…"

It was dark ahead. Dark behind. Dark everywhere. Rollo lay at the lip of the wadi, tucked under a scrub, battling to stay awake. *Isn't right for a knight to be crawling around in the black like a wounded bat. Not natural, either.*

He took his turn at watch, like the others, and yearned for dawn, like the others. His weary mind careened from this to that. At times he bit a knuckle to stave off sleep, and tried not to fret for Finn, and tried not to ponder Jean. He never cared much for Jean, nor Jean for him; one was too Godly, one not Godly enough. Their relationship was like summer and winter, hot or cold, though most often cold. Seasons were long but the shifts between them abrupt. The Frenchman was calm, calculating, and Rollo assumed these skills presaged a long life. *Certes he'd live longer than me.*

Yet now Jean was gone Rollo felt lessened. Unsettled.

Finn said Gerard's stupidity got Jean killed, and Mael, and others. Which was true.

But Finn, in his haste to snap at Gerard, chose to ignore one thing — brothers take vows knowing they might die. That's what happens in war. Jean was a warrior. He fought. He lost. Rollo scrubbed a calloused palm over his cheek. Still. Cackhand was gone.

A sudden muttering brought Rollo's head up. Senses, dulled by the wait, surged to life. He stared, unblinking. He listened. Sniffed. *Night can play tricks on a weary mind...* No — there, again, closer now. To the north-east.

Finn wouldn't make such a ruckus.

Shapes flitted single file down the track like ghosts. Only these ghosts carried circular shields, and bows, and swords. *Sandpigs.* His heart thumped — loud enough even the Sandpigs must have heard it.

His sword lay next to him, and he slid a hand to its pommel, felt the cold steel wheel, slid on and coiled a hand around the leather-wrapped handle. Having steel in his hand steadied him, and he lay still as a rock, quiet as a mouse. Thus did the ghosts pass, one at a time, and he counted each; ...*seven, eight, nine...*

He stayed rooted to give the Sandpigs time to drift off. After a while, he shifted, readying to crawl backward, when he heard another sound. Soft. Gravelly. Like a sandal scuffing in rocky dirt. More shapes coming down the track.

...*eleven, twelve, thirteen. And where are all you little ghosts travelling, I wonder?*

CHAPTER 13

"My God," Finn muttered, and half-heartedly made the sign of the cross to amend for his profanity.

He had seen an army at Montgisard. Learned men wrote twenty-thousand Saracens fought there, but Finn estimated half that number. He had faced Robert's army at the pass in the Samarian Hills, and neither was it twenty thousand, despite what chroniclers claimed.

Never seen twenty thousand of anything in one place at one time ... until now.

Row after row of tents spread into the distance — men moved about, busy at this or that. Banners hung limp in the desert air. Each marked a contingent of the Sultan's army. Bedouins. Egyptians. Armenians. Persians. Berbers and Nubians from Africa. Arabs of all tribes, and tribes of Turks. Kurds, Saladin's kin, were as numerous as the stars. Coloured standards were many. Red, green, yellow. Black or white was rare. Most bore exotic designs. Moons. Stars. Scrolling Arabic words.

A massive tent stood atop Tell Ashtara. A yellow banner drooped over it. Finn could not make out the design, though he knew it showed the red, double-headed eagle of Saladin. A sea of yellow Mamluk tents ringed the Sultan's.

Footmen. Spearmen. Swordmen. Axemen. Archers. Javelin-throwers and slingers. A dizzying array of men. And horses — herds of horses. Equine warriors milled and stomped in camps of their own, each larger than that occupied by men. Mounted archers. Light cavalry. Heavy cavalry. Each faris owned several mounts, some as many as a score, and it made for an impressive menagerie of horseflesh.

"Khurasanis," Elias whispered, and nodded toward a contingent. "From Persia. Armoured horsemen. Fearsome. They've not fought with Saladin afore."

Finn strained to see. Along the edge of the camp lay stacks of … something. The something went on for two, three furlongs, and was as tall as a man. "Firewood?"

"Arrows," Elias said. "Bundled in sheaves of twenty-four and stored in boxes. Keeps them straight, preserves the fletching. Must've taken an army of fletchers to make all that."

Archery was a mysterious art to Finn, one that had almost claimed his life, and seeing so many steel-tipped shafts made him edgy. They crawled down the ridge, then worked their way around the army's flank. More firelight flickered ahead. Finn nodded at it and mimed crawling closer and Elias rolled his eyes.

They found a second camp as large as the first.

Elias pointed at a series of banners and whispered, "Abna, kin of the Khurasanis. Also Persians but resettled in Mesopotamia. Footmen. Tough bastards. Fight over broken ground, in cities, on bridges. You name it. Once, in —"

Finn tapped Elias on the forearm, then pointed at the right side of the camp. Timbers lay there, stacked in endless rows, as well as stones the size of a child, mounds of coiled rope, hides, and wicker baskets. Slaves moved along the rows, mending gear and stacking wood.

"Trebuchets. Battering rams. Siege towers." The words tumbled out of Finn's mouth. "Never have I seen so many."

"Saladin brings all he has," Elias whispered. "He means mischief."

"He means to take Jerusalem. And Acre, and Jaffa, and all the cities." Finn dragged a palm over his face. "I've seen enough. Time to beat feet."

They slithered backward like snakes, then rose and scuttled back like spiders. Elias led the way. Finn trailed, deep in thought. Two armies, both larger than anything Guy could muster. Nations allying with a Sultan they had long denied. Piles of siege machines. Horses and men. A complex undertaking, war, especially when intended to conquer a kingdom.

Finn, deep in thought, did not hear Elias's hissed warning, nor the thump of hooves until too late. A hard-edged shout in Arabic straightened his swirling mind. Finn understood enough to know a watchword when demanded.

God's bones, not another watchword I don't know.

Three men on small-headed Arabians cantered from the early morning gloom. They wore yellow silk over lamellar mail. Ink marks shone on their arms and hands and faces. Their hennaed hair was rolled into braids that dangled from their heads like orange ropes. Ornate, curved *khanjar* hung at their hips.

Mamluks.

Rising fear scattered Finn's reason. He gawked at the first Mamluk's light eyes and red hair. *Harvested from the edges of Christendom, certes... It'll be odd to die at the hands of an enemy born Christian. God must have a keen sense of humour.*

The red-haired man slipped from the saddle, and in two strides he was barking at Finn in Arabic so guttural it sounded like throat-clearing from the poor souls that laboured in the dusty salt mines. Finn spoke Arabic, but not enough, nor well enough, to attempt a reply. Elias rattled off something, then said, *Mughafal, mughafal.* He laughed and patted Finn on the shoulder — *simpleton.*

He played along, bobbing his head and grinning like an idiot. The red-haired man stomped close and tilted his head to better peer into Finn's eyes, as if seeking something in those black orbs. His gaze dropped to the ink marks on Finn's wrist and forearms, and he furrowed his brow at them.

More men on horses were coming up, riding a narrow track. By ill-luck they stood on the east-to-west road connecting the two armies. Memories of the bound, broken, and burned scouts soured Finn's mind, and his hand crept toward Oathkeeper until by force of will he stilled it. Horsemen tramped by in a slow procession. Mamluks, in the main, and half a score of black-bearded men in black robes.

A man riding a glorious white Arab stallion came from the gloom. Red robes trimmed with yellow swathed a slight body. Delicate hands held a loose rein. His face was hawkish, sharp-chinned, hollow-cheeked. Hair and beard were an uncompromising black. And the eyes were piercing, keen, fierce. Kohl lined the sockets. A thousand schemes swirled in that gaze, yet also a self-assured calm, as if he saw the eventual outcome of his plans.

Last time I laid eyes on you, old friend, you were fleeing Montgisard on a racing camel, me snapping at your heels...

Saladin. The Devil incarnate.

Finn felt a sudden urge to yank out Oathkeeper and fling himself at the Devil. End it all. Here. Now. Save Christendom. Gain heaven.

Elias grabbed Finn's elbow, yanked him to his knees, then shoved his forehead into the dirt. Finn's last vision of the Devil was a slightly bemused stare from those piercing eyes.

Men babbled in Arabic. Rough hands heaved Finn to his feet. Someone clouted him on the side of his head, set his ears abuzz, and his breath gusted out as a fist hit his stomach. Then a sharp voice — edged with the long-vowel accent of the Svan, from the Caucasus Mountains.

The battering stopped.

Finn blinked and shook his head as Abram's grinning face swam into view.

A glance found the Sultan gone, and with him Finn's mad dream of death and heaven.

Mamluks ringed them. The red-head stood by Abram. Red Head's face was battered with pocks and welts, his eyes like blue embers under a brow like an anvil. He held Oathkeeper, the handle in one hand, the blade in the palm of the other. Finn could not recall his sword being taken, but there she was, in the hands of another man.

Abram barked at Red Head without taking his warning stare from Finn. Red Head tapped Oathkeeper in a meditative tic. He glanced up from under lowered brows, eyes cold, then grudgingly offered the sword pommel-first. The leather-wrapped handle felt warm in Finn's hand, and he slid the blade home. The Mamluks ringing him stepped back; one slapped him on the head as a parting gift. Red Head gave a last lingering glance, turned on his heel, and leapt onto his Arabian. He propped a forearm on his saddle, waiting for Abram and glaring at Finn.

Abram eased close, and in French whispered, "Life for a life. As I vowed. Now the debt is paid."

Finn wisely kept silent. Abram winked and turned away.

Goats. Damn goats. Never around when you were hungry, underfoot when you were not.

Rollo lay under the scrub at the lip of the wadi and eyed the furry bastards and their goatherd. The man strolled not more than sixty paces away. Sun-faded, loose-fitting robes shrouded his bony body and wrapped his head. Occasionally he used a crook to tap a goat on the rump or steer one this way or that.

The morning had begun pleasantly enough. Then Jerol heard bells. Copper bells, worn by goats. Shepherds used bells back home, in Caen, because men in different lands often devised the same solution to the same problem. Despite all that, Rollo still found the tinkle of bells on a desert landscape outlandish. Perhaps because they were so timeless.

Jerol lay not far away, tracking the man with his crossbow. With a dip of his chin, Rollo would send the goatherd to the other side, for Jerol would not miss at that range. His dun-coloured *shemagh* blended with the sandy ground, and he was nigh on invisible. The scarf hid his thick, fair hair on the sides and back, with a few wisps clinging stubbornly to his bald dome. Rollo liked Jerol, nicknamed Uncle because of his advanced age of forty-something. The man had been his sergeant for eight or nine years now. Jerol, despite his dotage, was hard as iron. Sharp-minded too.

He had come to the Order a wolf's head, as had the Irishman, Lugh. *I'd wager more wolf heads fight for the Order than lurk in all the forests of Christendom.*

Jerol shifted his gaze, somehow managing to keep one eye on the shepherd and the other on Rollo. He arched a thick brow to say, *Snuff him?* Rollo shook his head, then dipped it to the side to add, *Not unless he sees us.*

To be discovered beyond the Black portended trouble. Lots of it. And abandoning Finn, which would likely lead to his death. But this goatherd was an innocent, a man eking a living from his animals, from the land. He did not deserve death, certes, though he might get it.

Rollo was pondering all that when a foot — sandaled, by the feel — stepped on his back. Two surprised curses rang out;

one in Arabic, the other in French. Rollo rolled and yanked out his dagger in one move. He came out on top, his dagger poised in a backhanded grip as he stared into the white eyes of a brown-skinned lad.

"Bastard." Rollo climbed to his feet, hauling the lad up with him in a cloud of dust. He gave him a shake that set the lad flopping like a rag mawmet. "Who are you, eh?"

The lad shook his head stiffly at Rollo's *lingua franca*.

The goatherd trudged over, Jerol trailing with his crossbow levelled at the man. Goatherd skipped forward a few steps to catch the lad's elbow. Seeing the two side by side was like looking at the same person — with the same sharp eyes, craggy nose, and cleft chin. The man's leathery forehead and chin were ink-marked with swirls and lines. The lad was unadorned.

"Fall asleep, there?" Jerol said. "The lad stepped on you."

Rollo ignored that. He did not know much Arabic. Jerol's was passable. "Ask if they're Mahounds," Rollo said.

Jerol's query set loose a deluge of Arabic. After a moment, Goatherd turned to Rollo, making exaggerated pleading gestures and ending with a sad face that would put most mummers to shame. He began rattling off more Arabic. Jerol raised a hand, palm out, and patted the air in a conciliatory gesture until the Arabic trailed off.

"Says they're Bedouin," Jerol said. "Not Saracens — not the enemy kind, anyway. Vows on his honour."

"So I gather," Rollo said, voice dry. "Ask them where they're headed."

Jerol asked, which produced flailing toward the south-west, more Arabic, and some bad French. Goatherd clasped his hands together, brought them to his chin in mimicry of prayer, then tapped his chest. "Nasrānī." He patted the boy's head and said, "Nasrānī." He dared to touch Rollo's arm, then himself, then the lad. "You. Me. Him. Nasāra."

The man rattled off more and Jerol translated. "They're headed to the Cave de Sueth, to sell goats. Templars buy them. He insists they are Christian."

Jerol need not have translated that last bit, for even Rollo knew the word, *Nasāra*.

Rollo stared off, struggling to recall one of Hector's many tedious history lessons. Something about Nasāra being the word for a Christian community in Saracen lands. A treaty was made wherein Muhammad allowed the Christian Arabs to practise their religion and keep their property. Later, the treaty was broken, the Christians exiled. But the name Nasāra stuck and tribes of Nasāra Christians abounded. *Did one of Hector's droll stories once say Bedouin can be Christian? Can't remember...*

"Christians?" Owen spat and wiped a lip. "He lies to save his skin. Ask him to recite the Lord's Prayer. The lad too. Kill them when they can't."

"You couldn't recite the Lord's Prayer either, arse. Should I kill you?"

Owen frowned to acknowledge his grasp of the Lord's Prayer might need work.

Lugh, right hand tucked behind his back, ambled forward a few steps until he stood behind the lad. His stare was fixed on Rollo, and Rollo twisted his head to say, *Not yet*.

Goatherd peered over his shoulder at Lugh, at the feral look in his eyes, at the hand behind his back. He wrapped a protective arm around the lad and pulled him close.

Goats meandered around them. One nibbled at the ragged hem of Rollo's robe; he shoved it away with his boot and debated with himself to the soft tinkle of bells. The obvious choice was to kill the man and the boy, dig a shallow hole, and leave them in it. Take no chances. Leave no traces. The goats would do what goats do — wander about and eat things. By the time someone came for the goats, and found the missing goatherds, or not, Rollo and the others would be at Cave de Sueth.

Goatherd sensed Rollo's mood. "Friend … Christian … brother," he said in French. His grin showed more gaps than teeth. He patted his chest. "Nasārā," he repeated.

"Kill them," Owen said. "They'll give us up."

"Shut your hole." Rollo jerked his chin at Jerol, a man whose opinion he valued. The old man replied in Norman-French.

"They're Christians — sometimes, at least, and Mahounds when it suits them. Not Saladin's lackeys, though, I wager. And I don't think they'll give us away."

Rollo glanced to Lugh, who shrugged to say, *Say the word and I'll chib them.*

Rollo regarded Goatherd through narrowed eyes. "He claimed to sell goats at Cave de Sueth," he said to Jerol. "Ask him what Herson looks like."

Jerol asked and Goatherd's reply made him snort with mirth. "Like an overgrown, pale lizard, he says."

Rollo laughed and the tension flowed away like water from a stabbed skin. Goatherd grinned his gap-toothed grin and everyone else joined in.

Except Owen. "Sandpigs will torture them, if they catch them," he said. "They'll squeal."

Rollo ignored Owen and spoke to Jerol. "Uncle, tell them to get on their way. We'll be on their heels, so it's best if they don't dally."

The man and his son corralled their animals, then herded them south to the sound of soft goat bells and the occasional bleat.

"They'll squeal," Owen insisted.

"Shut your gob and go stand watch." Rollo watched Owen stomp off. He turned to Jerol. "This is the worst place to hide. Like a goddamned thoroughfare. Sandpigs in the night. Goatherds in the day. What was Elias thinking?"

"Goatherds work their herds here. Always have." Jerol slid the bolt from its track, dropped it into the quiver on his hip, and grunted as he unlatched the crossbow to take the tension off the cord. "Herds of Sandpigs shouldn't be here, though, and you can't fault Elias for that."

Rollo cocked his head to the side. "They're doing the same as us. Laying up by day and sneaking in the dark, but sneaking south-west. Only one reason for that — they're scouting a path for an army."

CHAPTER 14

Finn walked south as dawn warmed the sky. At his back the *adhan* echoed, an ancient song with no fixed melody, no fixed meter. It called the faithful to the first of five daily prayers. The mu'addin's voice was strong and euphonious, his style florid and melismatic. Finn found the song an unsettling reminder of where he was.

He doubled his pace, keen to leave the eerie refrain behind, to put distance between himself and the place that had almost become his grave. Elias explained all the Arabic back-and-forth as they walked.

Saladin had been riding out to inspect his men — as any clever leader would do. Red Head was *khassakiyya*, the sultan's retinue and bodyguard, selected from the Royal Mamluks. Best of the best, Elias said. Red Head, rightfully, thought them Christian scouts. The thought hardened when Finn, seemingly, did not understand Arabic. Elias told them he was mute and dumb at birth, which was not entirely a lie he said to Finn with a smirk. It was a flimsy ruse, destined to fail — until Abram confirmed the same. He said Elias, Yousef, and Finn were his men, who had come looking for him. Abram's real men, the Moor and the Armenian, jested with Elias at Finn's expense, to help sell the lie. Which did the trick.

Almost.

Red Head was mesmerized by Oathkeeper's watered steel, thought her too fine a blade for a simpleton, contemplated claiming her. Only Abram's threats stopped him.

Now I owe Abram a debt for saving Oathkeeper.

"And what was Abram doing with Saladin, do you suppose?"

Elias asked the obvious; Finn answered in turn.

"Doubling his pay? Working for Raymond and, at the same time, working for Saladin?"

"Bastard betrayed us, sold out the kingdom," Elias said.

"Did he?"

Abram was Godless but lived by a simple code. God does not exist, and if he does, needs no one to worship him. Thus it was better to think for yourself and not blindly follow anyone. But you had to believe in something, be it love, or brotherhood, or glory, and always treat others as you would want to be treated. Man could make himself as he wished. Edicts, deities, scripture — these were shadows. Honour, deeds, reputation — these were real.

Finn could not help thinking that betrayal, giving the Judas kiss to a brother, might come easily for a Godless man. Abram had been an agent in the Order's pay, and now took Raymond's pay. Why would he not also take the Sultan's coin to help topple the Kingdom of Jerusalem? The chaplain once recited the story of Samson. Delilah was paid to learn the secret of his strength, which she did, and to betray him. Was Abram like the Philistine woman?

And yet... Someone with a boot in the enemy camp would be invaluable. He could shed light on the enemy's plans, their strengths, their weaknesses. He could also sow false seeds. Certes Raymond saw this, knew the value in Abram, a man who could walk among the Saracens?

Finn prayed it was the latter. He said as much to Elias.

"That'd be best," Elias said. "No one wants that cold-blooded viper as an enemy."

There was no point holing up for the night. The quicker they returned, the quicker word would be in the king's ear. They walked under a sunny, cloudless sky and did their best to maintain stealth. They waded through the sluggish stream and slinked past the broken and burned scouts. A while later, they neared the lair and Elias made the distinctive call of a Hoopoe bird — *oop-oop-oop* — the agreed sign to forewarn of their coming. No one wanted Jerol's bolt in their eye.

Rollo met Finn at the shelter. "How'd it go?"

"Saw Saladin — up close, I mean. He was riding a white stallion. A slight man, but fierce. Eyes like fire. I almost yanked out Oathkeeper and —"

"Now is not the time for jests, Finn. How big is his army?"

"Armies," Finn corrected. "They're massive. Each as big as the other."

"How many men?"

Finn shook his head. "Too numerous to count. Siege engines. Piles of arrows. And horses, and…" He gave up trying to find the words. "Too many. Too much for Guy, Brother."

Rollo's scarred lip hitched, and Finn went on.

"Found the Sun Lizard's Turcs."

"What'd they say?"

"Nothing."

Realization settled on Rollo's face. "Dead. Well. Shite. Think I saw the culprits."

The Norman told what he had seen. Saracen scouts sneaking south during the night. The two goatherds. How he almost knifed them, though in the end he could not put steel into part-time Christians but full-time innocents. Finn nodded.

Saracen scouts … moving through the Black. The Sun Lizard's boyish voice filled Finn's head; *He can see there is no advantage to coming through the Black. Only risk.* Herson had spoken true if the Sultan's aim was Kerak, or Jerusalem, the ultimate prize. Finn's own words to Herson echoed between his ears; *Just because a man usually does something doesn't mean he always will.* Times were changing. Things were different.

Where is Saladin going? Finn stared into nothing before his eyes flared with an ugly thought. "Corral the lads. Grab your kit. I'll give you a head start, on account of your balky leg."

Rollo shook his head. "Safer to go at night."

"No. We go. Now."

Not waiting for darkness was risky. Images of two armies and piles of siege gear flooded Finn's head, and that, and what he suspected was the intended mark, drove him to recklessness. The larger risk lay in delay, for each hour that passed was time lost in preparing the kingdom's defences. The heat of the day was on them now. Dust caked his face. Rivulets of sweat pooled at the base of his neck, filled the shallow depressions between his collarbones with muddy water.

They neared the Yarmuk River gorge when his meagre plan soured.

Elias roamed ahead, Yousef trailed, and Templars stayed between the Turcs.

Rollo stepped off the track and a moment later came the patter of piss on dirt. "So ... much ... better..."

Finn stopped short of the splashes and raised a hand to shade his brow and study their backtrail. Nothing.

A sudden rustling in the bushes and a man shot up — gap-toothed, wide-eyed, and every bit as surprised to see Finn as Finn was to see him.

On instinct, Finn yanked out his biodag and stabbed — once, twice, three times: hard, underhanded thrusts that brought the man to his toes with each strike. Warm blood slicked his hand as the man folded and fell.

More rustling in the bushes and a blur hurtled at Rollo. The Norman stepped back, let go of his belt to pull his sword, and his braes dropped to his knees. He staggered and toppled backward in a flash of white arse and brown dirt.

The blur transformed to a black-haired youth — feet planted, curved sword hoisted in a two-fisted blow aimed to split Rollo's head. Rollo lunged up and stabbed, and the blade slid in above his guts and poked out the back between his shoulder blades. The youth moaned "*Ayreh feek*," and the sword dropped and thudded on the ground behind him. He toppled backward like a fresh-cut tree and landed with a louder thud.

Rollo's face was a snarl of anger, his arse so white it seemed translucent. The absurd contradiction was too much. Finn doubled over, hands on his knees, laughing in heaving sobs. "You stabbed him ... sitting in the dirt ... on your lily-white arse."

Jerol and Lugh sprinted up, saw Rollo and his bare arse, and joined in the laughter. Even Owen laughed.

Jerol pulled Rollo to his feet, and the knight commenced slapping dirt from his arse.

"Don't expect me to help with that," Jerol said, which brought more horselaughs.

Lugh cuffed his eye. "A man has his limits."

"Bastards," Rollo muttered, and belted his braes. "I stepped back, on my bad leg, and my braes... God's bones, I'll never hear the end of this."

Finn crouched, stropped the biodag clean on the dead man's robes, then poked the twitching body with the knife. "These your goatherds?"

"No." Rollo kicked the dead youth in the ribs. "Attack a man while he's taking a piss? Rotten bastard." Blood crawled down the youth's leather shirt, made of lozenges sewn together, like the scales of a giant fish. Light to wear. Easy to mend. Favoured by Turkmen. "Saladin's Scouts."

Elias held on the track, and when no one came up, he crept back until he found the Templars. He glanced from Jerol to Lugh, sensing he had missed something. "What?"

"Rollo fell on..." Lugh quailed at the Norman's warning glare, flapped a hand at Elias to say, *You had to be there.*

Elias jabbed a finger north-east. "Men."

His voice had a sharp edge that made everyone turn in unison. Backlit men stood on the skyline. Finn began counting them off: "One, two, three..."

Rollo shaded his eyes. "You can count them? I can barely see them. How many?"

"...fourteen, fifteen, sixteen."

"Sixteen," Rollo repeated, as if saying it again made it any better.

"About half have bows," Lugh said.

Finn prayed they give a friendly wave and stroll away. They did not. Someone must have spotted the dead men alongside the trail. *We sidled past their hide, by chance, but bumbled into their sentries.*

A bellow, then a harsh tribal chant echoed, *la-la-la-la.*

"Damn." Rollo slung off his haversack, then his blanket roll.

"Run," Owen said.

"No. Running is for Hospitallers." Finn held up a splayed-fingered hand, fanned it south. "Quick but steady. Face them. Overlapping withdrawal." He spoke slow, almost bored, though he was anything but bored. He turned to Lugh. "Rooster?"

"Boss?"

"Pair with Yousef. Uncle and Elias, do the same. Rollo leads. Owen, stay with Rollo, and you'd better be as handy with a crossbow as you brag you are."

To turn your back on an enemy to run led to chaos, and chaos led to ruin — they would be chased down and shot like antelope. Experience told them that; training told them what to do. Each twosome would hold; shoot when the enemy came nigh; fall back as the second duo covered them; cover the second duo as they fell back. And so on. Finn would support the front or the rear. They would move in unison. Slow and steady. With luck, they would be enough to keep the Turkmen at bay, and with more luck the Turkmen would take some lumps and give up the chase.

They gulped from waterbags, getting their last bit of water while they could, then tossed the bags. Haversacks and blankets went next. After a nod to say, *All ready here*, Elias and Jerol took a knee.

Turkmen whooped at the thrill of the chase, surged forward and disappeared into the scrub.

"Steady, Brothers," Finn said. "Not yet."

Waiting was no easy thing. Most men wanted to fight, some wanted to flee, but no one wanted to wait while death came at them. Time dragged by. It was up to him to read the moment. Sweat coursed down his spine. A yellow-furred squirrel frolicked in the bush where just moments before a man had died. Man-sized figures flitted through the scrub to their front, closer now, shuffling hunched and quick.

Heads of Turkmen popped up and down, in a parody of birds seeking worms.

Finn strolled backward, Oathkeeper braced on his shoulder. He felt naked and longed for a shield and mail. The longing was made worse when the first shaft whistled overhead. He waved a mocking hand at the archer. *Missed high, you arse.*

Turkmen broke from their cover, and Elias and Jerol fired — a Turkman dropped to his knees, and another reeled away with a shaft in his side. Jerol and Elias hustled back, Elias loosing shafts over his shoulder, Jerol reloading as he walked.

Turkmen slowed, stung. When they came again, they were wary, spread out. Jerol and Elias sprinted past a kneeling Lugh and Yousef, who stood and loosed. A Turkman squawked as a shaft thumped into his thigh. Lugh pulled at his crossbow cord while he walked backward; Yousef held and sent three shafts in quick succession, then scurried back.

Shafts answered in a hissing deluge. One nearly skewered Yousef.

Finn strolled backward, checked over a shoulder at Rollo and Owen. Not engaged. Yet. He turned back as the deadly dance of hold, shoot, and hustle played out again. Elias loosed an arrow, wheeled, loosed another over a shoulder as he moved. Jerol triggered his crossbow and a bolt hummed out.

Thus they went, foot by foot, furlong by furlong.

Turkmen rushed forward, loosing arrows as they came. Templars shot, scuttled back, then did it again. Somewhere in the fourth or fifth go-round Finn realized less Turkmen pressed them. *Others broke away. They are running ahead, flanking us...* He shouted a warning to Rollo and got a flailing hand in reply.

More holding. More trotting backward. Finn moved over a rise. He turned and held on the other side, eyes pinned on the backtrail, then Lugh trudged over the rise carrying Yousef's bow and quiver.

He caught the Irishman by the shoulder. "Yousef?"

Lugh, breathless, mimed catching an arrow in his chest, and made the pained expression that would come with having a shaft where it should not be. He slung his crossbow over a shoulder and nocked an arrow on Yousef's bow. Finn slid back to Elias.

Elias's stare asked what he could not voice, for Yousef was an old comrade.

Finn kept it brief. "Held too long."

And here we are. One man less.

A roar from ahead — Rollo. Finn broke into a sprint, Elias at his heels.

Finn loped between two bushes bordering the trail. Chaos awaited on the other side. Owen was reloading his crossbow. Two Turkmen were down. Rollo was twisting and cutting and sliding between three others. Two more burst from the scrub, angling toward Rollo's back. Finn sprinted to cut them off.

The first wore a round shield on an arm and held a straight sword in a fist. Finn glimpsed a shaved head, long black moustaches, slitted eyes. The eyes flared when he saw death coming. The man peeked out from behind the shield, just for a moment, but a moment too long. Finn stabbed him in the throat and shoved him away.

The second man charged with a roar. Finn swayed to the side, parried with the biodag, and thrust Oathkeeper through leather scales and the ribs behind. The man's triumphant roar morphed into a pained whine as he staggered and fell.

Finn turned as Rollo feinted outside, then chopped at the inside of a Turkman's sword arm. The man was confused by the deft footwork and chose the obvious defence — save his sword arm with his shield. He chose wrong. Rollo shoved his right shoulder into the shield, pinned it, then thrust over it with his left. The dagger punched into an eye and only stopped when the guard hit the man's nose. The man stood, blinked his remaining eye, then fell backward and slid off the dagger as he went.

Finn walked up, flicking blood from Oathkeeper, and in his best imitation of Father Henric's piping voice said, "You killed him ... stabbed him right in the eye."

"Would seem so."

Another Turkman lay with an arm canted awkwardly, multiple crimson blotches on his chest. Hallmarks of one of Rollo's favourite counters — grapple an elbow, snap it, then triple tap the chest with steel.

Finn nodded at the dead man. "And this one?"

"He started it."

They shared a laugh, fleeting and dreary.

"Yousef is gone," Finn said, and Rollo grimaced.

Owen had shot the third Turkmen menacing Rollo. The man lived, though his leg had seen better days. The man was older, slender, and wore a pointed leather hat lined with fur — an odd fashion choice for Outremer. Owen stood over him. The Turkman, whey-faced, huffing in pain, managed his best defiant glare.

Elias had not tailed Finn, and now the Turc came up the track with Jerol and Lugh. Finn jerked up his chin in mute question.

"Killed us some eejits," Lugh said. "Last three turned tail."

Turkmen proved fearless, but wild and poorly trained. They were skilled with the bow. Less so with the blade. Finn caught himself thinking his band had fared well. *Lost just the one. Yousef.* Then he noticed Elias's pinched face, his bulbous eyes welling up.

"Can't leave Yousef to the jackals," Elias said.

"I'll go with you. Say some words. We'll cairn him up proper." Finn tapped Owen and pointed to the wounded Turkman. "Tie his hands. Wait with him."

"Why?"

"We're going to chat with him."

"About what?"

Finn stared with an icy gaze. "It's a polite way to say we're going to knock him around until he spills Saladin's plans."

The Turkman needed little knocking about. A shattered thigh bone made him delirious with pain. A whack here, a smack there, all on the leg of course, and he sang like a bird. Not that Finn learned much he did not already suspect. Saladin was going to attack through the Black, around the south end of the Sea of Galilee, and on to Tiberias. Details were lacking. The Turkman did not know if the Sultan would send one army for the city and the second elsewhere, or use both to swallow Tiberias in one gulp.

Tiberias.

Not Kerak. Not Jerusalem.

An old horse can jump new fences.

They left the Turkman with his shattered leg and an extra hole in his neck, courtesy of Lugh, and a while later they dropped into the Yarmuk River gorge. They worked down the trail in single file, Elias in the lead, Rollo at Finn's back.

"I wager Master Gerard will be conflicted," Rollo said. "Does he celebrate our success, or fume we went over the Black and came back in one piece?"

"Came back with our arses in one piece, you mean," Finn said, and smiled.

"*Lily-white* arses," Jerol threw in.

Rollo growled in his throat.

The sun was fading when they came to Cave de Sueth. They swapped leather armour for mail, filled their waterskins, and saddled their mounts. Herson came off the ledge. He wore a loose, flowing Templar mantle, barelegged underneath, and walked barefoot.

"You live," Herson said, more than a little surprise in his boyish voice.

"Aye. But your scouts don't."

Finn explained the sacks of broken and burned men.

Herson glanced to the heavens and crossed himself. "And Saladin prepares to attack Kerak?"

Finn nodded and shared what he had learned. Saracen scouts sniffing a path south, toward Tiberias; two armies; siege engines; tribes honouring Saladin that previously slighted him. He left out the part about Abram and his role, whatever it was, in Saladin's plans. He finished by advising the Sun Lizard to leave Cave de Sueth and ride to Acre.

Herson stared unblinking over the gorge.

"Saladin will not leave you at his back," Finn said. "You will be sieged. Against such numbers you will fall."

"I cannot abandon my post without the Master's leave. Which he will not give." Herson shifted his pale gaze on Finn. "A wise man once told me brothers watch what their leaders do and follow their example. So I will heed the advice of that wise man, set an example of obedience, and fight here until ordered otherwise."

"Heeding the advice of an imbecile is the easiest way to become one," Finn countered.

Herson smiled, wooden, and in that simple gesture Finn could see the man was decided. "God protect you, Brother."

"God protect us all," Herson said.

CHAPTER 15

Emma started and ended each day with prayer. Now she prayed all day long.

O Mary, Mother of God, you who are above all creatures in heaven and on earth, more glorious than the Cherubim, firm bulwark and protectress. You are the consolation of the world, the ransom of captives, the joy of the sick, the comfort of the afflicted. Mother Mary, cover Finn with the wings of your mercy. Protect him. Protect his brothers. They are consecrated to your service. O immaculate Virgin, watch them with your protecting eye.

Emma prayed and waited, and paid waifs to be her eyes. One lad watched the south road into Tiberias, another the road to Cafarsset, the Templar *casale* outside town. Days passed with no news. What else could one do but stay vigilant and pray? Then one of the lads came, breathless and sweating, and reported six Templars had arrived at Cafarsset.

Emma made the sign of the cross and kissed an imaginary crucifix. *O Mary, Mother of God, you who are above all creatures in heaven, I give my thanks…*

Finn came to her in the early afternoon, and she went out to meet him. A *shemagh* wrapped his head and sagged under his chin. It was a houndstooth pattern, once black and white, but now faded to grey so the houndsteeth blurred together. Under the scarf, his cheeks were hollow, his eyes ringed with circles so dark it seemed he wore kohl. Rollo and the others looked no better. The stink was overpowering, even for Templars, and the yard reeked like a bag of rotten onions mixed with campfire smoke. Fagan's head hung from the end of his long neck like a boulder on a rope. Arlo brought oats and Fagan came to life, pranced his head in celebration.

"You look nigh on dead," Emma said to Finn, knowing formal greetings were not his way. She wanted to touch his hand but refrained, and instead offered kindness. "Stay a while. Rest yourselves and your horses."

"Can't. Must get to Acre. We..." Finn glanced at Rollo, who was palming his battered forehead, more grim-faced than usual. "Saladin is coming for Tiberias."

For a moment she thought she had misheard. "Who told you this?"

"A broken-legged man in a pointy fur hat." He waved away her confused pout. "No time to tell the tale. Trust me."

"What happens next?"

"Many things." Finn took a swig from his canteen and slapped the cork home. "The king will sally. He'll manoeuvre early, I'd wager, and claim the favourable ground at the south end of the Galilee. The river is wide and slow there. Crossing it with an army will be tricky. But there is a bridge, Sannabrah, and Guy will destroy it, to force Saladin to find a ford and maul him when he tries to use it. Bowmen on the slope will rain shafts. A wall of spearmen will line the bank. Knights will charge and shove them back. We take it, we own it, we send him off."

A fire warmed his weary eyes — the fire some men got when talking of war, a timeless fire that said, *Meet me at the river; it's my river; I'll fight you for it.* Emma exhaled and rolled her eyes skyward.

Finn inhaled a breath and mended course. "The short answer is Raymond will not leave Eschiva undefended. Nor will her sons. Nor will the king."

Eschiva of Bures, Princess of Galilee, ruled the largest fief in the kingdom. She was widowed and had married Raymond and made a life with him. She was born in Tiberias, had deep roots there, and with her husband would battle for it tooth and claw. The city lacked stout ramparts, though, which made defending it nigh on impossible. Eschiva's citadel stood at the shore of the Galilee, and it was built to withstand an attack — thick battlements of ashlar stones, four towers, a moat that drew water from the lake. Impressive, certes, but not large enough to admit a town's population. The city would hold for a day or two, then Eschiva and the garrison would huddle in the citadel, leave the people to fend for themselves.

"Go to your villa in Acre," Finn said.

"I cannot — not yet."

Finn scowled. She explained.

"I have unfinished business with the Order. A reliquary containing toe bones of Saint Juvenal, a stone from Golgotha, and twigs from the tree the Lord himself planted. The reliquary is exquisite. We recovered it digging ruins at Saruniyya." Emma paused to take a breath. "Timothy said it was a Roman villa, thus too young for what we sought, but the archives at Acre suggested otherwise. An old treatise on the area, in Latin, mind you, contained writings that —"

It was Finn's turn to roll his eyes skyward and Emma's turn to correct course.

"There is a meeting three days hence. The Templar Treasurer and Archivist meet me at Castle Saphet to seal the deal."

Finn laughed, though it was a tired, humourless sound. "Make the deal another day. Go to Acre. Who cares for coin? For musty bones?"

"I care, Finn. They are my trade. This sale has been in the works for months — nigh on a year." Emma made a placating gesture to sooth his scowl. "How long do I have afore Saladin arrives?"

"An army that size … two armies that size, will take time to herd into place, march down the Golan, and across the Black. Four, five days?" Finn pulled the head scarf and ran fingers through his hair. "Better to play it safe. Leave for Saphet tomorrow and find lodgings in the town. There is an inn close to the south gate — the Lost Shepherd. Wait there, make the deal in a few days, then depart to Acre."

Emma pondered and Finn carried on.

"Also hire a man or three as men-at-arms. Retired sergeants haunt the taverns. Arlo could pick old salts skilled with blade and bow."

"Wonderful. How I love the company of old soldiers." Emma's tone said otherwise. She gazed at her villa for a moment, then took a cleansing breath. "Arlo will make the arrangements. We will be on the road in a day or two — hurry but do not rush, my father used to say."

"We Templars say *Festino lento*."

"*Festina lente*," Emma corrected. "It means to make haste slowly. A favourite adage of Emperor Augustus. He did not mean slow, in the literal sense, but slow in the sense of moving with care and purpose to maintain precision. Do not rush. Do it right." She wagged a finger at Finn. "You said 'we Templars say,' though certes you meant Hector? He speaks Latin. You do not. Or did you intend to steal his saying and make it your own?"

Emma was learned and lettered, unlike most women of her day, and she could not help but flaunt it. Finn admired it, unlike most Godly men, and she found his confidence and humility an endearing combination.

"Aye, guilty." Finn fanned a hand in surrender, grinning at her sharp wit, though the grin wilted quickly. "Guy is no Augustus, certes, but even he can see what needs doing."

"His eyesight is not in question, Finn." Emma tapped a finger on her temple. "He is prone to fits of daftness because jesters whisper in his ears — foremost among them your Master."

"Aye." Finn's flat tone said he had nothing to say in defence of Gerard, nor did he care to think of any.

They said their goodbyes with curt nods and sly grins. Her own words echoed in her ears as she watched him go. *Make haste slowly. Do not rush. Do it right.*

Finn found the Red Wolf on the road to Acre.

A long row of men and horses mingled in the distance. A lone figure broke away. Raynald. Finn reined in and slid from Fagan. Two knights followed their lord — both salts of Raynald's many tussles.

"Well met, Brother Finn," Raynald said, voice bored but affable. He carried a loaf of bread, tore it, and handed half to Finn. "You look like you could use a meal."

"Too true, and God's blessings." Finn tore his piece and handed half to Rollo. "Seeing the sights, Lord Raynald?"

"Travelling to join Guy. The king proclaimed the *arrière-ban.* We are summoned to war." Raynald flashed a grin at the prospect. He had his war. His gaze swept Finn's meagre banner. "You are diminished. Brothers Serlo and Hector?"

"Hector got broke at Cresson and mends at Saphet. Serlo is in Gerard's guard."

Raynald cocked his head to say, *Good for Gerard, unfortunate for you.*

"And your knight..." Finn trailed off, the name of Raynald's old knight eluding him. "The gassy one."

"Alain? He is too old to fight. He says otherwise. But I am his lord, so I win. He and two score of men-at-arms hold Kerak."

"His flatulence will be missed."

"Funny man, for a Templar. You could make a living as a jester," Raynald vaguely waved vaguely with a crust, "if ever you grow weary of fighting to earn your bread. Where are you bound?"

"To Master Gerard, in Acre."

"Acre? We're past that. Everyone is at Saffuriya. The king is there, and wherever you find the king, you'll find your Master."

Saffuriya, as spoken by Arabs, or Le Saforie, as spoken by Franks. It was the birthplace of Mary, mother of Jesus, and a place sacred to all faiths. Now it was a place of war. A castle and watchtower occupied the hill. A drainage system, dug by the Romans, channelled water from springs. Saffuriya was the mirror to Tell Ashtara, at least in antiquity and function, and Christian troops formed there before campaigns.

"How did you find the Black?"

Finn raised a brow. "You know of our scout?"

"Certes." Raynald gave an exaggerated sigh. "You know the ways of Outremer. Countless species of folk here and too many religions to count. So many traditions to remember. Most ancient. Some young. But all bonded by the love of gossip. The more salacious the better. Master Gerard wants you gone — dead, preferably."

Finn smiled to show he was not thrown by Raynald's sudden shift. "Aye? And where did you hear this?"

"Rumour. Even laymen speak it."

"Well. Once layfolk speak a thing, you might as well write it in the chronicles."

"Chroniclers make a mess of history." Raynald scratched at his bearded jaw. "No doubt my finer deeds, of which there are many, will go unmentioned. Instead, I will be chronicled as a madman, tempestuous, murderous. Prone to fits of violence."

They'd be half right… "Folk love gossip, the more salacious the better," Finn said.

Raynald twitched his lip at hearing his own words. "Gerard sent you beyond the Black and prayed you would not return. Yet here you are. What did you see, by the way?"

Finn chewed bread to buy time. His inclination was to hoard knowledge and share it only with the Master. Secrecy was the Templar way. A Templar did not expect praise or acclaim for his labours. Service itself was reward enough. Yet neither should a loyal servant suffer the gall of insult nor the wormwood of mockery. *Gerard treats me like a dog while the Red Wolf treats me with respect — grudging respect, at least.* He nodded to himself in silent decision and told Raynald what they had seen. Saladin's two hordes. Siege engines. Horsemen. Spearmen. Bowmen. Scouts sneaking south through the Black.

Finn pointed with the bread. "And the Devil is coming for Tiberias."

Raynald arched a red brow at that. "Tiberias? Well, well. Won't our friend Raymond be fretted by that."

"He will," Finn said. "But shouldn't we all be fretted? Death of Christians is no small thing."

"I'd sooner stab myself in the cods than aid Raymond. I fight Saladin for my own reasons."

"You are Christian, as is he," Finn insisted.

"Is he, though?" Raynald cupped a bread crust in his hand and fed it to Fagan, then wiped his hand on his surcoat. "Raymond is a breeze-sniffer. A dealmaker. Yet despite his back-room dealings with Saladin, which are many, the Devil comes for him. Same way he comes for me, the thorn in his arse, a man he swore to kill with his own hand." He grunted in amusement. "Schemers like Raymond think they can bargain their way out of death — but they can't. It catches them by surprise, even when they should see it coming."

Finn spoke softly. "I wonder if we'll be surprised when our time comes."

Raynald stared off before flashing a toothy grin. "No doubt we will."

"This goes too far, Gerard."

Goes too far? This is not far enough, fool. Gerard gave a sympathetic smile. "I understand your concern, Brother Odon. I do. But we are in dire times, and dire times call for dire measures. The decision stands."

Odon de Erail scowled, creasing his stern face in a score of places. He sat rigid at the Master's campaign table, impeccable in a white cappa, red cross *pattée* like a splash of blood, every dark hair on his pale skull combed to perfect attention. Odon was Commander of the Kingdom of Jerusalem. He oversaw the finances and shared authority with Master Gerard. The Master could not access the Order's treasury on his own; he held one key and the Commander held the second. Yet somehow the vault doors had been recently opened with but one key. Decisions made by the Master alone.

Gerard had an irritatingly calm air that said the matter was decided.

Odon felt otherwise.

"You stole coin," he said. "Coin sent to us for safekeeping, and not yours to take, Gerard. It is God's. Given in penance by Henry."

Henry II, King of England, also known as Henry Curtmantle because of his odd habit of wearing a short cloak, and sometimes called Henry the Lion of Justice — though some folk might have said that last name was misplaced. Curtmantle had appointed his chancellor, Thomas Becket, as Archbishop of Canterbury. The king, in return, expected royal supremacy over the English Church to be reasserted. Shortly after Becket's consecration, though, the archbishop changed his tune. He had lived lavishly, but now lived as an ascetic, and often wore a cilice as mortification of the flesh. He also refused the role of Curtmantle's lapdog and even dared champion Church rights.

Arguments led to exile. Thomas returned to England. More arguments. More threats. Finally, Henry uttered the notorious words, 'Will no one rid me of this turbulent priest?' Then four knights did, and hacked Thomas apart at Canterbury.

Curtmantle performed public penance and allowed each bishop at the cathedral to give him five blows from a rod. Each of the eighty monks gave him three blows. Were they hard blows? Probably not — Curtmantle was a king, after all. The king also laid gifts at Becket's shrine and conducted a vigil at Becket's tomb. The final penance was sending coin to the Templars for safekeeping; coin to be spent at Henry's direction when he arrived in Outremer.

Holy coin Gerard had just stolen.

"As you say, the coin was to fund the war against Saladin," Gerard said. "Which is what I used it for."

"Used?" Odon gawked and slumped back. "You already spent it?"

"Most of it. To purchase two bands of men-at-arms and one of crossbowmen." Gerard ignored Odon's rising ire. "The men-at-arms are Normans, in the main, but also Bretons and Gascons. The crossbowmen are Genoese — the best."

"You bought freelances...?" The words stuck to Odon's tongue before he spat them out. "You contracted with routiers — murderers, rapists, thieves? Using the King of England's penance?"

"I did. Well, I should say I gave the coin to King Guy, and he contracted them." Gerard beamed. "Routiers is a harsh term, though. Their resumé is impressive and I am assured they are professional warriors-of-fortune. Most are hedge-born, aye, but only a handful of murderers and rapists are among them."

"Only a handful? Ah. Well. Not so bad, then." Odon dragged a palm over his forehead, then murmured, "The Master of the Temple made off with the King of England's alms. Our name is soiled — ruined."

Gerard had been calm, a touch bored, but now his eyes turned sharp as flint. "Cresson gutted us, Odon. You know this. We are undermanned yet expected to defend the kingdom. Men were needed. Men were available. The means were there. God laid these coincidences at my feet for a reason — it is as simple as that."

"The king leads the defence of the kingdom, Gerard. The Order supports him, aye, but our sacred duty is defending pilgrims and —"

Gerard slapped a palm on the table. "The Order *is* Jerusalem, Odon. We own it, we protect it. Do you think Guy could find his own arse without help? I assure you he could not."

The Commander regarded the Master with a look of disdain.

"The Order strays from the righteous path," Odon said. "God will punish us for our arrogance. Mark my words.

Templars do not steal." He flicked a finger heavenward and whispered, "We certainly do not steal from Him."

"Steal ... what an ugly word," Gerard said. "We borrow to ensure the kingdom's survival. We would never do it otherwise."

Odon said, "*We?* This is your doing. Yours alone. I plan to write to the Holy Father, and King Henry, to wash my hands of *your* sins. Then I will pray God's wrath does not fall on us."

"*We* need not fear, Brother Odon. God loves the righteous."

"And He hates the sinner. But what if that is us?"

CHAPTER 16

Finn reached Saffuriya at sundown, just as the citadel's gates were closing. The day's heat had been oppressive, like living in a bread oven, and the misery made coarse men commit crass deeds. Knights and sergeants and Turcs filled the streets, overflowed from taverns, and brawled drunk in the alleys. More camped in an empty field below the hill; the sprawl of tents stretched to the horizon; the reek of thousands of men and horses drifted to points beyond. Finn went there.

Master Gerard's tent was easy to find — large as a castle, white, with a black-and-white battle flag flying above. Finn slid off Fagan, handed his reins to Lugh, and strode toward two brother knights standing guard at the flap.

Both wore crisp cappas, fresh as the day they were woven into brown linen and bleached by a soaking in wood ash lye. Field brothers, like Finn, wore cappas dirty, their mail dark with patina. His garb was mended, the hem in tatters, which gave him pride, for he had earned each hole and patch in service.

He recognized neither knight, but dipped his chin in greeting and made to walk past.

"None shall pass without the Master's blessing," said the first.

The second laid a hand on Finn's shoulder. "Who are you?"

Finn made a point of staring at the hand, clean and unblemished, then in a level voice said, "I'm the man who is going to break your hand if you don't remove it."

The weight of the hand lessened but stayed, presumably to show the knight had no fear. He was sun-browned and salted, with a broad and battered face. The second was pale, younger, and certes not a field brother. The pair made odd battle companions.

The salted knight made a point of sliding his hand from Finn's shoulder to his chest. "Master is busy. Come back another time."

"Oy, Ivin," said Lugh, coming up. "You're putting a hand on Finnláech o' Struan. Might want to rethink that. And why you playing dress up? You're a blackcoat, same as me."

"Was a blackcoat." Ivin squared his shoulders. "I've been raised."

"Raised?" Lugh gave a mocking bow. "Well met, Sir Ivin of Cesspit. Whose arse did you spit shine for the raising?"

Master Gerard's, Finn thought.

A sergeant raised to knighthood — a rare event in the Order. Sergeants were commoners, lacking at least eight quarterings of noble blood, though extreme acts of bravery or skill could be enough to overlook a lack of proper breeding. A lack of manpower might be cause, too.

"How proud you must be, remember to write your ma," Finn said. "Now, step aside."

"None shall enter — Master's orders," Ivin said, and leaned into the hand.

Finn puffed out a breath. "I warned you."

He grabbed Ivin's hand, twisted it inside and upside down, and at the same time caught his elbow with his free hand and torqued it up. In a flash, the arm was bent into an unnatural, s-shaped curve from elbow to fingers. Ivin yelped like a kicked dog as Finn steered him away a few hopping, cursing steps, then swept his feet from under him. He fell to his arse cradling the arm.

Pale Knight went for his sword — feebly. With one hand Rollo pinned the man's hand to the sword handle, then slapped a palm on his chest and shoved him into the tent's anchor ropes. The brother sprawled in a tangle of legs, arms, and rope.

"Only go for a blade if you're serious about using it, boy," Rollo said with a toothy sneer that made his scarred chin and lips more hideous.

Finn pushed through the tent flap, Rollo at his heels.

Oil lamps lit the inside with a flickering light. A campaign table stood in the middle and Templars crowded around it. A map was spread over the boards. Master Gerard tapped at it with a pointing stick. Denis lingered at the Master's elbow.

Urs de Alneto was there. He was the Seneschal, the Master's right-hand man, and salted by two decades of warfare. An eye had gone missing somewhere along the way and he covered it with a crude, leather patch.

Two of the brothers Finn knew. Nicholas of Hertfordshire had replaced Jakelin as the Templar Marshal. He was responsible for all things war — planning, supplying, doing. He was tall, heavy-jawed, handsome, with close-cropped hair the colour of gold. Pons de Sellón, the Turcopolier, administered the sergeants and Turcopoles. He was shorter than Nicholas. Dark and brooding, wide and thick. Both spoke the language of warfare. Terrain and manoeuvre. Discipline and morale. Rate of march.

Between Finn and the table stood three attending knights for the Seneschal, Marshal, and Turcopole. Each was as fresh-faced as the other, each head bobbing in unison at everything Gerard said.

Odon, Commander of the Kingdom of Jerusalem, was absent.

As Commander he should be here, certes. He too has grown weary of Gerard.

"Greetings, Brothers," Finn said.

Bearded faces shot up. Gerard stared a moment, then exhaled loudly and set down the stick.

"No one is to enter." Denis grinned in confusion. "Payens…?" he called. "Ivin…?"

"Payens?" Rollo made a snorting sound. "The pale oaf is named Payens?"

Hugues de Payens was a founder of the Order. A brother of legend.

"Aye," Denis said, the one word defensive and awed at the same time. "He comes from a prestigious line of Templars traced back to Hugues de Payens himself."

"Well," Rollo said, and spat. "Somewhere the First Master is rolling over in his crypt."

Ivin and Payens came in fast, with intent, but wavered between putting hands on Finn or politely requesting he leave. Gerard raised a hand and flicked his fingers, and like obedient dogs Ivin and Payens shuffled back outside.

"Brother Finn, Brother Rollo. God held his warding hand over you both. How kind of Him." Gerard's tone said he was presently a touch disappointed in God. He regarded Finn for a long, cold moment. "You are not invited to this council. Come back tomorrow."

"If this be a council of war, Master," Finn said, "then you should hear our report."

Gerard dithered between anger and interest. Finn stepped forward uninvited, sent the fresh-faced knights back with wrinkled noses, and leaned over the map.

Finn stared for a few heartbeats, getting his bearings, then dropped a finger on Tell Ashtara. "Saladin gathers here." He tapped a little to the east. "He forms a second army there. Twenty thousand fighters, at least, and again that number in haulers, labourers, farriers, attenders. Has new allies, too, from Mosul and Irbil and other places. Heavy horsemen and engineers. Turkmen from Mardin and Nisibin." He dragged his finger south-west, across the Black, then tapped the south end of the Sea of Galilee. "They'll travel this direction and cross the Jordan using the bridge of Sannabrah. Saladin goes for Tiberias."

Voices erupted at once, a burble of confusion and outrage, until Nicholas held up a hand for silence. "You know this how?"

"The Jordan is too marshy near the Galilee. He'll have to use Sannabrah or risk a river crossing on soft ground."

"No. I meant how do you know he goes for Tiberias?"

Finn told them the tale. Moving at night. The Turkmen scouts. The broken-legged man. His instinct for what it boded.

"What a story you weave, Brother Finn," Gerard said. "Perhaps you should have been a troubadour and not a knight, though your singing voice leaves much to be desired."

Gerard's tone was light-spirited, as one would expect with a jest, but Finn heard the mockery in it. He ignored it. Two of the young knights did not. One leered like the village pervert while the other barely suppressed a giggle — the Master's arse-lickers, obligated to laugh at his drivel. The third knight, to his credit, was stone-faced.

This one seems familiar...

"You are misinformed, Brother," Pons said, and offered a courteous nod. "Two days past, one of Saladin's sons, Al-Afdal, marched from Damascus and began ravaging Oultrejordain. He began the attack only after Raynald departed. Kerak and Montreal stand but every town between is razed. Saladin is preparing the ground, obviously, and plans to lay siege to Kerak. He expects King Guy to sally and relieve it."

"Same strategy used many times," added Nicholas.

"A ruse to keep your gaze on Kerak while he moves south," Finn said. "This time is different, Brothers. Saladin is too cunning to try the strategy again when it has brought only failure."

Nicholas and Pons swapped a quick look.

"He shows us what we expect to see, but does what we least expect," Finn said. "So we must claim Sannabrah, force him to find a ford, and savage him in the crossing."

Gerard made a show of raising his gaze heavenward, as if pondering, waiting for inspiration. The others fell silent.

Make haste slowly. Finn glanced to Rollo, who puffed out his cheeks in frustrated boredom.

"We cannot wager the kingdom on your instinct, Brother Finn." Gerard sliced a hand in the air to still Finn's argument. The Master bowed his head, and six other heads did likewise. Finn and Rollo stared at each other wearily while the others whispered prayers.

"Tiberias. Kerak. Jerusalem." Gerard spoke in a stage whisper. "Saladin's attack will be ... at Kerak." He made the sign of the cross, as if to acknowledge some heavenly revelation, and the young knights mimicked him with a flurry of waving hands. "Cilicia sent men, good Armenian Christians," Gerard went on. "Not many, granted, but the king awaits their arrival and desires their participation in the war council. This will be tomorrow, perhaps the day after. Point is, we have time to develop a strategy, Brothers."

Sombre nods all around.

"A sore fight awaits, certes, but we will triumph. God be praised."

A chorus of "Forever and ever," echoed in the tent.

Finn tried once more. "I respectfully disagree, Master," he said, fighting to keep the ice from his voice. "We must claim the bridge of Sannabrah and —"

"We heard you, Brother," Gerard said, his gaze now pinned on the map. "Our thanks for your diligence, though you are mistaken."

"Please reconsider the evidence, Master."

"You wear out your welcome. Leave us." Gerard picked up the pointing stick, flicked it toward the tent flap, then tapped it on the map and spoke to Pons. "The Devil will move here, to Amman, and after he will..."

Finn shuffled away, rigid of body, and Rollo muttered, "You can lead a horse to water, but you cannot make it drink."

"Brother Finn?"

Finn glanced over his shoulder. "Aye?"

Gerard's smile did not reach his eyes. "Seek Under Marshal Denis at Terce. We have another task for you. Try not to make a mess of it."

Anger began singing its song, buzzing and humming in his veins, and Finn let Rollo steer him outside. He found himself at Fagan's side, blinking and breathing hard through his nostrils. *Gerard is an arse.* His hatred for Finn deafened him to the obvious and his deafness doomed the kingdom.

"Fools. All fools but us," Finn growled.

"You've noticed too?" Rollo asked in a mock whisper.

Finn sighed and almost laughed, then insight hit like a thunderclap. *Tiberias is undefended — and Emma might be there.*

Saffuriya was cloaked with tattered offcuts of Jewish finery, and Persians, and Romans. Other drab remnants rotted here, too, in nameless layers thicker than any made by Franks. Now

Christians held Saffuriya close to their bosoms and founded a bishopric and churches, including one dedicated to Saint Anne, the mother of the Virgin Mary.

Finn's band tented near a row of age-pitted marble columns. A statue of some Roman notable lay on his back in the brush. He wore a breastplate, moulded with bulging muscles and eagles and lightning bolts, and greaves on his legs, though they had not saved him from whatever broke him off at the ankles. His hand was held aloft in benevolence, or perhaps arrogance, though now he seemed to be pleading for someone to help him up and mend his broken ankles.

Not far off, Gerard's groom brushed Azrael in the wan morning light.

If only Gerard were as crafty at war as he is at stealing horses...

Finn sat outside their tent, sliding skull-shaped prayer beads through his fingers, trying to ignore Rollo's snoring. The sun peeked above the skyline and with it would come the infernal desert heat. Day would be dry as dust, hot as hell. Finn longed for rain. A downpour. A soft Highland *smirr*. Anything. Back home, folk said a day could be *dreich* — dreary, grey, sunless. A *dreich* day could be rainy. Or not. Some days were *plowetery*, with a bit of it all — rainy, windy, cold.

He had longed for Alba when first he came to Outremer. Home was a hole in his heart made wider by memories of the weather, the land, his kin — and his longing for Agnes, though she must be married now. Time passed. Things changed. Rarely did he ponder the old life now.

One scrap of home remained — Da's biodag, given at his death, granted by the Order. He set aside the prayer cord, slid the knife free, and propped it across his lap. The single-edged blade was spear-shaped, wide at the plunge, and tapered to a wicked point. It had been cut down from a broken sword wielded by his grandfather, then given a black bog oak handle carved with loops and spirals. Twin humps of wood crept onto the blade like a pair of bollocks. She had an ancient soul, the knife, and carried the souls of those she claimed. *Garg 'nuair dhùisgear,* the Clan Donnachie motto, was etched into her spine. He ran a finger over the script; *Fierce when roused.*

Truer words have never been written. Yet he had learned over the years to temper fierceness, or to at least try to. *Bide your time until it is time to strike, then strike hard,* might have been a more apt motto. A shadow fell and he looked up to see Marshal Nicholas. A young knight stood by his side.

Nicholas offered a hand, pulled Finn to his feet, and tipped his head toward the young knight. "May I introduce Henri de Mailly?"

"Well met, Brother Finn," Henri said. "I have heard much about you."

"Some of it good, I pray?"

Henri grinned. "Most of it. My brother, Jakelin, wrote to tell me of your deeds, and those of your brothers."

Henri's face was familiar and now Finn knew why. Hair like straw, eyes the colour of a winter sky — like Jakelin de Mailly, minus the weathered face and crow's feet at the corners of his eyes. Unwanted memories crept in; the bloody field at Cresson, Jakelin's last stand, his body laid out by Mamluks.

"I've something for you, I think," Finn said. "Rooster?"

The sergeant arose from the campfire and came over. Finn told him what he wanted, and the Irishman nodded and walked away. Rollo staggered out of their tent, squinting into the rising sun. Finn made introductions and for a moment four knights chatted about things mundane. A lull came and Nicholas filled it.

"I congratulate you on finishing a hard task — going over the Black and coming back, I mean. Well-planned and bravely done. Pons thinks so too."

"But not the Master," Finn said.

"He sees what you did," Nicholas said, "though he does not rejoice in it."

"He ignores it." Finn stabbed a finger toward the east. "Saladin comes for Tiberias. Gerard's puppet king needs to be on the move. Now."

"I agree," Nicholas said, and held up appeasing palms. "As do others. We make use of your report, as much as we can, and work with Raymond to steer the king's council. All is not lost."

"Unlike the thoughts in Denis's head," Rollo said, and chuckled at his jest.

"Speaking of whom," Nicholas said. "Denis had orders for you, but I wanted to give them myself."

"You do me an honour," Finn said. *Partly because the muttonhead would make my chore, whatever it is, a long and humiliating slap in the face.*

"Well, I suppose one could think of it as an honour," Nicholas said. "You are to go to Acre, await initiates who are to arrive within the month, then escort them to their posts. They carry writs with individual assignments. Return to Acre. From there, patrol the Road to Antioch."

Acre. Antioch. The two names held all the bitterness filling Finn's heart.

Nicholas eyed Finn, then Rollo. He wrapped an arm around their shoulders and pulled them close. "If I were Master, I would celebrate your successes, which are many, and reward you with positions befitting your experience and skill. Alas, I am not he, though I pray for you — nightly, and recite the ancient prayers known only to Templars."

"Do you fight for us, argue our cause?" Finn asked.

"Well, no." Nicholas gave their shoulders a squeeze and eased back. "I lack the seniority, and the allies to challenge the Master presently. So, I bide my time, pick and choose my battles. But rest assured, I do not agree with your degradation, nor do I disparage your name."

Finn's hard stare said, *How kind of you.*

"Gerard has enemies, and not just amongst the Saracens. A faction within the Order seeks to remove him from office. Recent acts shamed us — the tragedy at Cresson, scheming with King Guy, stealing King Henry's alms." Nicholas rolled a hand to say, *And all the other shames.* "We cannot afford Gerard as our Master. God wills better men to lead."

Gossip was forbidden to the brothers, as was disparaging the Master, yet healthy doses of both spewed from Nicholas. Finn kept his silence, waiting for the inevitable.

"Will you support me, Brother, when the time comes?"

Support your bid for the Master's mantle? Likely not... Finn gave a vague answer, for he found such intrigues tiresome. "I'll support any brother who earns God's favour."

Masters were like squalls, Finn had learned. They arrived from afar, raged and sputtered, and in their passing left you rumpled, grumbling, but otherwise hale. He had suffered several — Odo, Arnold, Gerard. His career had died and been resurrected under each. Odo esteemed only himself. Arnold held Finn in high regard but was gone too soon. Gerard, well, he bent to the king's breezes. At his worst he saw Finn as a wayward brother in need of mending, and at his best saw him as a brother useful for dirty tasks. But Finn knew himself — and his place in the Templars, and the way of things. Men led, flawed men, thus one might assume the Order flawed. For a while Finn had confused God and the Order; thus for a while had doubted both. But God was not fallible. God was good.

Lugh came up with Finn's great sword yoked over his shoulders. He swung it off, and with a flourish presented it handle-first to Finn. Finn in turn offered the handle to Henri.

"I took this from Jakelin's... I recovered it after he died, at Cresson. It's not a blade made for the Order, nor given by the Order, as you see." Finn tapped the pommel, engraved with a prancing stag and three hammers. "This is a family crest, aye?"

Henri held the sword aloft; his gaze wandered along the blade — grey with age, worn narrow by years of resharpening, edges nicked here and there. His eyes flared with recognition. "Our father's blade. He gifted it to Jakelin the day he made his vows. How did you know?"

Finn patted the biodag on his hip. "I carry my da's blade, too, though admittedly it's not as fancy as your da's."

"I am moved, Brother," Henri said, eyes glistening. "You have my endless thanks. I would be honoured if you would count me among your friends."

Finn bowed his head and held it for a long moment.

"You saw my brother's death?"

"I saw his fight."

"Was it as glorious as folk say?"

"More. I've never seen anything so brave, so defiant, so honourable. He and that sword..." Finn took a ragged breath. "I strive to be like Jakelin, though I often fall well short. But I see him in you, and I pray you have as noble a life as his."

"May we all have a life, and death, as noble as Jakelin's," Nicholas said.

In the morning a squire brought Finn Henri's great sword. It was offered in exchange for Jakelin's sword, and Finn gladly accepted. The Order assigned knights the same weapons — a great sword, an arming sword, a mace, a dagger, and two knives. Some also carried axes. Giving Jakelin's sword to Henri left Finn without a great sword, so he sent thanks with the squire, a pimple-faced lad in a man's body.

"Must be nice to have an errand boy," Rollo said, though his derision was toothless.

Finn and Rollo once had squires. Denic served Finn; the lad owned a lively mouth and livelier sword arm. Now he served as a sergeant in Acre. Rollo's squire, Cedric, had died in Robert of Saint Albans' camp. Rollo blamed himself for the death. Now neither Finn nor Rollo wanted a squire badly enough to have one, and besides, keeping one alive was a constant chore. Sergeants were better equipped to the rigours of war.

He wrapped a fist around the handle of Henri's present. It was typical of swords crafted for the Order — straight guard, round pommel, blade three fingerbreadths at the guard and three feet long. The grip was cord-impressed leather over wood and long enough for two hands. The steel was bright, never used, and Finn revelled in the beauty of a freshly made weapon.

Finn dragged his heels, loath to go to Acre, for Acre was too far from Tiberias for him to act. What action he would take, he could not say, nor did he have the inkling of a plan. Two days he spent thus, in hesitation and rumination, his nights spent over too many cups of elixir.

He put his new sword through its paces while he dawdled. Several practice pells suffered a splintery death. A training ground had been set up and knights of every stripe trained in a flurry of thrusts and cuts and curses.

Finn sparred with Lugh. The Irishman was skilled and quick. Years of training and fighting had trimmed away the recklessness, and now he was lethal and quick, with just a dash of bold. Lugh took four of twelve bouts from Finn, to his shame, though he also felt pride in seeing the beast a rooster could become.

Finn worked with Owen, too. Normally he was distant. Gloomy. Training with Finn made him crazed, brought out a fever. The sergeant used a sword like a cleaver, chopping and hacking, in his frenzy forgetting a sword also had a point for thrusting. He attacked with bared teeth and deadly seriousness, like he wanted to kill and skin Finn. During previous bouts he had tried to break Finn's head. This morning he went for an arm.

Lugh and Owen readied to come at him. Owen stared at Finn like a starved man at a slice of meat, breathed like a bellows, and clenched and unclenched his hand around the sword handle.

The Irishman slapped him on the side of the head as he sidled past. "Oy, eejit, can ye rein it in this time?"

Owen could not. Finn cut along the edge of his shield, thrust over the top of it, and sent him away clutching a bruised chest. Lugh fared better, fought for a while, but still lost. They went away, bickering like children, Lugh giving pointers Owen ignored.

Now Finn was back to a pell. Cuts from the true edge. Cuts across the angle. Thrusts paired with slashes. Pommel strikes. The routine was ingrained, beaten into him by a Bavarian swordmaster when young, and he shifted effortlessly between combinations. Chips flew. Sweat flowed. A blade in his hand centred him, focused him, connected him to an ancient tradition.

"Why are you here?"

Finn froze, the sword held in two fists in the high guard, and glanced at Denis. "To practise, Under Marshal. You should try it. Trains the body. Trims the fat."

"No, I meant why are you here, now, and not in Acre?"

Finn swirled the sword around, stuck the point into the dirt, and draped an arm over each end of the guard. "Nicholas told me to go to Acre, aye, but he did not say when to depart. Thus I await further instruction to avoid impertinence. Impertinence riles Gerard, does it not?"

"*Master* Gerard to you," Denis said. "And you have a smart mouth."

"I think of myself as sophistic."

"What?"

"Sophistic. Someone who makes effective arguments, though they're not entirely true, and often intentionally misleading. Brother Hector said it once and I liked how it sounded."

Denis squinted, suspecting a game at his expense, and given another day or two he might have picked it apart. He stabbed a finger to the south. "Ride for Acre. Now."

Finn tipped his head to the north-west. "Acre lies that way. Besides, it is too late in the day to depart, so with your blessing we'll leave tomorrow."

"Fine."

"Fine what?"

"Fine … as in, fine, tomorrow will be acceptable."

"Perfect. That matches my plan."

"Matches your…" Denis trailed off, mouth gaping like a cod. "You arrogant arse. I will talk to Gerard —"

"*Master* Gerard to you," Finn interjected.

"— he, I, we … we will make plans for you." Denis recovered his wits and tried for a withering stare. "We will make them soon. Very soon."

"Very well, Under Marshal," Finn said, and flicked his fingers dismissively.

Denis doubled down on the withering stare, then gave up and stomped off.

Finn hefted the great sword as Rollo came up. "Your left hand is too low; slide it up a hair," the Norman said.

Holding a sword is like shaking hands — similar, yet a slightly different grip for everyone. Rollo and Finn were always debating which of their grips worked best.

"Up a hair ... is that how you manage to wield a sword like a peasant swings a sickle? How many times must..." Finn trailed off, eyeing a dust plume on the road.

It grew larger until a rider emerged wearing the livery of the Armenian Principality of Cilicia — a red lion, rearing on a white field. The rider reined in before two Hospitallers, flailed his hand toward the camp, then nodded and spurred toward the king's tent. Not long after, a score of knights wearing the red lion emerged, followed by another score of men-at-arms.

"Cilicians, Armenian knights," Finn said. Cilicia was a small but fervent ally of the Kingdom of Jerusalem.

"Here to see Guy." Rollo took a swig from his canteen. "Now the king can hold the war council, and soon, I wager. You should be there."

"Gerard will toss me out."

"Onto your arse, certes."

Finn mulled it over.

Two squires, stripped to the waist and sheened in sweat, rolled a barrel back and forth between them. The barrel was filled with sand and a mail coat, and the rolling motion and the grit scrubbed the rings clean. As a boy, Finn learned of two kinds of rust. Red rot, degrader of steel, and dark patina, protector of steel. Dark mail was his way. He did not care to be the knight in shining armour. Nor did he wear a bright white cappa over his mail, unlike so many others, but let the white turn to dingy tan.

"Many new brothers these days. Don't know half of them." Finn spoke over his shoulder. "Oy, Rooster, go sniff out the council meeting, then go to the drapier and fetch me a cappa. White as snow, if you please. You know how I loathe shabby clothes."

"You loathe…" Rollo scowled, then his face lit up with comprehension. "Forced to skulk among our own brothers now, eh?"

"I don't think of it as skulking."

"Then what?"

"Hiding in plain sight."

CHAPTER 17

The king's tent was as large as the king's chamber in Jerusalem — and almost as opulent. The floor was covered in red and yellow rugs, woven in Persia, and imported at immense cost. A silver-edged table stood in the middle of the space. A silk curtain hung along the back of the tent and through it showed the outline of Guy's palliasse. He would not sleep on the ground. Nor would he eat dried food or drink stale water, for a side table heaved under roast lamb, fruits of every shape and colour, jugs of wine and chilled water. A coat of mail and a shield, bright and shiny, was draped on a wooden frame to give the veneer of a warrior-king.

Knights and lords filled the tent. Finn stood at the back with Templars from Cyprus and next to the Armenians from Cilicia. Lugh had done well, and Finn wore a cappa so white it glowed.

Guy sat on a small, gaudy chair — a gross parody of his throne in Jerusalem. Nothing he uttered had weight or went anywhere. His powers of self-deception were endless. He was fixated on battling and defeating Saladin, being a hero-king, a man of legend. Alas, he had no idea how to do it, yet, strangely, acted as if he already had. A menagerie of advisors, each with their own aims, only made the situation worse.

Aimery of Lusignan, the Constable of Jerusalem and Guy's older brother, hunched over a map on the table. The Lusignan brothers were gifted diamond-shaped faces, soft brown hair, and green eyes. The resemblance ended there. Aimery was thicker, greyer, and lacked an earlobe. He had gained the constableship, rumour said, through a love affair with Agnes de Courtney, King Baldwin's mother. Being the king's brother helped ensure it. But Aimery was no fop. He led the defence of Jerusalem during Robert of Saint Albans' attack and there showed his mettle.

Balian of Ibelin stood to one side of the king's table. He was accompanied by a knight wearing the Ibelin livery of a red cross on a marigold background. The man was pale-eyed, dark-haired, and crooked-nosed. And glaring at Finn. He looked familiar. *Padrig ... Rooster flattened his nose at Saint Stephen's Gate.* Finn gave his toothiest smile, nodded a greeting, then tapped his nose. Padrig's glare darkened.

Gerard and his lackeys, Serlo among them, entered the tent in a sombre procession. Finn pulled the hood on his cappa up, to hide his face, and stepped deeper into shadow. The Master managed to appear proud and humble at the same time. Marshal Nicholas stood by his side, but not too close. William Borrel, *ad interim* Hospitaller Master, scowled at Gerard and any Templar that dared look his way.

Opposite Balian stood Raynald, the Red Wolf of Kerak. Joscelin, Count of Edessa, Seneschal of the Kingdom of Jerusalem, stood by his side. The County of Edessa had ceased to exist some years prior, yet the count lingered, like a rakefire none dared disinvite. Joscelin was small and lean, Raynald thick and tall.

Reginald, Count of Sidon, was trying his best to appear stern. He was native-born and spoke fluent Arabic. Folk claimed he was 'extremely ugly and very wise,' and Finn agreed he fulfilled the first part. Raymond, Count of Tripoli, Prince of Galilee, paced over to join them. His brown hair was splattered with grey. Princess Eschiva's four sons, Raymond's stepsons, lingered behind their stepfather. The four were cut from the same cloth — big, brooding, dark, clad in blue slashed by a stripe of yellow.

Finn's gaze sought Abram among them. He was nowhere to be found.

Various nobles made grand entrances and soon the tent was stuffed with knights and nobles — some old, some young, most glaring. Lords abounded. Lords of Hebron, of Caesarea, of Toron, of Jubail, of Tyre, of Nablus, of Caymont. They surged close, drifted apart, nudged by ancient allegiances until they sorted themselves into one clique or another.

"Sire." Raymond stepped forward to begin the debate. "Some of us have feuds, and grievances, and factions. But I say let every man set these aside for the greater good. Forget past wrongs and face the Devil together, as one, as Christians."

A plea for unity. It was a strong opening argument. There were many nods of agreement and a few smirks of contempt. Raymond carried on.

"Not long ago a rider came from Princess Eschiva, my wife, bearing word Saladin moved south, down the Heights and through the Black. His horsemen crossed the Jordan, claimed the springs at Kafr Sabt, and surrounded Tiberias. More of the fiends roam the countryside unchecked. The Sultan encamps at Al Qahwani, south-east of the Galilee, and tomorrow he will cross the Jordan to join the siege. We are too late to take the bridge at Sannabrah, too late to force a wet ford, too late to oppose his crossing."

A murmur of surprise and outrage rolled around the room. Saladin had moved sooner than expected and had travelled fast. The Saracen vanguard must have been at Finn's heels as he re-crossed the Black. *Gerard, you half-wit, even a novice knows to avoid what is strong, to strike what is weak. Sannabrah was his weakness.* His gaze leapt to the Master — fingers interlaced over his chest in a Godly pose, his face a mask.

One of the Armenians whispered to his neighbour. "How did no one foresee this? Did no one keep an eye on the Sultan's war camp?"

Finn nearly laughed aloud.

The king raised a hand for silence, then nodded at Raymond to finish.

"We are on a back foot, Sire. Hasty deeds will only worsen it. Thus I advise caution."

"Tell me why."

"In a word — water." Raymond stared at Raynald, awaiting his riposte, then carried on when it did not come. "It is summer. Water is in short supply. There are springs at Saforie, which we occupy, and Kafr Sabt, which Saladin's horsemen have taken. There is an ample supply in the Sea of Galilee, of course, but soon it will be on the wrong side of Saladin. Several towns have wells, though their quality is unknown, nor do we know if they can provide enough for an army."

Balian spoke. "Water will win or lose the war, Sire."

"Aye," Reginald of Sidon said, just to be heard.

Raymond nodded in stern agreement. "We must control the water to control the field. The ground between us and them is desert. No trees. No shade. Only scrub, open terrain." He swept the crowd with his gaze. "Wait for him to come to us. On our terms. On our ground."

Guy stroked his chin, made a show of pondering the advice, then looked to Raynald.

Raynald stepped forward, grinning and shaking his head. Lamplight flickered on his long red locks. "It is but a day's march, two at most, from here to there. We'll carry water with us. And we'll have all the water we need after we send Saladin running."

"The bastard is at Tiberias. Go to Tiberias. Kill him there!"

The voice came from the crowd, loud but anonymous, and Raynald swung a hand in the vague direction of the mystery speaker. "See? Simple. Find him. Kill him."

Balian gave a scornful snort. "Have you learned nothing in your time here? Nothing is simple. Especially tussling with Saladin."

Raynald nodded at the jewel-pommelled sword on Balian's hip. "You ever use that bauble?"

"Many times. Once to trim your Lady's low toupee."

Raynald snarled and stomped toward Balian, but Aimery's arm stopped him. "No quarrelling," he barked. "We must set aside our differences, as Raymond advised."

Raynald and Balian glowered at each other. Gerard, who had been suspiciously quiet, twisted to scan the room. Finn tipped his head and the Master's gaze swept by.

Joscelin spoke. "We must attack. Quickly. Before Saladin has a chance to set his defences, or take Tiberias."

It's a trap. The Devil wants you to come to him, to ground of his choosing...

Raymond shared Finn's mind. "Saladin seeks to lure us from water. Tiberias is bait." The count fixed his gaze on Guy. "My wife is in Tiberias. I have much at risk. Yet I, who stand to lose the most, am the one advising caution. Consider that, Sire."

Finn's thoughts raced to Tiberias, and to Emma, and the number of days since they had last spoken. *She should be travelling to Saphet. Could be there already.*

The king asked, "Will the city hold?"

"Alas, no, Sire." Raymond breathed out sombrely. "But the citadel will hold until Christ returns in his glory. Two wells for water. Food for a year. Eschiva commands a sizable garrison."

Raynald's head came up. "A woman defends Tiberias?"

"Aye. What of it?" one of her sons barked.

215

"Princess Eschiva is braver than most of the men in this room. Smarter too." Balian made a point of staring at Raynald. "She will not fail. Saladin will dull his teeth on Tiberias's ramparts. Just as he did at in Nablus in 1184 — on my citadel, mind you, defended by my wife. I am the most skilled knight in Outremer. I know of what I speak."

Balian did not boast. Did not bluster. He spoke simple fact.

Raynald smirked. "There are lots of skilled knights about these days. More than a few in this tent. We say you're full of shite. And you are suspiciously familiar with Princess Eschiva. Know her well, do you?"

Balian refused the bait. Most of the lords and knights looked at Raymond. Seeing their collective gaze, he ignored the childish aspersions cast on his wife and friend and rallied to higher ground.

"The Citadel of Tiberias will hold." He paused to nod at Marshal Nicholas. "Templar scouts report Saladin's numbers are thick as the stars. My agent reports the same. A perceived strength can be a weakness, for an army that large must be maintained — men fed, horses fed, illness kept at bay. He cannot maintain a force of that size for long."

Raymond gave a dramatic pause. "We have water here, and good, defensible ground. Best if we continue to gather our forces here while Saladin weakens by the day. He will be forced to move afore disease and infighting tear his coalition apart. When he comes, it will be in desperation, and we will destroy him." He bowed to the king. "We wait, with your blessing of course, Sire."

The soft hissing of oil lamps was the only sound. All eyes settled on the king. Guy glanced at his brother, Aimery, who gave a small nod.

"We stay," Guy said, voice high and haughty. "Make him come to us, on our terms."

Half the room let out a collective sigh, the other half a groan of frustration.

"Shame there are so many cowards among us," Raynald said, staring at Balian.

"Shame you are so thick-headed," Balian shot back, then in a softer voice added, "Keep it up, old man. I can make you look like an arse all night long."

Raynald and Joscelin wheeled away in unison and ploughed toward the tent flap. The crowd formed a disorderly queue like sheep being herded into a pen. The indistinct babble of a hundred voices filled the space. Finn kept his head down as nobles and knights filed past.

Raymond spoke of an agent among Saladin's camp. *Abram? Must be.* A comrade switched sides? Again? Finn hoped it was not so. He felt a kinship with the exiled Mamluk.

Finn had scouted over the Black, gleaned Saladin's plans, reported back — and was promptly dismissed. Ignored. The bridge was not taken by Christians. The riverbank was not lined with archers and spearmen and knights. It was plain the Marshal had shared Finn's report with Raymond and Balian, a small consolation, but opportunity had been squandered. Perhaps fatally.

But all is not lost.

Guy had refused Saladin's bait. He had not ordered an attack over a waterless desert. Had not traded a position of strength for a position of weakness.

Finn watched Gerard angling toward the exit. He had not spoken during the council. Not a word.

What are you up to, deceiver?

"The king will see you, Master Gerard."

The king's page held open the tent flap and Gerard slid through. Inside was as before, except for the absence of men. The table was there, and the faux throne, and the faux king sitting on it. Memories of the night prior to Cresson came to mind —Gerard steering Guy to a decision, Balian waiting outside, the king changing his mind after Balian's visit.

Guy heeds whoever last whispers in his ear. Balian used this. Now I use it.

"Outremer," Guy said by way of greeting. He sat with a blanket wrapped over his knees. "I often marvel at how a day, hot as a furnace, turns so cold at night. Why is that, do you suppose?"

"Men of God say it is because the Lord made it thus," Gerard said. "Learned men say the desert air cannot hold the heat. Sand heats and cools rapidly, too, and at night the ground loses its warmth. These quirks of nature make for extreme temperatures."

Guy blinked as if Gerard was speaking a foreign tongue. "I prefer God's way, I think," he said. "Simple that way."

Simple like you. "Most wise, Sire."

Master and king regarded each other through the lamplight. The king broke the impasse. "Why are you here, Master Gerard?"

"I fret for you, Sire."

"How so?"

"Count Raymond —"

The king's hand shot up. "Allow me to guess … Raymond is allied with Saladin?"

Gerard tilted his head to acknowledge the well-trod argument. "A snake might shed its skin, but it is still a snake. You cannot, must not, believe the count's word. You know he

218

has no love for you. Even now, after bending the knee, he lusts for your crown. He wishes you to be shamed, to lose your kingdom, and will go to the ends of the earth to achieve it."

"Raymond spoke well tonight. Aimery assures me the count has a sound mind for tactics."

"Any good warrior knows the best form of defence is attack," Gerard said. "This attack, by Saladin, is the first challenge to your rule. Fail in this and the nobles will turn on you. The Sultan will take Tiberias, then come here to overwhelm you. Hesitation brings dishonour. Retreat means shame — shame which Raymond so badly wants you to suffer."

"Raymond has much to lose," Guy said. "He would not sacrifice his wife and Tiberias merely to score a black mark on my name."

"You are certain?"

The king thumbed his ear.

"There is more to consider," Gerard said.

"What?"

"We borrowed Henry's alms without his consent. No doubt he will see our reasoning — we are, after all, using it to fight the Devil." Gerard breathed out a ragged breath. "Still. We are obliged to not misuse his coin. To do otherwise…"

Guy's lips pinched tight as a purse string, and suggested he had not considered a slighted, powerful king until now. "Can we cancel the contract? Return the coin and send the freelances away?"

"No, Sire," Gerard said, voice soft as a father teaching a son. "The contract is for this campaign season. Waiting here will diddle away the campaign season, which means wasting Henry's coin. Thus we cannot wait. The freelances need to have a go at Saladin, and soon, or more coin will be needed to keep them employed."

"Which is coin I do not have," Guy said, taking the bait.

"You also do not have history on your side, Sire." Gerard grasped that great deeds mattered to great men — more so for men who sought to be so, like Guy. "Recall the invasion of eighty-three?"

Guy had been King Baldwin's regent in 1183, during one of Saladin's invasions, and led one of the largest Christian armies assembled in Outremer. He had marched carefully, screened knights with infantry, and avoided committing to a pitched fight — despite the Sultan's attempts to lure him out. A solid if not spectacular job. But war-hawks said he squandered a rare chance to kill Saladin. King Baldwin lost faith in Guy and stripped him of the regency.

Prudence had cost Guy; he needed no reminding of 1183.

"Raymond wagers you will, as before, manoeuvre with care. And if you hold here, he will blame you for the fall of Tiberias, call you a coward, then put himself forward as the man to fight Saladin." Gerard's voice dropped to a hard-edged whisper. "Nobles have the memories of fleas, alas, and none will remember it was Raymond preaching caution. Do not stumble into his trap, Sire."

Guy fidgeted with the hem of his blanket.

"There are those who conspire to drag you from your throne and make it their own." Gerard brought his palms together, upright, pleading. "Sire, to guarantee your kingship, we Templars would sell all we own — even our white mantles, which are most sacred to us."

"You would give all you own for my kingdom?"

I would not. A soft smile, and Gerard said, "To inherit eternal life, Jesus preached, 'Go, sell all your possessions and give to others, and you will have treasure in heaven. Then come, follow me."

Guy rested his chin on his fist, a picture of royal contemplation, and Gerard struck the killing blow.

"Templars believe in you, Sire, and God believes in you," he whispered. "With us at your side, and with God at your back, you will triumph."

Guy stared, pondering, and in a soft voice said, "The life of a king is not all glory and respect, I have found. Far from it. Mostly it is days filled with paranoia, nights haunted by doubt, thoughts slathered in mud." He raised his chin and tapped a ring-encrusted finger at Gerard. "But I can always rely on you, good sir, to clean away the muck."

"You are too kind, Sire," Gerard said, and offered a half-bow. "Though I am but God's humble servant."

CHAPTER 18

The tranquil morning was sundered by the blast of a trumpet.

Finn was torn from a dream in which an angel called to him from the heavens, its voice patient, soft and kind. It said, "See to your own, see to your own…" He sat up in his bedroll, slack-jawed, as trumpets took up the call in a brassy symphony.

"Cease the ruckus," Rollo groaned from across the tent, head buried under a cloak.

Finn arose and went outside. The pre-dawn camp moiled with half-dressed, bleary-eyed Templars. Sergeants and squires hurried past. There was no discernible flow; men came one way, went the other.

Finn grabbed a sergeant by the elbow. "What's all this?"

"The king ordered everyone into the saddle," the man said. "We're going on the attack."

"You jest?"

The sergeant shook his head.

Inside the tent, Rollo yelled, "Tell me he didn't just say we're attacking."

"We're not — they are," Finn muttered. He grabbed a fistful of beard and tugged in rhythmic, futile frustration until the anger settled to a dull burn. *Fools.*

Not long after, a rumour trickled through the camp that Cave de Sueth had fallen two days past. None of the brothers surrendered. No Templar should. But the ill news put a hitch in Finn's heart. He was fond of the Sun Lizard, his quirky habits, his unfailing loyalty to the Order.

The campfire was resurrected and fed sticks and branches, then a battered pot was hung over it. The pot had begun life as a *chapel de fer*, the brimmed helmet issued to sergeants. This one lacked its metal brim, though the riveted cap remained sound enough to boil water. Lugh made pottage in it. He hummed 'Deirdre's Lament', an ancient Irish tune, and every so often broke into song. It was supposed to be played on a knee harp and accompanied by a *bodhrán*, a goatskin drum, but Lugh made a fine solo of it.

"...*Deirdre lay down by the grave, and they were digging earth from it, and she made this lament after the sons of Usnach.*

"*Long is the day without the sons of Usnach; it was never wearisome in their company; sons of a king that entertained exiles; three lions of the Hill of the Cave.*

"*Three darlings of the women of Britain; three hawks of Slieve Cuilenn; sons of a king served by valour, to whom warriors did obedience.*

"*Three heroes not good at homage; their fall is a cause of sorrow...*"

Rollo dragged himself to the fire, blanket draped over his shoulders, and dropped next to Finn. "Shouldn't we be gearing up?"

"We've not been ordered to gear up. We're supposed to be in Acre, remember?"

"So, are we obedient for not making ready, or disobedient for not being in Acre?"

"Too early for philosophy."

Lugh spooned pottage from the battered *chapel de fer* into crude wood bowls. Jerol handed out pitta cooked over coals. Hot food was a luxury after days spent gnawing dry horsebread and air-dried meat. They sipped *maramiya* tea, soothing and floral, as the camp was unmade around them. Those labouring glared and cursed them as lazy.

Finn's thoughts raced. Too often plans were made poorly, then reality came and broke them to bits. What came after was a lot of scrambling to mend them. *Emma's in Saphet. Must be. But what if she isn't? And what do I do then?*

"Pottage needed more salt," Jerol said.

"Then you make it next time, ye old whinger," Lugh shot back, though with little sting.

The camp gradually emptied, leaving only the waste and wreckage of thousands of men strewn over the ground. Empty feed bags. Broken pottery. Dirty rags. The stench of the shite pits came and went, depending on the breeze. The army had left thousands of round, cold fire rings, like countless kohl-lined eyes in mother earth. A dirty yellow dog yapped and wheezed at them, as if they were intruders in his den, before it eventually grew bored and padded off to rummage through the refuse.

Gerard rode up on Azrael. Sunlight glinted off the stallion's well-groomed black hide. Denis was there, grinning, as always. A pack of knights and sergeants shadowed their Master.

Finn arose but ignored the men, instead stroked Azrael's muzzle. "Oy, handsome, you are a Templar now, I see. Shouldn't you be a Hospitaller?" He glanced up at Gerard and fanned a hand over the empty camp. "This foolishness your doing?"

"No one else had the backbone to do it," Gerard said. He leaned from the saddle, eyes cold and flinty. "Guy is mine. I made him. Did you think I would allow Raymond to make a fool of my king? Dawdling would be our undoing. Already I am proved right, for riders came, just now, to report Saracen demons encircle Tiberias. The only way to kill a pack of demons is to snatch up weapons and take the fight to them. Or do you lack the stomach for it?"

Finn said nothing, flashed an irritating grin.

"This is for disobeying me," Gerard snarled, and struck Finn on the side of the head. "Never disobey me again, you dog-arse Scot. I command, you go, that is how it works."

Finn did not flinch from the blow. Nor did his grin falter. He heard Rollo climb to his feet. Denis watched Rollo and rested a hand on his pommel.

"You think I do not know of your schemes?" Gerard's nostrils were flaring rhythmically, like a pair of small bellows. "I have ears and eyes everywhere. I know everything you do!"

"Here is what I know, *Master*." Finn's voice was cold, for Gerard's ears only. "Raymond denied you. You wormed into the Master's mantle. Now you throw stones and hide your hand. Arrogant heart. Wounded pride. Weak soul. These fuel your sins. But God sees into the darkness, sees what you do, and He will cut you down."

Gerard bared his teeth and hefted a fist. Finn stared back, wearing a humourless smile that said, *Do it, I dare you.* The fist sank. The anger did not.

"So says the prodigal son." Gerard snorted and got back a burst of sycophantic laughter from his lackies. "It is you, Brother Finn, who will suffer God's rebuke — and soon."

The Master jerked Azrael around, then spurred after an army with his entourage eating his dust.

"Such a lovely man," Rollo said, coming to Finn's side. "How's your head?"

"Fine. Your sister hits harder."

Which was not exactly true — no lass had ever set Finn's ears to ringing, as they did now. Nor had a man struck him and not paid a price. He lived by rules. Loyalty. Courage. Discipline. Dedication. *Have humility, always a challenge, and at the same time have pride, for you should never diminish yourself. Respect is high on the list — respect me, I respect you. Disrespect is not tolerated. Ever.* But today was not the day, Saffuriya was not the place.

He stared at Gerard's dwindling back with eyes black and burning.

Rollo shrugged. "Surprised you didn't yank him down and stomp him."

"I'm being less of a contrary man, for you and the lads," Finn said. "Remember?"

"I like the old you better." Rollo laughed, then squinted at the dusty road, where three figures rode toward them. "And who's this?"

Riding toward them was a familiar wide-shouldered frame and the gleam of a just-shaved dome.

"Serlo. With Ivin and Payens."

Thus did Brother Serlo find them, lounging beside a smouldering fire in the ghost of a camp.

Serlo reined in and dismounted. He tossed his reins to Ivin, a subtle insult, though the newly made knight was not sharp enough to see it. He strolled toward Finn with two sergeants, Amic and Diego, at his heels.

The Norman settled by the ashes of the fire. Finn spooned pottage into a bowl, handed it to him, then motioned for Amic and Diego to serve themselves. Amic was Serlo's sergeant. Like Serlo, he was Norman, and muscled like a Greek statue. Unlike Serlo, he lacked two front teeth, and probably several of his molars. Diego, from Aragon, was reed-thin and thick-haired. For a while he had been Hector's sergeant.

"Needs more salt, Rooster," Amic said around a mouthful.

Lugh threw up his hands and stomped off, Jerol's laughter ringing in his ears.

Serlo ate much and said nothing, and Finn and Rollo sat with him in companionable silence. His voice, when finally he spoke, was hoarse from disuse.

"Hector can walk," he said. "Bit of a hobble. Steady in the main."

Finn tipped back his head and breathed out. "God blesses us."

"Amen." Serlo set down his bowl gently, as if it were priceless porcelain and not rough-hewn wood. He fixed his gaze on Rollo. "We are to escort Brother Finn to the Home for Wayward Brothers. Master Gerard's orders."

"What's this?" Rollo's gaze darted from Serlo to Finn, then back to Serlo. "We're to toss Finn into the Devil's cesspit?"

The Home for Wayward Brothers was in Acre. Finn thought it a quaint name for a dungeon. It was said to be a deep, dark hole where shameful sinners were thrown to wither and die from lack of hope. Light and sound were denied the miscreant, purity of milieu intended to strike despair into the dishonoured.

Finn guessed the answer but asked anyway. "Why?"

"Disobedience. Arrogance. Chastity." Serlo tugged out a leather tube that hung from a cord around his neck. "Charges are written here."

Serlo knew Finn could barely read, thus spared him the indignity of offering the writ for his perusal. Accusations would be declared before the Council, as part of an inquisition, but only after he rotted for a while in the dark. Vile images ran amuck in his head — himself dragged from the pit, squinting into the blinding sun, broken of mind, a reeking sack of skin and bones and beard.

Other bits of Gerard's scheme drifted until settling.

Finn began speaking slowly. "He gave this chore to you and Rollo, companions who served under my command, to further humiliate me. And as penance for you. Because he assumes I had ... relations with Emma. Certes you and Rollo knew, thus are complicit." He gazed at Ivin and Payens. "These two churls, no doubt eager to amend their previous humiliation at my hand, are to ensure the plan doesn't go awry."

Serlo nodded once. Rollo made a low growl in his throat.

Gerard, you mean-spirited bastard...

"Did you break your vow, Brother?" Serlo's voice was deep, yet somehow soft.

Serlo did not say the word, *chastity*, but Finn knew which vow he meant. Finn looked him in the eye and held his gaze. "No. Never. But I care for Emma. I cannot deny that. She saved my life twice, and I will not abandon her."

Finn did not say that he thought about her daily, nor that in his mind he had broken the vow of chastity many times. The guilt of sinful thoughts was his. Serlo and Rollo knew, somehow, perhaps because they often shared similar notions about the fairer gender. Vows were severe by design and severity begot discipline of the soul and body. At least in theory.

An awkward silence settled. Finn broke it.

"I'm sorry I put you on the Master's blacklist, Brothers."

"Been on it for years," Rollo said. "Nothing new for me."

Serlo shrugged. "God willed it. Besides, Gerard is an arse."

Serlo swearing always brought a laugh. Seeing the devout dip a toe into the pool of the improper was perversely rewarding for those who bathed there often.

Laughter receded and Finn spoke. "Take me to Acre, if you must, Brothers, but first I've an unfinished task. Deny me, and

I'll fight you; allow me to complete it, and I'll go meek as a lamb."

Rollo started laughing, as if this were all some grand jest, but Serlo was stone-faced. Like Finn, he lived by rules, and unflinching obedience was at the top of his list. Two causes fought a war behind those sober blue eyes. Loyalty to an institution, to his vows, to his Master. Or loyalty to a brother — flawed, aye, but a man he loved.

"You needn't come, Serlo," Finn said. "Go to Acre. Say I ran. You lost me. Whatever. I'll not think less of you."

"Time in Gerard's company taught me much. I know him. I know you. And I choose you. Same as Rollo. Same as Hector."

Serlo and Hector were battle companions. Had been for years. The erudite, convivial Catalonian and the mute, sombre Norman made an odd pairing. But they, like Finn and Rollo, had forged deep bonds while guarding the other's back. Such links were not easily broken. Not by Serlo, not by Finn — certainly not by a wayward Master.

Elias asked, "We're not going to Acre, are we?"

"We're taking the long road to Acre." Rollo, who knew Finn best, spoke up. "Patrol on our way, mayhap, like the diligent Templars we are. Roads hereabouts can be perilous — on account of bandits and Sandpigs, and whatnot."

"Saphet is north-east of us, Acre to the north-west," Owen said. "Why travel out of our way?"

No one answered the obvious question; Owen glanced from face to face.

"Your cogs are dull, Owen." Lugh was saddling Fagan and spoke over his shoulder. "Your *brain* cogs, I mean, in case you didn't grasp the reference."

"I only seem dull," Owen said, and Lugh fluttered a dismissive hand.

"So," Rollo said, "what's the plan?"

"Simple. Ride to Saphet. Find Emma. Escort her to Acre." Finn climbed to his feet, dusted off his arse, and dipped his head at Ivin and Payens. "First we need to rid ourselves of two pesky curs."

"Kill them, bury the bodies, and hide the knives." Rollo spread his palms as if to say, *Problem solved.*

"We'd get in trouble for that, big trouble," Finn said.

"Hit them over the head?"

"That might kill them."

Serlo eyed Finn and Rollo from under his brows, as if suddenly doubting their intelligence. "Just leave them behind."

Ridding themselves of Ivin and Payens proved simple, for a knight's horse is his strength, and his weakness.

Serlo led them from Saffuriya and they settled into a habit practised by horsemen since time immemorial. Travel at an easy walk. Halt to adjust straps, inspect hooves, give water. Then a sequence of walking and trotting, to avoid wearying the mounts by endless repetition of the same gait, with regular breaks for water and hoof checks.

They did the deed during the mid-morning breather.

Ivin was making water at the edge of the road; Payens was taking water in the shade. Jerol tied Diego's courser to the pack rounceys while Diego watered Payens' destrier, like any useful sergeant would do. Finn gave a nod. Brothers slid into their saddles, except Diego, who vaulted onto Payens' destrier. Lugh grabbed the reins of Ivin's destrier, offered Sir Ivin of Cesspit a mocking bow, then spurred after Diego. Everyone else followed — apart from Finn, who reined in and dropped two waterskins in the road.

"That should see you to Saffuriya." Finn pointed at the mail *chausses* covering their legs and feet. "I've found walking easier if you strip all that off. Cooler, too." He touched a finger to his brow in a mock salute. "God's blessings, Brothers."

Finn left Ivin and Payens in a cloud of dust — flailing, pleading, shouting. A faint, "Rot in hell, shite-stink Scot," was the last he heard. That had to be from Ivin.

Finn's band carried on until out of Payens' and Ivin's sight, then turned north, off the main road. They used meandering trails and travelled parallel to the coast. Stony ridges came down from the east like ribs, degraded rock tumbling off, and they scattered tiny stones from a narrow trail packed hard by the passage of countless feet and hooves and paws. Near midday they rested in the shade of an acacia tree, ancient as Moses, and ate stringy desert hare with flatbread. Afterwards they turned east, into a land dotted with dense stands of cedar.

Elias said they were now pointing toward the north end of the Sea of Galilee.

Finn reined in on a hill to study the terrain. The low ground unfurled like a lumpy tan blanket, broken by wadis and marked by low hills. Dry. Drab. The dead land was alive with men, some Saracen, some Christian. Dust mushroomed on the eastern skyline. To the south, a pall marred the sky like a low-hung, dirty cloud. Columns of oily smoke interlaced it and marked Saracens at their labours — burning, looting, destroying. The Horns of Hattin, long-dead volcanoes, shimmered in the heat haze.

A smudge to the south-west marked the Christian army marching east. Sundry dirt clouds, east and west, drifted ominously toward each other. Toward the Horns of Hattin. *Chaos will break where they meet.*

Finn was staring, squinting.

Lugh chuckled and said, "You fret too much, Boss."

"I call it thinking," Finn said. "You should try it sometime."

He gave the ill-omened landscape a last look, then turned north, toward Castle Saphet.

Saphet sat atop a mountain. Getting there required wending their way on a road that looped over the slopes like a discarded ribbon. A crowded town lolled precariously along the hillside, houses packed one on top of the other until they bumped drunkenly against the castle. Cobble-lined streets were narrow, winding, a miniature of the mountainside road but with less dirt and dust.

Hector met them at the castle portcullis.

The Catalonian's face was hollow-cheeked, eyes sunken, black hair streaked with thin lines of grey. He limped when he walked and leaned on a stick when standing. There was much embracing and slapping of backs.

"Still on the correct side of the ground, I see," Finn said.

"Too dry here to push up corn, so I thought I'd stay alive awhile." Hector flashed a grin. "We're getting the banner back together?"

"Alas, no," Finn said. "At least not yet."

He laid out the tale and spared no detail. Gerard's folly in convincing the king to sally. The Master's retribution. Finn's planned residency in the Home for Wayward Brothers. Tricking Ivin and Payens. Emma's dealings with the Order's Treasurer and Archivist. Hector, in turn, explained that most of the brethren at Saphet had ridden off three days ago to join Gerard — including the Castellan, Brother Maban. Hector led in his absence and, with a score of sergeants and another knight, was charged with holding Saphet until Maban's return.

The other knight strolled through the gate. Hector made introductions. The knight, Brother Lando de Sicilia, wore a patchy beard, and had a narrow head topped by a shock of curly hair. Finn took an instant dislike to Lando, even though the man had not uttered a word. It was easy to sniff out such brothers — too overbearing, too judgmental, too serious. He offered Lando a curt nod.

Finn fixed his gaze on Hector. "My last chore as a free man is escorting Emma to Acre."

"Did the Master tell you to do this?" Lando's accent was hard, strong, quick.

"He didn't tell me not to," Finn said, without taking his gaze from Hector.

"When did you say Emma was to join us?" asked Hector.

"No later than this morning. You've no visitors?"

"A handful of refugees from nearby villages. The Treasurer and Archivist have not arrived, nor has anyone from Tiberias. Yesterday some..."

Hector's words faded out as a cold shiver ran down Finn's spine. Emma was not here. She must be trapped in Tiberias. Soon to be razed. Frustration and despair surged in his veins, and he wanted to scream, to claw his face, to tear his hair. *All for a box of bones and a sack of dirty coins.* He realized Hector was still talking.

"...refugees should be streaming along the roads, fleeing Tiberias, fleeing Saladin, but they are not."

"Why, do you suppose?" Finn's words came out in a rasp.

"Turks report Saladin marched around the south end of the Galilee, but also sent desert horsemen around the north end, to encircle Tiberias, to cut off escape. Kurds and Turkmen, mostly, riders who sleep and eat in the saddle. They moved over the land like blown clouds, struck fast as lightning. No one expected them."

"Emma is in Tiberias," Rollo said.

Hector glanced at Finn and arched a brow.

"What is all this furore? For a woman?" Lando spat the last word. "There are vows to uphold, remember?"

Finn fixed an icy glare on Lando.

Rollo slipped between. "See to your men, Brother Lando. I hear them calling you."

Lando took a few halting steps toward the gate. He had fallen for the same ploy used by children to rid themselves of an annoying mate — though the children's version was usually, *Oy, I think I hear your ma calling you to supper, better run along now.*

Hector clasped Finn's shoulder. "What can I do, Brother?"

"Nothing," Finn said, and returned the clasp. "Nothing at all."

CHAPTER 19

"Why will she not burn?" a knight said.

"A witch is bred and born in flame, you clod," another said. "She cannot burn."

The hag hunched over the flames sputtering at her bare feet. Smoke flowed upward and interwove with strands of her dangling, stringy black hair. The fire's glow showed a face as dark as her hair, blue ink marks, eyes cinched against the smoke. A crude stake had been pounded into the ground, and she slumped from it in poorly tied ropes. Balian's men fussed around her, some trying to add wood, others trying to spark new flame.

"What are they doing?" Gerard asked.

Denis gave a confused grin. "Burning a witch, Master."

"I see that." Gerard tried but failed to keep the annoyance from his voice. "Why burn her when Mahounds bite at our flanks undeterred?"

"She cursed the army," Nicholas said. "If she burns, the curse is ended, and her evil foiled."

"Makes sense," Gerard said, voice as dry as the air around him.

The witch began shrieking, high-pitched and horrible, and men scurried away. Gerard could see no reason for it. The flames were weaker now, the smoke dying in sad little wisps.

Gerard stood in the stirrups and scanned the road. An endless line of spearmen stood there; those near wore the red and cream colours of the Balians, those further on were an indistinct red-cream blur in the dusty haze. Raymond, as Prince of Galilee, led the army's vanguard. This was his land; he knew the lay of it, and he would play the hero. Then came the king and other lords. The True Cross, a fragment of the cross on which Jesus was crucified, resided with the king and Rufinus, the Bishop of Acre.

Balian of Ibelin, Hospitallers, and Templars formed the rearguard. They had not guarded the rear, yet, and spent most of their time guarding the flanks. The attacks started not long after leaving Turan, a small village several miles from Saffuriya. Horsemen. Sometimes they held off, content to chant, sing, and taunt. Mostly they wheeled along the Christian line like flocks of angry birds, riding close to shoot arrows at the destriers, or feinting and shooting over their shoulders as they veered away. Some dismounted to bare their arses, or pretend their mounts were lame, either ploy an all-too obvious attempt to prod Christians into leaving the safety of the line.

Balian's men were old hands at this game, as were the Templars, and no one took the bait. Arrows still found their mark. Men and horses limped and staggered back to Saffuriya in a miserable line. The occasional dead horse lay beside the road. Blue-bodied flies plagued both dead and living in huge, shifting black clouds, and the steady drone of countless wings sounded like a giant beehive.

Two roads went from Saffuriya to Tiberias. Raymond chose the road that cut north-east across the Galilean Hills, onto a plateau, and dropped to the Sea of Galilee a few miles north of the city. The second, called the Sannabrah Road, went toward the bridge of the same name, then branched north to Tiberias. Much of Saladin's army sat astride the Sannabrah Road at Kafr Sabt, blocking it and guarding the springs there. Christians used the better of the two and, despite the harassing faris, should have been making good time. They were not; they had been stalled for an hour or so now.

Is it the witch's curse?

Gerard twisted, caught the gaze of his sergeant, Eudo, then pointed at the witch and made a throat-slicing gesture. Eudo pulled an axe from behind his saddle and trudged toward the smouldering pile of wood. The sergeant shoved into the throng of Balian's men, bumped them right and left, ignored their curses until he stood in front of the miserable woman.

Eudo planted his feet and swung the axe. A sharp scream rang out that was cut short by a dull crunch. The sergeant turned away, wiping blood from his axe with a rag, as a burble of outrage arose.

"He killed her..." someone mumbled.

"Does steel break the curse, or must it be flame?" another asked.

Gerard swiped a hand over his sweaty brow. "Damn this heat," he said.

"Shall we move off the road and around these laggards, Master?" Nicholas asked.

"No. We wait for..."

Gerard lost the thought as a rider came galloping down the line. Balian's man, Padrig, a Poulain with dark hair and pale eyes. Someone had recently broken his nose, for it was crooked and lumpy.

"Lord Balian reports we are almost cut off, Master Gerard," Padrig said in a nasally voice. "Bedouins and Kurds are between us and the king. He requests your aid breaking through."

Gerard ordered Nicholas to lead the rear guard and rode forward with two score knights and sergeants. At last. Someone to fight, something to do. Boredom fled, and he said a silent prayer of thanks to Mary, and another to Saint George.

Gerard reined in alongside Balian. The Lord of Ibelin spoke without turning his head. "Would you be so kind as to charge their middle, Master Gerard? I'll hit the bastards at the flanks. We'll break them open and hold them off while the footmen wade through."

Bedouin swirled and screeched, disorganized, but a band of Kurd faris sat unruffled astride the road. There were three, four score of them, grouped in a low spot. They fought to take it, lost much in the doing, but could not hold the trough without reinforcements.

"Gladly, Lord Balian, though please encourage your footmen to make haste. They tarried too long with the witch."

The back and forth was curt, calm,, though Lord and Master both knew that getting cut off and encircled would be their doom. Templars dropped from their destriers. They stabbed the points of their swords into the dry ground, knelt, and bowed their heads to the sword handles as makeshift altars. Prayers merged into a babble of voices. A burly knight was rocking on his knees and chanting, *Non nobis, Domine, non nobis, sed Nomini tuo da gloriam…*

Balian hitched a brow to say, *Can we get on with it?*

"God winnows the righteous — battle is his sifter." Gerard was tying his ventail and paused to add, "The tougher the fight, the nobler the trial, and trial brings us nearer to God."

Balian raised a brow to say, *If you say so.*

Eudo handed Gerard his lance — ten feet of ash capped with pointed steel. At impact all the force and weight of man and horse was transferred to the hand-sized needle. Simple. Brutal. Inescapable. Templars formed a wedge, with Gerard and four knights at the point, then seven, then nine, then eleven. Sergeants would follow on coursers in a staggered line.

Templars shouted hosanas to God and drove off the rise like demons.

The Kurds huddled, tired and wasted, and arched up a feeble spray of arrows. Gerard guided Azrael with his knees, aiming his lance with one arm, and they struck and rolled over the Kurds like an avalanche of steel and flesh. Screams of fear and rage. Snaps and cracks of wood and bone. A strike shuddered up the shaft to his shoulder. He glimpsed an open-mouthed man skewered like a bug, felt a hitch and a drag and the lance snapped.

Templars broke through and swung and reformed. The Kurds scattered, the Bedouin too, leaving behind a carpet of bloody men and broken horses. A wail went up from the wounded, 'Mercy, mercy,' in halting French. They would get none.

A shout went up from Balian's men, and they trotted through the low spot, red-faced and huffing. Some stopped to spear lamed Kurds, or to loot the dead, which was the way of war since Cain had swung the stone that killed Abel.

"Damn. That was a good lance." Gerard held out a hand. "Water."

A half-empty skin, floppy and warm to the touch, slopped into his hand. Gerard's throat felt dry as sand. Hot liquid from a reeking bag did little to soothe it.

"We're saving most of it for the horses, Master," Eudo warned.

Water. Raymond said it was the key to victory. Doubtless he was right. Thirst. It could strip a man's spirit, lay it bare to the sun, drive him to madness. Gerard closed his eyes and listened to the tromp of booted feet and grumbling men. Warriors bellyache, always, and their complaints are an endless parade of the real to the absurd. Poor rations. Late pay. Inept leaders.

Bad omens. The itch tormenting their nethers since that last visit to the camp whore.

Today's gripes were the same — all of them. Water. *When will we have it, and how much, and will it not be wonderful to have a drink, and pour cold water over your hot, stinking face. And will God ever favour us with cold drops and a gentler sun?*

Gerard shoved the thoughts aside, for there was nothing to be done about them now, and turned to his sergeant. "Ride and tell the Hospitallers I order them to move up with haste — no, better to say, *I request* they move up with haste."

"Aye, Master."

"And sergeant?"

"Aye, Master?"

"Never mind. Just go."

Gerard had been about to ask for water from the Hospitallers but thought better of it. They would only laugh and ride on. Pour some of it on the ground out of spite. The sergeant nudged his courser around and spurred away as Nicholas and Henri were coming up, their men trailing in a line with their heads hanging.

Nicholas reined in alongside Gerard. "How much further to Tiberias, do you reckon?"

Too long... "Not long now," Gerard said.

Nicholas made a pained face. "Throat's dry as sandstone. Perchance do you have water to spare, Master?"

Emma sat in the garden to watch the goldfinches frolic. Normally they brought simple joy, an expression of nature, of God's creation. Today their charm went unnoticed.

She stared to the east, over the Galilee, at the mountains rising beyond. Desert riders had flooded off those drab brown heights, wrapped around Tiberias, with no warning, and with such ferocity that Christians scattered from the storm. Arlo was readying their horses for departure to Saphet — alas, too slow, too late — when word came that Saracens had come in the night. The city was encircled. Confusion abounded.

Emma was trapped like a hare in a snare. *By one day, one cursed day...* Recrimination and regret took turns pecking at her. The blame lay in her own stubbornness and contempt for danger. She would never hear the end of it from Finn. *If I see him again, that is...*

At least she had heeded part of Finn's advice. Arlo hired on three men-at-arms. The first, Benik, was a retired Templar sergeant. His face was sweaty and flushed pink as a pig's snout, even in the cool night, and he boasted a stout belly but lacked fingers on one hand. Arlo assured her Benik's remaining fingers were skilled with a blade. The second, Omar, was an old Syrian, swarthy and stocky, but with kind and delicate eyes.

The third ... well, he took her coin eagerly enough, but used it to buy passage aboard a fisherman's skiff and flee across the Galilee. All the fishermen and their families fled over the water, though a few entrepreneurial souls ferried townsfolk from the city for a ridiculous fee.

Should have bought a boat, not two old men and a coward.

Arlo came into the garden, saw her at the plank table, and came to sit by her.

"Talked to men on the wall," Arlo said. Dark bags lay under his eyes. "Saracens crossed the Jordan in the night. Crafty bastards. Part of Saladin's force encamps at Kafr Sabt while the other part, the part encircling us, gets ready to take Tiberias. Word is Saladin made Eschiva an offer — surrender and the people will be spared; resist and everyone dies. She has one day to decide."

"She will not surrender," Emma said.

Arlo nodded to say he thought the same, and told her more of what he had learned. Townsfolk fled for Lady Eschiva's citadel. Only a few were admitted — the noble, the connected, the entitled. Arlo had gone to the citadel but was denied by the sergeant at the gate. There was no room for layfolk. Entreaties fell on deaf ears. Reminders of Emma's name brought confused scowls.

Do they not remember me? Nor recollect what I did for the Order?

In the grey morning she dug a hole in her garden, under the apple tree, and there buried the reliquary and a sack of coins. She made several false holes, the true hole was one of many, but it held riches of the soul and of the world. She prayed for its protection and to someday recover it.

The ruckus at the city walls said it was unlikely. The rising columns of smoke said the same.

She had given Benik coins and sent him to find passage on a boat. Now the portly old man dragged himself into the garden. Lady Eschiva had commandeered the boats. They wallowed, overloaded with folk, and neighbouring fishing villages refused to send more. Too dangerous, they claimed. Lady Eschiva negotiated. Maybe some would come. Maybe not. For certain no amount of coin-waving changed her prospects. Benik joined Omar in the house, watching the street.

With luck, the city walls will hold for two days or so, Emma thought. *Then horror will be unleashed. Townsfolk will die. Tiberias will burn.* Emma took a calming breath and let it out. Yet her voice, when at last she spoke, had more pleading in it than she liked.

"Can we break through on horses?"

Arlo shook his head. "The road is blocked by an army. Besides, if by some miracle we got through, bands of Turkmen rove the countryside. They'll track us, hunt us down. They're notorious for…" He trailed off.

"What do you suggest?"

Arlo stared at the plank table and ran a hand down it. "Can you swim?"

She almost laughed, but saw the serious set of his eyes. "Not well. My people are horse breeders, remember?"

Arlo patted the table. "Then I say we make a boat. And some paddles. Wait to see what Lady Eschiva decides. Cross the lake if we must."

Attempt to cross it, you mean. "Things are so desperate?"

"They are."

Fear surged and she fought for calm. The last time she had felt such despair was in the Wadi of the Dead, with the killer Shabh, and with Finn.

"My villa is not defensible. My neighbours, Yitzchak and Hanna, though … their villa is practically a castle. High walls. Stout gate. Upper windows. Backs onto the water." Emma picked up speed. "We must haul the table to a place we can ably defend, if need be, while we work it into a boat."

Arlo barked a short laugh. "We'll make a warrior of you yet. But will Yitzchak admit us?"

"With open arms." Emma had grown close to Yitzchak. He was a ceramic merchant by trade, wealthy, learned, and affable by nature. She often dined with the couple, spending hours discussing Jewish history and culture. They had a girl and a boy, Mina and Ravi, and Emma enjoyed their company as much as that of their parents.

She had a plan. She breathed out.

Finn will not abandon me. He will come. I know he will.

Finn rode from Saphet with guilt and regret. He tipped back his head, let Fagan find the way, and watched the clouds slide through the sky. Bad judgements had been made. Robert often said a capable leader cannot chew over the bad ones, neither can he help but chew himself over for making them. Leaving Emma in Tiberias had been daft, aye, but dwelling on it did no good. Finn had done right by her at the time, with what he knew, and now all that remained was making success from failure.

But how?

The wisp of an idea was swirling in his head as they dropped toward the Galilee, glittering in the distance like an oversized blue jewel. The plumes of dust and smoke were closer now, thicker, more numerous. A wispy idea began to take form. He pondered Tiberias as he would a riddle, ignored false notions, considered promising clues. What he landed on was not complex, and, since complex plans had a way of failing, it offered a glimmer of hope.

Finn peered over his shoulder at the line of Templars. Hector had asked, 'What can I do, Brother?' and Finn had answered, 'Nothing.' But Hector, being Hector, did what he could. He loaned five sergeants and begged forgiveness for not being able to spare more. Finn embraced them with open arms — though he knew not their names. Experience taught him not to learn a man's name until he stuck around a while; war had a way of winnowing new arrivals, young ones especially, before they learned how to stay alive. Two hailed from Normandy, one from Brittany, one from Gascony, and one was a Poulain, a local-born Christian.

Elias reined in and Finn came alongside. A deep wadi gouged the ground to the east. A village sprawled on the flat land beyond.

"Wadi al-Amud," Elias said. "It flows to the Galilee."

"And the village?"

Elias scowled to say he did not know the name of every settlement in the Galilee. "Let's call it, 'Village'."

"How creative." Finn nodded at the wadi. "So we go there, follow it down, then over to Village. Easy."

Except it was not easy.

The sun sat on the western skyline like a dollop of molten iron. Finn was thinking of camp and a mouthful of dry horsebread when a score of Turkmen in fur hats vomited out of a crease in the ground, whooping and screaming, loosing arrows as they came.

"Shields," Finn said. Piebald boards were swung off backs and slid onto arms. "Tighten the line." The knights kneed the destriers together, facing the enemy, and Finn glanced at Lugh. "At my word, make it rain."

Lugh was yanking his crossbow free but nodded to say he had heard.

The sergeants, ten of them now, slid from their mounts. They hid on the shady sides of their coursers, sidelong to the Turkmen, and loaded crossbows by fitting a foot in the stirrup, pulling back the cord with a prong, and slotting in a bolt. Elias held his bow in a hand and shafts in the other. Preparations were methodical. Practiced.

The Turkmen were coming on fast — close enough now that Finn could make out their quaint hats and shaggy ponies. A handful of arrows pattered down. Sergeants argued over targets.

"I'll take the skinny one riding the black horse..."

"I got the man three to the left, the one in red..."

"The muttonhead at the end of the line is dead; he just don't know it yet…"

"Hold." Finn lowered his shield to cover Fagan's head, just in time for a shaft to hit and ricochet away. "Patience, lads," he said.

The Turkmen, emboldened by Templar inaction, slapped their heels to their mounts and came on with more whoops and shouts and shafts.

Arrows hissed through the air.

One tonked off Rollo's helmet. "Bastard," he said, but did not flinch.

Amic's courser took a shaft in the chest, then a second, and skittered backward as the sergeant fought to keep it in place.

"Why don't we charge?" Owen squawked, then ducked as an arrow flew overhead.

"Because they want us to, but then they'll turn on us, wrap around us in a blink." Finn spoke over his shoulder. "Make ready, lads."

Sergeants dropped to a knee and aimed under the bellies of their coursers.

"Send them," Finn said, casual as a man hunting ducks.

Strings thrummed and quarrels shot out. Elias loosed two arrows in the time it took the bolts to cross the field and hit home. Turkmen went backward off their ponies as if they had been snared by an invisible rope. One reeled in the saddle with the vanes of a bolt jutting from an eye. His mount veered, collided with another, and went over in a medley of screaming horses and cursing men.

"You missed," Jerol grunted, as he pulled on the cord of his crossbow.

"Didn't," Lugh grunted back. "Mine wore red. Owen missed."

Elias's eyes were slits and the tip of his tongue poked from his mouth in a rictus of concentration. Each shaft found a target. A second volley of bolts buzzed out. More men went down.

Turkmen wheeled, fired arrows in an aimless scatter, and fled in a cloud of dust and yelps. One lagged, hunching over the neck of his pony with an arrow in his back. Elias gave him another for good measure. The field was littered with twitching men and kicking horses. A dusty Turkman wandered aimlessly, squatting every so often to peer at the ground, as if he had set down a tool and could not remember where it was.

"To the wreckage and back, Brothers," Finn said, great sword propped on his shoulder.

Three Templars trotted forward in a line.

A Turkman broke cover like a wounded rabbit, staggered left and stumbled right. Rollo spurred alongside. His axe came up, held, then dropped and finished the rabbit.

Another crawled away, raising dust as he dragged a broken leg. Serlo slipped from his mount, mace in hand, and crushed his head. The blow was firm, not too hard, but hard enough the get the job done.

The wandering Turkman found his tool — a long-bladed sword. The man lumbered forward hissing maledictions from a beard-rimmed mouth.

Finn heel-tapped Fagan and clicked his tongue. The man bobbed and weaved. Fagan jouked, danced, then surged and dropped a shoulder into the man. A grunt and the man landed on his arse. Finn thrusted down, felt ribs crack, then a sucking pull as steel slid free.

"Cheat," Rollo said, coming alongside. "Letting Fagan do all the work."

"He's a good lad." Finn laid the great sword across his lap and patted the destrier's neck. "Odd thing, though ... the Turkman seemed surprised a horse could fight."

"Ducked when he should've dodged, I'd say." Rollo checked over his shoulder.

Turkmen swirled, reformed — silent now, less enthusiastic. Between them was bare ground, salted here and there with tufts of weeds, sun-cracked rocks, stunted scrub. Dead men littered it, too, their carcasses awaiting the arrival of carrion birds.

Knights re-joined the sergeants and Finn's company drew up neat, everyone in order. Amic sat astride Ivin's destrier. Serlo handed Elias three quivers of arrows salvaged from the dead; Elias dipped his prodigious chin in gratitude.

Templar and Turkman stared at each other across a field of dead. Templars blinked first.

"Turn away, lads," Finn said. "Slow. Like we haven't a care in the world."

The Turkmen let them go, content to bury their dead, see to their wounded, and seek softer prey elsewhere. Finn's company travelled toward Wadi al-Amud and Village. Every so often they turned to make certain the Turkmen were not making another go at it. Jerol and Lugh watched their trail. Elias roamed ahead.

The Turc found a trail winding into Wadi al-Amud. A clear stream ran down it and, to no one's surprise, Elias named it Stream Amud. Sergeants filled waterskins and watered horses, though not too much, and they lazed awhile in the shade. Another trail brought them up and to the other side. Night fell and they made camp, an arrow shot away from Village, and close to the sharp edge of Wadi al-Amud. Elias went to Village to assure the headman the Templars had no ill intent. He came back with a basket of warm bread.

The Turc handed Finn a slab. "You'll never guess Village's real name."

Finn shook his head to say, *You're right, I won't.*

"Kaphar," Elias said, and laughed. "It means 'village' in Hebrew."

CHAPTER 20

Heat. Thirst. Sweat. The sun had no pity.

"Dry as a dead camel." Gerard kicked the empty bucket lying on the parched ground. "Why was no one sent ahead to check the well?"

"King Guy did not think of it, apparently," Nicholas said, then pointedly added, "nor did his closest advisor think to recommend it."

Gerard huffed at that slight and might have spit in contempt if he had moisture to spare. The Master scanned the line of Templars. Every rank was there. Every knight of renown. Urs, the Seneschal; Pons, the Turcopolier; Maban, the Castellan of Saphet. Other Castellans. The Drapier. Commanders of Houses. And the Commander of Jerusalem, Odon, though he was yet to speak to Gerard since the repurposing of King Henry's alms.

"The dry well of Lubieh," Nicholas said, as if the name held some grand meaning, and chuckled to himself.

The town of Lubieh surrounded them in a sprawl of crumbling stone huts. Lubieh was a ghost town, so empty and lifeless even the ghosts had long since abandoned it. The Horns of Hattin jutted up not far away, past the end of the plateau, and beyond them shimmered the blue expanse of the Galilee. Gerard fought the urge to give Azrael spurs and drive him into its cool waters. But the Galilee was a mirage, of sorts; there, but farther away than it appeared. His mind laboured. *How far was it? Three, four miles? And around ten thousand Saracens in between.*

Gerard became aware that Denis was nudging his elbow. Everyone had sun- cracked, bleeding lips and moved slow as snails. Denis still wore one of his grins, though now it was a grin of suffering.

"Master?"

Gerard squinted and forced his gritty eyes to focus. Before him sat one of the king's squires. The squire said something. Gerard did not recall tailing the squire, but he must have, for now he stood in front of the king and the nobles. Someone handed him a flask, a pilgrim's flask, he noticed with a bleary eye, and he took a long pull. The water was hot, tasted foul, but was manna from heaven.

The king's gaze twitched north-east, at the glittering host to their north, then north-east, at the host there. "Might we…" Guy wavered, never considering the best course might be south-west, back the way they had come.

"We told you," said Reginald, the Count of Sidon. "We told you Saladin would not seek you, nor did he. We told you he would lure you out and control the water. And he did. We told you —"

Raymond froze the count with a stare that said, *Not now.*

Balian redirected course. "The army is out of water, Sire. We will be encircled, if we are not already, and to camp here will be our undoing. Breaking through is our only play. Get to the springs of Hattin or, better yet, all the way to the Galilee."

Raynald looked at the ground, arms folded over his chest. He held the pilgrim's flask in a hand. He had given Gerard the water. He noticed everyone staring at him. Guy most keenly.

"We…" The word came out as a croak, and Gerard began anew. "We have been in the saddle all day, running off attacks and breaking blockades, as have our Hospitaller brothers. Our horses will collapse under us, and soon, if we do not rest. An hour or two will suffice."

William Borrel, the *ad interim* Hospitaller Master, stared at Azrael, as if he recognized the beast from somewhere. "Charge," he said, and fixed Gerard with a taut stare. "Charge all the way to the Galilee or die in the attempt."

The king's gaze meandered the half-circle of nobles, halted on each, then settled on Gerard. He nodded once.

"Excellent," Guy said, "excellent," though it was unclear what was so praiseworthy. "We have marched hard and our men are not fighting fit, at the moment, as Master Gerard said. Rest is the remedy. We camp here. On the morrow we reform, tighten the lines, and march onward with renewed vigour. God favours us. Victory awaits! We will seize it!"

Gerard frowned. *I advised an hour or two of rest, not all night.*

Raymond dared to grasp the king's arm. "Fool! You started this march of folly, and you cannot stop it. Not now. We will be hemmed in —"

"Unhand me!" Guy flung off Raymond's hand and wheeled away with his entourage in tow. One of them glared indignantly over a shoulder to say, *Lay a hand on the king? How dare you, Sir!*

Raymond turned to Raynald. "And you?" he snarled.

Raynald looked up, tossed the pilgrim's flask to one of his knights, and climbed into the saddle. "Camp here, I say. Those loyal to the king will stay with him. We'll end up with two small forces and Saladin will pluck us one at a time. Better to forge on together, in strength, with numbers."

"What a firm grasp on strategy you have," Balian said. "Most impressive. Still think leaving Saffuriya was wise, I wonder?"

Raynald's silence spoke volumes.

Raymond stared into the distance and blurted, "The war is over. The kingdom is finished. We are dead men."

The council broke apart with that cheery pronouncement. Men trudged off in a score of directions. Raynald and Gerard remained.

Raynald looked askance. "Is the rear under constant attack, as you said?"

Gerard snorted, intended as a mocking laugh, though it came out dry and pathetic. "Has been all day. One side, then the other. The imps target our destriers. Not a lot of dead, but a lot of wounded, and we fight one long, running battle."

"Can you do it again tomorrow?"

Gerard nudged Azrael in a half circle and spoke over his shoulder. "Do we have a choice?"

Finn sat on a boulder under the stars and watched the campfires encircling Tiberias. He wore only braes and the night air was cool on his bare skin. The stars looked down, bright and knowing, and he studied them, and wondered what they knew and where God was in all this.

He idly palmed the scar on his chest where Shabh had carved away an ink mark, one of several made in his wayward youth. It bled incessantly, too wide to suture, so Rollo had burned it. Fire purified and healed — but it hurt like hell. Worse than any wound before or since. Emma witnessed the skinning, thus a bit of her resided in that puckered welt. The killer Shabh strung him up naked in chains. Finn should have been cringing in fear, yet all he could think was, *When was I last nude afore a woman, let alone two?*

Rollo lay at the base of the boulder. "The town is encircled."

"Except for the lakeside."

"Except for that."

They sat in silence awhile. Neither mentioned the plan, though both knew what needed doing.

A grin split Rollo's beard. "Gerard will be … beyond enraged."

"Wish I could be there to see it." Finn was numb to the Order, done with Gerard, done with scampering to obey orders. All that mattered now was love. Brothers. Emma. Jesus. He would do anything for them. Everything else — the Order, the kingdom, the Master — could rot.

He had changed much, he realized, as he contemplated the stars.

His thoughts meandered to his youth. It had been a blood feud. Dark. Brutal.

All because of hairy cows.

Legend had it a MacDougall stole a herd … or was it a Donnachaidh stole MacDougall cows? It did not matter now. What mattered was a feud erupted and, years after, his father died by Tomas MacDougall's hand.

Rage came, and a few nights later Finn left Tomas a bloody mess with a blade wedged in his ribs. He left two of Tomas's sons the same. The youngest fled and hid in the pines. *Never heard what became of the lad.*

Some called it murder. Finn called it revenge. Still did. The holy book said that revenge belongs to the Lord, leave it to Him, but Finn had never agreed with that part.

The deeds earned him a dark name, *Cù-Sìth*, the Black Dog, and a dark reputation. The MacDougalls could never let the Black Dog live. Finn's kin, the Donnachaidh, decided Finn should leave. At least for a while. Folk on both sides were the kind to keep the fires of feud burning bright, stoke them every so often, and carry grudges all the way to the grave. Finn lived hard in the forests awhile. Eventually he took vows with the

Order, partly to dampen the blood feud, but mostly for forgiveness of his sins.

The Order proved a new world.

In the zealous authority he found a master worthy of his soul. He welcomed structure. Revelled in austerity. Devoured the discipline. Finn never questioned, never balked, never disobeyed. Any doubt he buried. The severity of it, married to his affinity for violence, made him a rare beast. He fought with reckless abandon.

Lately, though, the Order riled him at every turn. He could not say why. The blame might lie with Gerard — how he hated that man. Or perhaps it was inevitable with time, with reflection, with hard-knock wisdom.

A bag of elixir sloshed at his hip. It was the Order's brew of aloe and hemp steeped in palm wine. Elixir furthered healing and health, and was to be taken in moderation, though Finn was finding moderation more of a challenge by the day. He filled himself a cup, then one for Rollo, and passed it down. They drank awhile. Finn heard Serlo come over and drop to his arse against the boulder.

"What are you going to do?" Serlo's voice was deep and hoarse.

"You know what I'm going to do."

Serlo said nothing, which was nothing new.

What Finn planned was a rope that, once cut, could never be retied. Rollo had lost the habit long ago. Finn would soon lose it, or worse. Serlo need not suffer the same indignities. He was innocent, decent of soul.

Finn had offered Serlo a way out at Saffuriya. He tried again.

"You needn't come," Finn said. "You're a good man. You'll climb high in the Order."

Still Serlo said nothing.

Finn drained the cup and poured himself another. "I'm not going to Acre. I'll not abide being tossed into a hole to rot. Not after all the service I've given. I'll leave the Order, just walk away, be a free man."

"Amen to that," Rollo muttered.

Finn ploughed on. "My escape means you'll be punished. Probably lose the habit."

"Certes," Serlo said.

"Then go to Acre," Finn insisted. "Tell Gerard I turned rabid, bit you on the hand, stole away in the night, whatever."

Serlo dragged a hand over his fresh-shaved pate.

"You ask me to lie. To abandon brothers. I will not." Serlo's voice grew hard. "God bids me to fight for light and virtue. Gerard is neither. Emma is both."

Finn wanted to slap himself for doubting the man. Instead, he knocked back the cup, poured another, then hefted it in a toast. "To you, Serlo. Often the hardest thing and the right thing are the same thing."

"Ooh — someone needs to write that down." Rollo stretched and was rewarded with a satisfying crack. "So, now that we're all aboard the same ship, how do we sail it?"

Finn stared out across the lake to the darkened city. Points of fire danced. It was hard to separate the land from the lake, the torches of men from the lights of buildings. All was a confusion of light and dark, each swirling and flowing around the other, intangible and indecipherable. There was only one real thing in it. Emma. She was there. Somewhere.

"This lake," Finn said, and waved the cup toward the Galilee. In the darkness neither Rollo nor Serlo could see the gesture, and Finn realized he was a bit drunk. He tossed the cup and heard it break in the darkness. "Did you know Jesus fished here? On this very lake?"

"Aye," Rollo said.

"Well, I had forgotten, and it set me to thinking. We need a fisherman."

"Capernaum?" Rollo scrunched up his face. "Should I know the significance of this hole?"

"You should," Finn said. "It's an ancient fishing village, as old as the lake itself, and a place loved by Jesus. He was born in Bethlehem, raised in Nazareth, and preached in Jerusalem. But Capernaum is where he performed many of his miracles. He lived here after facing temptation in the wilderness. Met Peter, James, and John here, and most of the other lads."

"Been talking to Hector again, I see," Rollo said, and spat.

They had ridden from Village to Capernaum in the dark morning. Already the day simmered with heat. Finn adjusted his headwrap. Everywhere he turned folk were staring at him. A stone breakwater curved out into the harbour; three piers jutted from the shore toward the harbour wall; Finn stood near the lesser of the three. He paced the shore of the Galilee and gazed south across the water. The smoke was there, but not much thicker or taller, which was a good portent. Tiberias remained intact, for now. The crunch of feet on rock made him turn — Elias, with the chief of the fishermen.

The fisherman walked barefoot, wore a threadbare linen shift, and boasted a beard more grey than black. He had skin brown as leather and, despite his advanced age, a body rippling with lean muscle. The man was not unlike the fishermen of old — sinewy men that had worked this lake for eons, back to Adam. Finn had spied from afar as Elias conversed with the chief. The man flailed his hands as he talked and used exaggerated faces, which made up for his poor *lingua franca*. Kinsfolk stood in a knot on the beach.

"Sunny day, calm waters," the fisherman said, apropos of nothing.

"Aye," Finn said. There was no reason for small talk, nor did he have the time for it. "Will you take us across the lake? To Tiberias. We'll pay."

"Tiberias? No, no, no, kind sir. No. Sail is broken. Look and see?"

Finn turned, eyeing the boat at the pier. "I'm no sailor, certes, but even I know oars work just fine in gentle waters. And I see you have oars."

"No, no, no." The fisherman flailed a hand, then held it in the air for added emphasis. "Too hard. Much rowing. Much work needed."

"You'll be paid, as I said."

The fisherman perked up, then deflated. "You have taken vow of poverty. No coin in Templar purse."

"I don't have coin, no, but our Temple in Jerusalem does. The Temple will pay." Finn did not know if the Temple was good for the coin, but he would find a way to pay the man, one way or the other.

"No, no, no, kind sir." The fisherman made a sad face. "No Temple. Gone soon."

Thus they bargained. Round and round. Finn tried what little charm he possessed. He appealed to the man's decency. To reason. He applied guilt. The fisherman deftly evaded every hook. Trepidation was the cause, Finn could see, for only a fool or madman would willingly sail to a doomed city. The fisherman was neither a fool nor a madman. In the end, his patience exhausted, Finn resorted to what he knew best. He draped an arm around the man's shoulders, corded with muscle from a lifetime of pulling oars and nets, and leaned toward his ear.

"You'll take us to Tiberias, fisherman. In two boats. Drop us off where I say. Wait for us. Then, when our work is done, you'll ferry us back to Capernaum."

"No, no, no, kind —"

Finn dug his fingers into the man's neck and squeezed. Hard. "You'll do as I bid, or I'll stab you in the guts, then leave you to die. Have you seen a gut wound? I have, and it's a long and painful death." Finn slacked off and pointed at the man's kin, bunched like a flock of nervous sheep. "I'll stab them, too. All of them. One by one. I'll feed your corpses to the fishes and take your boats. You hear me?"

Finn would not resort to murder and theft — it was a bluff, though past deeds gave him the guile to sell his empty threats. Something in his cold, calm voice told the fisherman as much.

"I hear you." The fisherman papered a smile over his fear. He kept the papery smile as the entrepreneur in him floated to the surface. "You say the Temple has coin?"

"Finn."

Something in Rollo's voice made Finn turn from the fisherman.

Across the waters, smoke fumed in a massive plume. The wall climbed higher until it hung over the lake like an ashy club. It veiled the sun and cast them all in a murky shade.

"The light went out," Rollo said.

Finn could not help thinking darkness had swept in to blot out Tiberias, the kingdom, and all that was good.

CHAPTER 21

Saracens came at dawn. Bells rang, unremitting, booming and brassy, then stopped abruptly. Perhaps the bellringer grew weary of yanking the rope and took up spear and shield; mayhap an archer, vexed by the ruckus, sent a shaft into the poor man. Townfolk were mostly gone from this part of Tiberias, fled to the citadel or the docks, and the streets were unnaturally quiet and still.

Emma sat in Hanna's garden and tried to ignore the sounds of war drifting from the city's walls — faint shouts, whistling thumps, the occasional scream. Yitzchak and Hanna's villa was down the road from her own. It boasted stout walls on three sides, a stout metal gate at ground level, and the lake at its back. She had Arlo, Benik, and Omar, and an ample supply of arms and food. Their strengths were not insignificant.

Still.

Emma was no salt, certes, but even she grasped that the villa could not hold for long.

Another of her Jewish neighbours, also named Yitzchak, joined them, along with his wife Chanta and three children. Yitzchak was a too-common name hereabouts, so Arlo took to calling them, 'the Fathers', or 'First Father' or 'Second Father', to avoid confusion.

Benik and Omar kept watch from the villa. Arlo and the Fathers laboured, putting the final touches to their boat — though barge might have been a more accurate term. They used the top of the plank table, broke away the legs, then lashed other pieces of wood to give depth and add stability.

Arlo tested it in the shallows of the Galilee and it floated — poorly, with water sloshing over its boards.

Emma dressed like a Bedouin, as she did when afield, and carried a long knife at her belt. Her former bodyguard, Baret, had taught her a few tricks with the blade. Arlo taught more. Stab a man in the groin, slash his eyes, thrust for the neck. Go fast. Hard. Nasty. Do not dance. Knife fights are not an exquisite dance of parry and counter, Arlo said. The game is to make as many holes as you can, as quickly as you can, and take none in return. One does not keep score. As they drilled with sheathed knives, he called out, 'Point to me,' with every blow, just to mock the notion.

Arlo bought her a latchbow, small and easy to load, and lethal at close range. She practised until her fingers bled, Arlo's training mantra ringing in her ears: *Place the prong, pull the cord, slot the bolt.* She added the obvious: *Aim, breathe, squeeze.* Many an apple died. After, she braided her hair, a soothing habit that also infused her with strength, like an Amazon of Greek myth.

"Ready?" Emma asked.

"Ready as it'll ever be." Arlo glanced up from tying rope. "All aboard now."

The Fathers climbed on, the raft rocking in the waves, then pushed in makeshift oars to stabilize the raft. Wives and children clambered aboard, then Emma. The raft plunged, struggled to right itself, then Arlo's weight sent them into the lake. Benik and Omar went back to their posts while the others spluttered in the water.

They sat at the shore and dried themselves in the sun, jested about how so few folk could weigh so much, and tried to ignore ugly sounds from the ramparts. Arlo teased the children, claimed their weight had sunk the boat, though they were skinny as freshly peeled poles. He scratched his chin. Peered at the raft this way and that. Then with the Fathers set to improving it. Perhaps adding an outrigger would keep it from diving and tipping...

Benik whistled from the house. Emma shared a look with Arlo, motioned that he should stay, and clambered up from the shore to check the goings-on. The walls of the villa were stone. Two upper windows faced the street; Benik and Omar watched from there.

Emma climbed the stairs and moved down the hall to Omar, who reclined against the casing with a bow in one hand and arrows laid out on the sill. Benik was in the next window, whistling a lively, circular tune — *Ierusalem mirabilis*. It was a song to inspire travel from Christendom to Outremer, to take Jerusalem, and a simple ditty meant to rouse simple folk to difficult deeds. Outremer was where Jesus lived; go there, die there, join Him in paradise.

"Trouble?" Emma asked.

Omar nodded at the street and Emma peered out. Her stomach knotted.

Two men lay before the gate. Another lay in the road. The manner of their death was not apparent, though she could hazard a guess — Omar and Benik must have shot them while she dried at the lakeshore. Shapes moved across the road. The villa there had an open yard bordered by a row of wooden posts, the beginnings of a wall never finished. The shapes wore scaled leather armour, head wraps, flowing robes.

Omar grabbed a shoulder and yanked Emma back — just as something blurred through the window, careened off the wall, and clattered down the hall.

"Javelin throwers, Kurds," Omar said.

"Saracens." Emma could not keep the tremor from her voice. "The wall has fallen?"

"I don't think so. We'd be overrun." Omar adjusted the fit of his thumb ring by twisting it. "Walls don't always fall in one go. A city can be taken in bits. Attackers get over the weak spots. The professional gets behind the defenders, fights for a toe hold on the wall, but the amateur sets off into the city to loot and claim the fat houses. These are —"

A javelin lodged in the sill, sudden, thrumming.

Omar tilted into the window and pulled the string of the short Turkish bow in one sinuous move. The stick flexed, he loosed off the leather ring on his thumb, and the shaft was gone. Curiosity prodded and Emma peeked out. A man staggered and dropped to his knees in the road. A wet shaft quivered in a post beyond.

"That had to hurt," Benik said, and Omar grinned.

"Can you hold them?" Emma managed to sound steelier now.

"If they keep coming in twos and threes. More of them will get over the city wall, I'd wager. We're a tempting morsel. But the gate is stout, in our favour, and they'll need something heavy to batter it, which will take time to steal or make. We'll murder them while they hammer away."

Benik had spoken from his window. Emma could imagine him, holding a crossbow with his good hand and whistling *Ierusalem mirabilis*. Omar watched her from the corner of his eye, and seeing her gaze, he winked and flashed a grin. Suddenly she rejoiced for spending coin on two old men — though a well-made boat would also have been nice.

Emma went back to the lake. Arlo met her while the Fathers worked on the raft. She told him about the Kurds; he shrugged but said nothing. Emma and Arlo watched the Fathers labour, the children chase each other up and down the beach, and the wives at once scold the children and help the Fathers. Emma had never been a mother, never held her own creation of flesh and blood and spirit, never felt the mix of love and fear every parent must feel daily. God had never blessed her in this. But she saw it in the mothers and their children, and in that moment understood the seriousness it must be to cultivate another soul.

"City walls won't hold much longer." Arlo's gaze ran along the wall from the house to the water's edge. It was two feet taller than a man, the gap between the end of the wall and the water ten feet or so. "Saracens will get around our back, sooner or later, and then we'll be in trouble. Daft idea, the boat. Can't take all of us and stay afloat. You, me, and the old men. Or the families. But not all of us."

It was a gentle way of saying Emma had an ugly choice to make.

"The children must go." She spoke without a moment's thought. She suffered a twinge of fear, but there was no unsaying it now.

"Knew you'd choose them." Arlo tore his gaze from the families and fixed it on Emma. "Ugly things happen when cities fall. Worse things than you can imagine. Women and children, sold as slaves. Women suffering indignities and depravities innumerable. When the ramparts fall…" He paused, then found his backbone. "Don't let yourself be taken. Say the word and I'll do it. If I'm gone, put the knife tip to your chest, slightly left of centre, and run the handle into a wall."

"What awaits is no mystery, Arlo, but my thanks for the advice … I think." Emma smiled, flat and pale. "So, shall we help the Fathers cast off?"

The fisherman drove a hard bargain. Thirty silver shekels to ferry them to Tiberias and back, plus another three to tend their horses. Finn threw in five gold bezants, which raised the fisherman's brows. It was enough to buy a fleet of boats. He did not care — wealth was nothing to him, and it was the Order's coin anyhow, not his own.

The fisherman was named Cephas. He said it meant Rock, though somehow it was also the name for Peter, a Jewish fisherman from Capernaum who had become one of Jesus's favourite apostles and the first Pope. Finn could not unravel how Cephas morphed to Saint Peter.

Neither did he understand the mysteries of sailing. What little he knew entailed bobbing up and down, spewing breakfast over the gunnels, and praying for landfall. Much time was spent tacking away from the wind — or was it into the wind? Whichever, travel on water was rarely a straight line, and a boat had to zigzag many miles to progress a few. Two boats rocked at the pier, but Cephas insisted they wait until mid-morning, when the winds would pick up, otherwise they would waste strength rowing but not getting far.

Waiting was misery. Smoke roiled over Tiberias. Smuts drifted down, light as snow.

Finn sat at the water's edge and ran a whetstone down Oathkeeper. The sound of stone on steel was a lullaby, a centrum for meditation, and he lost himself in the work. Every so often he rested, deliberated over Tiberias, or watched the water. Schools of silvery minnows flitted through the shallows. A bigger fish would sometimes pounce from deeper water, then whirl away, and the minnows would reform like nothing had happened. *Do they not notice they are one less than before, or do they notice and not care?*

Owen came and sat by his side. He flexed his fingers incessantly. Finn ignored him until he spoke in Scots-Gaelic.

"Do ye fear death?"

"I don't." Finn did not mention the rare occasions when dark moods came upon him, when he sought death. Instead, he said the expected. "Paradise awaits me."

"Ye think it does?"

"Why wouldn't it? I'm a Templar."

"Vows, piety, a few noble deeds ... none of these make up for all the bad ye've done."

"We've all done bad things, Owen. Ye. Me. Doesn't mean God doesn't love us."

Owen smirked at that.

Finn fixed him with a frosty stare. "Why do ye hate me so?"

Silence.

"We're well-nigh kin," Finn carried on. "Bred and born in Alba. We speak the same tongue. Know the same tales. Should be thick as thieves, ye and I. Yet you're always crabbit."

Owen seemed amused by that. "Dinnae fret. It's not just ye. I hate everyone."

"Aye, well, I feel better for knowing."

Owen grinned, forced, like a madman, and the hairs stood up along Finn's neck. He wearied of Owen — the po-faced demeanour, the steady grumbling, the rapid flights between content and offended. Emma's warning, in Acre, came to him; *Never turn your back to him, Finn.* A woman's intuition? In his estimation such insight was not often wrong. Yet what was one to do? Finn needed sword arms, now more than ever, and could not spare leaving the sergeant behind.

Keep brothers close. Keep enemies closer.

Lugh gave a whistle. "Cephas says God favours us. An early breeze is tickling his short hairs. Time to go to work."

"Don't trip and fall," Lugh said. "In all that steel, you'll sink fast as a rock, and I can't swim well enough to save your arse."

Finn grunted to acknowledge the obvious advice, then strode down the pier with as much confidence as he could muster. His carried Oathkeeper, Da's biodag, and a mace tucked into his wide leather belt. A piebald shield was slung on his back. All this he dropped over the boat's edge. He clambered in while Lugh and Diego made room, Owen and Elias shifted to the opposite side as counterweights, and Cephas belly-laughed at the sight.

Water sloshed onto Lugh. "God's bones, we'll never get the rust off," he grumbled.

Donning mail always made Finn feel impervious — protected by something grander. Wearing mail near water made him edgy and vulnerable to whims beyond his control. He had stripped the mail *chausses* off his legs and feet, which lightened the load, and wore just the thigh-length hauberk with sleeves to his elbows. Still he fretted.

Rollo, Serlo, Amic, and Jerol rode in the second boat. Hector's five sergeants were there and looked as fidgety on water as they did on land. Rollo gave a cheery wave, as if setting off on a leisurely day of sightseeing and not into a city encircled by Saracens.

The boats were Cephas's babies and, he claimed, no different than the boat Jesus sailed. Each measured thirty feet long, eight feet wide, and were made of cedar planks joined by pegged mortise and tenon. Boards of varying colour and grain showed the boats had been mended more than once. Keels did not extend far beneath the waterline, like a Norse ship of old, and were made to work in shallow water. Four staggered benches allowed for rowing. A central mast gave the boat its power, though, and a sail made it skim through the water. Each could carry twenty people, though Cephas insisted less was better.

"You wear steel, weigh the same as two men." Cephas paused to mime a wobbly boat. "Makes us slow."

The breeze was rising and Cephas raised a grinning face into it. Two shaggy-haired youths rowed them away from the shore, then pulled the oars in and began raising the sail. Cephas manned the rudder. His brother, Yoshiah, and another man worked the second boat.

Finn had rolled out the plan after the ride from Village to Capernaum. Go to Tiberias by boat. Find the harbour near Emma's villa. Land there. Fetch her. Sail back to Capernaum. The success of the plan, oddly, depended on Saladin's meticulous preparation. The Sultan boasted hordes of horsemen, spearmen, archers, swordsmen. Siege engines. Stacks of arrows. The list was endless. But there was a blank line where 'watercraft' should have been written. The Sultan brought none. No balingers. No birlinns. No cogs. Not even a skin-lined currach. He enclosed the landward side of the town, aye, but the Galilee was the rent in his net.

Finn got back flat stares. Rollo spoke what they were all thinking.

"What if Emma isn't at the villa? How will we find her? And what if the walls fall — how will we fight a city of Sandpigs while we search?"

"Pray she's there." Finn sighed. "Few plans survive meeting the enemy. We know that. So, we'll improvise, if we must. Do what we do best. Go on the hunt."

It sounded simple. But it was also reckless.

"Tiberias," Rollo called now, and pointed south-west.

The city staggered up along the shore like a row of broken teeth. Tall houses. Low houses. Some dingy yellow, some gleaming white. Old and new intermixed and made a disparate mess. Emma, ever fond of old things, lived in the old part of town. Streets there were narrow. Blank walls and blind alleys abounded. Make a wrong turn on most days and one might stumble into a haven of cutpurses and throat-slicers. A wrong turn in a city soon to be teeming with Saracens meant death.

Harbours and piers dotted the shore. Boat traffic was but a trickle, which was a bad sign, though the shore bustled like a kicked ant mound.

The citadel stood proud, glimmering and white, rising from the lakeshore in the old Jewish Quarter. It boasted thick walls made of ashlar stones. The Galilee lapped at the east wall. A moat encircled the fortress and drew water from the lake. The main gate was a steel portcullis. The lintel over it was adorned with floral patterns and a wreath of Heracles, which Hector had claimed was borrowed, or stolen, from the ruins of the synagogue in Capernaum. Other rummaged bits decorated various nooks and crannies — a basalt ashlar with a five-branch candelabrum, ornate cornice stones and capitals, column drums, fragments of Italian marble. Finn found the marriage of Jewish and Christian elements inspiring, a physical representation of Outremer, though a Jew would likely think otherwise.

Psalmody echoed from the citadel and, judging by the high, crisp notes, it was a boys' choir. The singing was calm and smooth, and in God's note — an angelic voice so serene it warmed Finn's soul. The song had a touch of defiance, too, and a subtle vigour calling for Christians to stand firm.

Serlo's head was bowed in prayer. Rollo cuffed his eye. Even Cephas seemed awed.

Most folk seek omens. The habit is ingrained in their very fibres. Even Christians look for omens — though few admit it.

Finn sought them. In the dust blowing off the desert, in the croak of a raven, in the way a loaf of bread breaks. He chastised himself for being irrational, and murmured a prayer of forgiveness, but not long after found himself thumbing his iron crucifix for good luck.

Heavenly singing was the best of omens. It defied belief, creed, and calling, and warmed every man, no matter his place of birth. Omens could be hard to read, but this one was undeniable. *God favours us...*

They passed the occasional boat, all heading in the opposite direction, all stuffed with people and riding low in the water. Cephas hailed one. A shouted response drifted over the water. He said something to Elias in Hebrew; Elias translated for Finn.

"The city holds. Heavy fighting on the walls. Common folk flee or hide."

Owen nodded at Elias, then spoke to Lugh. "Is there a language he doesn't speak?"

"The language of love." Lugh shaded his brow, then crossed himself and blurted, "Father, Jesus, and Mary — either the Lord almighty is walking on water or I've gone mad."

Finn tracked the Irishman's gaze — there, not far off, a man stood on the water, waving frantically. Several others, too. As they neared, Finn saw the people were not standing *on the water* but *in the water*. It sloshed around their ankles as they see-sawed on a flat-bottom cog. No ... not a cog, but a tabletop made into a poor imitation of a raft, and sinking fast. The first man, a short man with greying hair, called out in Hebrew, and Cephas flailed his arm toward Finn.

Finn fanned a hand to say the obvious, *Can't leave them to drown*. Cephas moved their boat alongside and the lads tossed over a rope, then hauled the wallowing craft in. Lugh and Jerol helped the folk clamber aboard — two men, two women, and five children.

The grey-haired man came to Finn and dropped to his knees, hands in a pleading gesture, eyes wet with tears. He spoke in Hebrew but stopped when Finn tapped his ear to say, *I don't understand*, then pointed to Elias. The two conversed, the older man doing most of the talking, Elias doing most of the nodding.

Elias turned to Finn. "He pleads we rescue his friends. They're holed up in his villa at the lakeshore. Four of them. One woman and three rough men."

"Tell him we've friends of our own to find," Finn said. "Tell him we'll grab his if we have time and room to spare, though I make no promise."

Elias spoke to the man, listened, then turned back to Finn. "He repeats words I don't know ... something about the woman. Says Kurds attacked but were driven off."

Finn gave a half-nod to say he had heard, but his gaze had settled on a child, a girl with eyes as dark as his own. In her was everything pure, and innocent, and good. She stared back, lips tight with fear. He offered a comforting smile, but it only frightened her more. A sudden realization soured him.

There is a city full of children, each as innocent as this one, each waiting for a saviour.

CHAPTER 22

Finding Emma's villa was simple. The stone breakwater curved into the lake like a crooked finger. The pier, wood boards set over wood posts, was on the shore side of the barrier, shielded by its embrace. Two stone pillars marked the juncture of the pier and the lakeshore.

Cephas angled toward the pier, Yoshiah wallowing in his wake.

Finn rode the prow like a berserker of Norse legend — helmet on his head, boot on the rail, shield rim up to his chin. The ship bumped the pier and Finn leapt out — and on sea-stiff legs stumbled across the planks and almost tumbled off the other side.

That would be bad...

Jerol was left bobbing in place with Cephas because the old Norman had the stomach for it and, well, because promises of gold could only go so far. Finn reeled down a swaying pier with the others at his heels. He dropped onto firm ground, made a fist and held it out to his side to say, *Line abreast*, then signalled, *Forward*, with a wave of splayed fingers. They crept up the trail and over the vacant ground next to Emma's villa, formed up at the wall, then rolled around and into the garden in force.

It was empty — and ransacked. Holes pocked the ground. Broken ceramic pots lay in jumbles of brown and orange shards. Plants had been yanked up by the roots and flung aside, the apple tree stripped bare as a skeleton.

"God's wounds," Lugh said. "Eejits even stole the table."

"No one here." Rollo nodded to himself, as if some earlier claim had been proven right, though Finn could not recall what. "Don't mean to gloat but —"

Whatever bragging Rollo planned was cut short as Elias drew and loosed. A shape fell from the roof of the villa. A muffled thud marked his landing.

A chorus of calls in Arabic, and men in blue and yellow robes poured out the door yapping like a pack of demented jackals. Finn glimpsed round shields, curved swords, domed helmets. A grey-haired man came at Finn with a lopsided gait, toothless mouth open and screaming a challenge.

A part of Finn did not want to kill a limping, toothless old man. Except now the old man was raising a *saif* with surprising swiftness and strength. Finn took the blade on his shield and hacked low at the old man's good leg. He tried to twist away on the gimpy leg, a bad idea, and Oathkeeper bit deep. *There, now you have two gimpy legs.* A hiss of pain was cut short as Finn punched the shield corner into his forehead and used the shield face to knock him down.

The air was filled with noise — clang, scream, clatter. Arrows buzzed in the freshly raised dust — Elias sending shafts left, right and centre.

Rollo shoved past to hack at someone coming at Finn's side. A crunch and a groan. The Norman contorted the other way. Took a chop on his shield. Gave one back. A man scuttled close, trying to get inside the radius of the axe, thrusting and probing around the piebald shield. Rollo lunged with the top corner of the blade and slashed the edge down and away. Bright ruby droplets sparkled in the sunlight.

Finn slid into the battle madness. Fiery hate surged in his veins.

Movement to the left. A man coming in. Finn twisted and stabbed him in the mouth. He risked a glance right.

A man in a domed steel cap slid out of the dust and thrust overhand with a short-handled spear. The blade clanged off Finn's helmet and he stabbed blindly along the edge of his shield, felt his sword bite. He skipped aside. Swept Oathkeeper in a graceful arc. Glimpsed a head rolling in the dust, yellow teeth between red lips, heard blood spattering down like rain.

Lugh ghosted into the corner of his vision. The Irishman pivoted forward at the hips and thrust over his shield. A black-bearded man reeled away with a hand pasted over his eye. The thrust was so precise Finn had missed it — as had the black-bearded man, until the steel slid in.

I taught him that...

An arrow buzzed past Finn's ear. *God's bones, Elias, that was too close for comfort!*

A pained shout, then a burly man stomped toward Finn, his *saif* pulled back and his shield pushed forward. Steel chopped into his board. Finn countered with a stab over his shield and felt it batted aside.

Silver flickered — Rollo's axe, glinting in the hazy light. A wet crack and half of the burly man's face vanished in a spray of red.

"They're legging it!" Amic shouted.

Men in blue and yellow robes scattered through the garden like roaches exposed to sunlight. Elias loosed and a man staggered forward, collapsed with a shaft quivering in his back. Another. And another. Only two made it to the villa.

Hector's sergeants took a few hesitant steps.

Finn held up Oathkeeper. "Let them go." He tapped one of the sergeants, nodded at the villa, and said, "Watch the street and give a shout if they come back with friends."

Diego slumped against the apple tree, then coughed a spray of red froth and slid down the trunk. A hole was bleeding in his chest.

Amic pulled back his lips and spat through the gap in his teeth. "God's bones, balls, and arse," he moaned.

There was nothing Amic could do to help his friend but hold his hand, and whisper in his ear as he passed. Serlo knelt by his side and prayed. "O God, accept your faithful servant, Diego, and admit him to the land of light..."

They found one of Hector's sergeants face-down in a shaded corner of the garden. They dug hasty graves and planted the sergeants in the dark, rich soil. The garden had been a place of life. Now it held death. If you passed away back home, you would get a funeral with mourners and Godly words. If you got killed here, you would be lucky to get a lumpy hole with a few rocks stacked on top of you.

Now our school of fish is two less than before. Finn felt nothing. He should have been twisted by grief. But he was hollow. *People die. It happens.*

Rollo propped the axe head on the ground and leaned on the handle. He seemed to read Finn's mind. "Wouldn't be war if folks were all smiles and hugs after, would it?"

"You're a hard bastard," Finn said, and Rollo grinned at his words put back on him.

Elias was there, head lowered, rubbing a thumb down his lacquered bow. "Now where to?" he asked.

Finn dragged a palm over his face and stared over the lake.

Where is she? He closed his eyes and thought. *Where would I go, if I were Emma?* The citadel. Would they admit her, though? The citadel was stout but small, reserved only for those critical to the cause or close to Lady Eschiva. Emma was neither. Perhaps she had purchased a boat, sailed away, and made landfall somewhere safe. Even now she could be heading for Saphet. *All this searching could be in vain.* Such thoughts set his heart aflutter with a mix of calm and fret.

Elias's head shot up and he said something in Hebrew.

Finn quirked a brow and Elias explained. "The old Jewish man out on the water — he called the woman something in Hebrew. I think he meant a relic hunter, a dealer of souvenirs."

Finn stared a moment, blinking, then snorted a humourless laugh. "Where's the old man's villa?"

Arlo cuffed sweat from his eye. "Bastards won't give up."

"We're the biggest villa this side of town," Emma said. "Certes such a castle must be owned by wealthy folk — at least that's what they believe."

Arlo grimaced to say the notion had not occurred to him. He began gathering javelins thrown by the javelineers, sorted those still usable, and leaned them against the wall. They were short, light spears with a small, leaf-shaped point. The Kurds seemed to have an endless supply. Emma came from the house, fingering the handle of the knife, a new tic she loathed but could not shake. Omar watched from his window perch.

Benik lay against a wall. He had taken a javelin in the gut defending the narrow gap between the wall and the lake. Two dead Saracens now clogged the space. Both lacked their spindles, Arlo told her, which Omar had sliced away and nailed to the gate. The old Syrian shouted in Arabic for the enemy to come and see what he had done to their friends. The same would be done to them. Omar's trick, ghastly as it was, gave the Kurds pause, for now they knew the mettle of the folk here.

Emma looked to Benik, mouth gaping and face pale, then glanced at Arlo, who twitched up a shoulder to say, *Nothing we can do.*

"Can't hold both walls," Arlo said. "Either we move inside, defend the doorways, and wait for rescue —" he used a javelin to point east — "or we try to escape by wading along the shore. Swim into the lake if we must."

Emma's insides turned cold, as if a creature named despair had crawled in and made a nest. She tried to heave it out but found her finger stroking the knife handle.

It cannot end now. Not this way.

"Move quickly, stay keen, and strike first," Finn said. Oathkeeper filled his fist. The sword's weight and balance felt good. Death or life in a span of sharp steel.

They marched through the streets in a line. The knights were shoulder-to-shoulder, sergeants followed, Elias walked to the side with a shaft on a string.

Realization had dawned slowly. Emma had to be the old Jewish man's friend; her rough men were Arlo, and others she hired at Finn's urging — all of them the same folk the old man had begged Finn to rescue.

If I'd listened, then perhaps Diego might have lived.

The distance between Emma's villa and the old man's was not far. The streets were empty, eerily so. No city should ever be so lifeless. The only sound was heavy breathing, the scuffle of boots, the soft slush of mail. Finn's pulse thumped. They passed a broken cart. A pile of torn robes. Dead bodies — mostly townsfolk, rarely Saracens. A pale-bodied woman sprawled in a doorway; Finn forced his eyes to linger on things better left unseen. *Not Emma...*

Somewhere not far off a dog began barking, rapid and incessant, then stopped with a sudden yelp.

Finn caught a glimpse of the old man's villa rearing over a street corner — stone walls, two levels, two windows. He pointed right, held up a clenched fist, and they glided into the shade of a building and dropped into a crouch. Finn tapped Elias, indicated his eyes with two fingers, then the fingers toward the villa. Lugh made a stirrup with his hands. Elias stepped into it and the Irishman hoisted him so he could slither onto the roof.

They waited, and in the lull fidgeted with shield straps, cuffed sweat, or habitually thumbed sword edges.

Distant shouting at the ramparts intensified — sporadic yells became a constant burble. The day was eye-achingly bright with sunlight, the brightness amplified by the street's pale limestone pavers. It darkened all at once and Finn peered up to a massive pall of smoke, larger than before and shrouding the sun.

That's not good, but at least we get to fight in the shade.

Elias's head appeared over the roof edge. "The old Jew's villa is one to the right of this one. Gate faces the intersection. Two walls extend back to the lake. Seventeen men, by my count. Kurds, by their look. About half linger in the courtyard opposite — you'd see their backs if you peeked around the corner. They run out in twos and threes and throw javelins at the villa. Others creep down the walls, work towards the lakeshore."

Finn nodded at Elias to say, *You know what to do.*

He waved the others close and spelled out the plan. Bearded faces beamed and nodded in unison. Finn kissed Oathkeeper on her flat, checked the mace was tucked into the back of his belt, and finished by making the sign of the cross.

Rollo propped his axe against the wall and slid out his sword. He gave the fuller an affectionate stroke, as one would a favourite dog, then grinned wide enough to show his pointy teeth.

Finn flashed a toothy grin of his own as they rolled around the corner with shields butted up edge-to-edge.

Arlo exhaled, long and slow. "We best get inside."

"They're coming!" Omar yelled from the house.

"So soon? Last time they —"

Emma was cut short by the scrape of boots on the north wall. A bearded face peeked over, leered at her with a mouthful of yellow teeth, then clambered onto the wall and hopped over. Then another. Two more appeared on the south wall.

Arlo snatched up a javelin and skipped forward and threw. One of the men on the wall folded over the stick with a groan, tipped backward and landed with a muffled thud.

Three more dropped into the garden and scuttled forward in a crouch. Emma's gaze latched onto the blade in one of their fists — single-edged and wickedly pointed. Sunlight danced along the polished edge. The shiny recurved steel was mesmerizing, like a cobra, swaying side to side to entrance its prey.

Arlo grabbed her shoulder and shoved her toward the house. "Get inside!"

Emma scooped up the latchbow as a blue-robed man appeared on the wall. She turned, aimed, and squeezed the lever. The bolt hummed out. The man's knees buckled and he disappeared the way he had come.

From the corner of her eye she saw Arlo, wide-legged, sword held in two-fisted in the high guard.

I will not run while he fights.

The prong was in her hand, though she did not remember fumbling it from her belt. Arlo's training mantra rang in her head; *Place the prong, pull the cord, slot the bolt.* She glanced up as Arlo wheeled away, blood flying from somewhere, and she aimed and squeezed the lever. They were intent on hacking Arlo apart and the Saracen only knew he was hit when fire lanced his side. He yelped and dropped next to Arlo.

The others swung toward her.

Damn. I'll never get it reloaded in time.

Emma flung the latchbow and one batted it aside. She pulled the long knife and waved it side-to-side as she shuffled back, heart hammering in her chest, mouth suddenly dry as dust. They followed, grinning like jackals over a carcass. Something nudged her heel ... a javelin, stacked against the wall. Arlo's words rang in her head; *Don't let yourself be taken... Put the knife tip to your chest, slightly left of centre...*

CHAPTER 23

"Kill everyone who isn't already dead," Rollo growled as they came around the corner.

"Then stick 'em again, just to be certain," Lugh added.

Finn paused to get his bearings. Sunlight filtered through the smoke. It looked like rumpled veins of yarn and made the air shimmer with a hellish play of light and shadow. Saracens jogged into the street, javelins held out, then capered forward and threw. A shaft blurred out a window in reply. More Saracens loitered around a stone-lined fountain with their backs to Finn. Those creeping down the walls were no longer in sight.

He dropped a hand and Templars charged in a running wedge of man and shield.

Finn steered toward the man in the middle, taller than the others, doing all the pointing while the others did all the nodding. Another man turned at the last moment but his bark of warning came too late.

They hit with a crash of wood and steel and flesh. A Saracen was struck so hard he flew like a thrown doll and landed on his face. Men were hammered down. Hacked in the spine. Skewered in the kidneys. Alive one moment, gone the next.

Oathkeeper, with all Finn's weight and momentum behind the wicked sharp edge, split Tall Man's head and carried on splitting until she lodged in his sternum. Tall Man toppled headlong. Oathkeeper went with him.

Finn yanked the mace from his belt just as someone fell into his. He sprawled but avoided smashing his face by snaking and falling on his shield. Boots danced around him in a parody of an ancient tribal war dance — a heel came dangerously close to stomping on his windpipe.

Being on the ground tempted death, so he scrambled up, flailing the mace to make space.

Silver flashed at Finn and he heaved up the shield in time to save his head from the same fate as Tall Man. A flurry of sword hacks banged on the shield. Something hummed past his ear — fletching bloomed on the swordsman's chest, and he grunted and folded sideways.

God's bones! Elias, too close again. He glanced at the rooftop, but the Turc was already gone.

A snarling Saracen wheeled toward Finn. He glimpsed a sword sliding greasily out of the man's sternum, vanish the way it had come, Lugh grinning over the man's shoulder. The man blinked, likely wondering why his vision was growing dark, and Finn used the shield to lay him flat.

A husky Saracen was hacking Owen's shield to splinters with a crescent-bladed axe, trying to beat him down with the weight of his blows. Owen crabbed backward to buy space but stepped in blood and slipped onto a knee. The axe whipped up, the Saracen barked a triumphant laugh, and Finn took two lupine strides and unmade the man's skull with a crisp swing of the mace.

Finn let the mace dangle on its wrist strap, gripped Owen by the forearm, and dragged him to his feet. "You all right?" he yelled in his ear.

Owen grunted a reply — just as Finn shoved him toward a blur coming from the right.

Finn went left toward another and nearly butted helmets with the man. He wore a conical helmet, fluted to imitate a turban, and swung a bright-edged sword that bit the rim of Finn's shield. The man yanked at the blade and Finn punched the mace into his teeth. *Should have let the blade go, fool.* A low blow broke his ribs, folded him over like a hinge, and a dropping blow crushed the base of his skull.

A sliver of light came toward Finn's neck. He parried it with the mace shaft, felt the blade scrape on the langets, pivoted and coshed a knee with the mace. The man wailed and flailed a hand at his mangled leg. Finn further maimed him with a crisp blow that broke his shoulder.

His gaze bounded right and left and behind.

Garbled war cries, howls of fear or pain, the smack and clatter of steel and wood. Dust billowed. A half-seen shape staggered in the haze, hitched, and toppled.

Rollo and Serlo stood side-by-side in the street, carving into the Saracens in a well-choreographed dance of destruction. Stab the bottom of a shield to tip the rim forward, grin as Serlo stabbed the exposed neck. Bat aside a thrust meant for Rollo, hack the man's hand off, slam the shield corner to break a jaw. Feint high and scythe low. Cover Rollo as he leans at the hip and stabs a man through the chest. Pivot hard right at the man crowding Rollo, skewer him in the armpit, kick him off your blade.

Knights were too skilled and too cruel for javelin throwers. Such men are trained to fling pointy sticks from a distance, which they do well, but not to stand toe-to-toe with a beast hardened by bloodshed since birth. To no one's surprise, what was left of the stick flingers broke and ran, and the only surprise was they had tried to stand at all.

The street was a butcher's yard. Dead men. Dying men. Pools of blood. An arm lay in the road, missing its owner, and one of Hector's sergeants lay in the courtyard. *One of the Normans, I think? Hector will never forgive me.*

Finn trudged over, placed a boot on Tall Man's shoulder, and levered Oathkeeper's handle back and forth until she came loose with a sucking, crunching sound.

"Ever hear of pulling your stroke?" Rollo mimed swinging from the high guard then drawing it back, just a hair, at the end of the swing. "Splits the bone but keeps the blade free."

Finn spat, in no mood for a ribbing, and swiped a wrist over his cracked lip.

Amic stumbled past and plunged his head into the fountain, came up with a gasp. Lugh ambled up. He bled from a nasty gash on his cheek, but was grinning, apparently happy to add the wound to his collection. He submerged his kettle helmet in the water. He hefted it, tipped it, and bathed in the cascade. Another brimming helmet streamed into his mouth.

Finn waved Lugh over, drank from his helmet-canteen, then poured the last of it over his face and blew water from his moustaches. His body was leaden, his head groggy from the cruel fighting and the crueller heat. The water was cool as a night breeze. Reviving. A sudden thought revived him further.

Emma...

Finn swung toward the villa just as a long, falsetto scream filled the air.

Emma reached behind for a javelin leaned against the wall, groping along the shaft until she grasped it just under the head. *This won't end now ... not this way.*

The javelineers crept toward her, gently placed their heels then rolled to their toes, as if sneaking up on a wild hare. *As if I don't see you?* The one on the left was grinning and licking his lips when the man on the right raised a placating hand and spoke in Arabic.

"Put down the knife, my love, and we will not hurt you."

Emma spoke passable Arabic, learned as part of the relic trade, and sweetly replied in kind. "You will not hurt me, my love?"

The man arched a brow at that. "You speak our language. Are you a believer?"

"I am," Emma lied. "There is only one God, Allah, who created the universe, and Muhammad, peace be upon him, is his messenger on earth."

To become a Saracen, a believer, one only needed to recite these words in front of two witnesses. Speaking it proved she knew it by heart, she hoped, and her blue Bedouin robes might help seal the deception.

"Ah, sister," the man said, and leered.

There was only ugliness in that look. It said he saw through her ruse or, if he believed it, he did not care.

Her hands trembled. Emma raised the long knife in her right hand, waggled it, then crouched and set it on the ground. The trembling stopped. She breathed out. And they rushed in — just as she had hoped. She grabbed and whipped the javelin around and up. The stab was with her left, her weaker hand, but the man's momentum gouged the small, sharp blade into his groin until it lodged in bone.

That was when the screaming began — high-pitched and piercing.

Point to me!

Emma snatched up the long knife and slashed at the other man's face while sliding away. Something hot spattered her face.

Another point to me.

The man pulled a hand from his cheek and a curtain of blood flowed from a gash just under an eye. "Sliced ... me ... you —"

Something blurred across the yard and the man's head flinched to one side, like an invisible hand had slapped him. He stared for a beat, lip curled in a snarl, then went backward in a slow fall.

A peek at the villa found Omar with a bow in hand. He gave a wink. The crotch-gouged man was no longer screaming, but was whimpering instead. Omar strode toward Emma, handed her his bow in passing, and pulled his long knife mid-stride. He crouched, stabbed, twisted the blade, and yanked it free. The whimpering stopped.

More men surged over the walls and Emma despaired. Then she saw they wore white, or black, and some were familiar faces.

Templars.

Finn.

His face was sweaty, crimson-spattered, his eyes sunken and wild. But he was a welcome vision of light and life.

"You came," Emma whispered.

"Aye," Finn said, then flashed a grin, the first in days. "*Festina lente*. I made haste slowly."

She snorted a laugh. Relief flooded her and she wrapped her arms around his shoulders and hung there. Her mouth was at his ear, and she whispered what she had longed to whisper so many times.

"I love you."

She felt warm tears on her cheek, though they were not hers.

"Rest a moment," Finn told Emma. "Then we go to the harbour."

Finn explained that Jerol was there with boats. Emma breathed out at that.

The fight had taken a toll. Finn's blood felt muddy, his bones achy to the marrow. His left elbow throbbed, though he could not say why, and his ribs burned from at least two hits. It was mid-afternoon, he guessed, and night came fast in Outremer. Emma was here, but they were not safe. Not yet.

The others guzzled water from the fountain, poured it over their heads, . splashed it at each other like children at play. Finn drank deeply, wondered how the Christian army fared and if Gerard was dead, and felt a twinge of guilt for thinking it.

Butterflies fluttered from plant to plant in a medley of colour. A black and yellow type with long tails was common, and an orange and white breed, and others with spots in yellow, crimson, and cream. A blue butterfly caught his eye; it was iridescent and the size of his palm. Finn wanted to curl up in the shade of the garden and nap awhile. Here it was easy to forget the horde battering away at the gates of Tiberias. He forced his weary mind to the task at hand.

Lugh and Amic tended to Arlo. Amic unstoppered a vial and poured its contents — a brew of vinegar, garlic, and oregano — over the wounds. Lugh tore his *shemagh*, used the cleaner strips to wrap a slash on his shoulder, and another to plug a hole in his chest.

Emma held bandages, likely in a futile attempt to hide her quivering hands, and chewed a lip. An old man, grey and weathered, stood next to her. The man's bearing and the short, recurved bow slung on his shoulder said he was once a Turc. Elias, who had been collecting usable arrows in the street, now came into the garden. He saw the old man and grinned.

"Omar. Still plucking a string, I see."

"Barely." Omar embraced Elias. "Good to see you, you surly arse-face."

"Likewise, you drunken old turd-licker."

"You seem fond of each other," Finn said, voice dry.

"Reared this bonehead from a pup." Omar spat without looking where it landed. "Taught him most of what he knows about, well, everything."

"Ah, so you're the one to blame for all his meanness," Finn said.

Rollo shuffled over, wringing water from his beard, and nodded a greeting to Emma. "Came to rescue you and found you stabbing Sandpigs in the cods."

Emma shrugged. "Should have come earlier, if you wanted to do it yourself."

She affected a calm and confident air. But Finn felt the quiver in her shoulders when they had embraced, had heard the tremor in her voice.

He stared at Emma; she stared at him. Much had happened. Her whisper in his ears, the heat of her mouth, the import of her words. He nodded at her to acknowledge the unspoken; *I will not abandon you. Ever.*

One of Hector's sergeants whistled from the rooftop. "There are a lot of men in the streets, hundreds, running away from the walls."

"Saracens?" Finn yelled back.

"Christians. Wearing the yellow and red livery of Galilee."

"The ramparts have fallen," Finn said, and cursed himself for dawdling. "We go. Now."

CHAPTER 24

"Should never have left Saforie. Christ's bones, what fat-kidneyed arse-head thought it wise?"

"Shut your mouth," Denis told the muttering sergeant over his shoulder.

Gerard, too tired to care, chose to ignore the sergeant's profane critique. He shifted to Denis, who was grinning tiredly, and Nicholas, a study in forced calm. They all painted a picture of misery. Lips cracked and bleeding. Eyes sunken and staring. Gerard's tongue was so dry he had long since given up trying to wet it and come to think of it, he could not remember the last time he had passed water.

Saracens came in the night. They encircled the camp and every so often loosed arrows or screamed insults. Some brought drums and commenced banging them in a discordant mockery of song. Others chanted praises to their heathen god. Gerard could do nothing but grit his teeth. Sleep was impossible. *Come to think of it ... when was the last time I slept?*

The sun peeked over the horizon and promised another day of suffering. Some devious Saracen arrayed dry brush along the windward side of the camp. It was lit, and now the Christians coughed, and cursed, and rubbed heat-sore eyes. Faris swooped from the smoke as if a company of demons just arrived in the mortal realm. Harassing attacks were regular enough to be timed with an hourglass, if they had thought to bring one. Destriers were the targets, and footmen, less valuable than a destrier, marched alongside the horses as human shields.

Faris charged thrice, and thrice the Templars and Hospitallers counter-charged, drove them off, but lost men and horses in the doing of it. Guy altered their line of march toward the Horns of Hattin. Wells were there, local men said, and the lure of water was strong.

"Hell," the muttering sergeant said. "We're in hell. Fire, smoke, ruckus, all we need now is —"

A sharp slap rang out and Denis hissed, "I said shut your mouth."

Gerard again did not bother to look around. Brother Nicholas began spluttering, tried to stifle it, then gave in to a racking, lung-rending cough. The sounds of coughing and spitting spread down the line like a contagion.

The army was unravelling.

Footmen carried on marching, a death slog, smoke shadowing them like a plague. The Saracens stacked brush along the route, too, and the stacks went up in flames one at a time, running just ahead of the vanguard. The Horns of Hattin were spectres in the haze. The southern horn was larger, flat-topped, but the northern horn rose to a sharper point.

They did not march for long before a squire came to fetch Gerard. He left Nicholas with one hundred or so knights and rode to the gathering of nobles. King Guy stood in the middle, awkward as a lump of mud, while Raymond did all the talking.

"Gökböri and his division shifted behind us, between us and Turan. There is no going back. Only forward. We must break through." Raymond paused for effect. "To do so, we must charge their centre, and charge hard. Lead with my knights, and the Templars, and follow with footmen. Knights will gouge a hole. Footmen will gouge it wider. Keep Saladin from raking our flanks."

"Smash the bastards open!" someone yelled, with no reply.

Gerard squinted into the smoky haze. The Horns were larger now, and between them strung Taqi al-Din's men, then a gap, then Saladin's men. Saracens sat astride the road to Tiberias. Footmen. Horsemen. Archers. Thousands upon thousands of men. Wan sunlight winked on steel. Christian footmen arrayed on the ground in front of the nobles, though the right flank drifted toward the northern Horn and the blue lake beyond it.

Gerard's mind was drifting with the footmen when Guy prompted, "Master Gerard?"

"God wills it." Gerard gave his usual answer to half-heard questions, then added a firm, "We'll bathe in the Galilee by end of the day."

Raymond shook his head.

"Taqi al-Din holds the left, Saladin the right. Their men are professionals; they await our obvious attempt. Thus they will hold." Balian pointed to the west. "The weak link is there, the footmen — the *muttawiyah* — the same bastard volunteers tormenting us with fire and smoke. Charge them and they will scatter like chickens in the yard."

"Water is that way," Raynald said, and jabbed a finger northeast, toward the Horns of Hattin. "The village of Hattin has wells. The lake is beyond. Best get to either, and soon, and to do so we must break Taqi al-Din or Saladin. Fight real warriors." He smiled at the prospect, then put on a mock fretful face. "Or do you only fight poltroons, Lord Balian?"

"I fight poltroons whenever and wherever I can. Easy way to win. Why, just last —"

Horns blared from the Saracen line.

"Here they come!" someone barked.

Balian stared into the smoke, blinking, then yanked his destrier around and spurred back to the rear guard. Gerard's gaze worked up the long, brown slope before them, stopping at the ridgeline above. A mass of steel-clad faris boiled at the crest, flowed over, then flooded down unchecked. Behind more were waiting and they came in three surging tides. The first row of Genoese crossbowmen, kneeling, triggered a cloud of bolts. The second row, standing, triggered another. Saracens went down, men were thrown, horses screamed — then, inexplicably, the Genoese turned and began shoving their way away from the carnage.

Most of Henry's coin spent on two volleys. Damn.

Gerard cringed as the tide of Saracens rolled in, hit with a smashing clatter, gouged into the footmen, wheeled away in unison. Screams rent the air. Garbled orders drifted. The second surge of faris closed in fast, hit hard, burrowed deeper into the footmen, sloughed along the front and wheeled away. Footmen held but teetered at the breaking point. Several contingents began shifting further toward the north Horn.

"Charge! At Saladin!" Gerard flailed a hand over his shoulder until Eudo shoved a lance under his arm. Eighty or so knights and twice that number of sergeants formed, crisply mended their line, then trotted out with shouts of, "For God!" And the Templar war cry, *"Beauséant!"*

Azrael, scenting blood in the air, went into a full gallop in three blinks of an eye. The Master swung the lance level, cinched it tight to his side, and steered toward a faris in shining mail and blue robes. Scores of heavy hooves rumbled like surf breaking on rock. Faris were reforming, not together yet, and Gerard glimpsed black beards and white eyes. Then his lance tore in, hit something hard, sheared away, caught something soft and snapped with a crack loud as thunder.

Azrael charged at a faris bringing a lance in line. Gerard leaned and coiled the lance shaft under his arm, then twisted and hauled the Saracen from the saddle. Eudo's courser trampled him in a medley of thumps and shouts. Ahead, a sea of Saracens stretched to the skyline — endless rows of spearmen, mobs of horsemen, clusters of archers.

Black streaks sliced the air overhead. It was endless. The sound was like a giant flock of hummingbirds in flight. Sunlight flickered with passing shadows.

Azrael lowered his shoulder and flattened a man, stomped on him for good measure, then snaked out his long neck to snap at another with his chisel-like teeth. The great sword filled Gerard's fist and he screamed, "For God! For Mary!" He found himself staring at a back swathed in green robes, and he ran it through, back to front. The man grunted in surprise and fell forward. Gerard hacked at another across the empty saddle.

Trumpets began blaring, loud and incessant, and he kneed Azrael around on his length and spurred him toward the Christian line.

He reined in beside the king and turned to study the damage they had done. Saladin's men milled, mended their line, then came back together. Seamless. Intact.

A count of his eighty knights found sixty or so. Urs was gone; his missing eye gave him a blind spot, and it must have finally been his undoing. Odon was gone too — his sullen resentment gone with him. A handful of knights and sergeants trudged back on foot.

Denis came alongside. Crimson spattered his helmet and coif. His destrier brayed like a donkey and dropped to his front knees. Denis made no move to dismount. Then Gerard noticed the multitude of shafts jutting from his cousin's chest, stomach, and shoulder. Denis grinned one last grin, then melted to the ground.

"Denis…"

A pained throb began in Gerard's heart, for Denis, then a throb in his ribs, from a blow he did not remember. His weary mind trudged off and he found himself home, in Flanders. There was Denis, a chubby lad, asleep under a tree. And there was Gerard. Japes filled their days. Hiding in the tithe barn. Shouting abuse at the serfs. Throwing rocks at their oxen. *I've known Denis all my life, and now he is gone...*

Gerard's mind came back with a rush and a crack. Men were yelling. Someone was waving the banner of Tripoli.

"Break them open!" Raymond bellowed.

His hundred thundered past the Templars trailing a cloud of dirt. Footmen let them pass, then charged in a mob of swaying spears and stomping boots. Templars had charged Saladin, probed his line, taken their licks and given a few. Now Raymond would try Taqi al-Din.

The *conroi* was tight, the charge short, but the Saracens ready. Trumpets blared just before impact. Taqi al-Din's massed troops parted like the Red Sea, the Christians flowed through the sudden gap, then the Saracens seamlessly closed. The *conroi* was gone. Disappeared. Swallowed. Like one hundred men had ridden off a cliff.

Eudo said, "God's blood, what in the..."

"Traitorous wretch!" Gerard shouted. "O God, smite him, curse his bones!"

But Gerard, despite claims otherwise, knew Raymond was no traitor. Taqi al-Din's horsemen refused the charge, swung aside, let it pass and reformed. *So neat — step lively and let them barge past, like a bull chasing a cape.* Now Raymond milled on the far side of the Saracens, downhill, and climbing back into the fight was nigh on impossible. Raymond was gone. Out of it.

The footmen had staggered to a stop, milled in confusion at the vanished *conroi*, then scattered like roaches. Many ran for the northern Horn. Faris howled at the thrill of the chase, spurred after and shot shafts into backs, or stooped from the saddle to spear or hack. Easy as spearing fish in a puddle.

Gerard watched laymen die, hunted for sport, and could do nothing to aid them. Horrid sounds drifted up — screams, clangs, yips. Vigour drained from the nobles, as if an invisible claw gouged into their collective chest and tore out their heart.

He slid from Azrael and threw the great sword point-first, expecting it to stick in the dirt and waver back and forth elegantly. It toppled over with a metallic clatter. *Suitable end to a bad jest of a morning.* Gerard dragged off his helmet and coif; his eyes were dry and hot, and he rubbed them with his finger and thumb, which only made it worse.

Their charges had churned the earth to a powdery dust. Dead and lamed lay between the Christians and Saracens. Most of the dead bristled with arrows. Thousands of them jutted from the ground, like a sinister harvest conjured from the earth itself.

King Guy was muttering, "Must get through ... must get through..."

Gerard wanted to slap his face, to bring him back, but his side hurt too much to lift his arm. He checked over his shoulder for the True Cross. Still there — a gaudy thing, encased in gold and studded with rubies. Rufinus, the Bishop of Acre, stood in front of it with a gaggle of priests and knights of Acre.

With it, we cannot lose; we must protect it. Gerard glanced north, intending to order the king to order a contingent of spearmen to shift nearer to Rufinus, but most of the footmen were streaming in a long, ragged line toward the north Horn. Thousands of men were broken and fleeing. Horns blared in the distance; Taqi al-Din's flank began shifting to let them pass. The scene stole Gerard's breath.

"Craven bastards!" Raynald roared.

Others joined him, and in loud voices cursed, jeered, and cajoled the footmen. To no effect.

Gerard's voice was a raspy murmur. "We will be exposed, shot like flies — the horses too."

His eyes darted about, seeking what, he was not sure. They settled on the south Horn, flat-topped and lower than the north Horn. He stared, blinking slowly, then shoved down the bile of fear rising in his throat. *I am Gerard de Ridefort, Master of the Templars, Master of the Poor Knights of Christ and of the Temple of Solomon. I will not lose to a rabble of heathens.*

"Get to the south Horn!" Gerard yelled. "Claim the top. Defend it. Make them come at us!"

Terror gripped the soldiers of Tiberias. Fear was so ripe the air carried its stench. Soldiers stampeded toward the citadel like a herd of cattle. Few held weapons. Fewer still paid the Templars any heed.

One slowed long enough to yell, "Oy, Whitebacks, you're going the wrong way! The wall is breached. Saracens are coming."

Templars ignored the stampede and battered their way through like lone fish swimming against a run of spawning salmon. They moved in the boar's snout formation — a moving wedge, a human spear. It was an old array, borrowed from their ancestors, and was meant to break an enemy line by sheer weight and force. Finn and Rollo were the point. Then Serlo and the sergeants arrayed back along two edges. Emma tucked into the middle. She lugged Arlo with an arm under his;

Owen lugged at the other arm. Elias and Omar came behind with shafts notched on strings.

Almost there...

The last street corner before Emma's villa lay ahead. They rolled around it — and came nose-to-nose with a pack of Saracens.

Finn glimpsed black beards and turbans - and had just enough wits to shout, "Kill them!"

Three hard strides and he shield-slammed the Saracen in the middle — older than the others, with the fanciest spiral helmet, wearing the shiniest mail shirt. The man went over backwards in a cloud of dust. Finn pounced on him, smashed his shield's point into his face, again and again, until the strap tore out of the board.

He dropped the ruined board on the man's ruined face and yanked out the mace. Shafts blurred past — Omar and Elias. Someone shoulder-slammed him. Finn was half-spun around and found himself staring at the side of a turban-wrapped helmet. He cut it from the wearer's shoulders and watched the helmet topple one way, the body the other.

Finn spared a glance.

Lugh was at his elbow, shoving a hunched man off his blade, and Rollo was barging in, carving a hole in the Saracens. A wide-shouldered Kurd stood firm and they met shield-to-shield, shoving, scraping and grinding, until Rollo levered the other man's shield back and stabbed over the top. A wet gurgle and the resistance disappeared so quickly Rollo staggered and almost fell.

Serlo and Amic ploughed into the hole Rollo had made. They moved like twin bulls, side by side, and Saracens were carved down or battered aside. A cow-eyed Saracen tried to make a stand. Amic's shield staggered him sideways and an eyeblink later Serlo's knocked him flat.

Sergeants and Turcs hustled Emma, Owen, and Arlo into the chasm and through the villa gate. Saracens milled, not certain if they should pursue Serlo's band or fight Finn's group, and Finn took advantage of their confusion.

"Turn," he said, and he, Rollo, and Lugh wheeled to face the way they had come. "Reverse!" The three shuffled backward toward the villa.

One of Hector's sergeants, the Breton, drifted in behind to guard their arses.

"Oy, well met, laddie," the Breton said, and snorted a laugh. Finn heard the bony crunch of a mace coshing a Saracen, and a moment later stepped over a twitching body.

Saracens shoved and barked at each other, reformed, and tromped after the Templars.

Finn shuffled backward into the gate, wide enough for two men to fight side by side, though the low wall to either side meant Saracens could come over and get behind. A wood cart, tipped on its side, lay in the courtyard with a smattering of dead Saracens. A sergeant, the Gascon, Finn guessed, twitched in the dirt. The Poulain lay further on. *Hector will never forgive me now, certes...*

Serlo, standing at the opposite end of the yard, caught Finn's eye, and motioned toward the harbour to say he would clear a path and hold it. Finn nodded, then jabbed Oathkeeper toward the street to say, *We'll deal with these.*

Saracen curs had been hounding him all day. He had thinned the pack a bit, but the remainder, which were many, would tell a different tale. Christians ran. Suffered dishonourable deaths. Soon they would convince themselves Tiberias was a glorious victory and nary a Saracen had died there. Their lies were of no concern to Finn, for men would say what they pleased, but he used the notion to sluice marrow into his weary bones. He breathed deep and his second wind arrived. Fire flowed into his veins and swirled there a moment, limbered his muscles with its warmth.

"Guard our backs and mind the walls," Finn ordered Lugh and the Breton.

These Saracens were better trained than the Kurdish stick flingers, certes, but still no equal to a Templar. He and Rollo stepped boldly to the dance.

"Just another day in the practice yard," Rollo said.

Saracens stood in a line. Bulging eyes. Bearded faces. Glittering mail. They were frozen by two knights, unafraid of death, perhaps mad enough to come at a score of enemies with smiles on their lips. One began trilling, *le-le-le-le-le*, a shrill tribal song intended to put fear into a man's heart. Finn had heard it so much over the years he was oblivious to the ruckus.

He ducked a thrust at his face. Then he hip-hinged forward and stabbed the man through the breastbone, and with the sword dragged him and flung him into the legs of those to his right. Finn jouked away from the congested mess and three spears swayed in time. Had they read his body, not the feint, they would have stayed centred. Their eagerness cost them. In a stride he was inside the length of their spears, the points rendered useless.

Finn swooped at the first and smashed his knee with the mace. The man hopped backward like a wounded hare. Finn leaned and thrust through the neck of the hare's neighbour, sawed Oathkeeper aslant, and closed his eyes against the wet spray. The third man, no longer trilling, shoved crosswise with a spear shaft. Finn shattered the shaft with the mace and stabbed him below the rib line.

Rollo was wreaking similar carnage. The Norman was grinning like a lunatic, humming a discordant tune as he laboured, the nag of old wounds forgotten in the bliss of a fight. Feint at a man's eyes, stab him in the groin; sway aside from a thrust, come back with a scything cut across the ankles. Shrug off a weak poke. Grasp the ricasso of the great sword and stab him through the guts.

Finn checked over his shoulder. Lugh was sliding and stabbing at two Saracens. One crumpled like wet paper. The Irishman shifted his feet, quick as liquid, and slashed at the second, sent him hopping back with a hand pasted to his thigh.

The dupes in the congested mess had freed themselves of their dead mate, and three came forward waving long, curved swords and crouching behind little round shields.

Instinct took over. Training and experience and meanness came with it. Finn fell into a rhythm.

One-handed grip in the high guard, cut across and feel her bite. Parry a slash; take a hit to the ribs and praise God for well-made mail. Slide and shift, nimble and quick. Mace-shove and thrust, boot the man off the blade; glide left and away, cut to the right out of the low guard. Carve a thigh. Block a dropping slice with the mace. Take a spear on the shoulder. Smirk in defiance. Stab a man in the liver, not too deep, and swirl Oathkeeper in a spray of ruby droplets.

Finn grinned at the shambles. The Saracen wall was breaking.

Spearmen and swordsmen needed training to fight together cohesively and effectively, and these had a small dose. But they also needed effective leadership, which had been denied them with the death of the man in the fancy spiralled helmet and shiny mail. Lamed Saracens jabbered and bled. Dead Saracens clogged the ground. Those still standing shouted orders at each other and managed to muddle a simple situation.

Finn and Rollo pounced on their confusion.

They carved in with disdain, like knights tilting with squires, yet with care enough to avoid a tragic miscalculation. Mark your prey. Listen to Oathkeeper. Keep the tail of your eye on Rollo; know he is eyeing you. Stab upward, under the floating rib, twist and pull out. Duck and weave. Pommel punch a man in the eye. *Didn't see that coming, I wager...* Finish him with an edge slash across the jugular. Ignore a weak poke to the ribs. Parry a cut with the mace. Slide past. Bat down a blade aimed for Rollo. Slice the swordsman across the face. Feint at a knee. Mace a man in the throat. Take a ringing spear thrust on the helmet; sway aside while Rollo unmakes the spearman's shoulder.

The last three undamaged Saracens hovered for a moment, swapped glances, then broke and ran. Finn and Rollo bobbed their heads at each other to say, *Job well done, Brother*, and shuffled backward through the mess they had made.

The Breton crouched over a Saracen, methodically smashing away with a mace.

Lugh was on his knees, open-mouthed and panting, leaning on his sword thrust into the dirt. Finn thought him fatigued. Almost taunted him for weakness. Then he saw the blood slathering Lugh's side, streaming through the links of his mail, pooling in the dirt.

God, no. Not Rooster...

"Lugh of Omagh, on your feet." Finn used the man's birth name and his sternest voice, like a father scolding a wayward child. "Get moving, lazy arse."

Finn waved the blood-mad Breton over, caught Lugh under the arms, and hauled him up. He and the Breton half dragged, half carried Lugh through Emma's garden while Lugh blathered on about being done for, about going on without him.

"And when did you grow so maudlin, eh?" Finn grunted.

"Irish. Prone to fits of maudlin."

Rollo guarded their backs. He strolled backward, gaze nailed on the yard, his red-slathered great sword yoked over his shoulders.

The carnage made by Serlo and Amic was easy to follow. A dead man here, a dead man there, a pool of blood still soaking into the hard-packed earth. And a hand, bronze-skinned, with pink palms and surprisingly well-manicured nails. *No Templar would be so neat and trim...* They went around the wall, found Elias and Omar holding there, then ploughed across the field and lurched their way down the trail. Two stone pillars, each just taller than a man, bracketed the pier at the lakeshore.

Emma sprinted up, took Lugh's shoulder from Finn, and with the Breton lugged him toward the boats rocking along the pier. Jerol pulled out a haversack of bandages, herbals, and remedies and began tending the Irishman.

Serlo leaned against a stone pillar like a wind-tipped palm tree. Blood oozed from a nasty gash over his brow and cheek, and more from a gash on his forearm. He was slathered from head to toe in crimson and shiny wet gobs. Most of it was spray or splatter from the Saracens he had mauled; his pale face said some of it was his own. Amic looked little better.

A throng milled on the shore — two score, at least. Women. Children. Haggard-faced men. Elderly couples. More waded in the shallows, drawn by the lure of boats. Their eyes flicked about like trapped animals, for trapped they were. They were local folk. Jews, mostly, some Poulains, and a handful of Maronites, by their dress. Three dogs circled and barked at the tumult.

"God's bones." Rollo fetched the great sword off his neck and planted the tip between his boots. He leaned on the pommel and said, "That's a lot of folks."

Serlo arched a brow to say, *Too many to take with us.*

CHAPTER 25

The late afternoon was filled with shouted commands, tribal chants and thumping drums, and the air carried the sour stink of smoke and defeat. Christians marched for the south Horn and Saracens shifted around them like water.

The slope was littered with spears, shields, swords, and dead or dying men and horses. A cart meant to carry waterskins lay on its side, empty. Gerard passed a dead horse; weak sunlight shone on bared yellow teeth. Clusters of footmen sat in the sun, bearing no wounds — on their bodies, anyway. The Bishop of Acre harangued them to stand and fight, but it fell on deaf ears; the True Cross was raised before blind eyes. The king had ordered tents to be set up at the base of the slope, changed course and abandoned them, and now sheets of red canvas draped the brush like waves of blood.

Fear had been a rarity at Saforie. Boredom, ignorance, and hunger were rife amid the laymen; confidence, contempt, and suspicion ran amuck among the nobles. Perhaps homesickness by those newly arrived in Outremer. But not fear. Never fear. Now it was everywhere, shared by commoner and noble alike, and it spread like a contagion.

Guy set up the royal tent on the south Horn and sequestered himself inside. Hospitallers came bearing word that Balian of Ibelin and Reginald of Sidon had charged from the rearguard, battered their way through, then rode to the south-west. Gerard watched from the Horn but could see nothing to confirm nor deny Balian's escape. Raynald muttered into his red beard but kept the words to himself.

An arrow had pierced Gerard's forearm neatly between the bones. Eudo snapped the shaft and slid it free without so much as a grimace from the Master. But pain enlivened him. Sudden fury rose like bile in his throat. He spurred Azrael and trotted along the row of remaining Templars, ragged and battered and thirsty, but still more than a hundred fierce and beating hearts.

"I swear never to shun combat with any infidel, and to never fly from an enemy." Gerard recited snippets of a Templar's vows. He raised his bloody arm and pointed at a tent behind the Saracen line. "See that tent? That is Saladin. We do not surrender to the Devil. We are hammers of God! Charge him, kill him, and we win the day!"

It was as reasonable a plan as any.

Nicholas made it a mantra. "Hammers of God! Kill Saladin!"

"Kill Saladin!" arose the cry from scores of parched throats.

Templars formed a *conroi*, sergeants and knights now intermingled. Hospitallers wedged Templars. God's warriors would ride together, a melange of white and black. The *Gonfanier* hoisted the black-and-white standard and a hundred voices sang, *Non nobis, non nobis, Domine, sed nomini tuo da gloriam.* They thundered off the Horn, holding swords and axes aloft and screaming, "For God!"

Azrael lowered his head, warming to the task, then stumbled and went down on one knee. Gerard toppled from the stirrups and came up on his knees. From there he watched the *conroi* roll on, Nicholas leading the charge now, and smash into the Saracen line with a mighty roar that shook the heavens. Screams and yells and curses rebounded.

The wedge ploughed in. Saracens fell before it, a cloud of dirt boiled behind it, and the furrow of destruction was long and wide. The black-and-white battle flag flew above the masses.

Turkish horsemen wheeled in and shot arrows point-blank as the wedge rumbled past. Templars and Hospitallers fell but the charge swept on and up the slope, into the teeth of volleys from Kurdish archers. These they reaped like ripe corn or sent running.

Ahead lay the massive tent.

Gerard glimpsed a man in black standing there, impassively stroking his beard.

Saladin … they're going to kill him!

And as he thought it, the storm of arrows redoubled, and a contingent of Mamluks, bright in their yellow silk, poured into the space before their Sultan. The black-and-white standard stalled, wavered, then disappeared into the dirt murk. Gone. Just like that.

The haze swirled and thinned, to reveal a smattering of Templar and Hospitallers fighting back-to-back in ragged groups. Pons, the Turcopolier, was reeling like a drunkard. Then he hitched to a stop and toppled slowly, like a just-felled tree. Black and white bodies lay like sea wrack but a stone's throw from the Sultan.

Sunlight flashing on steel caught Gerard's eye. There, on his feet, a lone Templar ran at the Sultan with his great sword hoisted back. Black streaks blurred out and the Templar, Nicholas, flinched and staggered as a hail of shafts hit home. He fell not far from the Sultan's black lacquered chair.

An uproar of voices, Saracen voices, arose in a mighty cheer. Drums and trumpets and song flowed like water over the land.

Gerard turned away, grinding his teeth, nostrils flaring rhythmically. Eudo was gone, doubtless dead, and Azrael was done. The destrier stood on widespread legs, head hung at the end of his long neck, his once-glorious hide dry and dusty as stone. He did the destrier the favour of removing the saddle and laying it in the ground beside him, then gave him one last shoulder rub. He propped his head on the horse's trembling neck, and a surge of pity, fear and despair swamped him for a moment until he pushed it aside.

"Put me afoot and put me in my grave, aye?" Gerard spoke into Azrael's ear, with a half-smile. He slipped off the bridle. "No need to fret, Brother. You are too fine to be lashed to a cart. Some faris will see you for what you are."

He left Azrael there and limped up the Horn.

Saracens came up the slope in waves. Templars and Hospitallers met them at the edge and drove them off. Odon fought there and died, and his reproach with him, and Maban, the Castellan, and other Templars of note.

"Dogs behind us!" someone yelled.

Templars wheeled. Kurds clambered over the far lip of the Horn and seven knights from Acre charged them. Each was hemmed in and hacked down. The True Cross was there, held by two squires, and Rufinus stood wide-legged, bellowing maledictions. A blue-robed Kurd with a crescent-bladed axe split the Bishop of Acre's shoulder and his bellowing stopped with a wet gurgle. The Kurd straddled him, and with business-like precision began hacking him limb from limb, like a butcher preparing a boar for market. Sunlight glinted on the axe as it rose and fell.

Gerard dimly thought he should go to the bishop's aid, but then the Hospitallers did, and drove off the Kurds. Too late. The True Cross went with them and disappeared over the precipice of the slope.

It had happened so fast — like a spider scuttling from its lair, snagging its prey, then dragging it away to some dark corner. Gerard came back to the front, bones grinding in their sockets, and the scene further unnerved him. Mamluks formed at the base of the slope.

Death was upon the Christians.

Gerard's throat hurt, his arm hurt, his chest hurt. He looked to the sky. Perhaps he hoped to see Michael there with his flaming sword, coming to their aid, but saw only ravens and vultures wheeling over the field.

"Let us pray, Brothers," Henri said, voice calm. His fair hair was plastered to his head with sweat, his lips bleeding, but his eyes shone with the light of bliss, the fire of defiance.

I've gutted a noble family. Killed the first de Mailly at Cresson, and now I've killed the second at Hattin. Nay, God's bones, I killed the Order...

Henri thrust his father's sword, Jakelin's sword, into the sun-baked ground. Rosaries hung from the guard, the long blade quivered, and the quivering swung the cords in a rhythm. An iron cross tapped against the blade and made a metallic tune. Templars and Hospitallers knelt around the sword-shrine. Words from the Seven Penitential Psalms, the Psalms of Confession, dribbled from a score of cracked lips. Several tongues prayed at once. French. Catalonian. English. The multitude of languages and prayers made a cacophonous loop.

O Lord, hear my prayer, and let my cry come unto thee... No one who practises deceit will dwell in my house; no one who speaks falsely will stand in my presence...

Have mercy on me, O God, for I know my sins, and my sin is always before me ... deliver me from the guilt of bloodshed ...

O Lord, rebuke me not in thy indignation; have mercy upon me, for I am weak; O Lord, heal me; for my bones are vexed, my soul is sore vexed...

Gerard stared at the altar-sword, at its aged pommel, its well-worn edges, and something stirred in his breast. Warmth radiated from the steel, surged into him and soothed him. Hate passed. Pride withered. The fire of vengeance was quenched and shame settled in its place.

God cut you down. You've been an arrogant churl, Gerard. He thought he weaved grand schemes, burnished his name while burning Raymond's, though all along it had been nothing but falsehoods. Lies. Vanities. He spun webs in the corner of a dark room alone, round and round, gaining nothing, hurting everyone. His body shuddered with racking sobs, but no tears came, for he was dry inside.

And Finn. I did you grievous wrong, Brother, when you could have aided God. I pray you not suffer long in the Home for Wayward Brothers, and beg your forgiveness, Finn —

"They're coming," someone said. The voice sounded hollow and lifeless.

Henri took up his sword, wrapped the rosaries around his wrist, and eyed Gerard from under lowered brows. The Master tried to rise but his legs refused to obey. Other brothers, feeble, wasted, wounded, lay on the ground praying for a good end. Henri lurched to the edge of the Horn and Nicasius de Burgio, a renowned Hospitaller, went with him. The first Mamluk over the lip died, as did the second and third. Templar and Hospitaller fought side by side in a blur of white and black, a harmonized dance of flashing steel. The knights were stone-faced. Frugal in their movements. They called out quarry, each to the other, with voices steady as a labourer reaping corn. Mamluks reeled away, broken and panting.

Knights and sergeants staggered over to join the fight. Such defiance stirred Gerard. *I will not die on my knees like a cur.* He climbed to his feet and stood there, swaying.

A Mamluk with a mace wheeled toward him. Gerard was one-on-one with a demon, nothing new, though just then the demon fixed him with the glassy stare of a killer. His sword came up, too late, and the mace arced in and clanged from his helmet.

His knees caved and the ground punched him in the back. He gazed up at the sky and blinked.

The last thing he saw was a blue expanse of nothingness.

"Here he is. Still breathing too."

The speaker's French was impeccable, the accent tinged with English. Strong hands hauled Gerard into a kneeling position.

"Take this water, Master Gerard."

A figure held out a cup. He was backlit by sunlight, haloed, and for a moment Gerard thought it the Saviour come to greet him. Then he felt the throb in his head, the agony in his arm, the ache in his back and chest. *No, I am alive, sadly.* Gerard took the proffered cup and drank. It tasted of ash. He took the man in. Body like a megalith, beard the colour of straw, pale eyes below a black *shemagh*. *Not a Saracen, but I know this man…*

Gerard gaped while his memory sifted for the name to match the face. "Conrad of Warwick," he said after a moment. "You served Robert of Saint Albans."

Two of Robert's band of apostates had escaped God's justice — Conrad, and Simon of Durham, both Englishmen. The Order, in the years after, continued the hunt with paid killers — to no avail. Gerard should not have been surprised to find Conrad with Saladin. *Where else would he be?*

"Aye, and well met, Master Gerard." Conrad tipped his head, as if inviting the Master's reproach, then smiled to say he did not care if it was offered. "We shall forgo reminiscences — and good, I say, for there are other pressing matters to discuss."

Gerard managed a defiant air. Conrad carried on.

"I am sent by the Sultan. He is magnanimous in victory, generous of heart, and offers life. My Lord will spare you, on the condition you convert to the one true faith, and likewise your brothers."

"Your *Lord*?" Gerard tried to spit in disgust but only sputtered. "Dog, tell your *master* I will not convert to save my skin, nor will my brothers. We will not forsake our God, unlike you, apostate. And unlike you, who shall bathe in eternal hellfire, we will live in perpetual bliss with our benevolent Lord. We cannot lose, you see, and victory is ours come what may."

"Aye?" Conrad laughed like a jackal barking. "Even now buzzards feast on the lords of Outremer. Why, you once bragged Templar lances would prop up the sky, should it fall, and lo, it has fallen and you and yours grovel on bended knee."

"The Order is eternal and will not be dimmed. Ever."

"Fool, nothing is eternal. There is no heaven or hell, just as there is nothing to be gained in your death." Conrad's voice hardened. "Take the offer. It will not be proffered again."

"We choose death. We choose paradise."

Gerard and Conrad stared at one another, neither blinking, then Conrad shook his head to say he should have expected such stubbornness. He gazed over the Horns. "The Koran forbids killing defenceless prisoners. It preaches compassion for the defeated." He fixed his gaze on Gerard. "But you will be given no mercy. Saladin will not allow Templars to live, nor

Hospitallers. The Sultan decreed your heads shall be hacked from your bodies by men with no training at arms. Mullahs. Scribes. Sufis. Your ending will be messy."

Gerard scowled at that final insult. Then his beard split in a smile.

"Your *master* is unnerved by our fierceness, by our willingness to die, and lacks the will to fight us again. He chooses the coward's path."

Gerard shifted away from the apostate as a demonstration of his disdain. A savage bliss filled him. He knelt at the precipice of something grand, transmutation perhaps, and soon he would meet Jesus and Mary. Pain smoothed to a minor nuisance. Thirst no longer tormented him.

"To your feet!" someone barked in heavily accented French.

Gerard ignored the order, and was bodily lifted and carried toward the Sultan's tent, where no doubt he would gain paradise.

Saladin stood in the filtered shade of his tent awning. The Sultan was smaller than Gerard had expected, at least in body, though in the moment he seemed large as a giant. He boasted sharp lips that never said *please*, ears that never heard the word *no*, and a nose that rarely smelled defeat. A long, black beard glistened with oil. Kohl lined his eyes. He applied kohl to his right eye three times and twice to his left eye, like the Prophet was said to have done, which made the right eye larger and fiercer. He wore a snow-white turban now, and a matching vest, wrapped with a brilliant red sash.

Kurds brought the noble prisoners to him, Gerard among them, and King Guy, and Raynald. Guy stepped forward, then froze, seemingly uncertain of how one king should treat another.

"Bow to the Sultan, cur," Conrad said.

A red-headed Mamluk shoved Guy's head, and Guy bowed. A ripple of laughter arose from the Sultan's entourage. Saladin did not laugh. He stared, chin lifted expectantly, as if willing to hear a request but unlikely to grant it.

"Greetings, Sultan," Guy said, in French. "I beg you spare my men. They fought nobly, and for their God, not for me."

Saladin stared, unmoved, and said, "Your men, those fit enough, shall be sold in the slave markets of Damascus. I give them life, of a sort. Your Turcopoles defied the one true faith to take up the yoke of Christianity, a sin punishable by death, thus all shall be executed as the traitorous dogs they are."

"You are mistaken, Sultan. They were born Christian. They did not convert —"

Saladin cut Guy off by slicing a hand though the air. He waved a Mamluk over, and from him took a silver cup, which he handed to Guy.

"Iced rose water. For you."

The silver was dewy with cold. Guy shrank from it. He passed the cup to Raynald without taking his gaze from the Sultan. Raynald raised the cup to Guy and downed it, the apple of his throat working up and down.

"Splendid," Raynald gasped, and made a show of smacking his lips.

"I did not give this drink to that man," the Sultan said, his voice as icy as the cup. His dark eyes narrowed to knife-like slits. "Custom prescribes that a man who gives food or drink to a prisoner cannot harm him, but you, King Guy, gave the cup to Raynald without my consent."

Saladin considered his cadre of advisors, his dark gaze seeking one, until a wizened man in resplendent robes stepped forward and pronounced his agreement in a speech of some length.

"Just so." Saladin's voice was a purr. He added a vicious smile to say some notion had been confirmed. "Raynald of Châtillon, demon of Oultrejordain. Brigand. Blasphemer. You are lower than a dog. A stain on the world."

Raynald placed a palm on his chest and offered a mocking half-bow.

"Oath-breaker." Saladin hissed the word.

Raynald shrugged. "Kings have always acted thus."

These were the last words uttered by Raynald.

The red-headed Mamluk held a sword and tilted the silver handle toward the Sultan. Saladin grasped it and stepped and struck. The strike was fast as a serpent. Raynald did not so much as flinch, then his head toppled forward, his body backward. The silver cup fell with a clatter and rolled in a small circle before coming to a stop. A murmur of awe for a deed well done coursed through the Saracens.

Saladin handed the sword to the Mamluk. He took two steps and kneeled, palms fitted together in a pose of gratitude, then dipped two fingers into Raynald's blood and smeared it on his forehead as a sign that his vow was met. He shifted his stare from Raynald to Guy, then grinned like a cat — a mix of scorn and arrogance, a promise of death and reckoning. *You are mine to toy with as I please*, it said.

Guy was spattered with crimson, trembling, and muttering, "My God, my God."

Saladin arose and wiped his fingers on a towel handed to him by the Mamluk. He regarded Guy and said, "A lion does not spill the blood of lions, just as a king does not kill a king." He nodded at Raynald's twitching boots. "But that man's perfidy and insolence went too far."

Gerard visibly sagged at the knees. Raynald, the Red Wolf, once larger than life, was now dead by the Sultan's hand. His death was one of biggest horrors in a day full of horrors. The Sultan took a chair and was given a cup of iced rose water. He gave a languid hand roll to say, *Begin the show.*

Gerard followed the Sultan's gaze to a cleared area, where holy and learned men were handed swords, then guided toward a Templar or Hospitaller.

The horrors began anew.

Learned men killed men of war. Some struck neat blows. Most did not, and chopped and hewed and sawed until the grisly deed was done. The watching Saracens jeered and laid wagers on how many hacks it would take to carve off a head. For their part, Templars and Hospitallers did not cry, nor beg, nor try to flee. Kurdish guards ordered them to bow their heads, to better accept the blade, but none did, and they perished with their faces raised toward heaven.

CHAPTER 26

Serlo was right; these are far too many folk for our two boats.

Finn was a killer of men. Inured to death, hard-hearted, cold-minded. But he was also a Templar, a man of God, and sworn to do virtuous deeds. Snippets of vows rolled through his head. *Never flee an enemy... Protect the weak and defenceless...*

He waved Cephas over.

"Fill the boats. Women and children. The elderly. Ferry them to Capernaum. Then come back for us."

Cephas opened his mouth, perhaps to argue, maybe to haggle for more coin, but he took in Finn's fierce, black stare and the drove of innocents awaiting salvation. His teeth clacked shut. He barked short, crisp orders in Hebrew. Folk milled and sorted themselves. Some of the men would have to wait, and husbands kissed crying wives and hugged their children.

A queue began forming.

Finn, Rollo and Serlo, battered and bloody, pasted on benign faces and nodded politely as folk passed by. A mother and daughter stopped before them. Each was the mirror of the other except for twenty years or so. The girl was slim, dark of hair and eyes, and possessed immense dignity for one so young. She hugged a rag doll against her bony chest and put on a stern, brave face. Finn was painted with splashes of crimson, now dried to brown, and his cappa was torn and tattered. He dipped a chin in greeting, expecting to cause more fear than comfort, but she gave him a warm, gap-toothed smile. Finn could not help but smile in return.

"There was a cart by the gate. Bunch of crates, too." Rollo was musing aloud. His eyes flared with an idea. "Elias and Omar are up there. We'll build a bonfire from the wood. Block the courtyard with a wall of fire. That'll keep the Sandpigs at bay."

Serlo breathed in, like he was about to speak, then his eyes rolled up and his body collapsed in on itself.

"Shite," Rollo cursed, and bent to the man.

Finn was already there with two fingers on Serlo's neck. "Sluggish, but it beats." He probed Serlo for holes and found a few, then patted for broken bits and found none. "No mortal wounds. Must be loss of blood." He peered up at Rollo. "Uncle and I will plug Serlo's leaks. Go start your fire."

Rollo and the Breton sprinted up the trail. Jerol dropped by Serlo and was fussing in his haversack for linens and ointments. A cord peeked from under the collar of Serlo's mail. *The leather tube at the end of that cord holds my condemnation.* Finn took the cord between his finger and thumb, pondering, then yanked and broke it. He slid the tube free and tossed it into the Galilee. He watched the tube fill with water and sink, wobbling and weaving like a pebble tossed into a pool. A twinge of guilt needled him for meddling in the Order's judgments, then he snorted at his own folly. *Fools were going to toss you into a hole like rubbish...*

Finn and Jerol mended Serlo, as much as they could, then carried him aboard a boat. Amic was fading fast and, on Finn's order, climbed into the boat next to Serlo. Jerol dashed off to find Rollo, and Finn ambled back to the lakeshore. He laid Oathkeeper, his helmet, and Serlo's shield at the base of a stone pillar, then drank from the lake and washed his hands and face. He reclined against the pillar, somewhat refreshed, and watched skeins of smoke wraith over the city. A butterfly fluttered past — one of the iridescent blue ones. He waited and listened to the lapping waves, the hum of life in the boats, the not-so-distant scream of a city being razed. All of it was at odds. A city turned to hell on earth while he sat in the garden of Eden.

An inky black column of smoke draped itself over the harbour.

Rollo's bonfire...

Owen had been loading boats, and now stomped down the pier to Finn's side.

"This is madness. Christians could die while Jews sail away." Owen nodded toward the boats and whispered, "Jews murdered Christ. We owe them no favours. Leave them."

"Christ was a Jew," Finn said. "Besides, the Jewish people didn't kill Jesus, it was the high priests, in league with the Romans. Why does no one blame Rome's descendants?"

Owen was in no mood for intellectual debate. "They're Jews. Leave them," he insisted.

"Is that what Christ would do? Abandon innocents?" Finn fixed Owen with a withering stare. "They're humans. They're made from the same dust as we, breathe the same winds, drink the same waters. Their days are lit by the sun, their homes shadowed by the moon. Their hearts flow and ebb with desires and dreams. They love and are loved in return. Just like me and you." He started to turn away but came back hard. "Like me, I should say. You're a churl."

Finn and Owen glared, then Owen wheeled away and shuffled off to stand by himself.

Glare at me from over there, you arse.

The blind hatred of some had grown tiresome over the years. Finn had arrived in Outremer as close-minded as Owen. But life outside the glen of home opened his eyes to the sameness of people. All folk had a soul. Even Saracens, his sworn foe, offered much to admire. Abram, an ex-Mamluk, a once-hated foe, proved more akin than most Christians. Robert often said, 'A man should not spare an enemy, nor cease to learn his arts,' but some men never learned to appreciate each other, and their hate only deepened with time. *Owen will be one of these, I wager, or perhaps he'll not live long enough to learn to love neighbours, to hate enemies, and to know the difference.*

Emma came to him. "Boats are stuffed to the gills. Shall I tell Cephas to shove off?"

"Go with him," Finn said, voice soft but firm.

"No. I will not leave your side. Not now."

"You must. To ferry the children to safety. Uncle is needed here, and neither Serlo nor Rooster are capable of speech, let alone strong-arming fishermen." He eased close. "I don't trust Cephas, not much anyway, so I need you to make certain he gets the children away from here and comes back for us."

Finn, by now, did not doubt Cephas. The man would come back — he had seen purpose in the fisherman's eyes, the firm set of his jaw. But he wanted Emma gone from here; the harbour was small, tucked away, but Saracens poured through the city like a river. They would come here. And soon.

"Go," Finn said. "Do this for the children. For my brothers. For me."

"We'll be slow."

"Then you better get going."

"You'll be here when I get back?"

"Where else would I be?"

Words formed just behind his lips, against his will, words that should never be uttered by a man vowed to chastity. Emma nodded once, curtly, and turned away.

In a husky voice, Finn blurted, "Emma."

She turned back and he wrapped an arm around her waist and pulled her close. He whispered in her ear, "I love you."

Finn stood awhile, squinting into the sunlight coming off the lake, and watched the boats grow small. He breathed out and turned to the task at hand. He thumbed Oathkeeper's edge, found it still lively, then gathered three spears, strewn nearby, and propped them by his helmet.

Where is that arse, Rollo?

He took stock as he waited.

By his count, fourteen men remained behind, some old, most young fathers. Then more folk came down the shore. A family of five. And a family of four. They trod warily until Finn waved them over. One of the fathers, a rail-thin man with black hair and bright eyes, came to Finn and pled for protection in halting French. Finn explained that boats were coming, and soon, then smiled and swept an inviting hand towards the others at the end of the pier.

A silver-haired man garbed head-to-toe in black came from the group. He offered a bow of the head, then in passable French said, "My name is Ibrahim."

"God's blessings, Ibrahim. You are an Armenian Christian, aye?"

"I am." Ibrahim showed the cross ink-marked on his wrist, then fanned a hand toward the knot of folk. "They asked that I convey their thanks to you, for allowing them to use your boats."

Finn nodded. They stood awhile in amicable silence. Then Ibrahim asked what they were both thinking.

"What happens if Saracens come before the boats?"

Finn raised a finger skyward, at the smoke. "Fire should hold them. My brothers will hold them further. If they manage to get past, I'll fight them here, at the pier, where it's narrow and they have to come at me one at a time. You pray they don't carry bows."

"I can help, with fighting." Ibrahim was shaking, though it was a warm day.

"You're a brave man, Ibrahim." Finn toed a spear with his boot. "Ever use one of these?"

Ibrahim shook his head.

"It's simple." Finn used his boot tip to flip the spear into the air and his hand to snatch it. "You hold the wooden end and the steel end goes into the bad man, thus." He mimed stabbing the spear, then handed it over. "Give the other spears to your friends. But stay back. Give me space."

"And if you fall?"

For a moment Finn was quiet. He nodded at the others. "That is your family, aye?"

"It is. And a few other families. I'm not that fertile."

Finn smiled from under lowered brows. "Well. I'm no father, but if it were me, I'd decide if I wanted them to be sold as slaves. Or..."

Ibrahim glanced to the east. "We'll swim. Strong swimmers, my family."

You'll drown. "It's what I'd do," Finn said.

Ibrahim went away and Finn went back to watching smoke roil over his head.

Rollo should be back by now...

Owen had been glaring at Finn from the shore. Now he meandered over with a fist propped on his back hip.

"I pondered your earlier words, Brother Finn, and you are right." Owen gave a self-deprecating grimace. "I was a churl, about the Jews, I mean. I can be an arse sometimes."

"Sometimes?" Finn poked his shoulder to say it was a jest. "Don't fret, Owen. Time will teach you that not everyone is an enemy. You'll find there is much to commend the folk here."

Finn shifted his gaze to the villa, seeking Rollo. Something, instinct perhaps, made him glance back — just in time to flinch up an arm at the silver streaking for his neck. The blade sliced across his forearm and the point, knocked high by his parry, glanced over his cheek and temple. The bite of steel on bone was jarring — as was the searing pain that hit a heartbeat after.

Owen leapt on him.

The dagger hit like a punch. The tip gouged through a ring, scored a rib, but the blade lacked the weight to break well-made mail. Owen growled like a rabid dog. His hot breath blasted Finn's cheek and the reek of fish and onion filled his nose. The blade flashed madly, again and again. Finn grunted at each strike, used a forearm to parry blows, groped for the blade with his other hand.

Mail won't hold forever. Going to be daggered in the heart by a dark-souled arse...

Somehow he clamped both hands onto Owen's wrist. They thrashed and grunted and tugged. Owen was strong. Finn was stronger. He twisted the wrist, rolled and yanked it down, felt bone snap and slip. Steel clattered on wood. Finn stomped Owen's ankle, then again, and it splintered and folded in on itself. Owen groaned and dropped to his knees .

Da's biodag filled Finn's hand.

"Arse," he hissed in Owen's ear. "I'll kill you, you rotten —"

Finn had uttered those words into another man's ear. In Alba. Now the words cut deep. Memories blended to paint a picture. The odd looks. The cold words. The bad blood. Owen hacking at Finn's head during their training bouts. Lurking at

Finn's back, stalking him with a spear on the field of dead at Cresson. Lies about Elias saving him.

I know you. Why you joined the Order. What drove you to Outremer. You hunted me. I'm the devil in your tale.

Finn had caught but a glimpse of the youngest MacDougall fleeing into the pines. Now Owen MacDougall, if Owen was his real name, was here to finish a blood feud. To kill the man who had killed his father, and his brothers, and turned his young life into one of banditry and hardship. Finn would have done the same — he *had* done the same.

Vengeance.

He hauled Owen up and stared into his fiery blue eyes, watering with rage, hate, grief.

During the tales told around Templar fires, which were many, there was always a final exchange between hero and evildoer. Brief. Witty. Tense. The hero seeks to unravel the final knot in the web, tell the evildoer why he is going to die. The evildoer, not evil in his own mind, argues his just cause or snarls defiance. The whole performance is intended to give some last insight, some meaning, to all the schemes and deeds.

Finn did not care. Fireside tales could be spun later. This moment belonged in the real world.

"You bastard," Owen whined. "You took everything —"

Finn stabbed Owen in the hollow of his throat, just above the collar of his mail, then again for good measure. Owen coughed, a harsh, consumptive sound, and groped at the knife handle jutting from his neck. Finn grabbed him with both hands, dragged him down the pier, then shoved him. Owen tottered on his mashed ankle and fell backward into the lake with a booming splash.

Waves rocked the pier. Bubbles trailed up in a score of places, then a curly ribbon of crimson, but of Owen

MacDougall there was no more. The weight of a mail shirt ensured he would never again breathe air, never again see the light of day.

Nor will the knife stuck in his neck ever see the light of day.

Da's biodag...

Finn cringed and nearly dived in after it. He had left the knife stuck in Owen's throat to haul him two-handed along the pier. He let the knife go by accident. Now he let it go again, this time with purpose. Years past he left a blade in old man MacDougall's ribs, and now he decided it felt cleansing, fitting, to leave Da's biodag in young MacDougall. The feud was done. The knife would lie in Owen at the bottom of the Galilee, where fishermen would tromp the pier above and sail over his bones. It would degrade to iron. Some future person might find remnants of it wedged in a skeleton, Finn imagined, and conclude it had been murder.

And they might be right. I knifed a Christian. Committed a mortal sin.

Guilt threatened to weave a dark cord in his soul. Anger drove it off. *Bastard thought to knife me!* Compassion for those who would do him harm, even a Christian, was not something he possessed.

So much for turning the other cheek.

Emma's warning about Owen, all those months ago in her garden, needled him now. 'Never turn your back to him, Finn,' she had said.

He laughed.

Ibrahim came. "Why did that man, your brother, do such ugliness?"

"He didn't like me much."

Ibrahim frowned at that, as if seeking some deeper meaning, then unravelled Finn's *shemagh* and began tearing it into strips.

He wrapped the arm tight and tied it off. He pressed a wad to Finn's cheek and temple to stem the bleeding.

Finn slumped against a pillar, closed his eyes and listened to Ibrahim's rhythmic breathing, welcomed the weight of his hand and the burn that came with it. His various wounds merged into one body-wide torment. Coldness settled. Sudden shivers racked him. Worry came too — he fretted for Lugh, Serlo, Amic. He again wondered how the Christian army fared, and if Gerard was dead, though now he felt no guilt for thinking it.

Emma, lovely Emma, drifted through his mind and chased away the pain. Her crisp blue eyes, the sun kisses on her nose and cheeks, her warm brown hair, her protruding ears. He had whispered words that, as a celibate, he had not uttered in many a year. They were words that, once given, could never be taken back. Nor did he want to.

Rocks clattered down the trail. One tumbled into the lake.

"You're a kind man, Ibrahim," Finn rasped. He opened his eyes as the last stone tumbled down the path and bounded into the water. "But it's time you go. See to your family."

Ibrahim left without a word — or if he spoke, Finn did not hear it. He hefted Oathkeeper, heavy as a log now, and jiggled his arm to try to bring life to it. None came. He looped the *guige* of Serlo's shield over a shoulder and slid his left arm into the straps, but his hand would not close, no matter how he tried. It was like a stone. Numb. Cold. He let the arm slump.

Finn waited on wide-planted feet.. His blood should have been rising, thumping with anticipation of a fight, but it was thin and sluggish.

Rollo's head appeared above the scarp, and he lurched down the trail, sending rocks clattering into the water. Finn almost laughed in relief. He slumped back against the pillar. The

Norman staggered up and sagged against the pillar opposite. There was blood on his chest, fresh blood, his blood. He melted to his arse, but somehow made it appear as if he slid down the pillar on purpose. They regarded each other for a moment before Rollo spoke.

"The fire was gorgeous. Pure chaos. You should have seen it."

"I expected no less." Finn raised a shaky finger and pointed at Rollo's chest. "Bad?"

"Meh. Saracens rushed the wagon while the fire grew. I took a small poke."

"Elias and the others?"

Rollo fanned a hand toward the villa. "Watching the trail. The Poulain is a madman."

"Poulain? Thought he was the Breton?"

"The Breton is planted in Emma's garden." Rollo scowled at Finn's ignorance, then made a show of looking around. "Owen?"

"Fell into the lake. Won't be coming out."

Rollo's scowl settled on Finn's bandaged arm, the bright red spots on his chest, the fresh red seam over his cheek and temple. Realization dawned. "That bastard. Why?"

"Old sins, old grudges."

Rollo snorted. "Old friends become bitter enemies for small wrongs."

"The wrongs weren't small."

Tiberias burned. Ash and smuts drifted on an eastbound wind. A blue butterfly fluttered past. Peace filled Finn, and contentment, despite all the earlier cruelty.

"We did well today," Finn rasped. *Other than me killing Owen, I suppose...*

"Acted like proper knights, certes." Rollo reclined his head against the pillar.

Finn shaded his eyes with a hand and stared across the lake. The late afternoon sun angled off the water; the light was bright and blinding. "A boat comes."

Rollo breathed out a lengthy sigh, sluggish and ragged.

"Shall we?" Finn offered a hand.

Rollo shooed it away. "Do you take me for a weakling?"

"Well, you did just fall on your arse."

"You're the arse."

They laughed, short but sincere, in the way of old friends. Finn heaved Rollo to his feet, and together they walked down the pier toward the light.

HISTORICAL NOTES

The core events of *Blood of Lions* are historical and happened much as described in the novel. Where histories contradict, which they often do, decisions were made to patch the holes. Details were sometimes omitted, too, or the roles of some personages, such as Reginald of Sidon, minimized for the sake of flow. Fictional bits were created to augment the historic — such as Finn's trip to Kerak, his scout beyond the Black, and his foray into Tiberias. My apologies to any historical purists offended by the methods or results.

I care deeply for aspects of the past no longer well understood and weaving them into a novel takes care. Three or more hours can be spent researching historic bits to weave into one line of text — and often were. All this effort does not ensure I get it right all the time. No author does. Errors or omissions are few, hopefully, and entirely mine.

The death of King Baldwin V, at just eight, set off a series of events that changed the course of the Crusades. Baldwin's mother, Sibylla of Jerusalem, staged a coup with her husband, Guy de Lusignan. The Templar Grand Master, Gerard de Ridefort, and Patriarch of Jerusalem were in cahoots. Together they outfoxed Raymond of Tripoli and his allies, the Balians among them.

Templars were supposed to be free from worldly scheming. Not in this instance.

Several chroniclers claim the Templar Grand Master, Gerard de Ridefort, aided Sibylla's cause to further his own. Gerard steered Guy onto the throne so he could control the kingdom and in the same stroke deny the crown to Raymond, his sworn enemy. Gerard pressured the Hospitaller Master, Roger de Moulins, to give up his key to the treasury where the crowns were stored. Roger, loyal to Baldwin's wishes, at first refused, then in dramatic fashion tossed the key from a window in disgust. Gerard and the Patriarch, now in possession of the three keys and the crowns, proceeded to make themselves a king.

The whole sordid affair fuelled existing resentments between the Templars and Hospitallers, as well as widening rifts between the nobles of Outremer. Raymond refused to bend the knee to Guy and continued to make nice with the Sultan Saladin. Under truce, Raymond allowed a contingent of the Sultan's men to cross his land, though with certain stipulations, mainly that no Christians should be harmed. Guy in turn sent a force to bring Raymond to heel.

Those fateful events led to the harming of Christians, at the Battle of Cresson Springs, which was pivotal to the story — and to the history of the Outremer.

The battle is described in chronicles of the day, but accounts differ, often considerably, and are yet to be reconciled (the *Latin Itinerarium Peregrinorum et Gesta Regis Ricardi*, or *The Chronicle of the Third Crusade*, is generally favoured). Saracens are said to have numbered 7,000, though modern historians argue 700 to 1,000 is more likely. Christians numbered 130 knights and several hundred sergeants, Turcopoles, and infantry. Exact numbers are murky, then, but it is generally agreed the Christians stumbled into a larger force but charged anyway. The why is unclear. Hubris, possibly, or the enemy numbers were not so large as to rule out an attack. Knights preferred a hard charge, to break open enemy formations, so perhaps they hoped to catch the enemy off guard, as had happened at the Battle of Montgisard.

Roger de Moulins and the Templar Marshal, Jakelin de Mailly, argued against an attack. Chroniclers claim Gerard, as part of his harangue, said to Jakelin, "You love your blond head too much to want to lose it," to which Jakelin replied, "I shall die in battle a brave man. It is you who will flee a traitor." The lines stink of historical propaganda, meant to smear Gerard, and probably they were. Such tension is too juicy to ignore, however, and was put to good use in *Blood of Lions*.

Boldness and poor judgment, whether attributable to one or all, led to a catastrophe of epic proportions. The quixotic charge failed.

A hard fight ensued, which included Muslim forces withstanding the Christian *conroi*, then counterattacking. Losses were ruinous — especially for two Orders perpetually undermanned. Roger de Moulins and the Templar Seneschal, Urs de Alneto were among the fallen, as were 120 or so knights. Gerard, who had a curious knack for escaping sticky spots, was one of a handful of Templars to escape relatively unscathed (some accounts claim as few as three knights survived).

The *Itinerarium* heaps praise on Jakelin and a Hospitaller named Henry. Details are lacking, sadly, though it is generally agreed two knights made a valiant stand against many. The last stand went into Templar lore. Jakelin is said to have ridden a white horse, reminiscent of Saint George, then fought afoot in the rows of stubble until they were trampled to dust. His fight was fierce — so ferocious the enemy revered his bravery and urged him to surrender, which he refused. Layfolk from Nazareth even cut away strips of his cappa to venerate as relics.

Some historic sources attribute the Marshalship to Jakelin; others note the Marshal was Robert Fraisnel, and record Jakelin as a knight and leader of a *conroi*. In *Blood of Lions*,

Jakelin was given the role of Marshal, though the specifics of his fight are largely imagined. Jakelin's premonition of his own death was likewise fictional, though accounts of ancient warriors and modern soldiers presaging their own demise are widely known.

Losses at Cresson, brutal for the Orders, also affected the Kingdom of Jerusalem, and set the table for arguably the most significant tipping point in the Crusades: the Battle of Hattin.

Hattin, like Cresson, was a messy affair largely driven by competing agendas. Some, like Raynald, pursued an aggressive strategy. Raymond and the Balians and Reginald preached prudence. On the other side, Saladin was a clever commander and knew how and when to deploy forces, and how to use water and terrain to his advantage. He set a trap. The bait was Tiberias. A council was held, wherein the prudent camp won out, and King Guy wisely elected to stay at Saffuriya, where water was plentiful. Gerard had other notions. In the night, he visited Guy, and in the morning the army was on the march. Gerard, in essence, shoved the king into Saladin's trap, and along with him the nobles and army of Outremer.

What followed was a disaster. A witch supposedly cursed the army, an ominous beginning, and attempting to burn her failed to lift the curse. Sundry ills befell the army. Horses refused water. Constant harassment by enemy horsemen. Burning grasses. Blazing heat. A dire lack of water. In the end, Saladin controlled the field, and the Christians ended up encircled.

Some escaped. Balian of Ibelin and Reginald of Sidon charged south, broke out, and lived to fight another day. Templars and Raymond launched several furious charges to fight free. Raymond's charge (or his second charge, depending on the source) broke through. Several sources agree the charge was as described in the novel. The Muslim formation opened, let Raymond and his men ride past, then closed up behind, effectively sealing Raymond from the battle. Raymond, with nothing else to do, rode for Tyre and left his wife, Eschiva, to fend for herself. After a few days, she came to terms with Saladin and surrendered the citadel, then joined Raymond in Tyre.

Christians fought a last stand on the south Horn. Nicasius de Burgio, a Hospitaller, died at Hattin and, after his death, became Saint Nicasius, a Roman Catholic martyr. Confusion abounds regarding Saint Nicasius's death; some say he died at Hattin after refusing to convert to Islam, others say he died at the defence of Acre in 1191. In *Blood of Lions*, he died fighting at the last, with a fictional Templar, Henri de Mailly, at his side.

Guy, Gerard, and Raynald were brought to Saladin's tent. Saladin offered Guy iced rose water, a sign that the prisoner would be spared, but Guy was unaware of the Muslim tradition and passed the cup to Raynald. Saladin might or might not have struck the cup from his hands, but is recorded as saying, "I did not ask this evil man to drink, and he would not save his life by doing so." Some Muslim accounts claim Saladin then beheaded Raynald with a single stroke; others record that Saladin struck Raynald as a sign to his Mamluks to behead him. In my mind, Saladin would have struck the fatal blow, but either way the Red Wolf of Kerak was no more. Guy assumed he would die too, but Saladin let him live, and said, "Kings do not kill kings." To this I added, "A lion does not spill the blood of lions," because it seemed something the Sultan would have uttered — and because it made a great book title.

Christian defeat, placed under the lens of history, seems inevitable. Muslim nations vastly outnumbered the Kingdom of Jerusalem. Divisions among Muslim leaders bought the Christians time. But the arrival of Saladin, who united Syria and

Egypt under a single, charismatic leader, finally enabled Muslims to exploit their numbers. Hattin was arguably Saladin's greatest victory — and one of the most significant disasters in medieval military history. It resulted in the eventual downfall of the Crusader States and led directly to the Third Crusade. Despite minor successes, including a foray by King Richard the Lionheart and his famous war against Saladin, Christians would never again control Jerusalem unchecked.

One could never attempt writing such complex historical events without a great deal of research. Peter Lock's *The Crusades*, Steve Runciman's *A History of the Crusades*, and Thomas Asbridge's *The Crusades* were used to place events and players in order. Professor Helen Nicholson's translation of *Itinerarium Peregrinorum et Gesta Regis Ricardi*, or *The Chronicle of the Third Crusade*, was also an invaluable reference.

Several works were used for all things Templar: Malcolm Barber's *The New Knighthood*, and Professor Nicholson's *The Knights Templar: God's Warriors* (with David Nicolle); *Knight Templar: 1120–1312*; and *The Knights Templar: A New History*. Paul Hill's *The Knights Templar at War* and David Campbell's *Templar Knight Versus Mamluk Warrior* provided insight for organization, strategy, and training, as well as informing the battles of Cresson Springs and Hattin. David Nicolle's *Hattin 1187: Saladin's Greatest Victory* and John France's *Hattin: Great Battles* provided detailed works of the battle, including strategies, troop movements, and the tactical success and failures of that fateful day.

Research inevitably reached a common conclusion — Templars were highly revered, infamous among both Christians and Muslims. Paul Cobb, author of *The Race for Paradise: An Islamic History of the Crusades*, notes Muslims considered Templars their most fearsome Frankish opponents.

They were recognized as elite holy warriors, seen as honourable, zealously loyal, and doggedly brave. It is a compliment, of sorts, that Saladin, normally generous in victory, ordered the Templar prisoners executed because they were too dangerous to let live.

Yet there was also understanding. Usama ibn Munqidh, author of the twelfth-century volume *The Book of Contemplation*, recounts a tale wherein a Frank harassed him while praying in a Templar chapel. The Templars hauled the ill-mannered Frank away, apologised for his behaviour, and helped Usama continue his worship in peace. Holy sites were often shared, even if managed by one religion or the other, and hosting Muslims at prayer was part of a diplomatic code. Knights were noble-born many were reasonably well-educated for their day. These traits made them formidable at the disparate roles of warrior and diplomat.

Noble birth also meant they had trained in the knightly arts since toddlers, and came to Outremer as fully formed fighting men. Templars trained extensively after taking vows and incessant drill, combined with the rigours of combat, honed the individual into a fearsome beast. Templars fought together, and thus were an elite fighting force of their day — impeccably trained, well-armed, highly motivated. The Order's Rule also instilled a discipline lacking among other fighting units of their day that, it might be argued, was the equal of any modern army.

The phrase 'medieval warfare' suggests muscled brutes, crude weapons, and hacking. Some knights fought this way. Most were imminently skilled at arms, however, and erudite fighting systems existed in Europe for centuries. Techniques were time-tested, brutally effective, yet elegant. Armour was hand-fitted and comfortably functional, like a modern-day businessman's suit, and weapons were made by artisans with skills lost to the passage of time.

I make knives and axes, and occasionally attempt to make period-correct swords. Holding a tool in your hands, getting its feel, understanding its balance, then giving it a swing are critical to understanding what medieval warfare must have been like. Several works were also used to help craft lively but believable sword fights. These include *Medieval Swordsmanship* by John Clements; *Swordfighting* by Guy Windsor; and *Medieval Combat*, Hans Talhoffer's fifteenth-century manual on fighting. Ewart Oakeshott's *Records of the Medieval Sword* guided all things slicey and stabby. Hopefully these details are reflected here.

The Templars' body count is high with fewer deaths on their side. Some might think this unrealistic. But I assumed their skill, in comparison to most of their enemy's, was above and beyond. Something like a high-level martial arts master, but in a European fighting style, and with swords.

My father boxed competitively. He went undefeated over four years and rarely got hit. Then he joined the Army and boxed on the Army team. He did well, but lost more than he won, and knew what it was like to get hit. He also sparred with Panama's Olympian boxer, who had never medalled, but once fought in the Olympics. He was a virtuoso, and Dad was stunned, overwhelmed, outclassed. The Olympian's speed, foresight, insight, and decisiveness were next-level. Dad never put a glove on him; the Panamanian toyed with the gringo. Templars, to bring home the analogy, were gold medallists of combat fighting. There are others in their league, Mamluks certainly, but Finn and his men faced none so skilled in the streets of Tiberias.

And no matter how much a boxer trains, at the end of the day he goes home, eats a nice meal, and sleeps in a comfortable bed. So how much more extraordinary must the warriors of the past have been, when their lives were at risk daily, as well as notions of honour, brotherhood, and faith? Templars faced trained men, but not men trained to their level, nor as experienced. So, I think it realistic to assume that if you are that skilled, and your enemy that inferior, and the numbers close to equal, the Templars would take some licks but would mostly wreak bloody havoc.

Finn's knife bears the inscription 'fierce when roused,' the battle cry of Clan Robertson (aka Clan Donnachaidh). The slogan came after the twelfth century but was too good a fit for Finn's character to be ignored. National Museums Scotland holds a dirk inscribed with, *Fear God and do not Kil* (*sic*), so inscribed dirks are not unheard of.

Tattooing plays a minor role in *Blood of Lions*. Isabella Fusillo's *Tracing Stigma: The Evolution of the Tattoo in the Middle Ages* provides a wonderful summary of tattooing among Christians during the medieval period. Christian tattooing dates back to the sixth century in the Holy Land and was a mark of distinction among Christians, though early edicts distinguished between secular and religious tattoos. The tradition was also practised among Christians in Armenia, Ethiopia, and Syria. Many Coptic churches still require a cross tattoo to enter the church. Tattooing expanded to twelfth-century pilgrims seeking to commemorate their peregrination; the Jerusalem cross was, and still is, a common image inked into pilgrims. Legend also has it Hospitaller knights of Malta tattooed a cross on their wrist so, when killed in battle, they might be identified and properly buried as Christians.

Abram was ink marked as part of a supposed Mamluk tradition. There is little evidence Mamluks tattooed, but there is ample evidence that Janissaries, successors to Mamluks in the Islamic slave-soldier tradition, tattooed extensively. Mamluk tattooing is a literary invention, then, but not one without precedent.

Several characters are historical personages, like Gerard de Ridefort, and not the creations of computer and keyboard. Some of their historical traits and deeds were given fictional flourishes, to varying degrees, or were fleshed out from what little history tells us.

Finn and his Brotherhood are invented. Snippets of historic Templars were woven into each to make believable fictional knights. Some have sinful pasts but strive for absolution, like Finn of Struan. Others are devout and obedient, like Serlo of Bellême and Hector de la Roca. A few, like Rollo of Caen, are too strong-willed to be bent by the Order's rules. In the end, they share darkness, they share light, and in the sharing are forged into a brotherhood. A disproportionate number of Templars hailed from Provence, France, and from other regions of France, Normandy, Aragon, and Catalonia, thus a large portion of the fictional characters also come from these areas.

Name spellings follow modern conventions — such as Jakelin, not Jacqueline; Raynald, not Renaud; Saladin, not Salah al-Din, etc. Several historic persons shared similar names, especially Raynald, Raymond, and Reginald. Their names were maintained, though efforts were made to include nicknames, such as Raynald's moniker, the Red Wolf, to alleviate confusion.

Rendering Turkic or Arabic names into English is equally vexing, perhaps more so than the spellings of medieval French names, thus English versions were used for readability. The problem, essentially, is which spelling to use? For example, Khaddafi, Gadhafi, or Qadafi? Da'ud ibn Auda, in his 2003 work, *Period Arabic Names and Naming Practices*, best summed up the issue by citing correspondence between T. E. Lawrence and his publisher regarding inconsistent spellings of Arabic names in his manuscript, *Revolt in the Desert*:

Arabic names won't go into English, exactly, for their consonants are not the same as ours, and their words, like ours, vary from district to district. There are 'scientific systems' of transliteration, helpful to people who know enough Arabic not to need helping, but these are a wash-out for the world. I spell my names anyhow, to show what rot the systems are.

Names for fictional characters were gleaned from a range of sources, including the Academy of Saint Gabriel, a group of volunteers who research medieval names; the *Dictionary of Medieval Names from European Sources*; and *Behind the Name*, a database of medieval names. Each of these sources in turn draw names from medieval records, such as tax rolls and parish registers, and cover several geographies, including Normandy, England, and Jerusalem.

Place names attempted to mirror the time. Outremer, for example, was the name given to the four Catholic realms in the Middle East that lasted from 1098 to 1291. Many places in Outremer repeatedly changed name, and a given locale often bore multiple names. For example, Tiberias was named by the Romans and this name was adopted by the Franks, the generic term given to westerners in Jerusalem. However, the city had earlier names ascribed by Jewish people, Arabs, and others. The name in Western sources was used here and this choice was based on ease of use.

Religion drove conflict in Outremer. The war for Jerusalem was long, hotly contested, and bloody. One must remember that medieval peoples strongly believed in religious ideals —

piety, God's word, paradise. Belief, whether Christian, Muslim, or Jewish, drove a litany of deeds, many virtuous and noble, others horrid and repugnant. Depictions of violence in religion, such as the graphic murder of saints, were common practice.

Killing and death were also viewed differently during the medieval period. Daily life included violence in many forms — wars, tournaments, murder, revenge. Knights were raised from birth in a culture of warfare, then, and were hardened to bloodshed by adulthood. Most historians agree chivalry, as a code of conduct, developed around 1170 to 1220. Thus chivalric codes of conduct influenced war, treatment of prisoners, and what was and was not acceptable. The Christian fighting orders, likewise, attempted to instil a measure of discipline into an otherwise chaotic undertaking. History is rife with examples of knights, Christian and Muslim, breaking their codes of conduct and committing bloody, ruthless acts. Saladin's killing of Templar and Hospitaller prisoners is one. No attempt was made to judge practices of religion or warfare, nor place them under the scrutiny of modern morals, but simply to show them as accurately as possible.

GLOSSARY

The definitions provided here are fine-tuned to *Blood of Lions*. Words or phrases often have multiple meanings, spellings, or uses, especially when dealing with a melting pot of cultures, as was Outremer. Only those used in this novel are given. Some terms have been invented for the purpose of this book.

AKETON — Thigh-length jacket worn under mail to cushion blows, reduce chafing, and improve fit. Fluted, stuffed with cotton, and quilted. Aketon comes from the Arabic word *al qutn*, meaning of cotton. In Europe, the jacket was usually stuffed
with wool and called a *gambeson*, *haubergeon*, or *padded jack*.

ALBA — As in the Kingdom of Alba, the name for pre-eleventh century Scotland. Scotia was also used at various times and in various places, but by the eleventh century 'Scotland' was mostly used to refer to the Gaelic-speaking Kingdom of Alba north of the river Forth. The term 'Scotland,' as used today to refer to the entirety of Scotland, became common only in the Late Middle Ages.

ARMING CAP — Wool, cotton, or linen cap worn under a mail coif.

ARMING SWORD — A Templar carried an arming sword and great sword. Here, arming sword denotes a sword wielded with one hand (what Ewart Oakeshott might classify as a Type X or Xa). Arming swords often had a cruciform guard and round (wheel) pommel. Blades averaged 30 inches long and were broad, double-edged, and tapered to a usable point. A fuller, or longitudinal groove, often ran down the blade to lighten it without sacrificing strength.

BANNER — A band of Templar knights. Each band carried their own black-and-white banner. Banner is invented and used here to avoid confusion with similar terms used interchangeably, such as *conroi* or *eschielle*.

BAUCENT — Templar war banner. Variously spelled *baucant*, *bauceant*, *baussant*, *beauséant*, etc. The banner was black-and-white, or *piebald*, and called the *gonfanon baucent*. The origin is thought to be the Old French term for a piebald horse. Black might have symbolized ferocity to enemies and white kindness to friends. Medieval frescoes show the upper half white, the lower half black, with a red cross in the white field.

BEAUSÉANT — Templar battle cry. Spelled differently here to distinguish it from the battle flag of similar spelling. Full cry was, *À moi, beau sire! Beauséant à la rescousse!* Meaning: To me, good sire! Beauséant to the rescue! Shortened in the moment to *Beauséant*.

BIODAG — Gaelic word for dagger or dirk. The Scottish dirk was not known in the twelfth century (the earliest known dirk is on an effigy dated to 1502 in Ardchattan Priory). Here, biodag is used to denote an ancestor of the dirk. Single edged, spear-pointed, with a blade of 12 inches or so.

BLACKCOAT — Slang term for Templar sergeant. Non-noble. Included tradesmen and fighting sergeants. Fighting sergeants were light cavalry, some equal to a knight in training and skill. Not equipped as generously as a knight. Wore a black or brown mantle with a red cross.

BOARD — Slang for a shield, which was made from multiple wooden boards covered by leather.

BODKIN — Arrow point used to punch into mail. Generally a needle-sharp, squared metal spike.

BOLT, OR QUARREL — Projectile shot from a crossbow. Resembles an arrow, but shorter and heavier.

BOWL MATE, OR BATTLE COMPANION — Invented slang term for Templar tradition of two men sharing a bowl in compliance with the Templar Rule that a knight should never be alone.

BRAES — Men's knee-length pants made of linen. Tightened with a drawstring.

BROADHEAD — Arrowhead consisting of two blades, sometimes more, with a wide cutting edge. Often barbed (though not always) to prevent withdrawal.

CACKHAND, OR CACKHANDED — Slang term for a left-handed person. Likely derives from the tradition that one used the left hand for cleaning oneself after defecating and the right hand for everything else. *Cack* was an Old English term for excrement, thus the left is the cack-hand.

CAPPA — White robe, usually linen, that extends below the knees and to the wrists. Hooded, belted at the waist, and slit front and back below the hips. Marked with a red cross, though when marking began, the size and design of the cross, and placement is debated. Also covered mail to keep the metal from heating in the sun.

CATERAN — Scots Gaelic term for a Highland fighting man, but also raiders or cattle thieves.

CERTES — Medieval term for, sure, of course, or I assure you.

CHRISTENDOM — The wider Christian world, here used to denote Europe.

CHURL — A person of low birth, impolite, mean-spirited.

CILLICE — Garment made of coarse cloth or animal hair (a hairshirt) worn close to the skin. Also called a sackcloth. Used as a self-imposed penance, repentance, or mortification of the flesh.

COIF — Mail hood covering head and neck. Often included a leather-backed chin guard that was laced in place or left open when not fighting. Worn over an arming cap and under a helmet.

COMMANDER — Below the Marshal in rank. Each land had a Commander who oversaw farms, castles, etc. in their jurisdiction. The Commander of Jerusalem was treasurer of the Order and shared power with the Master. There was also a Commander of Tripoli and Antioch.

CONROI — A wall of cavalry, riding knee-to-knee in a charge (some sources use *eschielle*). *Conroi* is also slang for a band of knights that trained, lived, and fought together.

COURSER — Light, fast horse for riding, hunting, or battle. Templars had a courser or two, perhaps a rouncey, and one or more destriers. Here, destrier is used most often for simplicity.

CROSSBOW, LATCHBOW, ARBALEST — Family of weapon consisting of a short bow mounted horizontally on a wooden frame. Held and aimed like a modern rifle. Reloaded using a wood prong or both hands to pull the string and re-hook it over the locking mechanism; feet were propped against the bow or placed in a stirrup. Arbalests were heavier and reloaded with a hand crank.

CROSS PATTÉE — Type of cross with narrow arms at the centre and flaring in a curve to be wider at the perimeter. Several variants are known.

DAGGER — Double-edged, straight knife used as a secondary weapon. Primarily for thrusting.

DASTARD — Coward. Dishonourable person.

DESTRIER — War horse. Origins are murky, though it's argued they trace back to the Spanish Jennet, an ancestor to the modern Friesian and Andalusian horse. The Jennet had Barb and Arabian blood brought to Europe after the First Crusade. A destrier was well-trained and fearless, as well as strong, fast, and agile. Costly to breed and train. Sources refer to the destrier as the *great horse* because of its size. However, a destrier was not more than 15 hands tall, or the height of a modern riding horse (though more heavily muscled in the hind legs).

DISSECTION — Medieval term for a puzzle.

DONNACHAIDH — Clan Donnachaidh, later Clan Robertson. The clan system, as currently understood — with customs such as each clan wearing its own tartan — was not firmly in place by the twelfth century. The clan tradition was emerging by the eleventh century, however, if not much earlier.

DRAPER — In charge of the Templar garments and linens. The Rule states that, after the Master and Marshal, the Draper was superior to all brethren.

ESCHIELLE — Squadron ranging from 10 to 50 men. Includes two or more banners. Often used to denote knights formed for a charge, and here is interchanged with *conroi*. Once in an eschielle, a brother was not permitted to charge or break rank without permission of the Marshal, who alone gave the command to attack.

FARIS — Saracen equivalent of a knight or cavalier. Sources sometimes use the term to refer to Mamluks, though a faris need not be (and often wasn't) a Mamluk.

FRANKS — As used in the Levant, means any European (Latin) Christian, whether French, English, Norman, etc. (The term *Crusader* was not used in the twelfth century). Frank originates from the Arabic term *Frangistan*, a Muslim and Persian term meaning *Land of the Franks*, and it is generally thought to refer to Francia, which gave its name to the Kingdom of France.

FREELANCE — Used to denote a soldier who fought for pay. Term comes from "Free Lance," meaning the lance is not sworn to any lord's service and is open for rent. Later called mercenaries.

FURŪSIYYA — Arabic term for equestrian martial exercise. Covers the martial arts and equestrianism of the Mamluk period. Aspects were horsemanship, horse archery, the lance, and the sword.

GONFANIER, OR CONFANONIER — Knight chosen to carry the *baucent* (often spelled *bauceant*), the Templar war flag, or the *gonfanon baucent*.

GREAT SWORD — The second sword a Templar carried. Comparable to a hand-and-a-half, long, or bastard sword. Called a 'great sword of war' in historical sources, its blade was around 46 inches and the handle long enough to allow a two-handed grip (a Type XIIa or XIIIa in the Ewart Oakeshott typology). Slung from the saddle; often used after the lance was lost or broken.

GUIGE — A strap, usually of leather, on the inside of a shield. Used to hang a shield on the shoulder or neck when not in use or, when fighting, to wield a weapon with two hands without discarding the shield. The shield could be retrieved when needed.

HAUBERK — Mail coat with integral coif. Reached to mid-thigh, included sleeves, and was slit front and rear below the waist to allow riding a horse. Made by riveting links in a four-in-one pattern, where each ring is linked to four others. Some archaeological examples show a six-in-one pattern. Knights also wore mufflers (mittens) and mail chausses on the legs. Sergeants wore only a hauberk.

HORSEBREAD — Form of medieval bread. Inexpensive, coarse, made from one or more of beans, legumes, bran, and/or seeds. Fed to horses, but also eaten by people.

IFRANJI — Slang for Frank, or foreigner. Also Faranji, Franj, or al-Franj for *the Franks*.

ISM — Medieval Arabic names are composed of several parts. *Ism* is one part, and literally means "name," and is the individual's name given at birth, or today would be one's first or given name.

JAZERANT — A coat of armour consisting of mail sewn between layers of fabric or leather. The inner layer was padded. Widely used in Turkey, the Middle East, and Persia.

JUBBEH — A long outer garment, common to Muslims, worn by both genders of the upper class.

KETTLE, KETTLE HELMET — Shaped like a brimmed hat, open-faced with a metal rim all the way around, but made of riveted metal. Also called a war hat. Worn by sergeants.

KHANJAR — Curved dagger, usually double-edge, carried by Mamluks.

KINE — Scots Gaelic for cattle.

KUNYA — Portion of Arabic name that gives information about one's offspring. The Kunya begins with "Abu," which means "father of…" or "Umm," which means "mother of…"

LANCE — Close relative of the spear but heavier, more durable, and meant for a cavalry charge. Hardwood shaft measuring around 8 to 10 feet long; tipped with a narrow, spear-blade point.

LANGETS — Strips of metal extending from the head of a staff weapon (such as an axe) down the wooden shaft. Secured with nails or screws. Protects the wood, reduces handle breakage.

LAYFOLK, LAYMEN — Commoners. Ordinary people. Not nobility.

LOGGERHEAD — Medieval insult. A blockhead, incapable of understanding basic things.

LEG YIELD — Lateral movement used by a horse to travel sideways (or diagonal) in small hops.

LINGUA FRANCA — A pidgin dialect spoken in Outremer. Based on *langue d'oïl*, the language of Normandy and France, but borrowed from many languages, including Arabic and Italian.

MACE, OR TURKISH MACE — Blunt weapon consisting of a wood or metal handle and an iron or steel head, usually flanged or knobbed.

MAHOUND, MAHOUNDS, MOHAMMEDAN — Medieval slang for a follower of Mohammad, used as a generic term for Muslims, thought to derive from the Anglo-Saxon word *Mahun*, a generic pagan deity Christians thought (incorrectly) Muslims worshipped.

MAMLUK — Slave soldiers serving the Arab dynasties (also mameluke, mamluq, etc.). Many were Turkic or Eurasian steppes peoples, but others came from the Caucasus Mountains, Greece, or the Balkans. Harvested young and sold to Egypt, where they were taught Islam and Furūsiyya.

MARSHAL — Primary role was military advisor and organizing the Order for war. Consulted with the Marshal on tactics. His retinue was four horses, two squires, a turcopole, and a sergeant. An Under Marshal oversaw the footmen and equipment.

MASTER — Grand Master of the Order, worldwide, and led the Order in battle, as well as in spiritual matters. Based in Jerusalem and answered only to the Pope.

MAWMET — Doll. Also an idol, because in the Middle Ages it was believed (erroneously) that Mohammedans worshiped idols (dolls) representing Mohammed.

MUMMER — An actor, performer, travelling entertainer; usually wore a costume.

MUTTONHEAD — A dull or stupid person.

NASAB — Portion of Arabic name that gives information about one's descent. The *nasab* begins with "ibn," meaning "son of…" or "bint," meaning "daughter of…"

NASAL, OR NASAL HELMET — Helmet worn by Templar knights during the twelfth century. Worn over a coif. The helmet was open-faced, rounded or conical, with a metal strip (or nasal) covering the nose. By the early 1200s, helmets had evolved to a flat-topped affair with an attached face plate. By around 1240, helmets were totally enclosed with eye slits and breathing holes.

NISBA — Portion of Arabic name that gives information about one's place of origin. Can also show tribal, political, sectarian, or factional affiliation.

ORDER — Used here to denote the Templars, as in the Order of the Templars.

OUTREMER — Term for the Latin east and the four Christian states carved out by the first crusade. French, meaning beyond the sea (*outre-mer*, or beyond [*outre*] the sea [*mer*]). Included the Kingdom of Jerusalem (1099–1291); county of Edessa (1097–1150); county of Tripoli (1102–1289); and principality of Antioch (1098–1287).

PALFREY — A saddle horse, other than a warhorse, and usually a light, easy-gaited riding horse.

PIEBALD — Black and white. The colours of Templar shields and the Templar war banner.

POLTROON — Coward, craven. Middle French, borrowed from Old Italian, *poltrone*. Traced to the Latin *pullus*, a root that is the ancestor of pullet, or a young hen (poultry).

POTTAGE — Thick stew or soup. Made of boiled vegetables, grains, and, if available, meat or fish.

POULAIN — French slang for a baby horse. In Outremer, and in this book, used as slang for Frankish descendants of the original crusaders who captured Jerusalem in 1099 and remained in Outremer.

QAMA — Edged weapon from the Caucasus. Resembles the offspring of a Roman gladius and a dagger; distinctive for its wide, double-edged blade that tapers to a needle-sharp point. Handled with a single piece of horn, ivory, or wood, and lacks a separate guard or pommel.

RAKEFIRE — A guest that overstays their welcome, to the point they would rake the ashes of a housefire for more.

RICASSO — An unsharpened length of sword blade just in front of the guard. Allowed the swordsman to place their index finger above the guard, which improved grip strength and torque. Could grasp the ricasso to shorten their grip, allowing a large blade to be used in a tight press.

ROUNCEY — All-purpose horse. Could be used for riding, as pack animals, or in some cases, might be trained for war.

ROUTIER — Term for a French brigand, or sometimes French mercenaries.

RULE, OR THE RULE — The Rule of the Templars, first put to parchment in 1129, outlined sixty-eight codes governing Templar life. Rules for penance were included. Eventually covered several hundred edicts in multiple languages.

SAIF — Arabic word for sword; can refer to any sword, curved or straight (though early Islamic swords were usually straight and double edged; curved sabres developed over time). Here, saif denotes a straight sword with a wide, double-edge blade; reasonably sharp point; and fuller.

SALT — Slang, denoting a veteran, someone salted (experienced) by war.

SANDPIG — Invented slang for Saracens.

SARACEN — Used to denote any person who followed Islam. Originally applied to a tribe of Arabs living in the Sinai Peninsula. The term morphed to cover Arab tribes in general, and, after the establishment of the caliphate, to refer to all Muslim subjects of the caliph.

SARD — Medieval slang for sexual intercourse, can be used as an insult.

SENESCHAL — Right-hand man to the Master; acted as advisor, tackled administrative duties.

SHEMAGH — Scarf, usually a long rectangle of cotton, wrapped around the neck and face as protection from sun and sand. Sometimes also called a *keffiyeh* or *ghutrah*.

SHIELD, OR BOARD — Templar shields were triangular and curved along the edges to a pointed bottom; flat across the top; convex across the face. Covered shoulder to mid-thigh. Usable mounted or afoot. Wooden with a painted leather cover. A leather strap, or *guige*, allowed it to be slung over a shoulder or across the back. Frescoes from the thirteenth century show Templar shields as white in the upper half, black in the lower half, with a red cross in the white field.

SOT — Drunkard; sottered (drunk).

SOUQ — A marketplace in northern Africa and the Middle East.

SQUIRE — Knights were allotted one or two squires to see to their horses, gear, etc. Squires were often not members of the Order and were outside labour hired for a set period.

SWEETMEAT — More or less, medieval candy.

TIRKESH, WAR BOW, OR TURKISH BOW — Composite bow made of horn, wood, and sinew. Recurved, compact, meant to be used from horseback. Draw weight of 80 to 120 pounds. Pulled with the index finger and thumb; a ring on the thumb aids the draw. Effective range of 300 yards.

TONSURE — Cutting, plucking, or shaving the hair on top of the head and leaving a ring of hair around the sides. Confusion exists about whether Templars tonsured. Some medieval paintings show tonsures, though others show long hair, curly hair, etc. A thirteenth-century account mentions Templars with shaved heads. The Rule states only that hair be regularly trimmed. Long beards were encouraged in Outremer, where beards were a sign of masculinity.

TURCOPOLE, OR TURC — Worked for the Order as archers, crossbowmen, light cavalry, scouts, etc. Local Christians; usually Syrians, Armenians, Lebanese, Greeks, often half-bred with Turks. Turcopole meant *son of Turk*, though over time the term evolved to denote a profession.

WATERED STEEL, OR DAMASCUS STEEL — Steel made in a crucible. Homogeneous content and high carbon with low slag (impurities). Swords forged from watered steel were tough, resistant to breakage, and held a sharp, resilient edge. Showed banding, swirls, and mottling evocative of flowing water. Modern pattern welding (or forge welding) produces similar surface patterns, leading some to wrongly label pattern welded steel as Damascus steel.

WHINGER — Someone who complains a lot.

WHITEBACK — Slang term for a Templar knight.

WOLF'S HEAD — Term used in the medieval English legal system to designate a criminal, an outlaw, someone who could be killed without penalty.

A NOTE TO THE READER

Dear Reader,

All history interests me, but the world of twelfth-century Outremer and the Third Crusades speaks to me in a way only a few other eras can. The notion of fighting monks, serving God with their swords, is a long-held fascination. The focus of *Blood of Lions* were the Templars, though Hospitallers, as was true in history, play a parallel role at critical junctures. Both Orders were promised paradise for their deeds, answered only to the Pope, and were immune to the laws of kings or men. Writers of the day praised them as, "formidable rather than flamboyant." Religous knights, unlike silk-clad secular knights, chose to be humble in their mien and ragged in their attire.

They set aside distractions of the world to focus on one task — war.

The Templar Order included droves of priests, bankers, diplomats, and advisors, as well as a cadre of tradesmen. Templars owned hundreds of properties and, far from being secretive, lodged travellers and opened their churches to commoners. Historians quibble over details of the Order's founding, yet most agree it was to guard pilgrims, to keep the Holy Land in Christian hands, and to wage war. Members of the Order either fought or supported the fight.

This is not a tale of holy relics, secret societies, or of Christ's offspring. Those fanciful tales have been done. This is a story of Templars as a military order, facing enemies more numerous than themselves, fighting to maintain a claw-hold on the Kingdom of Jerusalem. They are presented as real people, with the virtues and flaws unique to our species — devout, fearless, dedicated, but also scheming, ambitious, backstabbing.

I hope you found *Blood of Lions* a great read, and thank you for your time! Reviews are critical to authors, so if you enjoyed the novel, please spare a moment to post a review on **Amazon** and **Goodreads**. You can also connect with me on **Facebook**, where you will find more information about upcoming books.

Thank you again!

Daniel Colter

Sapere Books is an exciting new publisher of brilliant fiction and popular history.

To find out more about our latest releases and our monthly bargain books visit our website: **saperebooks.com**